THE CHOICE OF A CAVALIER

LINDA RAE SANDE

Twisted Teacup
PUBLISHING

This is a work of fiction. The events and characters described herein are imaginary and are not intended to refer to specific places or living persons. The opinions expressed in this manuscript are solely the opinions of the author and do not represent the opinions or thoughts of the publisher. The author has represented and warranted full ownership and/or legal right to publish all the materials in this book.

The Choice of Cavalier

ISBN: 978-1-946271-33-4

All Rights Reserved.

Copyright © 2020 Linda Rae Sande

V1.3

Cover photographs © PeriodImages.com and 123rf.com.

Cover art by Linda Rae Sande

All rights reserved – used with permission

Edited by Katrina Teele-Fair

This book may not be reproduced, transmitted, or stored in whole or in part by any means, including graphic, electronic, or mechanical without the express written consent of the publisher except in the case of brief quotations embodied in critical articles and reviews.

PRINTED IN THE UNITED STATES OF AMERICA

The Cousins of the Aristocracy

The Promise of a Gentleman

The Pride of a Gentleman

The Holidays of the Aristocracy

The Christmas of a Countess

The Knot of a Knight

The Heirs of the Aristocracy

The Angel of an Astronomer

The Puzzle of a Bastard

The Choice of a Cavalier

The Bargain of a Baroness

The Jewel of an Earl's Heir

The Vixen of a Viscount

Beyond the Aristocracy

The Pleasure of a Pirate

Stella of Akrotiri

Origins

Deminon

Diana

PROLOGUE

A **Brother's Concern for his Sister**
Friday, January 4, 1839, Grandby and Son, 300 Oxford Street, London

"I say, Grandby, you've managed to make this space into quite a museum," Lord Michael said as he studied several artifacts displayed around a luxurious office. The rich woods, green carpet, and gas-lit chandeliers would have been expected in a gentleman's study in a Park Lane townhouse. They were not as expected in an office in Oxford Street.

"This is actually my father's office," Tom Grandby said as he turned to lead them into his own. "He's done far more traveling than I have, and his brother-by-marriage owns Wellingham Imports, so it's been easy for him to acquire his collection."

"Yours is not so bad, either," Lord Michael said as he hurried to a wall of shelves laden with interesting artifacts and a stunning Wedgwood vase. Unlike Gregory Grandby's office across the hall, most of these items were more ancient—a Roman glass bottle, a Greek vase, a globe made of agate, and several marble slabs carved with reliefs—and they were displayed appropriately. "But it looks as if there's something missing," he commented, noting the top of a caryatid was bare.

"That pelike from Greece was due to go on there," Tom replied as he indicated the central artifact on his display shelves. "But an archivist from the British Museum warned me it might be accidentally knocked off its pedestal should I mount it on the caryatid. When I learned the vase was from 350 BCE, I of course took his recommendation."

"350 BCE, you say?" Michael repeated in awe. "From where did you acquire it?"

"Lord Henley found it for me in Athens," Tom replied, referring to an archaeologist who was currently working on a dig in Greece. Tom indicated they should sit. "Tell me, my lord. What brings you to London?"

The second son of the Duke of Somerset took the proffered chair and settled into it just as Tom's secretary entered with a tea tray. He went about pouring cups of tea and placing plates of cakes before each gentleman, and then he exited as quietly as he had arrived. He left behind the tea tray which featured an array of biscuits and more small cakes. "I was about to say *business*, but I must admit, I miss this kind of hospitality," Lord Michael said as he lifted his cup. He held it as if in salute, and Tom did the same with his. "I'm in a quandary, and I'm hoping you can help."

Tom furrowed his brows. "What is it?"

"Nothing I say can go beyond this room," Lord Michael warned.

"I've never divulged any of my investors' business," Tom reminded him. "Nor will I start."

"My father does not fare well," Lord Michael said quietly. "And my older brother is taking advantage."

Tom straightened, his tea forgotten. "How so?"

"He's looking to get his hands on our inheritances."

"But—"

"He can't, not really," Lord Michael was quick to say. "But he'll go to great lengths if he runs short of his own blunt, and I expect he'll run out before he inherits the dukedom. With

Father's mind not always where it should be—he's become very forgetful, somewhat confused—I fear Jeremiah will only grow bolder in his attempts at taking over the dukedom before he's entitled to do so."

Tom dipped his head. "I'm sorry to hear it. What can I do?"

Lord Michael sighed. "My oldest sister is safe, since she's already wed and her dowry has come under her husband's control," he explained. "Not so with my youngest sister, however. She has her funds deposited with the Bank of England. I've just come from there. I spoke with her banker and told him to be sure to mention you when next she meets with him," he added.

"Oh?" Tom furrowed a brow, wondering what the spare heir of the Somerset dukedom had in mind for the sister.

"I've also told Vicky to contact you about an appointment, but... I don't know if she will. She's living in an unentailed property just north of town. I'm fairly sure her inheritance won't allow her to buy it from the dukedom, but I don't want Jerry getting his hands on it, or selling it out from under her, either." Michael paused and then indicated the leather satchel he had brought with him. "I actually have the deed to the property with me. I took it from my father's study. Just to keep it from Jerry."

"Probably a good idea, as long as someone else knows you have it," Tom hedged.

"Well now *you* know. I told Mother. She agreed I should keep it safe, of course."

Tom leaned forward, a frown firmly in place. "Have you told *her* brother?" he asked, referring to Michael Cunningham. Since the man had made his fortune for the Cunningham viscountcy with investments in coal and gas extraction, Tom wondered why the nephew didn't invest with the uncle. Why he didn't trust Michael Cunningham to know what was happening in his sister's family.

Lord Michael inhaled slowly and shook his head. "I don't

want to get other family members involved in this," he said in a quiet voice. "I had hoped as he grew older, Jerry might take his responsibilities to heart. Spend less at the gaming tables Spend less on... *everything*, I suppose. But his choice of friends has not helped in the matter. One in particular is the reason Vicky is living at Fairmont Park... well, never mind about that. She needs a sound investment for her inheritance—"

"Has she already reached her majority?" Tom asked, finding he was growing more curious than he should.

"Indeed. And she won't marry, although after what happened last year, I can't say I blame her."

Tom was about to ask what had happened, but thought better of it. Meeting a potential client for the first time was always more about discovering what they wanted him to know about them. What they wanted him to *do* for them. All the rest didn't matter. All the rest wasn't really any of his business. "Are you looking for an agent to sell the property?"

"No!" Lord Michael said. "Vicky has already spent blunt on improvements. Intends to live there for the rest of her life, if she's not pushed out by our brother."

"So... you just want her fortune secured in a long-term investment?"

"Yes."

"Is that what *she* wants?"

Lord Michael's eyes darted sideways. "I hope so."

Against his better judgement, Tom allowed his curiosity to get the best of him. "Tell me, does your sister know this about Lord Jeremiah?"

Lord Michael grimaced. "I told her yesterday."

"And?"

"Well, I'm still alive, but it was touch and go there for a time." The words weren't said with any amusement.

"Angry, was she?"

"And I was just the messenger," Lord Michael said, an eyebrow arched in annoyance. "If Jerry had been there, I think she would have done him bodily harm. Probably run over him with a horse, whipped him with a crop, and then stomped on him for good measure." He glanced around the office while Tom visibly winced. "Tell me, Grandby. Do you own a house or... a mansion somewhere?"

Tom blinked at the sudden change of topic. "I just took a room at Arthur's a couple of months ago," he replied, referring to the men's club in St. James Street. "My family's estate is Woodscastle, down in Chiswick."

"Woodscastle," Lord Michael repeated quietly. "Isn't that next door to Merriweather Manor?"

Resisting the urge to laugh, Tom said, "I wouldn't call it next door, exactly. It's just down the road, though. As well as on the other side of it. My father grew up at Merriweather Manor, so everyone who lives there now is a cousin or a relative of some sort."

"Oh? So you aren't betrothed to any of the young women who live there?"

"Although I rather like my cousins, I'm not of a mind to marry any of them," Tom replied with a grin.

Lord Michael's widened eyes suggested he was unaware of the current occupants of the estate. "Will you inherit it?"

"Merriweather Manor? No. I rather imagine my banker will end up with it," he replied, remembering it was James Burroughs' father, Lord Andrew, who had seen to renovating the pile two decades before.

"Will you inherit Woodscastle?"

"Mayhap a part of it. I don't intend to reside there, though," Tom replied, wondering at Lord Michael's interest in the estates. "Too far from town."

Lord Michael's expression brightened. "Is there any chance you're in the market for a house with a park and grounds? New stables? A track, perhaps?"

Tom paused and regarded the duke's son with a wary eye. "Wait. Are you thinking to sell me Fairmont Park?"

Lord Michael finished off his tea and sat back, his chest puffed out. "If Jerry bankrupts the dukedom, my father will need money to pay servants and staff. To pay bills. I will not see my mother left a pauper," he said in a quiet voice. "If I sell Fairmont Park, I can put that money into an escrow account. Protect it from Jerry."

"You would sell your sister's house out from under her?" Although he didn't intend to sound angry, Tom certainly felt it on the woman's behalf.

"With the condition it be let back to her until such time as she either marries or decides to live somewhere else," Lord Michael explained. "Besides, it's not really *her* house," he added. "She just... lives there."

"But she sees to the upkeep? Manages the servants? Pays the bills?" Tom guessed, ready to chide the man for taking advantage of his sister.

"Yes, yes, and... and she trains horses there."

The fact that the property had new stables and a track now held meaning. "Trains horses for... *what*, exactly?"

Lord Michael once again grimaced. "Racing, of course. She's damned good at it, which vexes Mother to no end but has Jerry all excited about the prospect of his nag winning at some of this year's races," he explained. "Something more for him to lose money on," he complained.

"Does she train your horse, too?" Tom asked lightly.

"Yes, but I don't bet everything I own on whether it wins or not," Lord Michael replied defensively.

"Hmm. Well, am I to expect her to come here to the office to meet with me?"

Lord Michael shook his head. "Doubtful. Could you go there? I mentioned I would ask you on her behalf."

"Was this before or after she threw a vase at you?"

Blinking, Lord Michael allowed a self-deprecating grin. "She values the vases far too much to throw them at anyone," he replied. "She's more likely to lash out verbally when she's vexed. Which is how I left her company yesterday."

"She was not happy with the thought of the house being sold?" Tom guessed.

Lord Michael rolled his eyes. "I didn't even get that far with her. I only told her what our brother was doing."

Tom had a mind to laugh, but he certainly felt no humor and managed to hold it in. "Where exactly is Fairmont Park?" he asked. "I can pay a call there tomorrow. Speak with her ladyship, *if* she'll see me."

Lord Michael pulled a paper from his satchel. A rather well-drawn map of the northern London environs filled the sheet. He passed it over to Tom. "Just there," he said as he pointed to where a vast estate had been circled.

"It's huge for so close to town," Tom remarked. "How is it a duke owns such a property and not the dukedom?"

"Father bought it with his inheritance expecting he and my mother would live there. Back when his older brother was still the Somerset heir apparent. And still alive," he added with an arched brow.

Tom stared at his client, just then remembering that Jeremy Statton, Duke of Somerset, was the second-born son. He had only inherited because his father and older brother had died in a boating accident. "Interesting," Tom murmured.

"Will you take a look, at least?" Lord Michael implored.

Allowing a shrug—it couldn't hurt to look—Tom said, "I will. But I am not going to be the one to tell your sister why I'm looking," he warned.

"Noted," Lord Michael replied. "Oh, and she despises being called 'Vicky' by people she doesn't know."

Not wanting to start off on the wrong foot with a potential client, Tom asked, "What *is* her name, exactly?"

"Victoria. Lady Victoria," Lord Michael replied. "And she was named long before our queen was born," he added as he gathered his satchel. He suddenly sighed. "Oh, dear. I haven't exactly painted Vicky in a very pleasing palette," he murmured. "She really is a rather pleasant young woman when you get to know her. But maybe not quite the kind of girl your mother hopes you'll marry when you're finally of a mind to do so."

Tom blinked, deciding it best he not mention his mother's preference for the kind of girls *she* wanted for her sons. They certainly couldn't be classified as young, innocent, insipid English misses. His mother wanted her sons to be challenged by their mates, mostly so she would have allies at the dinner table.

He absently wondered if Lady Victoria would fit the bill, but quickly shook off the thought.

He was not in the market for a wife.

"I do hope you can help," Lord Michael said, just before he took his leave of the office. "And thank you again for the tea and cakes."

Tom stared after his client, a dozen questions coming to mind. He only hoped Lady Victoria would know the answers. Especially if he was going to take her on as a client.

CHAPTER 1

PAYING A CALL ON A
BANKER

A few hours later, Bank of England, Threadneedle Street, London

An umbrella held in one hand and her reticule clutched in another, Lady Victoria regarded the huge building before her with anticipation as snow fell from gray skies.

"Would you like me to come in with you, my lady?" her driver asked as he assisted Cummings, the lady's maid, from the unmarked town coach.

"That won't be necessary, Mr. Thompson. I've an appointment." At least, she hoped she did. She had dispatched Cummings' husband, a footman, earlier that morning with a note explaining she wished to see Mr. Burroughs. Cummings had returned to Fairmont Park with word that he had left the note with a clerk and been told someone would see to her ladyship when she arrived.

Victoria bristled at the thought that she might end up in the office of a clerk who knew nothing of her funds, or worse, knew nothing about why she wished to speak with Mr. Burroughs.

Anxious for the protection of a roof and the promise of warmth, she hurried up to the bank doors. A footman was quick to open one as she closed her umbrella, and she and Cummings entered the venerable establishment.

Seated behind a counter, the receptionist immediately stood when she approached. "How do, miss? How may I be of assistance?"

"Miss Statton to see Mr. Burroughs," she said in a hoarse whisper. Having heard the echoes of her boot heels on the marble floor, she didn't wish to announce her presence to everyone who stood about in the lobby, nor did she want the receptionist to know her true identity.

The receptionist consulted a book and nodded. "He's expecting you. Would you like to leave your umbrella with me?"

"Thank you, but no." She handed it to Cummings.

"Right this way."

The young man led her down a wide corridor with wood doors on either side, some open to reveal carpeted offices while most were closed.

The door to Mr. Burroughs' office was open only a few inches. After knocking, the receptionist listened and then opened the door and held it as Victoria and her lady's maid entered.

"Oh, there must be some mistake," Victoria said when her gaze fell on the blond-haired, blue-eyed man who sat behind a massive oak desk. "I am scheduled to see Mr. Burroughs. Mr. *Andrew* Burroughs."

The receptionist's eyes widened. He dared a glance at the tall man who had quickly stood upon seeing his caller.

"Miss Statton, this is—"

"Lady Victoria, I am James Burroughs," the banker stated. "My father, Lord Andrew, is retiring from the bank this week," he added as he stepped around the desk and moved to take her hand. "I do hope you're not... *offended* I am taking this meeting instead of him."

Victoria watched as he lifted her gloved hand to his lips. "I suppose that depends on whether or not you can help me, Mr. Burroughs."

His reference to 'Lord Andrew' had her stiffening. The name implied his father was a duke's son, but not the eldest. She quickly wracked her brain in an effort to remember to which ducal family Lord Andrew belonged. Burroughs was the family name of the Ariley dukedom, which meant James was the grandson of the late Duke of Ariley. The nephew of the current Duke of Ariley.

"May I take your coat, my lady?" Before Victoria could even answer, James stepped behind her and helped remove the redingote, revealing an emerald wool carriage dress. Other than the black frog closures at the neckline and down the front, the gown was void of decoration. Lady Victoria's green eyes appeared especially striking given the color of her gown and the small emerald hat mounted to the side of her elaborate coiffure of raven hair. If James hadn't already developed a tendre for another young woman, he might have been tempted by the lady.

Lady Victoria didn't strike him as a woman in want of a husband, however.

Cummings was about to accept the coat, but the receptionist stepped in and had it hung on a coat rack before he bowed and took his leave of the office.

"Have you come far this afternoon?" James asked as he held the chair in front of his desk for her.

"Not far. I live just north of the city," she replied. "I have recently taken Fairmont Park as my own."

James furrowed a brow. "I fear I'm not acquainted with it. I've only been back in London a few days," he explained. "And am more familiar with estates on the southwestern side. However, I'm quite sure I can be of assistance with whatever it is you require."

. . .

*V*ictoria sighed, sure Andrew Burroughs would be more familiar with her situation. He had been the one to arrange her first withdrawal in order to cover the costs associated with the work she had already had done at the estate. Now she would have to explain her situation to his son. "Fairmont Park is an unentailed property of the Somerset dukedom," she said. "Now that I've reached my majority, I have agreed to see to its renovation."

Nodding his understanding, James moved a pile of papers from the side of his desk to the middle. "You've a good deal of money deposited with this bank," he murmured. "And it looks as if you've already completed some of the renovations?"

"Indeed," she replied, curious as to what was written on the paper he was perusing at that moment.

"Do you expect to spend *all* of it on the house and grounds?"

"I do not. In fact, I am looking for an investment opportunity."

*J*ames immediately thought of his friend, Tom Grandby. Following in his father's footsteps as an investor involved in a number of industries, Tom had been making money for his clients for over a decade. "Have you something in mind?"

She shook her head, then said, "I was hoping you might have some suggestions."

He settled back in his leather chair and regarded Lady Victoria a long moment. "As a banker, I'm not really allowed to advise you on investments other than what we offer here at the bank. Fiver-percenters, for example. But I can at least recommend an investment advisor. Someone who can set up a subscription for you, or find a long-term investment for your funds." He noted her look of disappointment and quickly added, "As a member of the *ton*, however, I might be able to suggest a few options."

"Whom might you suggest as an advisor?" she queried.

"The Grandbys. Tom, specifically, since his father, like mine, is on the verge of retirement. He's a master at making money for his clients in a number of industries, most recently railroads and steam-powered engines. He has his office in Oxford Street," he said as he wrote something on a card.

Victoria's face brightened at hearing the mention of steam-powered engines. "And the options you would suggest?"

"What is your timeline?"

"A decade or two," Victoria replied.

James blinked. "That long?"

"It's necessary, yes," she said in a quiet voice. "I need to ensure the money is not easily accessible. By anyone."

"Does someone have a claim against you?" he asked, suspicion evident in his voice.

Victoria sighed. "I've a brother who has managed to squander most of his inheritance, and I don't wish for him to lay claim to mine."

James understood her concern. With her funds tied up in a long-term investment, her brother wouldn't be able to access it. "And the rest?"

"I'll need it to continue work on the house and grounds," she replied. "For living expenses and the servants' pay, as well. So I would prefer if those funds could be... hidden somewhat. Deposited under a pseudonym. One that he would not know."

Furrowing his brows, James considered her plight. "I take it you are not yet married?"

"I am not."

"But you've already received your inheritance, so you have reached your majority."

"I have."

"You have no other male relative who could—?"

"Not here in London." She didn't mention her brother, Michael, only because she didn't know how long he would be in town.

James cleared his throat and regarded her another moment. Although he was usually attracted to a typical blonde-haired, blue-eyed English miss, he could imagine there were a number of young men in London who would find the raven-haired, green-eyed beauty who sat before him more to their liking.

Men like Tom Grandby.

At the age of four-and-thirty, the second-oldest Grandby son was still unmarried. Given the fortune he was accumulating with every investment, he would require an heir. Which meant he needed a wife to produce said heir. His friend hadn't yet made his choice, nor had he even courted anyone. Meanwhile, James had already decided to take one of Tom's sisters to wife.

Marriage to Emily Grandby promised a quiet life free of chaos, just the way James wanted to continue living his life. He hadn't yet told Tom of his intentions to marry Emily, but there would be plenty of time for that later.

He straightened in his chair as he devised a strategy for Lady Victoria and her funds.

"If you employ Mr. Grandby as your advisor, I would suggest you meet with him in person. Either at his office or at your home."

"Of course."

"He'll ask what your interests are in terms of an investment."

"What do you suggest I tell him?"

"Well, what are your interests?"

"I train horses, Mr. Burroughs. Race horses."

James blinked. He blinked again. "Your... your own?"

"My family's as well as a few from other stables. The Marquess of Reading has placed a couple of his colts in my care. But please understand, I have no interest in investing in horse racing."

About to ask why, James had to remind himself that horse racing was one of the most uncertain of all the possible money making ventures. Anything could and did go wrong in the world of racing. Even a sure bet sometimes lost a race.

And horses were expensive.

No wonder her eyes had widened at the mention of steam engines.

"Have you ever seen a steam-powered bus?" he asked.

Victoria said, "Of course. I've even ridden on one or two."

"Are you familiar with their operation?"

She shook her head. "Are you?"

James allowed a slight grin to lift his lips. "I recently moved here from Bath. We had a steam bus service from Bath to London, one in which I have an investment. Let me tell you why."

For the next half-hour, James explained all the benefits of steam buses as well as some of their drawbacks while Victoria took notes in a small notebook she pulled from her reticule.

"Where might I find more information?" she asked when he had finished his list of pros and cons.

James considered the query. "A library, perhaps. Or you might gain an audience with someone at the steam bus company that services London."

"Very well," she said as she stood. "I appreciate your time, Mr. Burroughs. If you could see to changing the name on my account to V. Statton, I won't take up any more of your time."

Quick to stand when she did, James stepped from behind the desk and moved to take her coat from the rack.

"I will see to it. I won't allow anyone but you to access your funds," he promised. He held the coat open for her, a grin forming as he considered what Tom Grandby would think of the young woman.

"Good day, sir."

He handed her his card. On the back, he had written Tom's

information. "Good day to you. I look forward to learning what you decide."

He walked her to the door, gave her a bow as he settled a kiss on the back of her gloved hand, and wished he could be a fly on the wall when she and Tom would meet for the very first time.

CHAPTER 2

OF BUMS AND HORSES

*S*aturday, *January 5, 1839, Fairmont Park, just north of London*

"An Arabian, is he not?" Tom Grandby guessed, hoping he wasn't far off the mark. His only knowledge of horses extended to the Cleveland Bays he had purchased for his town coach and a high-perch phaeton. He rarely had a chance to ride, and he didn't even attend horse races unless he happened to be in the same town as a race when it was taking place.

"He is a Thoroughbred, if that is your real question," Lady Victoria Statton replied. Her green-eyed gaze turned onto the interloper who had been watching her ride at the edge of a racing track. "And who might you be?" Despite the falling snow, she didn't wear a riding habit nor even a wrap of any kind.

Nonplussed by the annoyance the young woman showed him, Tom gave a bow. "Thomas Grandby, at your service, my lady."

She quickly dismounted, not bothering to ask for assistance as she swung a leg over the saddle and hopped down. Neither did she curtsy but instead returned her attention to the horse, examining the animal's left side with a look of worry. "Are you here about a horse?" Dressed in what appeared to be a jockey's riding habit—a tight-fitting jacket and breeches—and with her jet black hair pinned up and stuffed under a velvet jockey's cap, she looked as if she were a tall boy from a distance.

The young woman had been riding the animal astride when Tom first approached the track. Given she was the only person at the track and having been told he could find her there, Tom knew he had the right person.

At least, he hoped the stableboy had understood his query.

When he had asked as to the whereabouts of Lady Victoria, the stableboy had to give it some thought before he said, "Oh. You want Vicky." Then he had directed Tom to the track.

Victoria bent over to examine the horse's foreleg. When her caller didn't immediately answer her question, she arched a brow. "Are you staring at my bum?"

Embarrassed, Tom blinked and quickly glanced away. Then he noted the tone of her query and wondered if she were daring him to admit that he had, indeed, noticed and was impressed by the shape of the bottom encased in the tight riding breeches she wore. "Admiring it, if you must know," he replied. "I have never before seen a woman wearing men's riding breeches. Now I'm left wondering why more of you do not."

She straightened, her eyes wide with what might have been anger. About to admonish him, she couldn't when he added, "If you did not wish for me to notice your perfect bum, then perhaps you could have refrained from bending down in my presence."

The young woman rolled her eyes and returned her attention to the horse's foreleg. "Or you could have been a gentleman and simply turned your gaze onto the landscape... or the horse."

"I prefer scenes of beauty when I am given the option," Tom responded, nearly shocked upon realizing he had spoken the words out loud. "And I cannot believe I just said that," he murmured. "I meant no offense. Truly."

What the hell was wrong with him? He wasn't a rake, or a scoundrel. He never behaved this way with a woman, and he had a mother and five sisters who could attest to it.

Something about Lady Victoria had him behaving in the oddest manner.

*V*ictoria Statton, second and youngest daughter of the Duke of Somerset, couldn't decide if she should feel offense or humor by her caller's odd comment. Learning the man thought she had a "perfect bum" had her deciding against expressing anger toward him. Annoyance was enough. "I cannot train a horse dressed in a women's riding habit. Especially for racing," she said on a sigh.

"I'm sure I wouldn't know," Tom replied.

She dared another glance at him. "Because you've never owned a racehorse?" Her eyes narrowed. "Or because you've never *ridden* a horse?"

*I*nhaling slowly, Tom decided the truth was best. He had already annoyed her, and he didn't wish to further anger a potential client. "I have never owned a racehorse, it's true. I can ride, but..."

Victoria straightened, her gloved hands gently smoothing both sides of the horse's leg and up to its withers as she did so. "You do not?"

The oddest sensation passed through Tom as he watched her rise and then direct her green-eyed gaze entirely on him. At that moment, a thought of riding *her* was quickly replaced with one of her riding him—astride, atop his prone body—and him helpless but to allow her to do so.

Where had that thought come from?

It hadn't been that long since he had ended his liaison with his mistress. Although Liza had been perfectly fine when they were in bed together, she lacked an education. As such, she couldn't keep up her end of a conversation involving any of his interests. She couldn't understand his concerns for events that occurred hundreds of miles away when she knew only of what happened in the neighborhood in which she lived.

After two years of twice-weekly trysts, he had given her a bracelet, paid off her debt with a Bond Street modiste, and said his farewells. That had been six months ago, and although he had missed the intimacy of their relationship, he had not missed the boredom that came with it.

Tom swallowed and felt grateful that his greatcoat was hiding the evidence of his sudden erection. The fashion-forward tight trousers with a front fly instead of the breeches featuring fall-fronts of the past few decades made hardened manhoods that much more apparent.

"I can ride a horse. I just... I do not find I have the time for it these days," he explained.

"If you are not here about having a horse trained, then why are you here?"

With all the talk of bums and horses, Tom had completely forgotten he had come to the manor house for a reason that did not include bums and horses. "Lord Michael asked that I pay a call. This is Fairmont Park, is it not?" he asked as he gazed at the back of the estate home. It was by no means as huge as some country estates tended to be, but the grounds were extensive. As were the stables. He thought the building might be large enough to hold twenty or more of the beasts. Then there was a manse for the grooms, a separate carriage house and, at the other end of the house stood a long orangery built of brick.

It was Victoria's turn to blink. "What was your name again?"

"Grandby. Thomas Grandby. Your brother asked that I call on you regarding—"

"An investment, yes," she murmured. "Forgive me. I thought you would be *older*."

His eyes darting to one side, Tom wondered if she was expecting a visit from his father instead of from him. "My father, Gregory Grandby, started our firm some forty years ago, but he is for the most part retired these days."

The familiar refrain—Victoria remembered James Burrough's comment about his father's retirement—had her nodding her understanding. She took up the reins of the Thoroughbred and indicated they should walk toward the stables. "Have you your father's same knack for making money?"

Tom gave a start at hearing her query. Unless it was a mention of pin money, women rarely spoke of blunt. "I do, although I will admit I'm a bit more conservative than my father in my approach to choosing investments."

"Why is that?"

He allowed a shrug and then noticed she was about to step onto a pile of horse manure that lay in their path. His reaction was to quickly reach out, lift her by the waist, and carry her over the excrement, which had her letting out a yelp of surprise.

"Whatever are you—?"

"Forgive me, but you were about to foul your boots," he explained, as he set her down beyond the manure.

"It would not be the first time," she replied, her annoyance apparent as she seemed to struggle to regain her balance. After a moment, her expression softened, and she said, "I am grateful you saved my boots from excrement, however. Thank you."

The comment had Tom nodding. "Hobys, are they not?"

She regarded him with an expression of curiosity. "They are." After a pause, she added, "I am surprised a man who does not ride would know such a thing."

"I am well aware of Hoby and his custom boots, my lady." Tom didn't add that the original owner of the boot maker's shop was a client of his father's, nor did he allow his gaze to return to the boots. For a moment, he was sure one of them was different from the other, the shape of the sole much wider.

Victoria led the horse to a stableboy, who took the reins from her. "Wrap his left foreleg, will you, Jemmy? And just to be safe, keep him in his stall for the rest of the day."

"Yes, my lady," the boy said before hurrying off.

"Is something wrong with the horse?" Tom asked when she returned her attention to him. "He was quite impressive in his run."

"Possibly. And I cannot take a chance." At seeing his continued interest, she added, "He's one of Lord Reading's two-year-olds. I am training him for the racing circuit."

Tom was secretly glad Lord Michael had told him about Lady Victoria's avocation. Otherwise his expression would have betrayed his shock. "But... I thought the marquess had his own trainers," he murmured.

"He does," Victoria acknowledged. "Just not enough of them for his current crop of colts."

"Ah. I understand he is one of the best horse breeders in the country," Tom said. He knew that much because the marquess was another of his father's clients. Lord Reading's investments in horse racing meant his fortunes might require more conservative investments to help cover the losses for years when his nags failed to win at the track.

Which was rare.

"I do believe his wife is the horse breeder in that family," Victoria remarked as they made their way to the back door of the Portland stone manor house. Despite the weather, a gardener was seeing to trimming the boxwoods that bordered the base of the house.

"You refer to the Marchioness of Reading?" Tom asked, hoping to gain a bit of respect from the young woman. He knew Constance Fitzwilliam Roderick. Knew of her skills when it came to matching dams to sires to achieve horses who could display both stamina and speed.

Randall Roderick, Marquess of Reading, was always quick to sing his wife's praises. With Constance having given birth to three boys during their twenty-year union, the marquess had his heir, a spare, and a jockey, not to mention the four bastard sons he had fathered prior to his marriage.

"And you said you knew nothing of horse racing," Victoria accused as she allowed him to open the manor's back door.

Expecting to step into the kitchens, Tom was surprised when they instead ended up in a wide, carpeted corridor.

"I'd like to change clothes before we speak," Victoria said, noticing the leather satchel that hung from one of his hands. "Can you afford the time? I can see to it you have a comfortable place to write letters."

Impressed she would consider his time valuable, Tom nodded. "Much appreciated." The extra time would give him an opportunity to look at the house.

They passed several doors before she led him into a parlor. At the back, a card table was set up near a window. A pot of ink and several quills were on display in a silver-handled carrier.

"This will do nicely," he said as he admired the inlaid table, sure it was a Chippendale.

"I like to write letters here instead of in my salon. The light is so much better," she explained. "Let me help with your coat." She moved to stand behind him and held onto the collar of the greatcoat as Tom pulled his arms from it. Then she draped it over one arm. "I'll have Clark see to some tea and cakes."

Tom bowed before she turned and took her leave of the parlor.

At the sight of her retreating figure, he swallowed.

Hard.

Besides the perfect shape of her bottom, she displayed a slight limp that had her hips swaying in a manner that could only be described as arousing.

Her unusual attire not withstanding, Victoria Statton was

unlike any of his other clients. As to whether or not he would take her on as a client, he wasn't yet sure.

But he found he didn't mind waiting in her well-appointed parlor as he wrote a letter, drank tea, and occasionally remembered what she had looked like in her riding clothes.

Perfect bum, indeed.

CHAPTER 3

A FOILED ATTEMPT AT
PRESSING A POINT

eanwhile, Carlington House, Mayfair
The sound of someone entering his house
had David Carlington, Marquess of Morganfield, moving to the
threshold of his study and angling his head around the door
frame. The servants had the day off—it was Sunday—and
Alfred, the butler, was spending the day with his aged mother in
Cheapside.

When David realized the identity of the intruder, he stepped
out of his study and regarded his son from head to toe. Then he
frowned. "Where have *you* been?"

Christopher, Earl of Haddon and heir to the Morganfield
marquessate, tapped his fencing foil against his right leg before
he lifted it in front of him. "Paris," he replied. "Bertrand finally
had time for me."

Bertrand referred to Francois-Joseph Bertrand, a fencing
master who emphasized speed and mobility in the sport. Having
received a missive that the master could accept Christopher as a
pupil, but only for a fortnight, the earl had taken the next ship
to France without so much as a word to anyone.

At least, to anyone but his mother, Adeline.

Christopher thrust the foil forward and then stepped back,

his weight evenly distributed over both feet. Other than the lacy cuffs that extended beyond the sleeves of his navy topcoat, he was dressed in the current fashion—buff trousers, tasseled boots, and an embroidered waistcoat featuring a shawl collar. The aforementioned topcoat, pinched in at the waist, flared out in pleats and nearly reached his knees. "I've had to unlearn everything I learned at university," he said.

Unimpressed, the marquess arched a brow. "I should hope not." His son had studied political affairs at Oxford and actually seemed to have retained much of the information when he had returned to London in 1818. In the past two decades, he had taken on the day-to-day responsibilities of the marquessate in addition to accepting a writ of acceleration so that he might attend sessions of Parliament before his father's death.

"I meant about fencing, of course," Christopher countered. "This new style is quite economical and far easier to learn. I can hardly wait to employ it when I'm next at the fencing academy," he continued. Then he glanced around the hall. "Anything of note happen whilst I was away?"

"Two weddings and two betrothals," his father replied. "Which means four fewer eligible ladies to choose from."

Christopher gave a start. "I was only gone three weeks!"

David allowed a shrug. "It seems the parson's trap works quickly when a young man—or lady—is of a mind to marry. Given your age, you really should consider it, and soon."

Bristling at the reminder he hadn't yet taken a wife, Christopher allowed a sigh. "Anyone I know?" he asked as he and his father made their way into the Carlington House study.

"Lady Angelica and Sir Benjamin—"

"I knew they were betrothed."

"Lady Anne and Lord Hexham—"

"She was far too young for me." Christopher furrowed his brows. "I have a niece Hexham's age," he said, referring to his sister Elizabeth's second child, Christina. "Who's betrothed?"

"I expect Gabe Wellingham will marry a ceramist whom he met whilst working at the British Museum."

"That's unexpected."

"And James Burroughs—Lord Andrew's son—has set his cap on one of the Grandby daughters."

Christopher's eyes darted sideways. "Hmm. I think Emily was the only one left unmarried, but it's not like she was royalty. Her father doesn't even possess a title."

"No, but he has *money*. I rather imagine her settlement will be huge," David remarked as he poured them both a brandy. "And I rather doubt Burroughs was in need of any of it."

Dropping his foil on the room's only sofa, Christopher regarded his father with a look of suspicion. "When I left, I was under the impression all was well with the Carlington coffers," he said in a hoarse whisper. "I've been seeing to the books."

"They still are," David quickly replied. "What I'm trying to make you understand is that your options for a wife are growing more limited."

"Nonsense," Christopher argued. "I'm not even—"

"If you're about to say 'forty,' then allow me to set you straight right now, son. You are *one*-and-forty and not far from *two*-and forty. There are those at White's who are placing bets that you're trying to follow in your godfather's footsteps—"

"There is nothing wrong with Torrington's footsteps," Christopher argued, referring to Milton Grandby, Earl of Torrington. "He waited to marry, and his countess still gave him an heir."

"Who is now married," David was quick to say. "And in Italy. He's probably already got an heir on his new wife." When Christopher rolled his eyes, he added, "I got Elizabeth on your mother during our wedding trip in Rome."

"Really, Father," Christopher said with disgust. "I didn't need to hear that."

"No? Then hear this. I'm about to have your *godfather* arrange something for you."

"You wouldn't dare!" Not that Torrington would choose a poor match for him—the man had done rather nicely for some of his godsons, at least for those who hadn't arranged their own marriages—but he really didn't wish to have a wife forced on him. Especially one not of his own choosing.

Outside, snow was falling again, the gray skies casting a gloom over Mayfair that was made even more gray from the coal soot that erupted from the rows of chimneys atop every single mansion and townhouse in London.

"Not that I would expect you to wed a daughter of the aristocracy, but it's past time you wed *someone*," David murmured. He took a drink from his rummer and set the glass down on his large desk. "At this point, I would have suggested your mistress, but apparently she quit you sometime back. Something about you being an arrogant ass?"

Christopher recoiled at hearing his father's words, more so because his father knew he'd had a mistress than that she had quit him. "Did Delilah come to you for money?" he asked in alarm.

"No," David replied. "I have my own source when it comes to learning about who's bedding whom in this town. What worries me is *why* she would say such a thing about you. Are you behaving poorly with the fairer sex?"

Anger building—why would Delilah make such a claim?—Christopher shook his head. "Not that I'm aware."

"You are awfully proud," his father argued. "Which probably works well on the piste. But it does you no favors elsewhere."

Christopher raised his chin but then thought better of providing a retort and quickly lowered it.

Yes, he was proud. He was educated. He was heir to a marquessate. He was handsome, at least to those women who were attracted to his dark auburn hair, decent height, and hazel eyes. His nose was more hooked than he would have liked, but it suited his angular face. And he had a chin, which was more than he could say for some of the other men his age.

Thanks to his inheritance, some of which he had claimed upon his twenty-fifth birthday, he had a fashionable wardrobe, several pairs of custom boots, his own town coach with four shires to pull it, a phaeton, his own cologne from Floris, a membership at White's and another at Brook's, and his own table at his favorite London coffee shop.

He could have any woman he wanted.

"I will prove to you that I can find a suitable match," Christopher said. "Why, I may have to choose from among many," he boasted.

"Make it quick," David replied. "You're not getting any younger."

Pulling his shoulders back, Christopher downed the rest of his brandy, retrieved his foil from the sofa, and took his leave of the study, determined to prove his father wrong.

CHAPTER 4

LEARNING ABOUT A LADY
OVER LUNCHEON

*M*eanwhile, back at Fairmont Park

"I do hope Clark has seen to tea for you," a female voice said from the door to the parlor.

His attentions entirely on the letter he was penning to a fellow investor, Tom gave a passing glance toward the door, thinking a housemaid was addressing him. "Yes, he's been very attentive, thank you."

He did a double-take when he realized the woman wore a coral day gown, the neckline decorated with a white eyelet collar. Her black hair was pinned up in a neat bun atop her head. She looked familiar, but for a moment, Tom couldn't remember where he might have seen her.

Rising to his feet, he gave a bow. "Good afternoon, my lady."

He watched as the young woman made her way into the deep parlor and dipped a curtsy. "Good afternoon, Mr. Grandby. I apologize for taking so long. My lady's maid insisted my hair be repinned," she said.

Tom blinked. "Lady Victoria?" Despite having spent nearly thirty minutes in her company only the hour before, he hadn't recognized the young woman. She looked positively elegant. Her bell-shaped skirts hid any evidence of what her breeches had so nicely displayed, but her fitted bodice accentuated her slim waist—he had learned of it when he lifted her over the manure—and a modest bosom. Whilst she was walking towards him, he didn't see any evidence of a limp.

"Yes?" Her reply was hesitant, especially after she glanced behind her to ensure there wasn't anyone else in the room.

He gave a shake of his head. "My apologies. I did not recognize you."

Victoria allowed a nod. "Well, I suppose that's a good thing?" she guessed, reminded that he had seen her in breeches only the hour before. "I wondered if we might talk over a luncheon? I've not eaten since early this morning, and I am in need of more than just tea."

"A luncheon would be welcome," he replied, glad for the opportunity to see more of the house. He'd been tempted to wander whilst she changed, but he didn't want to be caught by the butler. The servant might think he was there to steal something. "Let me just put away my things." He moved to stuff the parchments into his satchel and then turned to indicate he was ready.

"A footman has seen to a table for us in the orangery. With the sun out now, it should be warm enough for us in there."

Tom offered his arm. "Lead the way." He was secretly glad for the change in venue. Although the parlor had been comfortable for writing letters, the other furnishings were from the century prior and lent a stuffiness to what he had thought was a more modern estate located just beyond the northern borders of the city. "Have you lived here long?"

Victoria gave him a sideways glance. "Only on occasion until recently," she replied. "Usually during a Season. I expect I shall be spending more time here, though."

"Oh?"

"There isn't a suitable location to exercise the horses at my father's house—to train them for racing. Besides, it's too far from the racing towns," she said as they stepped out to a covered loggia. The air, still chilly, carried a few snowflakes as they made their way into the brick orangery.

Warmth and tropical scents immediately surrounded them. Tom closed the door behind them and took a quick look around. Potted orange and lime trees, already heavy with fruit, lined the front windowed wall. Palms and bromeliads filled the rest of the building. In the middle of the terra cotta-tiled floor, a white painted iron table was set with a cold collation of meats and cheeses. Instead of the usual floral arrangement, a soup tureen sat in the center of the table.

"Quite a contrast to the weather outside," he commented as he pulled out a chair for her.

She settled into the tooled iron chair and said, "Indeed. I much prefer eating here than inside. I don't care for the furnishings in the main house. They're far too stuffy." She reached over and ladled the rich soup into a bowl. "Would you like soup? It's probably lobster bisque."

"I would, thank you," Tom replied as he took the chair opposite. "It smells delicious."

"Father has always managed to employ good cooks," Victoria said as she set the bowl on the table and filled a second one. "Anything to keep my mother happy."

Curious, mostly because Lord Michael hadn't mentioned it, Tom asked, "Where do they reside now?"

"Wiltshire, of course. Although my mother used to love coming to the capital in her younger years, she has no use of gossip or soot-filled air and now prefers to stay at the ducal house."

Tom quickly reviewed her family connections in his head, glad he'd had the chance to meet with Lord Michael the Friday prior. Her father was Jeremy Statton, Duke of Somerset. Her mother was Elizabeth Cunningham, daughter of Viscount Mark Cunningham.

Tom wracked his brain in an effort to remember how many children there were in the Somerset family. *Four?* Two boys, two girls, which meant Victoria was...

"I am the youngest," Victoria stated, as if she could read his mind.

He gave his head a shake. "Tell me. Why would your brother ask for a meeting with *me* when your uncle has been so successful with his investment strategies?"

Victoria finished a spoonful of soup and then sighed. "Uncle Michael has done well for my father, it's true, but I wish to go a different route with my inheritance."

"You already have it?"

She nodded. "My birthday was last week. I find myself in possession of..." She was about to tell him how much her father had settled on her and then thought better of it. "A good deal of funds, most of which I would like to see invested—somehow protected—should I end up married to a fortune seeker."

Tom paused in lifting his spoon to his mouth. "You're not already betrothed?" Although Lord Michael had said she would probably never marry, he wanted to hear her side of it.

"I am not." She hesitated before adding, "Does that surprise you?"

Giving his head a shake, Tom said, "Somewhat. I suppose I expect all the daughters of dukes to be married off when they're of an age."

"I've done my best to remain a secret to the *ton*," Victoria whispered as she leaned over her soup. "Staying in Wiltshire these past few years has helped a great deal."

"No come-out? No Season or two in London?" he queried.

She shook her head. "Only in Wiltshire, and only because my mother insisted on something. She still holds out hope I will marry and produce a couple of colts," she added with a quirk.

Tom couldn't help but wince at the reference to babes as colts. "You wish to remain unmarried?"

A shoulder lifted. "For now. Society won't label me a spinster for a few years yet."

"Will you be returning to Wiltshire?"

"Not anytime soon. I told my father I would see to the restoration of Fairmont Park until such time as he can decide if he wants to sell it or give it to one of us."

Tom straightened. "It's not entailed?" he asked, pretending he didn't already know the answer. Besides, it was rare the ownership of an estate the size of Fairmont Park was free and clear. With it's huge manor house, additional buildings and parklands, anyone would assume it was a Somerset ducal property.

"It is not. And since I am the only one who showed an interest in it, Father challenged me with it."

"Challenged?" Tom repeated, a grin teasing his lips.

"You should have seen it a few months ago. It was a ruin," she said. "We hadn't lived here in some time. I had to enlist the aid of an agency to employ staff for the cleaning and gardening. Most of the furnishings are still in need of reupholstering or repair, but one thing at a time."

"And the race track?" Tom asked, thinking the grounds and fencing around the turf track looked new.

"I had that done first," she admitted. "As well as the enlarged stables."

"The horses. Are they yours, or—?"

"Father's, mostly. One is mine and two belong to my brothers. Their difference in ages means we'll have entries in the various horse races every year from this season going forward."

"You're training all of them?" Tom asked, trying to decide if he should be scandalized or impressed.

"I am," she affirmed. "Have I thoroughly scandalized you?"

Shaking his head, Tom said, "You have thoroughly

impressed me, in fact. Although, to be honest, I do not own a racehorse nor do I know much about the sport."

"Given your profession, that's rather wise of you," she replied. "Horses are expensive, the sport is filled with ruffians and cheats, and a win at the track is rare."

"Which is why you want me to invest your funds in something... safer?" he guessed.

She grinned. "I was thinking steam-powered buses."

Tom dropped his fork, the implement clattering onto his plate.

"Oh, dear. Is there something wrong with the meat?" she asked, her attention going to the platter of sliced ham and various cheeses.

"No. No, it's fine. It's very good," Tom said quickly. "What do you know of steam-powered buses?"

Victoria sighed. "I see how they have replaced horse-drawn carriages on the roads outside of the city," she replied. "They can cover four-and-twenty miles in an hour—"

"But for only four miles," Tom put in.

"And twelve miles per hour over longer distances," she continued, ignoring his comment. "They can travel when road conditions are deemed too hazardous for a coach-and-four. They do not tip over, and since they cannot be spooked, they do not run away with their customers." She paused to take a breath, and when her guest didn't offer a remark, she added, "Their brakes do not lock and drag. The buses do not cause as much damage to roads as carriage wheels do. And they can operate at a cost of half of a horse-drawn carriage."

Tom stared at his hostess, a strange contraction occurring in his chest. She was speaking of features and benefits and costs as if she were an investment advisor.

And she was doing so intelligently.

"Be still my heart," he murmured as he stared at her.

Her dark brows arched. "I beg your pardon?"

He shook his head. "Apologies. I've just... I've never heard a woman speak so eloquently on a topic of investment before," he stammered.

"I am not like most women," Victoria countered.

"A fact well established earlier this afternoon," he said with a quirk. He allowed a sigh when he noted how her expression darkened. "I apologize. What you wear when training horses is none of my concern. But your fortune is. That is, if you wish me to assist you."

"I thought choosing a younger man might be in my best interest," she murmured.

"You thought I would be older," he teased.

She grinned, and damn if he didn't feel as if he'd been bamboozled. "A bit older, yes," she finally admitted.

"And as you surmised, it is in your best interest to hire me," he added.

"So why is it you don't seem sold on the idea of steam-powered buses?" she asked, returning her attention to her meal.

He frowned. "I never said I wasn't."

"But you have reservations."

Angling his head to one side, Tom said, "In the interest of full disclosure, let me tell you that I *have* invested my own funds in them."

A flash of anger crossed Victoria's face before she said, "Then why is it you wish to dissuade *me*?"

"I don't." He took a breath, still impressed by her foresight. He decided he best inform her of the risks of funding such a venture, though. "What you say is true, to a point."

"What point is that?" she challenged.

"Sir Goldsworthy Gurney and his associates as well as Walter Hancock have done a marvelous job with their inventions. They run reliable services. Should either of them prevail within the cities, hackneys will be a thing of the past. Buses are already providing transportation services to those who cannot afford their own horses, and they offer a quicker trip than the mail coach. I cannot help but think they will be all the rage in the next decade."

"I hear a very large 'but' in your argument," she murmured, her concern evident in her expression.

"Tolls."

Victoria blinked. "Tolls?"

He nodded. "I expect tolls will be assessed that will make them too expensive to run in place of the stagecoach services," he explained. "But until such time as that happens, they could be a very lucrative investment."

Her brows furrowed at hearing the confusing news. "How long until that happens?"

Tom allowed a shrug. "Ten. Twenty years? At some point, speed limits will be set that will undermine their main benefit."

"But why?" she asked in exasperation. "Speed is the very reason they're becoming popular."

"Because horses are a way of life," he argued. "Which given your avocation has me a bit befuddled as to why you're not *protesting* steam buses."

She allowed a sound of impatience. "My avocation has to do with *speed*, Mr. Grandby," she countered quickly. "If it could not be achieved with horses, then I would be doing it with something else."

The thought of her interest in speed had Tom wondering if she was fast. He could think of a few things they could be doing, and not all of them quickly. A kiss. A tumble or two...

"What other reason can you provide that might dissuade me?"

Pulled from his brief reverie, Tom considered the query and allowed a sigh. "Because sometimes innovation and advancement are prevented from occurring. Every new invention has its critics."

"Luddites," she murmured, understanding his reasoning.

"Indeed. But that doesn't mean we can't capitalize on steam buses and their benefits now."

"Then what do I do?"

Tom considered options, knowing many of the overland routes would be served by trains in the coming decade. "Perhaps we propose a different city—or cities—in which to provide a bus service."

"You mean between them?"

He shook his head. "Trains are already doing that. Or they will in due time."

"But in the meantime?" she argued. "It's taken years to lay the tracks for the routes that are just now opening."

"True," he responded, his attention on his fork. "You're thinking the buses could be used in the interim?"

"Yes, and then redeployed to other routes once those railway lines are put into service. It will be years before the trains reach all of England."

"My Father and I have investments in some of those railways," he murmured. "Offering a quick travel solution until the track is finished is an excellent idea." He looked up when he heard her sound of protest. "You don't agree?"

"I didn't share my idea with you so that you could go off and do it without me," she replied.

Tom blinked and then understood her concern. "Oh, but I wouldn't," he said with a shake of his head. "I promise. It's your idea. You would hold the majority stake in the enterprise, depending on your level of investment, of course."

Victoria stared at him. "How do I know you won't double-cross me?"

Offended, Tom straightened in his chair. "I... I assure you, my lady, I am an honorable businessman," he argued. "There would be a contract, of course." He sighed and then inhaled. "Several, actually, since we'll have to procure the buses and arrange for a supporting infrastructure before any service can commence."

"Infrastructure?" Victoria sounded out the word, as if she had never heard it before.

"Buildings to house the buses when they are not in operation. Maintenance men to fix them. Drivers. Spare parts and whatnot," Tom explained.

She dipped her head. "That all sounds as if it will take a good deal of time."

"Some," Tom acknowledged. "But it's been done in Stratford for the route to London," he added. When he noted her continued expression of disappointment, he said, "The first one is always the most expensive. And usually fraught with problems. Mr. Hancock has everything working with the Stratford to London line."

"You're saying we could learn from Mr. Hancock's mistakes?"

"Yes, exactly."

"But... what incentive would he have to provide his knowledge?" she asked. Men rarely shared how they managed to get something to work. How they trained their horses, or how they won at cards, or how they managed to land the most unlikely woman to be their wife.

Tom allowed a brilliant smile to appear. "We make him a partner, of course," he whispered.

"But... not an investor?"

He shook his head. "Well, he would need to be to some extent. He would be required to help in the acquisition or construction of the buses and in the training of the people who will drive them and repair them," he argued. "So he would be investing his time."

"And if Mr. Hancock cannot be compelled to accept the offer?"

Tom angled his head back and forth. "We offer more or we take our offer to Sir Goldsworthy."

Seemingly satisfied by his answer, Victoria gave a nod. "Would you tell me if I was being foolish?"

"About what?" he asked, his attention having returned to his lunch.

"About this. About steam buses," she replied.

"Oh. Well, of course," he assured her. When he noted her look of expectation, he added, "If you're waiting for me to tell you you're being foolish, you will have a long wait."

A smile finally split Victoria's face, and Tom was struck in more ways than one.

He almost looked over his shoulder to discover if Cupid had taken aim and fired on him.

Damn the chubby menace.

CHAPTER 5

RUMINATING

A half-hour later, still in the orangery at Fairmont Park
Their luncheon finished and the last of a bottle of wine poured, Victoria regarded her caller with curiosity. "Tell me, Mr. Grandby, why is it you have agreed to take me on as a client when you don't even know how much I have to invest?"

Holding the stem of his wine glass between a thumb and forefinger, Tom gave her query a moment of thought before he responded. "I am intrigued."

"Intrigued?"

"I have four sisters, and only the youngest is not yet married," he explained.

Emily would soon be, given what he had learned the day before and then last night at White's.

Newly returned to London and a banker in Threadneedle Street, James Burroughs had admitted to a fascination with Emily. A common desire for a simple and quiet life as well as their easy rapport with one another meant they would make an excellent couple. The fact that James had his own fortune meant that neither Tom nor their father needed to be concerned with Emily's.

"If Emily had come to me wanting to protect her fortune

from her future husband, I know I would do whatever I could in my power to see to its safety," he explained. "I would do nothing less for you."

Victoria narrowed her eyes. "And if my future husband took exception to such an arrangement?"

Tom allowed a guffaw. "You would never agree to marry a man unless he approved the arrangement."

Allowing a wan grin, Victoria nodded. "Well said." She seemed lost in thought for a moment before she suddenly added, "Pray tell, what is the time?"

Tom pulled his Breguet from his waistcoat pocket. "Half-past three," he said with some surprise. "I cannot believe we've been in here for two hours."

"Neither can I. I am so sorry, but I really must be going back to the stables," she said. "It's past time for the next horse."

"Of course," Tom said as he stood up. "I'll get started on a proposal this evening."

"Fifty-thousand pounds," she stated.

"Fifty-thousand?" he repeated, startled by the amount.

She nodded. "That will leave me with enough to live on for some time," she added. "And pay for some new furniture for the house."

Even though he was curious as to how much she was holding back, Tom didn't ask the amount. He trusted she would spend it wisely. "If you're thinking of buying furniture, does that mean you're keeping the house?" he asked as he held the door for her. He offered his arm as a blast of cold air greeted them. They hastened their steps along the loggia until they reached the house.

Victoria took a deep breath. "I think I will tell Father I wish to keep it," she murmured as they entered, warmth once again surrounding them.

"Might I make a suggestion?"

She led him to the ground floor parlor, to the table where he had left his leather satchel. "Of course."

"Choose what you like and make this place your own," he murmured. "They might just be things, but... well, you'll enjoy the house much more if you like them."

Victoria angled her head to one side. "Spoken as if that is what you do with your own home."

"My office, actually. I like to surround myself with beautiful things." He paused, gave a leg, and lifted her hand to his lips. "Good day, my lady. I shall send a formal proposal when I have it ready for your review."

About to reply that she would see him to the door, she instead dipped a curtsy. "Good day, Mr. Grandby."

*V*ictoria watched as her caller made his way to the front door, her hand held at her waist as she relived the moment his lips had touched her knuckles.

How was it possible the simple courtesy could leave her hand tingling?

How was it possible he would say words she never thought to hear a man utter?

Be still my heart.

Had he said it in jest?

Perhaps.

But there had been that odd flicker in his eyes, as if he was seeing her in an entirely different light.

You have thoroughly impressed me.

That comment had been sincere, she was sure. She remembered how it warmed her, how it had changed both the way she regarded him as well as their conversation for the rest of the meal.

For two hours!

How was it possible his cologne could surround her as they ate their simple luncheon, the citrusy odors of the lime trees mixing with his amber and sandalwood to form such a warm and comforting scent?

And how was it possible she had wanted nothing more than to have him kiss her on the lips when he took her hand in his?

They hadn't spoken of anything intimate. They hadn't alluded to anything too personal. Well, except for his comment about surrounding himself with beautiful things.

Now that she knew that about him, she wanted to know what those things might be. Wanted to see them for herself.

And she wanted to know more. Much more.

Everything.

Oh, Mr. Grandby, what have you done to me?

Whatever it was, she didn't have time to consider it at that moment. She had a two-year-old colt who needed his daily run and a yearling in need of a workout.

She made her way up to her bedchamber to change back into her riding clothes.

CHAPTER 6

BRANDY WITH COUSINS AT WHITE'S

The following night at White's men's club in St. James Street

Tom Grandby entered the venerable White's at half-past nine o'clock and allowed the butler to take his hat and great-coat. He glanced about the first room past the entry as he made his way to his usual chair. Although there was no sign of his friend and second cousin, James Burroughs, another gentleman he was expecting caught his eye.

Gabe Wellingham, the illegitimate son of the Earl of Trenton and his second cousin, hurried toward him and shook hands.

"Well, this is fortuitous," Tom said with a grin. "I half expect Burroughs to join us. I invited him when I spoke with him this morning."

Earlier that day, Tom had paid a call at Woodscastle, the Grandby family home. His youngest sister, Emily, continued to reside there while rest of the Grandbys were in Derbyshire for the holiday. They weren't expected to return to Woodscastle until the end of February.

Meanwhile, Emily had insisted James stay in one of the

guest bedchambers at Woodscastle until such time as he could find a living arrangement in town. He had moved in a week ago.

Until that morning, Tom had no idea James intended to marry Emily.

"Thank you for the invitation," Gabe said, noting a footman was already seeing to his drink. "I take it all was well when you arrived at Woodscastle this morning?"

Tom rolled his eyes. "It was. I may have overreacted," he said, referring to what he claimed he would do if he found his sister in a compromising position with the banker.

"What exactly did you expect to discover?"

"Emily, in bed with James."

Gabe blinked and then allowed a shrug. "Although I do not know Mr. Burroughs well—I've only met him the one time—I do know Emily. Why, I think she would make a fine match for him."

"You are right, of course," Tom agreed. "And thank you for agreeing to meet here tonight."

"I admit I am glad it was for tonight and not last night," Gabe said with a chuckle. He had spent the night before in the company of Frances Longworth, an expert in pottery restoration at the British Museum. Their dinner at Trenton House had been interrupted when she insisted she had to be home by a certain time. Gabe accompanied her, only to discover the reason for her need to be home was her seven-month-old son. Once Gabe learned of her circumstances, and having developed a tendré for the young woman, Gabe insisted Frances reside at Trenton House where the nursemaid could see to her son while she spent her days at the museum.

Just that morning, he had proposed marriage to Frances.

"She did say yes, I hope?" Tom teased.

Gabe inhaled. "She did."

At that moment, Gabe and Tom looked up in unison to

find James regarding them with an expression that suggested he, too, had news.

"Did I hear the word *wife*?" he asked with a grin.

Gabe stood and shook hands with the older gentleman. "You did. Within a week, if I can secure a license."

"Is this the same woman you said was *prickly*, I believe was the word you used?" James reminded him.

"She... had a reason to be, but I believe I have seen to it she will no longer be." Gabe paused. "Prickly, that is. I still expect she will be *particular*. Which is a necessary trait in our line of work."

James leaned forward. "What have you done?"

Gabe inhaled before he said, "I proposed. This morning. She accepted... finally, and we're to be married. Soon, I hope."

James looked to Tom. "Well, it seems you were telling the truth this morning."

Tom gave him a look of chagrin. "Of course I was."

They continued to tease Gabe about his circumstance. He explained he would be claiming the babe as his own and then shocked them both when he turned to Tom and said, "I was wondering if you might consider being his godfather?"

A laugh erupted from Tom before he sobered. "I am honored, of course," he murmured. "But... I am not married—"

"Your cousin Milton was not, either," Gabe reminded him, referring to the Earl of Torrington, "but he took on over twenty godsons and goddaughters before he took a wife."

Dipping his head, Tom said, "True." He gave the request a moment of thought. No one else had requested he be the godfather for their offspring. "Perhaps it's time I consider such matters."

Gabe straightened in his chair. "From the manner in which you just said that, I have to wonder if changes are in *your* future."

Looking ever so uncomfortable, Tom finally shrugged. "Possibly," he hedged.

James cleared his throat, which had both Tom and Gabe turning to regard him. "I probably should mention that I, too, have proposed marriage on this day."

Having already learned what had happened at Woodscastle earlier that morning, Gabe allowed a huge grin. "Emily?" His gaze quickly turned to find Tom displaying a blank expression on his face.

"I, uh, thought to speak with you about it this morning —*before* I proposed," James said to Tom in his own defense, "but then Emily interrupted us, and I didn't get the chance."

Tom dipped his head. "Emily has certainly learned how to keep a secret," he murmured. At no point had she said anything to him about her intent to marry.

"What other secrets do you suppose these women are keeping from us?" James asked as he settled back in his chair.

Gabe finished off his brandy and allowed a wan grin. "I cannot imagine Frances having any more secrets, but I shall endeavor to learn them. Starting tonight," he said as he stood up. "Gentleman. I am going home, and tomorrow, I'm paying a call in Doctors' Commons for a marriage license."

James straightened in his chair. "If you'd like, I will join you on the morrow." He drained his brandy and dared a glance at Tom. "I think I, too, will be taking my leave so that I may learn all of Emily's secrets," he said as he stood.

Tom rose and straightened to his full six-foot, two-inch height and said, "And I will come learn with you. About time I spent a night at Woodscastle," he said, one eyebrow arched.

Giving him a quelling glance, James said, "I am not going to like you as a brother, am I?"

Tom shook his head. "Probably not."

With that, James took his leave of White's.

Tom stared after his second cousin, an odd sensation having gripped him just then. With two of his best friends due to marry within the week, Tom was left wondering if he, too, should consider matrimony.

He quickly put aside the thought. With the snow falling as it was, he needed to leave now if he truly intended to spend the night at Woodscastle.

CHAPTER 7

A DEMONSTRATION OF SKILL

*M*onday, *January 7, 1839 at Angelo's Fencing Academy, 32 St. James Street, London*

The crowd around the piste was three deep by the time George Bennett-Jones, Viscount Bostwick, took his place at one end. At the other stood his equal in terms of skill. At least, the earl had been his equal prior to his disappearance from London three weeks prior.

"You're late," Christopher Carlington, Earl of Haddon, called out, annoyed with his brother-in-law of over two decades.

"I came as soon as I received your missive," George replied. "No word for nearly a month, Haddon, and suddenly you want a match. What's this about?"

"A demonstration."

From the gleam in Christopher's eyes, George knew the honorary earl was up to something. The note George had received only the hour before was brief but demanding.

Bostwick,

I am back in town and ready for a rematch. Angelo's today at two o'clock. Bring your best foil.

Haddon

Demanding had become Christopher's way of late. He had also adopted a pompous manner that he hadn't possessed a few years ago.

Back then, the heir to the Morganfield marquessate had been a pleasant fellow. A good friend to have whilst drinking. A welcome partner for an invigorating ride in the park. An excellent opponent on the piste.

George wondered now if Christopher's recent entry into his forties had been responsible for changing his wife's younger brother into someone with whom he no longer wished to spend time.

Nearly one-and-fifty, George hoped he wouldn't suffer the same change. He was a good-natured man who enjoyed an active life, traveling when he was in his twenties and learning how to run the viscountcy in his thirties. This was the year his oldest son, David, would finish university before embarking on a Grand Tour of Europe. His daughter, Christina, would make her come-out this spring. His younger son, Daniel, was safely ensconced at home, challenging a tutor he had probably exceeded in knowledge. He was also frustrating a dance master whom George had overheard referring to Daniel as the genius with two left feet.

And then there was Adeline, ten going on twenty. Too smart for her own good, too cute to discipline, and too much like her mother for the two of them to get along.

As for Christopher, he was nearly nine years younger and hadn't said a word about marriage or siring heirs and spares. It was as if the earl was intent on pretending he was still in his twenties.

"Gentlemen! Watch and learn," Christopher shouted as he raised his foil in a salute.

Rolling his eyes, George followed suit with a salute and then frowned as he watched Christopher begin an attack before George could even make his way to the middle of the piste.

"You are just warming up, I hope," George said as he was forced to step back.

But it was apparent from his opponent's moves that Christopher was not just warming up. Cursing under his breath, George studied the placement of Christopher's feet, his odd stance, and his unexpected movements. His weight seemed equal on both feet as he quickly moved forward, whereas George always held his head back to protect it from an errant swing, which meant his weight was usually on his back leg.

Christopher's attacks didn't follow the usual pattern, either. Of the eight parries he had learned while at Cambridge, Christopher now only employed four. He followed each with an immediate riposte, which kept George on the defensive.

George parried when he could, but mostly he retired until he was finally forced off the piste.

"Have a care," he cried out when the tiny knob at the end of Christoper's foil nearly took the sleeve off one of those who stood watching. Those nearest the unfortunate man allowed a round of startled gasps, and two of them caught George and righted him before he could go down on his back side.

One of the fencing masters stepped onto the piste and whispered something to Christopher. George saw defiance in his brother-in-law's eyes, and for a moment, he wondered if Christopher would aim the tip of his foil at the master.

Aware of quiet bets being made between those who watched, George lifted his foil and made to attack before Christopher had a chance to lift his own.

The clash of metal had the crowd shouting as George completed his attack and a series of thrusts that had Christopher backing up to the opposite end of the piste.

The entire time, George was aware of how his opponent balanced his body. How he positioned his feet. How he began his own attack run.

Halfway through it, George ducked and stepped off the piste completely. "I've an appointment," he announced to no one in particular. Annoyed by his relative's behavior and determined not to make a fool of himself in front of the growing crowd, he stalked off to the changing room. A murmur of disappointment sounded from the onlookers.

Left in the middle of the piste, Christopher was about to make a chiding comment, but he noted heads were shaking—and not from George's sudden departure. Another moment and the crowd's attention was turning to a match on the next piste.

Christopher hurried off to the changing room, nearly colliding with George as the older man made his way back out. He stumbled and aimed a look of annoyance at George. Remembering what George had said on the piste, Christopher said, "Have a care."

"Was that Messier Bertrand's style, perhaps?" George asked, once Christopher had regained his footing.

"You recognized it?" Christopher's surprise was evident. "How?"

"You are not the only *fop* who has gone to Paris for lessons on how to impale someone," George ground out before he headed toward the front door.

"Fop?" Christopher repeated. He quickly grabbed his greatcoat and topcoat from a bench in the changing room, not bothering to stop and pull them on before he stepped out the front door and into a flurry of snowflakes.

"Where are you going?" he called out, discovering his brother-in-law was already well down the street. Cursing, his foil in one hand as he attempted to pull on his topcoat with the other, Christopher whirled around. A blast of cold air hit his sweat-soaked face.

The blade of the foil rounded with him, arcing through the air until it suddenly wasn't.

The rectangle of metal, stopped by the thick wool of a bright blue redingote, was jerked from Christopher's hold and clattered to the pavement below.

He was left staring into the bright blue eyes of a rather startled young lady. Eyes that were positively mesmerizing. Eyes that blazed with sudden fury.

"How dare you?"

The lips that said those three little words caught his attention next. Red from the cold, they begged to be kissed. He didn't think their owner was of the same mind, but he could dream, couldn't he?

The voice that went with those blazing blue eyes and beautiful full lips was just as captivating. Just as bewitching. Christopher was suddenly reminded of the Sirens in Homer's epic poem. He understood perfectly how it was a man would do whatever a voice would tell him to do.

He was awaiting instructions when another blast of cold air stung his cheeks and chilled his arms. He remembered where he was. On St. James Street. Blocking the way of a rather fashionably dressed young woman whose arm was interlocked with another young woman's arm.

Her companion, no doubt. Or perhaps a lady's maid, given the simplicity of her coat and hat.

His topcoat only half-pulled on, his greatcoat draped haphazardly over an arm, Christopher stared at his victim for a moment before habit had him bowing. "Apologies, my lady," he managed to say, his gaze tearing from the blue eyes to where one of her kid gloved hands was pressed into her side. "Oh, my God. Are you hurt?"

Although reason would have reminded him that his foil had a rectangular blade that wouldn't necessarily slice through several layers of fabric and then into skin, he wasn't possessed of reason at that point. He was imagining a wound. Creamy white skin sliced with a sharp blade. A deep wound, with blood just beginning to pour from it.

And at the thought of bright red blood, Christopher's vision wavered until stars appeared to replace the image of the lovely young woman who stood before him, and he fell to the pavement in a dead faint.

CHAPTER 8

A PUNCH IN THE GUT

eanwhile, in front of Angelo's in St. James Street
Rooted to the pavement, Juliet Comber
stared down at the man whose fencing foil had whipped—hard
—against the side of her waist at the very moment her arm was
raised to hail a hackney. She turned to her maid and said a
delayed, "*Ouch,*" in a low voice.

"Are you all right, my lady?" Beeker asked with worry. The
lady's maid was only a few years older than Juliet, but she
appeared far more shaken than her mistress.

Juliet nodded. "I am, although I'm quite sure I'll have a
bruise for a few days," she complained.

"I'll apply some arnica just as soon as we're back at the
house," Beeker said before turning her attention back to the
prone man, realizing just then that the reason she couldn't move
was because her booted feet were pinned beneath one of his legs.

She was about to mention it when a gentleman rushed up
and regarded them a quick moment before he bowed and tipped
his hat.

"Apologies, my ladies, but... what happened?" His brows
furrowed and then his eyes rounded at seeing Juliet. "Miss
Comber?"

Juliet dipped a curtsy the moment she recognized the gentleman. "Lord Bostwick. How do?"

"Better than him, I should think. What happened?"

Juliet exchanged a quick glance with Beeker before she said, "He attacked me with his blade and then fell down. Do you know this man?"

George rolled his eyes. "Unfortunately. This is Haddon."

Juliet recoiled. "As in, *the Earl of?*"

He nodded as he used his cane to nudge the prone man. "He's my brother-in-law," he added. When Christopher didn't move, George crouched and shook his shoulder. "Wake up, you fool. You're blocking the pavement."

Christopher groaned and attempted to lift himself up before he simply bent his body and then settled onto his bum with a curse. His coats, in various states of entanglement, took him a moment to sort before he slowly finished pulling on the top coat. "What the hell...?"

He clamped his mouth shut upon seeing the bottom half of two women. The front half of one pair of booted feet were trapped beneath one of his legs while a bright blue redingote grazed the side of his face.

"Get up, you fool," George hissed, the hand that wasn't holding the cane reaching beneath Christopher's armpit to assist. "Miss Comber, are you hurt?"

She shook her head. "I'll be fine, my lord. Thank you for asking."

Christopher managed to stand, mostly of his own volition, and then moved to tip a hat that wasn't on his head. He absently glanced around for it and then remembered he had neglected to grab it when he was gathering his coats in the changing room.

George stood off to one side, trying to decide if he should simply bow and take his leave or wait to be sure the earl apologized. One thing he knew for certain—Christopher Carlington, Earl of Haddon, was no longer in possession of shoulders and a neck large or strong enough to support his enormous head.

He had become that vain. That arrogant. An ass of truly monumental proportions. And George had every intention of informing his wife of the situation when he returned to Bostwick House. After giving birth to two sons and two daughters, Elizabeth Carlington Bennett-Jones was quite capable of bestowing a scolding that might actually get through to her brother. George knew this because Elizabeth knew all of Christopher's names and, like her mother, used them as a prelude to a thorough scolding or a dressing down.

Once he had his greatcoat pulled on and then his gloves, Christopher bowed before the two women. "I apologize, my lady," he said before noticing his foil was still on the ground. He bent to retrieve it and then couldn't help but notice how the young lady with the striking blue eyes and beautiful red lips and probable bleeding gash of a wound stepped back as if to be sure the blade couldn't once again connect with her person.

"I meant no harm, of course," he murmured. "Are you...?" He struggled for a moment before he added, "bleeding?" He let out the breath he had held in his attempt to say the word out loud.

Juliet couldn't suppress the sound of disbelief she uttered, but now that he had mentioned the possibility of a wound, she couldn't help but angle her body so that Beeker could take a look.

"Your coat is fine, my lady. There might be a bit of a mark there—"

"I'll pay to have it replaced," Christopher said quickly. "Just... have the modiste send the bill to me at Carlington House." He nearly grimaced at hearing the words, hoping his father wouldn't notice the bill of sale before he had a chance to pay it.

David Carlington, Marquess of Morganfield, hated paying bills, which was one of the reasons Christopher had begun seeing to the day-to-day operations of the marquessate. But that didn't change Morganfield's practice of paying with coins or cheques whenever he could.

"Sir, we have not been introduced," Juliet said just before she quickly glanced around, fearing they were being noticed by those who had to walk around them. Despite the wintery weather, there were a number of people making their way up and down St. James Street.

"Ah. I am Christopher, Earl of Haddon," he said as he bowed again. He moved to take her gloved hand, but she had pulled it into the folds of her coat.

"I feel awful about what's happened—"

"As you should," Beeker piped up, one of her plump fists moving to rest on an ample hip. "You hurt my mistress with that... that blade of yours. Whatever are you doing swingin' that about—?"

"Beeker!" Emily said under her breath. "That's quite enough," she scolded. Usually the lady's maid knew enough to keep quiet when they were in the presence of aristocrats, but the earl's behavior had been rather odd. And rude.

"You are right, of course," Christopher stated. "I should think an eye for an eye is appropriate in this case."

Juliet blinked. "Pardon me?"

"Slap me, my lady."

Juliet blinked again and then gave a sideways glance in Beeker's direction. She wasn't about to give her a full glance, because she knew the lady's maid would just encourage her to do the man's bidding. "I will do no such thing," she stated. "I am a lady."

"I deserve it. A gentleman is never supposed to lose sight of his weapon, let alone allow it to hit another's person. Especially a young lady's. Please, slap me." He straightened and angled his head as if he was preparing for the assault.

"If I slap you, I should think it will hurt my hand more than it will hurt your face," she replied, quickly adding, "My lord," when she remembered that the man was an earl.

Then she recalled his introduction. Remembered what Lord Bostwick had said.

This was Haddon. The Earl of Haddon. The one rumored to be an arrogant ass. The one who, the older he got, the more full of himself he seemed to be. The one who was apparently considering another form of suitable punishment even as she considered simply walking away.

"So, punch me. Anywhere you'd like," he countered, holding his face in the other direction as if he were giving her a clear shot.

Juliet pulled her shoulders back and regarded the earl with a look of disbelief. Sighing, she balled up a fist, but rather than taking a swing at his face, she did what her father had taught her to do should a horse misbehave.

She punched him in the gut.

Unprepared for such an assault, Christopher gripped both hands to his belly, made a sound of astonishment that might have also been a curse, and doubled over in pain.

"Damnation," Juliet whispered as she shook out her gloved hand.

"Did you just say *damnation*?" Christopher managed to reply as he unbent his body.

"Are you wearing a wooden corset?" she countered as she cradled the injured hand in her other palm.

Christopher shook his head. "Of course not. That was just... *me* you hit. A rather effective hit, by the way. I shouldn't wish to anger you further."

Juliet's eyes widened a fraction. Most men the earl's age were soft in the belly. A bit round, too, as if they were with child. But his middle was solid. Hard. He obviously exercised a great deal. Probably fenced, given the foil that dangled from one hand and the fact that they were standing just beyond the entrance to Angelo's Fencing Academy.

"A word of advice if I might?" Juliet asked as she regarded the earl in a different light.

"Very well," he replied. He looked as if he was about to lean down and kiss her, his attention entirely on her lips. "And please know that I am very sorry for what happened."

Ignoring his last comment for the time being, Juliet said, "Do watch where you point your weapon." She hooked her arm with her maid's, dipped a curtsy, and made her way around the earl. "Good day, Lord Bostwick," she called out, realizing he had only stepped off to the side of the pavement, probably for his own protection. "So good to see you again. Do give my regards to Miss Christina," she added, referring to his daughter.

George tipped his hat and gave her a wink before turning his attention to the earl. He inhaled and slowly let out the breath, a white cloud surrounding his face as he did so. "Well, if I'd known a punch in the gut would have your head decreasing in size, I might have tried that last year."

Christopher jerked back at hearing the harsh words. "What are you saying?"

George glanced down the street, watching the backs of the departing women. "You're going to treat me to a drink at White's, and then I'm going to tell you what you need to hear."

About to argue, Christopher heard the seriousness in his brother-in-law's voice and saw the flash of anger in his eyes. Perhaps it would be best to hear the man out. "Agreed," he said.

The two turned in the direction of Jermyn Street and covered the short distance to the men's club in quick fashion.

CHAPTER 9

A VERBAL LASHING AT WHITE'S

*M*eanwhile, at White's men's club, 37–38 St. James Street

"Brandy," George said when asked what he wanted to drink. He hoped the liquor would help warm him as well as provide the courage he required to tell his wife's brother what he needed to hear.

"One for me as well," Christopher said as he settled into a wingback chair. Nestled into a corner of one of the smaller salons, it was near the fireplace and adjacent to the chair George had taken. He couldn't help but notice that they were the only ones in the room, although they had passed several occupied salons on their way to this one.

"Thank you for your assistance in front of Angelo's," Christopher said when the footman had hurried off to the tap.

"Have you taken to falling prostrate in front of beautiful young ladies now? Is this what French men do when they wish to stop a woman in her tracks?"

Christopher blinked at hearing the rebuke in George's voice. "I didn't fall deliberately," he argued. "I..." He paused and took a quick look around the otherwise empty room. "I fainted."

It was George's turn to blink. "Fainted?" he repeated. "Oh,

so now you're *fainting* at the sight of beautiful young ladies? How is *that* working for you?"

Holding up a staying hand, Christopher said, "No. It's not like that. I thought... I thought my foil had drawn blood, and I..." He wavered a bit before he took a quick breath and straightened in his chair. "The thought of blood just..." He grimaced before lifting a fist to his mouth.

"It's a good thing you weren't the second-born," George commented, finally understanding the earl's squeamishness.

"I could lead men into battle," Christopher claimed. "After that, I'd spend the rest of the time on my bum or passed out. I simply cannot abide the sight of blood."

"How is it I've known you this long and never knew this about you?" George countered.

"I never saw you bleed."

They had met at his sister's wedding, and although they had engaged in a number of spirited fencing matches, their persons hadn't suffered damage. George was about to do some now, though, although Christopher's wounds wouldn't require a surgeon or bandages.

"You, sir, have become an ass," George stated. He was about to say more, but the footman appeared with their drinks, and he was forced to wait until the servant had taken his leave.

Meanwhile, Christopher's brows had furrowed as if in confusion. "Is this some sort of—?"

"I am not joking," George said. "I am, however, forced to confront you on the matter of your behavior of late."

"Behavior?"

"I am your brother. No one else is going to tell you that you have become a pompous ass—"

"Oh, so now I'm not just an ass, I'm a pompous—?"

"Shut up. I am speaking," George stated firmly. "Upon the occasion of your fortieth birthday, your head grew too large for your body."

"My head?" Christopher's hands lifted to the sides of his head, as if he was testing the comment.

"You've grown vain. You're demanding. You have begun to act as if the entire world revolves around you, which it does not."

"I was at that lecture. The world revolves around the sun," Christopher said with some excitement.

"It's like I'm talking to an idiot," George said as his hands went to his own head in frustration.

"I am not an idiot," Christopher countered.

George settled back into his chair and took a sip of the brandy, hoping the fortified wine would give him some courage. "Are you even aware of how despicable you've become in the past year or so?"

Christopher's eyes darted to one side. "Despicable?"

Clearing his throat, George said, "You've become terribly full of yourself. You've become a braggart. You're no longer a pleasant fellow to be around."

"Since my fortieth birthday?"

"Yes. And perhaps even the year before that."

"Why the hell has it taken you so long to—?"

"I had hoped your *father* might mention it to you," George said quickly before he allowed an exaggerated sigh. "And if not him, then your *mother*, who I know is capable of reducing you to a blubbering idiot."

Christopher seemed to think on this last point a moment. "My father's only comment of late has been with respect to my lack of a wife," he replied, his voice quiet. "Seems I'm not allowed to behave as Torrington did for all those years and marry at six-and-forty as he did."

"He was lucky. And he knew who he wanted as his wife," George argued. "Do you even have anyone in mind?"

The image of bright blue eyes came to Christopher in a flash, as did the memory of her red lips. The thrust of her fist into his belly had him wincing, but even the memory of that hadn't diminished his fascination with her. "Who was that young lady I nearly impaled with my foil?"

George gave a start at the query. "You mean Miss Juliet? Juliet Comber?"

"Comber?" Christopher repeated, his brows furrowing.

"Alistair Comber's daughter. I think you might have employed him to find the team for your phaeton," George explained. "Expert horseman? Used to be at Tattersall's for nearly every auction? He's Aimsley's son," he added, referring to the Earl of Aimsley.

Christopher's eyes widened. "He's the one who married Lady Julia," he said with some excitement.

"And Juliet is the oldest of their children."

"How old is she, do you suppose?" Christopher asked in a faraway voice.

"Young enough to be your daughter," George replied, bristling at the thought of Christopher with the young lady. Juliet was gently bred, but she was also her father's daughter, blessed with keen skills in horsemanship and a way with the beasts that had them doing her bidding.

Christopher didn't deserve such a fine young lady.

"I wish to gain an introduction."

George winced. "Your fainting spell must have been worse than I thought. Did you hit your head on the pavement?"

"Why do you say that?"

"I already introduced you to Miss Juliet. In front of Angelo's."

Making a sound of disgust, Christopher said, "I was not at my best. In fact, I'm rather hoping the young lady has completely forgotten the incident."

George blinked. "I rather doubt she will *ever* forget that particular incident," he replied. "Poor thing probably broke her wrist doing your bidding to harm you, and besides that, she has a marred redingote due to your negligence."

"I will pay to replace it," Christopher stated.

"She probably has a bruise to go with it, too." Since he'd been walking away at the time, George hadn't paid witness to the actual incident. He only learned what had happened when he turned around on the pavement, wondering what might have become of Christopher when the earl hadn't come up alongside him. Despite his verbal rebuke in Angelo's, George knew Christopher wouldn't stay back and lick his wounds. He was too full of himself to believe he had done wrong on the piste.

"Do you really think so?" Christopher asked, his face displaying the first true expression of sorrow George had ever seen on him. "I could offer to kiss it. Make it better," he murmured.

George dropped his head back on his shoulders and stared up at the ceiling's plasterwork. "You really did hit your head when you fell to the pavement."

Christopher regarded his glass of brandy a moment before he lifted a hand to his wavy hair and gingerly pressed his fingers against his scalp. A grimace appeared when he touched a particularly tender spot on one side. "How did you know?" he asked in awe.

Rolling his eyes, George said, "You've a concussion," he replied. "Which explains some of why you've been behaving so strangely."

Strangely, but not badly. Ever since George had lifted him from the pavement, Christopher's manner had been that of an apologetic simpleton. Not the least bit arrogant. He wasn't his usual cocky, self-assured self.

"I do sort of feel... *off*," Christopher agreed. "Like there was something there that's been banged out of my head."

George stiffened in his chair. "Do you... do you recall what we were doing *before* you fell?"

His brows furrowing, Christopher took a moment before he said, "Walking?"

"And before that?"

"Fencing?" The word sounded more like a guess than a true memory of what they'd been doing at Angelo's.

George leaned forward in his chair. "Do you remember our match?"

"I remember arranging it." Christopher blinked a couple of times. "I remember telling the driver where to take me when I stepped into the town coach." Another moment went by, and his eyes widened. "Good God, why are we here drinking when we haven't yet performed our match?"

Dipping his head, George considered how to reply. "We had quite a spirited match, in fact. You showed off your new skills. From whom did you take your latest lessons?"

Christopher inhaled slowly as his eyes darted about. "I went to France. I spent a couple of weeks with Francois-Joseph Bertrand," he recalled. "He's quite adamant about turning fencing into a sport rather than leaving it as an art form."

"His way is definitely fast," George remarked, "but I rather prefer to fence the way I learned it. Long phrases, few hits."

"Predictable," Christopher murmured.

"Perhaps."

When Christopher returned his attention to his brandy and didn't say anything else, George did the same with his own. Another entire minute went by without a word before Christopher said, "So, are we going to Angelo's now?"

Blinking, George regarded his brother-in-law with concern. "As I said, we've already been. You gave a commanding display of Bertrand's technique."

"I don't remember doing that."

"But you remember Miss Juliet?"

Christopher's face lit up with a brilliant smile. "Oh, yes. Blue eyes," he replied. "Gorgeous lips and the most beautiful voice. Why, I think I would do whatever she told me to."

George grimaced, until he noticed how Christopher suddenly sobered, and a hand went to his middle. "What is it?"

"She has a wicked right fist. I think I love her."

Despite his brother's serious expression, George burst out laughing. "Come, I think we'd best get you home while you still remember how to get there."

"But, what about our match?"

George sighed and said, "Another day. Now, do you remember how you got to Angelo's this afternoon?"

"I walked."

"From Mayfair?"

"Don't be ridiculous. I..." His eyes darting about, Christopher once again appeared confused. "Rode in a coach, of course."

"A hackney?"

Christopher's faced screwed into a grimace. "Doubtful."

George led Christopher from the men's club, hoping he could spot a town coach with the Morganfield crest parked somewhere along St. James.

"Haddon!"

The shout had both of them turning to find the Marquess of Morganfield leaning his head out of a lowered town coach window. They both hurried over, and Christopher climbed in as his father started to scold him for not being where he was supposed to have been when his fencing match ended.

"My lord? Might I have a word?" George asked as he stepped up next to the coach window.

"Bostwick? What is it?"

"He hit his head on the pavement, and he hasn't been himself since," George said in a quiet voice.

"Not himself?" Morganfield repeated.

George allowed a wan grin. "Quite refreshing, really. Just thought you should know. I'll give your regards to your daughter." He tipped his hat and hurried off toward Jermyn Street.

The marquess regarded his son for a moment before the town coach lurched into motion, deciding he would take up the matter over dinner.

CHAPTER 10

SEEKING AN EQUINE
EDUCATION

eanwhile, in the stables at Tattersall's, Hyde Park Corner, London

Alistair Comber, second son of the Earl of Aimsley, regarded the horse who stood before him and asked, "How did you get to be so damned tall?"

The black shire actually angled his huge head to one side, as if about to answer his current caretaker. At nineteen hands, he was larger and taller than any of the other draft horses currently set for the following day's horse auction, which meant it might be difficult to sell him.

There wasn't another the beast could be matched with to make a perfect pair.

His manner seemed amiable—most shires were gentle giants—and his black coat was lustrous and his white stockings were bright white. Given those qualities, Alistair decided it might be possible to sell the horse by himself, perhaps to someone with a fashionable phaeton.

"There you are," Tom Grandby said as he approached the stables, a cloud of white air surrounding him as he made his way.

Alistair tore his attention from the horse and gave Tom a

huge grin. "Me? Where the hell have you been?" he asked. "Oh, let me guess. Derbyshire, for the holidays?"

Tom shook his head. "I didn't go with rest of the family this year, but I was up north for a few days. With Father," Tom replied. "Just seeing to our railway investments. I arrived back in London a week ago." He regarded the horse with wide eyes. "Is... is that a horse?"

Grinning, Alistair nodded. "Meet Jake. He's nineteen hands tall and in need of a phaeton, or perhaps a barouche to pull. He's far too beautiful for the plow."

Tom stared at the shire a moment. Knowing so little about horses was the reason he had come Tattersall's. He wanted to learn more about the beasts, especially if Lady Victoria accepted his proposal and became a client. Even if she didn't, he would at least have the knowledge to be able to converse with her on the subject should they spend more time in one another's company.

If anyone could give him a quick tutorial on the beasts, it was Alistair. The man was a consultant for the horse auction house. He was also in charge of the Earl of Mayfield's stables, and his wife was the earl's daughter.

"I own a phaeton," Tom remarked as he continued to gaze at Jake.

"Do you have a horse to pull it?" Alistair asked.

"Of course," Tom replied, his brows furrowing. "Well, one of a pair that really belongs to my father. To the stables at Woodscastle," he added, referring to the country estate where he had grown up with his parents, nine siblings, and an aunt and uncle and a cousin. "I take it Jake is for sale?"

Alistair nodded. "He's due to go up for auction tomorrow, but truth be told, I want him to go to someone I know," he explained with a look of worry. "Given his size, I fear some bloke will want him for hard labor."

"Isn't that what they're for?"

Alistair rolled his eyes. "Not back-breaking hard labor," he countered. "I delivered a team of horses to the British Museum yesterday. Have you seen the size of the stones they're using to build the new wing?" When Tom shook his head despite having paid witness to the largest construction project in all of Europe —he was on the museum board, after all—Alistair said, "All those stones are transported by dray carts. Overloaded dray carts, if you ask me. I hate to see horses subjected to that sort of labor."

Tom angled his head as he considered the comment. "Sounds as if you think something else would work better."

"You would think that with all the inventions that have been made of late, there wouldn't be a need for these beasts to be employed," Alistair replied.

A sound of disbelief erupted from Tom. "I admit to surprise at hearing you say that. I would have thought you would be one of those who eschewed steam-powered engines in favor of horsepower."

Alistair shook his head. "You will not hear me protest anything that prevents a horse from being abused." He turned his attention back to Jake. "I've a mind to buy you myself, Jake, but I'm not sure you would fit in the stables."

"He would fit in the mews behind Arthur's," Tom commented, remembering the stable boy bemoaning the lack of horses and therefore the lack of tips he could make in a day. Most of those who took rooms at Arthur's simply hired hackneys to take them about London. "Will you sell him to me?"

"You're serious?"

Tom inhaled and said, "I am, actually. Can I buy you a drink and prevail upon you to share some information?"

Suspicious but intrigued by the offer, Alistair nodded. "I am chilled to the bone and could use a brandy about now."

"Good. My town coach is parked at the front," Tom said as he regarded the shire one last time. "Jake," he said as he gave the horse a nod. "I look forward to seeing you again."

The shire nodded as if in reply, and Tom turned his astonished gaze on Alistair.

"They're not as dumb as some people think," Alistair remarked as he led the way out of the stables, shoving his gloved hands into the pockets of his greatcoat.

"What else?"

"What else?" Alistair repeated.

"I have a need to know as much about horses as I can learn," Tom said as he opened the town coach door and held it for his friend.

"Could you be a bit more specific?" Alistair asked, once they had settled in the coach.

"I've just met with a potential client who is training Thoroughbreds for the race track."

"Here in town?" Alistair's furrowed brows made it apparent he was trying to come up with the client's name.

"Just north of town. At Fairmont Park. I rather doubt you—"

"Oh, you mean Vicky," Alistair said with some excitement.

Tom blinked and straightened from the squabs. "Vicky?" he repeated.

"Now that's a woman who knows her horses," Alistair said with enthusiasm. "And knows how to train them. Why, she gets a halter on them before their second day out of the womb and a bit in their mouth before they're weaned. She has them broke for riding almost before she sets a saddle on them."

"You're speaking of Somerset's daughter," Tom said, stunned by his friend's cavalier manner about Lady Victoria.

"When it suits her," Alistair replied. "Which is rarely."

"What do you mean?"

Alistair suddenly seemed at a loss for words. "Well, ever since the accident, she hasn't had much use for Society," he said. "My wife thinks she might be living at Fairmont Park without a companion."

Remembering they hadn't had company whilst they ate their luncheon—not even a lady's maid had been in the orangery with them—Tom was about to confirm Alistair's comment. He was more interested in what else he had said, though. "Accident?"

Alistair nodded. "A horse stepped on her when she was younger. Broke her foot in several places, and the physician who saw to her couldn't set the bones properly. It's a wonder she can walk as well as she does."

"I noticed one of her boots was different from the other," Tom murmured. "Custom made at Hoby's."

Arching a dark brow, Alistair said, "So you've seen her in her riding breeches?"

Tom hesitated before he confirmed that he had, indeed, seen her dressed in the men's breeches. "What of it?" he asked, attempting an air of nonchalance.

It was Alistair's turn to blink. "Last I knew, you were a red-blooded man."

"I still am."

"Well, even though I'm a happily married man, I found I had to bed my wife just as soon as I made it back to our townhouse that day," he claimed. "Almost had a pair of breeches made for Julia."

Tom rolled his eyes. "Lady Victoria does have a shapely bum," he agreed, furrowing a brow when Alistair stared at him, as if he was waiting to hear more. "And I told her so."

Alistair blinked again. Twice. "You *what?*"

"She accused me of staring at her bum, and so I told her if she didn't want me admiring her bum, she shouldn't have knelt in my presence," he admitted.

Alistair vibrated with good humor until he suddenly sobered. "Why was she kneeling?"

Tom shrugged. "She was using her hands to feel the horse's leg," he said as he pantomimed what he had seen her doing earlier that day.

"Which part?"

Angling his head to one side, Tom said, "This is why I

wanted to treat you to a drink," he replied. "I don't know withers—"

"The ridge between the shoulders."

"—from a flank."

"End of the ribs, just in front of the back legs."

Tom sighed. "She told the stableboy to wrap the horse's foreleg."

Alistair sighed. "I was afraid of that."

Furrowing his brows, Tom asked, "What's wrong?"

"She's working with one of Reading's horses. He's a perfectly bred horse. Has it all—speed, agility, endurance. But he tends to favor one of his forelegs when she rides him. She asked me about it last week," he added, when he noted Tom's questioning glance.

"Perhaps the horse noticed her foot and is merely being sympathetic." Now that he knew *why* one of her boots had been different from the other, he remembered how her hips had swayed more than he was used to seeing in a woman's walk. Why she had tended to favor the one leg when they walked from the house to the conservatory.

Alistair stared at Tom for a long time. "Damnation," he murmured.

Tom recoiled at hearing the curse. "What is it?"

"You, sir, may be onto something," Alistair murmured. "Her one boot is different. Sam may be sensitive to that difference when he's running. Sensitive to how it sits in the stirrup."

"Sam?"

"The horse with the problematic foreleg."

"Who names a horse 'Sam'?" Tom asked in a whisper.

"It's a nickname," Alistair replied. "Short for 'Samuel Knickerbocker of York'. Connie named him after some distant relative in New York City."

"Connie?"

Alistair rolled his eyes. "Constance, Marchioness of Reading," he explained. "She's the horse breeder in that family. And probably the nicest woman in all of the *ton*."

"I know about the marchioness, of course. But you call her Connie? Isn't that rather... informal?"

"She insists on it when we're not among the *ton*," Alistair replied with a grin, just as the town coach came to a stuttering halt in front of Brook's men's club.

Once inside the warm confines of the club, a footman saw to their drinks as the two gentlemen took seats at a corner table and resumed their discussion.

For nearly an hour, Alistair explained the anatomy of a horse, talked about breeding and the desirable traits for race horses, and regaled Tom with stories of some of his own horses.

Although Tom listened intently and learned what he could, occasional thoughts of Lady Victoria made it hard for him to concentrate. When Alistair moved to finish off his second brandy, Tom finally broached the subject of the duke's daughter with a simple query.

"How long have you been working as a consultant for Lady Victoria?"

Alistair leaned back in his chair and said, "It's nothing that formal, of course. Towards the end of summer, Somerset sent me a note asking me if I might stop by Fairmont Park to look in on the construction of the stables. She happened to be there."

"Overseeing the construction?"

"Indeed," Alistair replied. "I've known her since she was..." He held out a hand a few feet above the floor. "...So I knew she was passionate about horses. I just didn't realize they had become her entire life. She spends more time with those horses than she does with anyone or anything else."

Tom wondered at the disappointment he felt at hearing his friend's words. Then he remembered her comments about steam buses. Never once had she mentioned how she came to learn so much about them.

Or from whom.

"Given our discussion about a particular investment option earlier this afternoon, I would have to disagree with you on that," Tom murmured. "Who besides you has her ear?"

Alistair regarded Tom for a moment before he said, "Her father, sometimes, although..." He allowed the sentence to trail off before he gave a shake of his head. "Not so much these days, I suppose. Then there are two grooms and a stableboy at Fairmont Park. Other than them, I've no idea." He furrowed a brow. "May I ask what investment option she's considering? And is it something *I* should be considering?"

Tom rolled his eyes. "You are already invested in part of what we're talking about," he replied, referring to one of the railway lines currently under construction. For a moment, he thought to simply leave it at that. But Alistair's eyebrows were lifted, his anticipation at learning more apparent in his expression. "Steam buses, to cover the railway routes until such time as the trains can start running."

Alistair shook his head. "That make no sense."

"I beg to differ. It's an excellent—"

"For her," Alistair interrupted.

Understanding his friend's comment, Tom said, "I admit, I was surprised, too, given her life is wrapped around horses, which is why I asked who might have her ear. Who might have spoken with her about steam buses? She knew all the features. All the benefits. The potential return on investment. Why, it was so..." He stopped speaking, realizing too late how Alistair's expression had changed. "What?"

"You're in love with her."

"I am not," Tom argued.

"You're in *lust* with her, then. My God, but I've never seen you so aroused whilst speaking of one of your clients."

"I never talk about my clients."

"Exactly."

Tom stared at his friend for perhaps a moment too long before he averted his gaze. "It's just been a long time since I ended the contract with Liza," he murmured. "Nothing more."

"Liar," Alistair accused. "When will you see her again?"

Tom considered how long it might take to have the proposal and contracts written and for his clerk to have them copied. "A day or two. The investment details already exist for the steam bus line I'm going to propose for her, but the contracts have to be drawn up and copied."

"Well, if you go back to see her on the morrow, you'll probably find my daughter there. Juliet spends every Tuesday with her, and she's usually there at least one other day of the week."

"Oh?"

"We have Vicky over for dinner quite often. Two peas in a pod, those girls," Alistair said with a grin. "They're like sisters. And with Juliet gone all day tomorrow and Jamie at university, I intend to spend the afternoon in bed with my wife."

"But, what of the auction?" Tom countered, hoping the warmth from his embarrassment wasn't showing on his face.

Was his friend teasing him by mentioning a tryst with his wife? Or bating him with a snippet of what his life might be like should he take a wife?

"It'll be done by noon," Alistair replied. "Especially if you're buying Jake."

"I'll buy him for whatever the reserve is," Tom responded. "As for when I'll see Lady Victoria again, we'll see how far I get with the contracts this evening," he added. He pulled his Breguet from his waistcoat pocket and winced. "I have to return to the office. Would you like a ride back to Tattersall's?"

Alistair shook his head. "I'm going to walk down to Floris. Buy something for my wife. I'll get a hackney from there," he added as he stood.

"Perfume?" Tom guessed.

"Maybe." When he noted Tom's expression of curiosity, he added, "Or mayhap a hairbrush. It's the little things they appreciate, Tom. Given you have five sisters, surely you've noticed."

Tom wondered at Alistair's comment as the older man stood and took his leave of the men's club.

The little things.

Well, before there could be any little things, he had to see to his newest client's paperwork. Perhaps after that he might consider the client.

CHAPTER 11

A DAUGHTER RECALLS HER ASSAULT

An hour later in the Comber townhouse, South Audley Street, Mayfair

"There you are," Julia Harrington Comber said with obvious relief as Juliet and her lady's maid entered the hall of their home in Mayfair. "I was about to send a footman to Jermyn Street to look for you," she added.

Juliet exchanged a quick glance with her lady's maid, who held the blue redingote draped over one arm. Although the rectangular blade of Lord Haddon's foil hadn't sliced through it, it had left a mark in the fabric. "We were... delayed."

"Obviously."

"Due to the Earl of Haddon."

About to return to her ground floor salon, Julia regarded her oldest child with an odd expression and then motioned for her to join her. Once they were inside, Julia shut the door and crossed her arms. "What did he do and who witnessed it?"

Before Juliet could answer, the salon door opened and Alistair Comber stepped in, his gaze going from his daughter to his wife. He closed the door and said, "Did I hear you mention Lord Haddon?" he asked of his daughter.

Juliet looked as if she might be about to cry. "I did. I didn't do anything, though. He... had just come out of that fencing academy in St. James Street—"

"Angelo's?" he guessed, thinking he had just been near there not an hour ago.

"Yes. But he wasn't really paying attention to where he was going, and he was trying to pull on his coat," Juliet explained as she pantomimed some of his motions. "And he had his foil in one hand, and it swung around and struck me—"

"*Struck* you?" Julia's eyes were wide with concern.

"—Here," Juliet continued, indicating the side of her waist. "Just as I was hailing a hackney. He apologized, of course, but he was staring at me and then suddenly fainted at my feet."

"Fainted?" Alistair repeated, his brows furrowing. Then he asked, "Were you... bleeding?"

"No. It was just a hard hit. The blade didn't slice through the fabric, although he has offered to pay for a modiste to replace my redingote. It just has a mark where the blade struck it. Beeker said she will try to brush it out."

"Was anyone else there?" Julia had one of her hands on her chest, two fingers worrying the chain of her favorite necklace.

"Lord Bostwick. He came and helped the earl to his feet."

"And that was the end of it?" Alistair guessed.

A flood of tears dripped from his daughter's eyes, and she shook her head. "He insisted I slap him. He said it was only fair. An eye for an eye." She struggled to find a hanky in her pocket, but Alistair was quick to offer his. She took it and pressed it to her cheeks.

"Did you?" Julia's eyes were wide with worry.

She shook her head. "When I refused, he told me to punch him."

"Did you?" This time, it was her father who asked, and he did so with a bit of enthusiasm.

"I punched him."

"Good girl!"

"In the *face*?" Now Julia looked as if she might faint.

"In his stomach." Juliet shook her hand at the memory of how her knuckles and wrist had hurt from the impact. "Which is hard as a rock."

An odd sound emanated from Alistair just then, and he looked as if he were attempting to stifle a laugh. "Did you at least hurt him as much as it hurt you to do it?" he asked gently, his sudden humor having subsided.

"Alistair!" Julia scolded.

Juliet's eyes darted sideways. "He bent over and let out an *oomph* sort of sound," she replied. "When I accused him of wearing a wooden corset, he said he wasn't. That it was just him."

Alistair had trouble stifling another guffaw and quickly cleared his throat. "And then what happened?"

"I told him he needed to watch where he was pointing his weapon, and then Lord Bostwick led him away." She sniffled and sighed. "Am I in trouble?"

Julia moved the hand from her necklace to her mouth, covering it in an effort to hide her sudden amusement. "If his sister finds out what happened, he'll never hear the end of it," she claimed.

"Well, I'm certainly not going to require he propose marriage," Alistair said with a chuckle. "Besides, he's old enough to be your father."

"Alistair!" Julia protested before she turned her attention back to her daughter. "He's actually close to my age."

"Did he court you?" Juliet asked, her red-rimmed eyes wide.

"Of course not. He was away. He was at university when I met your father. I don't believe I ever even danced with the man before I married."

When Juliet turned her gaze on her father, he shook his head. "Don't look at me. I never danced with him, either," he said with a smirk.

"Father," Juliet said as she dimpled, the first sign of a smile since she'd been in one of the shops in Jermyn Street and had spotted one of her friends from finishing school.

"I barely know the man," Alistair continued. "I'm older than he is, and I was with the army in Belgium before I started working at the Harrington House stables," he explained. "As the only heir to the Morganfield marquessate, Haddon wasn't expected to help with the war effort at the time, but I've heard he fancies himself a cavalier. Fencing is his sport of choice."

"Then it's a good thing he didn't go to the Continent for the wars," Julia remarked. "I rather doubt a foil could beat a bullet on the battlefield."

Alistair turned and stared at his wife, astonishment evident on his features. "No, but a bayonet could," he whispered, remembering all too well what war against the French had been like. As the second son of an earl, he had been an officer, although he tended to spend most of his time working undercover, scouting ahead or spying on the enemy from behind their lines.

His wife stared at him a moment before she dipped her head. "Apologies."

He was quick to wrap an arm around her shoulders and kiss her on the side of her head. "No need. You spoke the truth," he murmured.

Juliet swallowed as she watched her parents in their moment of quiet. Her father rarely spoke of his time in Belgium. Rarely mentioned the war against Napoleon. Now she wondered if he had been wounded. If he had lost friends to bullets and bayonets. But now wasn't the time to ask about such things.

"It matters not if Lord Haddon considers himself a cavalier. You needn't worry about having to marry the man just because you punched him in the gut," Alistair said to his daughter.

Juliet nodded her understanding and let out a breath. "May I go to my room and change for dinner?"

"Of course," her mother replied as she stepped aside. She watched as Juliet took her leave of the salon, and then, when the door had closed again, her gaze settled on her husband. "You're incorrigible," she accused.

"But you love me for it," Alistair replied as he moved to take her into his arms. After a moment, when Julia didn't seem to relax into his hold, he asked, "What is it?"

"She's one-and-twenty. She doesn't have any suitors—"

"Well, not at the moment, but a new Season will start in a couple of months," he reminded her.

"I fear the time she spends with horses makes her less attractive to those that might otherwise consider her for marriage."

"Nonsense," Alistair argued. "She'll be that much more attractive to a man who deserves her. To a man who has an appreciation for horseflesh. Maybe someone who owns a race horse or two, or who likes to ride every day."

"Do *you* know such a man?" Julia asked as she lifted her head from his shoulder.

Alistair inhaled slowly. "I know of many, of course, but I cannot think of one I might allow her to marry," he murmured.

"She's an earl's granddaughter," Julia reminded him, thinking of Alistair's father, the Earl of Aimsley.

"Two times over," he said, a reminder that she was the only daughter of the Earl of Mayfield. "Do you want her married to an aristocrat?"

"Only if he loves horses in addition to her, I suppose," she replied. "I almost wish Haddon wasn't so pompous, or I might suggest you have a word with him. He's still not married."

"He's old enough to be her father!" Alistair claimed. "And he has become a bit high on his horse of late. I cannot even fathom why."

"I hear his mother is quite upset with him. Lady Morganfield wants a grandchild—"

"More?" Alistair interrupted. "Bostwick has given her four of them," he said, referring to George Bennett-Jones, who was married to the marchioness' only daughter, Elizabeth.

"An heir for him," Julia argued. "Whoever Haddon marries will want for nothing. There's quite a fortune there."

"Yes, but what's a fortune worth if you have to spend your life with a pompous ass?"

Julia gave her head a shake. "Indeed." She regarded him for a moment and then furrowed a brow. "Where did you come from? When you came in here?"

Alistair grinned, about to give her a cheeky answer. Instead, he said, "My study. I just arrived home a few minutes ago and was reading my correspondence. I heard you admonish our daughter about her late arrival and thought nothing of it until I heard her mention Haddon."

"Ah," Julia murmured. "Well, I should go up and change for dinner."

"I'll join you, and if you'd like, I'll attempt to delay your dressing by at least a half-hour." He remembered the bottle of her favorite perfume he had purchased at Floris, but decided he could wait until the morrow to give it to her. "What say you?"

Julia blushed, much like she had done with him over twenty years ago. "I'd like that very much."

The two hurried up the stairs.

They were only a few minutes late for dinner.

CHAPTER 12

EATING CROW

Meanwhile, at Carlington House in Mayfair

The commotion that sounded from the entry had Adeline Carlington, Marchioness of Morganfield, hurrying to the door of her ground floor salon to discover her husband and son had returned.

She stood on tiptoe, intending to kiss the marquess' cheek. At the last second, David turned his head and captured her lips with his own as an arm went around her waist and pulled her against the front of his body.

Having paid witness to his parents' lusty behavior on more than one occasion, Christopher rolled his eyes and headed into the study. He moved to the credenza behind the desk and poured a finger's worth of brandy into a glass, his mind on the events of the afternoon.

On the cutting words that George had spoken whilst they were at White's.

Pompous ass.

Is that really what everyone thought of him?

And when had it started?

He couldn't remember behaving in such a manner. He had thought he was well regarded by those in the aristocracy.

Mothers still brought their marriageable daughters to him at balls and soirées, insisting on introductions. His fellow unmarried bucks still invited him to the card tables at house parties. To play billiards. To ride in the park during the fashionable hour.

But more importantly, why hadn't he ever met the young lady he had nearly impaled with his foil this afternoon? She was obviously a young woman of quality. Her clothes were evidence of it, as were her boots, which he remembered seeing up close when he had regained consciousness and discovered he was on the pavement in front of Angelo's. A rather indignant lady's maid had been attached to her arm.

What had George called her?

The name was at the edge of his brain. A name from a play. A tragedy, although the only tragedy on this day had been what she must be left thinking about him.

A libertine. A rake. A rogue.

A dunderhead.

He had begged her to hurt him. To slap him. To get even for his having hit her with his foil, although he couldn't quite remember exactly what he had done to be caught on the pavement in the first place. Every time the memory flitted at the edge of his brain, it flew away before he could grab onto it.

When his attempt to remember failed once again, he instead concentrated on his memory of *her*.

On any other day, would he have been able to walk past her without a second look? Ignore her silken hair the color of honey? Avoid staring into her blue eyes? Skip thinking of the figure beneath the fitted wool redingote? Forget how utterly enthralled he'd been when she punched him and then seemed so sorry she had done it?

Her poor hand.

She probably hadn't punched anything harder than a pillow in her entire life, and now she probably wouldn't punch anything again for the rest of it.

Who was she? He closed his eyes and let his mind drift a moment. Her name finally came in a flash.

Juliet.

Such a beautiful name. So perfect for her.

Although the name didn't portend a happily-ever-after for Shakespeare's character, surely this young woman deserved one.

She was young—too young for him, surely—but what if she wasn't? What if she was really twenty or so? What if she wasn't betrothed? What if she wasn't being courted by someone?

What if he could marry her?

He blinked, stunned that the thought didn't have him recoiling in horror. The thought, in fact, was a rather welcome one.

Juliet, as his wife.

Kissing him with the same determination she had displayed when she had punched him. Scolding him when he needed a reminder he'd been bad. Praising him when he'd done something right. Making love to him with a fervor matched only by his determination to make her his.

He could imagine squiring her about town, firm in the knowledge she wasn't some shrinking violet. That she would stand up for herself should some old biddy imply she wasn't worthy of being his countess. That she would one day make an excellent marchioness.

That she would make him proud.

Christopher took a sip of his brandy and turned to make his way out to the hall in search of his mother, completely unaware of how his father stared at him from where he sat on the edge of his desk.

Until Christopher had the niggling feeling someone was watching him. "Father!" he said, nearly spilling his brandy.

"Son," David replied, his brows furrowing. "Are you all right?"

Christopher considered how to answer. "I suppose that depends. If I told you I had someone in mind to marry—"

"Did you hit your head?"

Blinking, Christopher stared at his father. "How did you know?"

David had to resist the urge to show too much humor. He had spent the last five minutes watching Christopher as he ruminated on something that had his attention so completely, Christopher wasn't even aware David was in the same room, sitting not five feet away.

Besides, his son had just said something about marriage.

"I'd about given up on you ever finding your future marchioness," the current marquess murmured. "At least, while I'm still alive."

Christopher glanced into the hall, sure his mother was back in her salon. "As had I," he replied. "I need to speak with Mother." He left the study, his father staring after him as if he'd grown a second head.

*A*deline looked up from her escritoire and regarded her son with an elegantly arched brow. "You look as if you've lost your best friend."

Christopher allowed a nod and settled into the chair nearest his mother's, the glass of brandy dangling from two fingers. "George told me I'm a pompous..." He caught himself and swallowed the last word.

"Ass," his mother finished for him. "'Tis true. At least it has been for the past couple of years."

"Mother!"

She shrugged in the way he remembered Italians doing it. As if whatever he had just said was being dismissed out of hand. "You turned forty and have been horse high ever since."

Christopher furrowed a brow. "Do you mean 'high on my horse,' perhaps?"

"That, too."

He couldn't help but grin even though he felt as if he

wanted to bawl like a baby just then. "Why didn't you say something? To knock me off my high horse?"

Adeline set down her quill and sighed dramatically. "You are a grown man. It's not my place to hit you."

Reminded of being hit earlier that afternoon, he said, "I encouraged a young lady to punch me today." He went on to explain what he remembered, including the punch to his stomach.

"Have you been introduced to her?" Adeline asked, her eyes bright with amusement. "She sounds perfect for you."

Christopher's eyes widened. He hadn't expected his mother to say such a thing, at least without first meeting the young woman. "Really? Because... I was thinking the same thing."

Adeline straightened in her chair, glancing about as if she thought she might be the brunt of a joke. "Who is she?"

Christopher inhaled to reply and then let the air out. "I was hoping you might know. I remember George saying her name was Juliet."

"Juliet Comber?"

Practically jumping out of his chair, Christopher said, "Yes! That's it." His eyes narrowed. "Who is she?"

Adeline giggled, a delicate hand moving to cover her mouth as the musical sound filled the salon. Christopher was quite sure he had never heard his mother giggle before. "Why are you so amused?" Then his eyes widened in horror. "Oh, God no, she's already married."

Sobering, Adeline shook her head. "No. Not unless she married this past week," she countered. "She's the daughter of Alistair Comber and Lady Julia Comber." When he didn't immediately react, she added happily, "Mayfield and Aimsley are her grandfathers."

Two earls for grandfathers?

"That's magnificent," Christopher whispered. "But why haven't I met her before?"

Adeline angled her head and said, "Probably because you're old enough to be her father. She's just one-and-twenty, I think."

No longer so excited, Christopher drained his brandy. "I wouldn't be the first to take a far younger woman to wife," he said defensively.

"True."

"And I do think she was impressed by how hard my belly is." At his mother's obvious curiosity, he added, "She asked if I was wearing a wooden corset. After she punched me," he felt compelled to add.

"She learned that from her father," Adeline said.

"Is he a bare-knuckle fighter?"

Adeline made a sound of disbelief. "I cannot believe you do not remember Mr. Comber. He helped at the auction when you bought your black shires," she replied. Then her brows drew together. "Did you hit your head?"

Christopher decided it better he not deny it. Apparently, it was evident to everyone he had. "I fainted just after I hit Miss Comber with my foil. So, yes, I think I hit my head on the pavement." His hand lifted to the side of his head, his fingers gingerly feeling for the knot that was now rather large. And painful.

"Was there blood?"

He shook his head, a sound of disgust coupled with frustration sounding from his throat. When she continued to stare at him, he said, "I only imagined there was, and that was enough." In fact, it was nearly enough again, for he felt a bit light-headed.

"I'll have Alfred send for a physician," she said as she reached for the bell.

"No, Mother. Miss Comber insisted she was fine. Her coat protected her."

"Not for her," Adeline countered. "*You're* the one who is..." She paused and angled her head to one side. "Different," she murmured quietly.

"Different?" Stars no longer danced in front of his eyes.

"It's as if you're back to the way you were before you turned forty," she said in awe. "You haven't said or done a pompous thing since you came in here."

At once relieved but growing concerned, Christopher wondered just how much of an ass he had been.

How had he not noticed?

But worse, who besides his mother and George Bennett-Jones had taken note?

Did the entire *ton* think he was a pompous ass?

As if his mother could read his mind, she said, "If you're intent on changing the poor opinion of you amongst the *ton*, you've a good deal of raven to eat. The entire *ton* thinks you're an ass."

His brows once again furrowing, Christopher allowed a grunt and said, "*Crow*, Mother. I've a lot of *crow* to eat."

His hand absently moved to his belly. Hard or not, he was sure he was in for a bout of indigestion.

One that might last a very long time.

CHAPTER 13

FRIENDS UNITE

*T*uesday, January 8, 1839 at Fairmont Park

Juliet Comber stepped out of the town coach and regarded the manor house at Fairmont Park with a huge grin. The first time she had seen the Portland stone pile, she had been a young girl hanging onto her father's hand as he paid a call on Jeremy, Duke of Somerset. A call that no doubt had to do with horses.

The only reason Juliet had been allowed to come along was because the duke specifically invited her. His youngest daughter, Victoria, had joined him at the estate for his short stay and was in need of company.

The three-year age difference between Victoria and Juliet didn't seem to matter. The two became fast friends due to their mutual love of horses, and every time Victoria returned to Fairmont Park, Juliet was invited for an afternoon of riding followed by tea and cakes.

Today was no different, and because Victoria had now taken up residence in Fairmont Park—perhaps for the rest of her life —Juliet paid calls every Tuesday and sometimes one other day of the week. To reciprocate, Juliet brought along invitations from her mother requesting Victoria join the Combers for dinner in their Mayfair townhouse. Although she didn't accept every invitation, Victoria could be expected for dinner at least once a week.

The driver held her valise until a footman hurried out to retrieve it. "I'll return to collect you at five o'clock tomorrow afternoon," he said as he gave the valise to the liveried servant.

"If you are late, I will not mind," Juliet replied with a smirk.

"If I am late returning you to your mother, she will mind," he countered, his brow raised in warning.

Juliet sighed and gave a wave as she followed the footman to the front door.

She wasn't even over the threshold when Victoria reached out and pulled her into a hug. "I am so glad you are here," Victoria gushed. "I have much to tell."

"As do I," Juliet replied. "I cannot tell you how excited I was when I received your request that I spend the night." Her gaze took in the deep scarlet gown her hostess was wearing and she lifted a brow. "I thought I would find you in riding clothes."

"I will be shortly," Victoria said as she led Juliet to the stairs. "I had a meeting with the colorman and two carpenters today."

"What are you painting now?"

"I'm not painting anything," Victoria replied quickly. "But it's for a bedchamber. The master suite," she explained as they reached the landing and turned to continue up the next flight of stairs. "I thought I would surprise my father and have it redone before his next trip here. If I'm satisfied, I might do Mother's bedchamber next."

"For her? Or for you?" Juliet asked softly. "I thought you were going to be the mistress of Fairmont Park."

Victoria dipped her head. "I am already sleeping in the mistress suite. In fact, that's part of why I asked you to come stay with me for more than just a few hours. I finally have a guest bedchamber restored to its former glory," she explained as they headed down a corridor.

"How many rooms do you have left to do?" Juliet asked as

they paused before the third carved wooden door down the corridor.

"Twenty, I think," Victoria replied as she opened the door.

Juliet inhaled softly. "Oh, Vicky, it's beautiful," she breathed as she entered the guest bedchamber. Garbed in pink and magenta fabrics—the counterpane, canopy, a pair of upholstered chairs, drapes and the walls—the room was feminine and elegant.

"Do you think it's too pink?" Victoria asked as she winced.

"Not at all. In fact, I think I shall insist my bedchamber be decorated like this if I'm ever married."

"Oh, you'll be married," Victoria replied as she waved the footman into the room. He set down the valise and quickly took his leave.

Victoria and Juliet exchanged knowing looks. "He is handsome," Juliet whispered.

"And married with two children," Victoria countered. "His wife is my lady's maid."

Juliet rolled her eyes. "For a moment yesterday, I thought I might be forced to marry."

Boggling at hearing the comment, Victoria motioned Juliet to join her on the bed and then said, "What happened?"

Settling her hip on the edge of the velvet counterpane, Juliet repeated the story of what had occurred with Christopher, Earl of Haddon, the afternoon prior.

Covering her mouth with a hand, Victoria's mirth was evident when Juliet described her punch to his gut. "There was a time not so long ago that Mother said she would have welcomed him as a son," Victoria said in a whisper.

"He is so vain," Juliet whispered, as if someone might be listening at the door.

"*Pompous* is how Father has described him of late," Victoria said before she allowed a long sigh.

"What?"

Victoria's green eyes darted to one side. "Haddon used to be so pleasant. He was a very agreeable gentleman," she insisted when Juliet *huffed* in disbelief. "He was a flirt, of course, but he's heir to a marquessate."

"He behaves as if he's heir to a *king*," Juliet countered in disgust. Then her blonde brows furrowed. "I wonder what happened to him?"

"What do you mean?"

"You said he was a pleasant gentleman. What happened to change him?"

Victoria gave the query some thought. "I know he has passed forty years in age," she murmured.

"My Mother is his age, and she has not grown full of herself."

Victoria arched a brow. "Nor has your father."

"But they are married to one another. Happily, I might add," Juliet claimed.

"Why would a gentleman change his manner to one so reviled just because he's past forty?" Victoria asked in a whisper. "It almost sounds as if he doesn't want a wife. For how does he expect to marry if he's not agreeable?"

"Doesn't need to be since he's rich," Juliet argued. Then she allowed a shrug. "Perhaps he doesn't wish to marry."

"He has no choice," Victoria replied, remembering the last time she was in the earl's company. "Haddon is heir to a marquessate. He has no younger brother. He must marry and sire an heir, or the Morganfield marquessate will go to... to a cousin, or back to the Crown."

"Spoken like a true duke's daughter," Juliet accused with a grin.

Victoria's expression darkened. "When it comes to Somerset, I am glad it has to be my oldest brother and not me," she murmured. "I could not abide living in Wiltshire for the rest of my life."

"Because of what you told me?"

Victoria winced. "You haven't told anyone, I pray?"

Juliet shook her head. "I have not. But I'm sure your brother will have his affairs well in hand before he inherits."

"He has to," Victoria replied quietly. "Which is why I want to be sure my inheritance will be tied up in an investment for at least a decade. I cannot take the chance he will attempt to gain it for himself."

"Has your sister protected hers?"

Victoria nodded. "She married just before I returned here. Her dowry is now part of the Rockford viscountcy, soon to be part of the Eversham earldom."

Juliet furrowed a brow. "How is it a duke's daughter could marry an earl's son and there be no mention of it in Mayfair parlors?"

"Because they married in the chapel at the ducal estate with only our parents and me in attendance as witnesses," Victoria explained. "Violet and Robert are on their wedding trip to the Continent now, though, so I expect an announcement to be in the papers any day." She inhaled and added, "Which is why I met with Mr. Grandby this Saturday past. Are you familiar with him?"

Juliet's tentative smile widened. "I am. He's a friend of my father's." When Victoria didn't say anything right away, she prompted, "And?"

Victoria explained what she and Tom Grandby had discussed.

"What was his reaction when you told him you wanted to invest in steam buses?"

Leaning in close, Victoria replied, "I think... I think he was *aroused.* You would have thought we were speaking of a brothel or... or a gentleman's club staffed with courtesans—"

"Vicky!" Juliet said in protest. "I'm quite sure Mr. Grandby is not like that."

Victoria gave a start at hearing her friend's comment. "Do you know him? Personally?"

Juliet lifted a shoulder. "I think my father has his investments with him. Or Mr. Grandby's father, probably. Thomas has been at the house several times. Even had dinner with us on occasion."

"Was he... is he courting you?"

Juliet's eyes widened. "Heavens, no! He's far too old for me, although..."

"What?" Victoria prompted.

She seemed to hesitate before she said, "He would make an excellent catch for anyone, except for the fact I hear he practically lives at his office."

Victoria pondered the comment a moment, deciding she rather liked that about a gentleman. If Mr. Grandby spent so much time at his office, then he wasn't a man of leisure. He was less likely to be like her brother, frittering away a fortune on gaming hells and mistresses.

And bad investments.

"For an investor, that would be considered an admirable trait," Victoria finally replied.

"Was he here long?"

"We talked for nearly two hours."

Juliet tittered. "So Mr. Burroughs was right."

Victoria nodded. "I owe him much for giving me the idea, and for providing me with all the supporting information," she said. "I feel as if I should compensate him for the time he spent with me."

"I still cannot believe you would do such a thing as give your fortune to someone you do not know in order to keep it from your brother."

"I am not *giving* it to anyone. I am investing it with an expectation that in ten or twenty years, I shall have far more of it."

"And then? What will you do?"

Victoria directed her gaze to the foot that barely touched the carpet. Hitched up as it was, her gown's hem only reached her calf, exposing the odd shape of her slipper. Although her boot maker could construct a sole that made up for her missing arch and the wider foot, the shoemaker she had gone to in Bond Street didn't seem to have those same skills. At least this slipper hid the worst of the damage. The foot encased in it appeared far more mangled when it was bare. "I'd buy a new foot if I could, but I think I shall use the funds to continue restoring the house. Enlarge the stables. Add some more horses. Maybe go to the Continent for a Grand Tour."

"You could do that *now*," Juliet suggested.

Shaking her head, Victoria said, "I have horses to train. And speaking of the beasts, would you like to ride with me? It's time I go back out."

"I brought my riding habit, of course," Juliet replied happily. "Perhaps you'd let me ride Sam?"

Victoria considered the request a moment. "Depends on his foreleg. He's been favoring it a bit these past two days, so I had Jemmy wrap it yesterday."

"I'll take a look at it," Juliet said as she stood and moved to her valise. "He might just be imitating your walk," she added in a tease. "Horses have been known to mimic their owners."

"Juliet." Victoria stared at her friend a moment but quickly determined no harm was meant by the comment. Still, the thought that the animal would do such a thing rankled. "He'd better not be. If he doesn't increase his speed over the short course, he'll be sent back to his owner with my recommendation that he only be used for steeple chases."

Wincing, Juliet gave her a quelling glance. "Sam is too good for that, and you know it." Remembering her father's comment about the horse when she departed their house not two hours before, she asked, "When did you have occasion to speak of his limp with my father?"

Victoria shook her head. "I have not yet had the opportunity. I haven't seen Mr. Comber in a couple of weeks," she replied as she made her way to the door. "Would you like me to send my lady's maid?"

Juliet regarded her with a curious expression. "Oh, no need. I'll meet you out at the stables."

Nodding, Victoria left the bedchamber, closing the door behind her.

Shaking out her riding habit and pulling her boots from the valise, Juliet was left wondering how it was her father knew of the horse favoring his foreleg if Victoria hadn't spoken to him in a fortnight.

She would have to ask him about it when she returned home the following day.

CHAPTER 14

REFLECTIONS ON AGE AND WOMEN

*M*eanwhile, at Carlington House
Christopher regarded his image in the shaving mirror and then turned in an attempt to see his profile.

"Damn nose," he muttered, sure it had grown longer in the past year. He smoothed a hand over his face, the overnight growth of his blond beard no longer apparent now that his valet had seen to his morning shave. Christopher pulled his face back from the mirror and frowned.

Were those lines always there? The ones between his brows and at the edges of his eyes? Damn, but where had the time gone?

He thought of the other sons of aristocrats who had married when they were in their twenties, those who had married in their thirties. They already had their heirs and spares, daughters and little dogs.

Did he even know anyone who had waited until his forties to marry?

Try as he might, he could only think of the Earl of Torrington and of widowers who had married for the second time. The widowers already had their heirs when they took their second wives, though, and Torrington had managed to father a set of twins that included his heir.

Perhaps he would be as lucky as Torrington.

What had happened to prevent him from taking a bride? Why hadn't he simply chosen from the hundreds of young women who had been paraded past him for the past two decades?

Reasons started coming to mind.

Too tall, too short, too fat, too thin, too giggly, too dour, too happy, too sad, too rich, too poor, too sweet, too bitter.

So what of the other ten or twenty left after that?

Too quiet, too talkative, too loud, too proud. Already married.

Why couldn't he have found one that was just right?

Because she doesn't exist.

The thought brought him up short. There had to be someone who met his criteria. Someone who would appreciate her future as a marchioness. Appreciate the wealth that went along with his title. Someone who wouldn't be tempted to cuckold him.

"I've been waiting for the perfect wife."

He wasn't even aware he said the words aloud until his valet said, "Did you say something, my lord?"

Christopher whirled around to discover the servant had emerged from the dressing room with that day's clothes. "I need a wife, Parker."

The valet lifted a white shirt from the collection spread out on the counterpane and said, "Do you wish for me to send a note to a matchmaking service on your behalf?"

Not expecting such a response, Christopher said, "No."

"Perhaps an advertisement in *The Times*?"

"No."

"A tip to the editor of *The Tattler* then?"

"Most definitely not."

The earl furrowed his brows but then caught his expression

in the shaving mirror and grimaced. Furrowing his brows only made him look worse. He tried a slight smile and noted how the lines were lessened. "I'm quite sure you've missed my point. I was merely making a comment."

"It's interesting you should bring it up now, sir."

"Why is that?"

"As opposed to ten years ago, when you might have had a better chance of marrying well," Parker remarked, his tone rather peckish.

"I'm not going to get any sympathy from you, am I?"

"No, sir." At seeing the earl's frown, he added, "You might want to avoid displaying that expression, sir. It makes you look old. And mayhap a bit *fearsome*."

Annoyed as he was, Christopher struggled to make his expression less fearsome.

Parker held open a white shirt, and Christopher pulled it on in a huff. "Have you considered Juliet?" the valet asked.

Christopher's eyes widened. "How do you know about Juliet?"

Parker held out a pair of cream-colored trousers. "You were saying that name when I woke you this afternoon."

His eyes darting to the side, Christopher turned to find the clock on the fireplace mantel displaying ten-before-two. "Is that the right time?"

"It is, sir."

"I slept past *noon*?" He took the trousers from Parker, but did so as if they might explode.

"You did, sir. As you usually do."

Christopher turned a frightened gaze on his valet. "Since when?" He sat down on the edge of the bed, mostly to prevent himself from falling down.

Parker regarded him with a perfectly arched brow. "Did you hit your head, sir?"

A sound of disbelief erupted from his master, but the valet

merely moved to the edge of the bed, knelt, and pulled stockings onto Christopher's feet. "If you don't mind me saying, sir. You're... *different* today."

"How so?"

"Like... you woke up and just realized half your life has passed you by."

Christopher struggled to keep a passive expression on his face, mostly to keep the lines from showing, but also because the valet's words were true. "Something like that," he murmured.

Parker helped him into his trousers and asked, "Is this *Juliet* the one then?"

Dipping his head at the reminder of Juliet Comber, Christopher wondered at the sense of peace that settled over him just then. At the calm that seemed to surround him like a warm blanket. He imagined taking her into his arms and kissing her senseless, stripping her bare and making love to her. Of waking up in the morning and finding her tucked against his body. Of her making love to him as the sun barely lit the sky.

Juliet.

"Juliet," he murmured on a sigh.

"Are you courting her, sir?"

Christopher absently shook his head. "She punched me in the stomach yesterday."

Parker jerked back and regarded the earl with a frown that added at least ten years to his age. "That would be a no, then." He suddenly grimaced. "Is that when you hit your head?"

Lost in thought, Christopher absently lifted his hand to where a goose egg had formed on the side of his head. He winced at the pain, but a slight smile touched his lips. "No," he whispered. "Before, I think it was." Knowing he was about to live that unfortunate moment when he had thought he had wounded her with his foil, Christopher struggled to come back from his reverie. "I fell at her feet, prostrate before her," he murmured.

Blinking, Parker cleared his throat as he held a waistcoat open. "She must be the one, then. I cannot imagine you doing that with anyone else. Or with *anyone*, for that matter."

Christopher stared at the waistcoat. "That's far too elaborate for the day," he complained. "Juliet will think I'm a peacock if I show up at her door wearing that."

Parker's jaw dropped. "Uh, yes, sir." He moved into the dressing room and brought out a more conservative waistcoat, one with simpler embroidery.

"That's more like it," Christopher said as he allowed the valet to help him into the garment before he did the buttons.

"It's good to have you back, sir," Parker said with a nod.

"Back from where?"

"From wherever you've been these past few years, sir."

Christopher remembered his conversation with his mother. "You mean, since I turned forty?"

Parker nodded. "Mayhap a year before that."

"Seems I have much to atone for," Christopher whispered. "But first, I must court and marry Juliet."

The valet's eyes darted sideways before he said, "Very good, sir."

Christopher was already in his town coach settling into the leather squabs when it dawned on him that he had no idea where Juliet Comber lived.

The trap door above opened and the driver said, "Where to, sir?"

"Do you know where Mr. Alistair Comber lives?"

"The equine expert, sir?"

"That would be him," Christopher replied, his opinion of the driver rising a notch.

"I do not."

The opinion dropped a notch.

"However, I can find out in a few moments." The trap door

closed and Christopher was left wondering who the driver would be bothering with such a query.

The coach lurched into motion and proceeded down Park Lane, but stopped after only a few houses. Christopher watched from the window as the driver hurried to the servants' entrance of what he just then realized was Harrington House, home to the Earl of Mayfield. A few minutes later, and the driver bounded back up onto the seat and the coach once again moved.

Curious, Christopher tapped his cane against the trap door. A second later, and the driver appeared, his head silhouetted against a wintery sky.

"Sir?"

"Pray tell, why did you stop at Mayfield's house?"

The driver's attention briefly turned back to the street before he said, "Mr. Comber is in charge of his lordship's stables at Harrington House. He's not there today, though, as there was an auction this morning at Tattersall's. The stableboy gave me the address for his townhouse, though. It's not far."

"Ah, very good," Christopher replied, his opinion of the driver going up two notches.

He watched through the window as they made a turn off of Park Lane and then were in South Audley Street. Before they had made it to the next intersection, the coach slowed and came to a halt in front of a fashionable townhouse decorated with green wrought iron fencing, window boxes topped with mounds of snow and a front door painted in deep blue.

The coach door opened and Christopher glanced west—he could almost see Hyde Park— and then turned to discover they weren't far from Carlington House in Park Lane.

"Good God, I could have walked," he murmured under his breath.

"Would you like me to wait for you, sir?"

"Please do," Christopher replied. If this meeting with Mr.

Comber went well, he might be taking Juliet on a ride in the park. If it did not go well, he would be heading to White's.

He stepped up to the front door, but before he could lift the brass mermaid door knocker, the door opened.

"Good afternoon, sir," a rather portly butler said as he gave a nod.

"Lord Haddon to see Mr. Comber." Christopher flicked a calling card between two fingers, the pasteboard landing in the butler's palm.

The butler opened the door wider. "I'll see if Mr. Comber is in residence. Would you care to wait in the salon?" The servant indicated the room to the left of the front door.

Christopher glanced in, his first thought that it appeared a bit pink. But he gave a shrug and moved to take a seat in a floral upholstered chair that faced the fireplace.

He sank into the cushions with a sigh, deciding it wasn't so bad to be surrounded by pink peonies. The chair was more comfortable than anything in his mother's salon.

Imagining a chair this comfortable in his own home, perhaps in his study once he inherited Carlington House from his father, Christopher barely registered the butler as the portly man turned and made his way in measured steps to the stairs.

Christopher turned his head and watched through the salon's open door as the butler climbed them, wondering on which floor Comber might have his study.

Or perhaps he hadn't yet returned from Tattersall's.

For a moment, Christopher felt a bit of panic. What if he couldn't speak with Juliet's father? Time was of the essence.

He wasn't getting any younger.

If the butler returned to tell him that Mr. Comber wasn't in residence, then he would ask for Juliet. He could apprise her of his desire to court her and reassure her that he wasn't the pompous ass his reputation claimed.

He was so lost in thought, he didn't realize Alistair Comber stood before him until a hand waved in front of his face.

"Mr. Comber," he said as he jerked into awareness. His host wore a banyan and sported hair that appeared as if feminine fingers had been playing in it. He also wore an expression that could best be described as one of annoyance. "It's very good to see you again."

Alistair's eyes widened. "I'm surprised you remember me. My lord, you'll have to excuse my lack of proper dress, but—"

"I've interrupted an afternoon tryst," Christopher said with some consternation. "Please, accept my apologies—"

"She's asleep," Alistair said. "Look, if you're here about what happened in front of Angelo's yesterday—"

"I am," Christopher affirmed with a nod.

"My daughter is uninjured, and there is nothing you need do to make amends."

"I am heartened to hear it," Christopher replied. "But that is not the reason for my call."

*A*listair frowned as he ran a hand through his hair in an attempt to put it back into place. The butler's knock at his bedchamber door had woken him from a blissful post-coital sleep, one in which his head had come to rest next to one of his wife's soft breasts. Her fingers had speared his dark hair, their nails sending shivers through his scalp just as the last of his release had left him sated and sleepy.

Two times in two days had him feeling young again.

He nearly fired the butler.

Instead, he had absently pulled on his dressing robe, his mind so addled and his manner so annoyed, he hadn't even thought of pulling on proper clothes. Now he stood before an earl—the heir to the Morganfield marquessate—and feared what was to come.

"Then, what is?" he asked, curious as to why Haddon would pay a call on him.

"I wish to court your daughter."

"Oh, that's not necessary," Alistair replied quickly. "Juliet has happily forgiven you. She knows what happened yesterday was all just an accident."

"Yes, but... I have given this a great deal of thought, and find I cannot put her from my mind. I'm quite besotted."

"*Besotted?*" Alistair blinked at the earl, quite sure he had never heard a man use the term before.

"It's very possible I have fallen in love with her."

Alistair frowned, suddenly wondering if he was still asleep and merely experiencing a nightmare. Yes, that was it. That could be the only explanation as to why the Earl of Haddon was in his wife's salon, sitting in a chair featuring pink peonies and claiming he was besotted with Juliet.

There was another possibility, though.

"Did you hit your head?" Alistair asked, an expression of concern replacing the look of shock that had appeared there only the moment before.

Christopher gave him a quelling glance. "She told you, did she? I assure you, this..." He raised a hand to the side of his head. "This *bump* is a reminder of who I truly am."

Alistair was about to say, "A pompous ass?" but caught himself in time. He was speaking to an earl, after all. One who had apparently developed a fondness for his daughter. "And what might that be?"

"Well, not a pompous ass, if that's what you were thinking." Christopher sighed when he saw the guilty look flash over his host's face. He was about to say more, but the butler appeared at the door with a tea tray.

"Ah, yes. You can just set that down over here," Alistair said as he moved to sit in a chair adjacent to the earl. The tray was placed on the low table in front of them, and the butler saw to pouring the tea.

"Would you like brandy in your tea, my lord?"

"Just a lump of sugar is all," Christopher replied, and then he turned to Alistair to add, "I'd best keep a clear head. This is my first time for courting anyone. And hopefully last, of course."

"A… about that," Alistair stammered as he accepted a cup of tea. "It's really not necessary for you to marry my daughter."

"But it is. I cannot imagine anyone else to be my wife."

Alistair was about to chide his caller for his lack of imagination, but the fact that the earl would one day hold the title of marquess stilled his tongue. "Surely there is a woman with closer ties to a duke or a… a marquess you should be considering."

Christopher seemed to ponder the comment before he said. "Perhaps, but Vicky—"

"Vicky?"

"Lady Victoria. Somerset's daughter. She's still unwed, and I've known her for years, but I'll not take second or third place to horses." He dipped his head. "That sounded a bit pompous, didn't it?"

"Surprisingly, not," Alistair replied. "It's interesting you should mention Lady Victoria, though, since she is hosting my daughter today."

"Oh?"

From the sound of the two-syllable "oh," Alistair thought he might have made a mistake in mentioning just where his daughter could be found. "Juliet spends Tuesdays with her ladyship. Riding horses, of course. Training horses. Talking about horses." Perhaps he could dissuade the earl from his interest in Juliet by extolling her interest in horses.

"I would expect nothing less from a young lady whose father is London's leading equine expert," Christopher stated.

Alistair blinked at hearing the earl's assessment of him.

Perhaps he should be encouraging a courtship.

"A young lady needs a hobby. A cause to champion. Something about which to be passionate. My sister has always had her charities," Christopher continued, referring to Elizabeth Bennett-Jones, Viscountess Bostwick. "And I would expect Juliet to be no different." He took a drink from his tea and said, "I don't want an insipid English miss for a wife, Mr. Comber. I want a woman who will stand up to me should I do something... pompous."

"Like punch you in the gut?"

Christopher rolled his eyes. "I felt horrid about that. Her poor hand. I'm sure she thought my belly would be soft, but I've been determined not to go fat with age. I fence and I ride. I do not stuff myself at meals, despite the urge to do so." When he noted Alistair's arched brow, he added, "I think that must be the Italian side of me."

Alistair nodded. "Ah. Well. If you are seeking permission to court Juliet, then you have it," he said carefully.

"That is all I ask."

"But I will not force my daughter to marry you if she does not wish to," Alistair warned.

Christopher nodded. "I understand. I must woo her. Convince her I am worthy of her. Treat her like a queen."

Alistair allowed a wan grin. "She is my only daughter."

"She will be my only love," Christopher promised.

Staring at the earl in disbelief, Alistair said, "You really did hit your head, didn't you?"

Christopher nodded. "Best thing that ever happened to me." He straightened in the chair and added, "Please give my compliments to Mrs. Comber on these chairs. I have decided I rather like pink peonies."

Blinking with his continued disbelief, Alistair said, "I will."

Alistair stood when the earl did and led him to the front door. When Christopher offered his hand, he shook it and said, "Good luck."

Christopher smiled, his face youthening at least a decade.

"Thank you." He took his leave as Alistair stared after him, the older man wondering how he was going to break the news to his wife.

Worse, though, was he couldn't imagine how he would tell Juliet.

CHAPTER 15

AN INVIGORATING RIDE

eanwhile, at Fairmont Park

Garbed in their riding habits—Victoria in her breeches and short jacket and Juliet in a traditional navy velvet habit with epaulets at the shoulders—the two met at the top of the stairs. "I thought you would already be at the stables," Juliet said as they started to make their way down.

"I had trouble with my boot," Victoria complained as she reached for the railing. Although she could usually make it down the stairs without assistance, she wasn't yet sure her bad foot was firmly ensconced in the box of its boot. She felt her foot shift a bit and she sighed in relief as it settled properly.

"Better?" Juliet asked with concern as she paused on a wide step.

"Much. Sometimes it just doesn't go in as it should."

Their attentions were drawn to the front door. Clark, the butler, was speaking to someone who stood beyond the door before he opened it wider to reveal the caller.

Tom Grandby.

"Mr. Grandby," Victoria said with some surprise. The oddest sensation, pleasant and entirely unexpected, had her moving her hand to her midsection as she took in the sight of the tall, dark-haired man.

As was the case the Saturday before, he wore exquisitely tailored clothes, his topcoat of a deep blue wool, his embroidered waistcoat a scarlet that perfectly matched the gown Victoria had been wearing only the hour before, and dove gray trousers. His top hat was tucked under one arm.

"Lady Victoria," he replied. He turned his attention to Juliet and bowed. "Miss Comber. I see I have come at an inopportune time. I will simply leave these—"

"Nonsense," Victoria said as she hurried down the rest of the stairs. Although she didn't offer her hand, Tom was quick to take it and brush his lips over the bare knuckles. He did the same with Juliet, although she had already pulled on her gloves. "We were just headed to the stables." She noted the papers he held in his gloved hand, and her eyes widened. "Is that the paperwork for the investment? Already?"

"It is," he acknowledged, his gaze briefly darting to Juliet. "My clerk completed the copies of the contract about an hour ago, along with the terms and such. I can come back and we can go over them in more detail when it's convenient for you."

Victoria and Juliet exchanged quick glances. "Tomorrow, perhaps?"

"Of course," he replied. "Should you be of a mind to sign anything, you'll note there is a line for a witness to sign as well, so you'll want to be doing the actual signature in someone's presence."

"Will that be you?"

He shook his head. "It shouldn't be, as I will already be signing as your advisor. I don't wish there to appear to be any hint of impropriety."

"Could I act as a witness?" Juliet asked.

Tom inhaled, about to say she couldn't when he thought better of it. "If you are one-and-twenty, and you are not married..." He allowed a shrug.

"I am not," they both said in unison.

Tom sighed, his brows furrowed. "Truth be told, I would be more comfortable if your father... or your brother could sign as a witness." He was fairly certain Lord Michael was still in London.

Victoria gave him a quelling glance. "My father is in Wiltshire. Besides, I have no wish for my older brother to know of this."

"I understand," Tom said on a sigh. "Will just one night be enough time for you to review the terms?"

Victoria glanced at the sheath of papers. "I should think so."

"If you have any questions... any whatsoever, please send word with a courier, or I can answer them on the morrow," he replied as he moved to take his leave.

"Would you care to join us for a ride, Mr. Grandby? There are more than enough horses in need of exercise," Victoria offered.

Tom hesitated. Despite what he had told her the day before, he had ridden a horse on occasion. "Do you have a docile mare in your stables, perhaps?"

Victoria displayed a brilliant smile. "Come. We'll find you the perfect mount," she said as she set aside the papers on the hall's round table.

Feeling as if the young woman might be setting him up for a fall, Tom offered both his arms to the ladies before they headed down the wide corridor to the back door. "I cannot help but think I have interrupted a ladies' afternoon."

Juliet giggled. "Lady Victoria has me join her for a ride at least once a week," she admitted. "And the timing of her invitation could not be better."

. . .

They stepped outside to find the sun peeping through the clouds. Snow no longer fell, and what little there was on the ground seemed determined to melt. "Has something happened?" Tom asked.

Juliet was about to tell him about Lord Haddon, but decided it would be better if as few people knew about it as possible. She rather doubted anyone who might have paid witness to the punch she had planted in Lord Haddon's stomach would share it in a Mayfair parlor, or worse, tell it to the gossip rags, but one never knew for certain.

Apparently of another mind, Victoria said, "Miss Comber was an innocent participant in an earl's accident with a fencing foil yesterday. I think she fears he will feel honor-bound to marry her."

Tom turned a worried look on his friend's daughter. "Were you hurt?"

Juliet shook her head. "No, not really. Just a slight bruise is all."

"Would you consider his suit if he proposed marriage?"

Juliet's eyes widened in horror. She hadn't expected Mr. Grandby to ask such a personal question, but then she knew her father and he were close friends. "Perhaps a few years ago, but certainly not now. He is..." She sighed and aimed a quelling glance in Victoria's direction just as they entered the stables. "He has grown quite *proud* these past couple of years."

"Some earls can be peacocks," Tom said as his gaze fell on the horse Victoria had been riding the day before. The stable-boy, Jemmy, was securing the saddle as a groom Tom hadn't seen before finished saddling a bay. When he saw that Sam's leg had a wrap on it, Tom asked, "Has his leg improved?"

Victoria crossed her arms. "We'll find out soon enough. Juliet will ride him today." She turned her attention to the groom. "Mr. Grandby will be joining us on our ride. Mr.

Danbury, would you see to saddling the other bay for him? Daisy could use a run."

"Right away, my lady," the groom replied as he led the just-saddled bay out of the stables.

"Daisy?" Tom asked in a quiet voice.

"Her real name is Desdemona of Dover," Victoria replied in a hoarse whisper. "And she *despises* it."

"I'll remember that," Tom promised, recalling what Lord Michael had said about Victoria's nickname. He watched the stableboy lead Sam to a mounting block. Juliet made quick work of stepping up and onto the sidesaddle. With her right leg wrapped over the pommel and the hem of her skirts artfully arranged in an arc along the side of the horse, she accepted a crop from Jemmy and used it to tap Sam's right flank. Sam stepped away from the block and moved to join the other saddled horse.

om watched as Victoria mounted the bay and put it through a few quick paces. Seeing her swing her leg over the horse and sit astride in the saddle had his nether region responding, especially when one of her hands gripped the pommel. He had to suppress the urge to moan when an image of her doing that to him formed in his mind's eye.

What the hell is wrong with me?

She was a client. A duke's daughter. The very last thing he should be thinking about was them, together, in a bed. Her atop him. Or them in any other position, for that matter.

When he sensed Victoria was about to look his way, he turned his attention to the groom and asked, "Is there anything I need to know about this particular horse?"

"Not particularly, sir," Danbury replied. "She's been chomping at the bit to get some exercise, though, so she may wish to run a bit 'afore she settles down."

"I'll give her the rein once we get out on the track."

A few minutes later, Tom mounted the mare and joined the two young ladies and their mounts as they made their way to the track, impressed by the restraint his mare displayed.

"We'll do an easy run to warm them up," Victoria said as she studied Tom's position in the saddle. "It can't have been that long since you rode," she said with an arched brow.

Tom allowed a shrug. "I managed time for a ride in the park just last week," he admitted, glad for the chance to prove he could ride a horse. After their meeting the day before, he'd been left with the impression he had disappointed her.

Once they reached the track, it was as if the horses knew what to do. Tom's mount was the first to go from a walk to a trot to a run, quickly followed by the other two, although Juliet kept Sam on the inside of the turns while Victoria moved hers, a faster Thoroughbred, to the outside. Before long, the three horses were abreast of one another and seemed to favor their positions, none of them looking to gain a lead.

Tom was quick to note Sam's stride. The horse didn't favor his foreleg. His own mount, behaving as promised, had settled into a steady run designed for distance. Even after they had made the circuit twice, the horses continued their run.

Exhilarated by the speed and the excitement of racing between two horses ridden by women, Tom felt a joy he had not experienced in a very long time. He didn't care if his clothes were splattered from the wet turf, or if mud stained his boots. He understood why it was some people were invigorated by riding a running horse.

After the third circuit, he sensed Victoria's mount slipping back while Sam suddenly surged ahead. Despite the increased speed of her stablemate, Daisy continued to run at the same pace. When all the horses had completed four loops, he followed the women's lead in slowing down their mounts to a quick trot for a fifth turn about the track. The three of them made their way back to the stables at a walk.

"It appeared as if Sam did not limp," he said to Juliet.

"He did not," she agreed. She leaned forward and said to Victoria, "Whatever was wrong yesterday seems to have disappeared."

"I am relieved to hear it," their hostess said with a happy sigh. "Can you stay for tea, Mr. Grandby? It may be some time before we'll be finished changing into proper clothes, but you're welcome to use the parlor for an office whilst you wait."

Tom considered the invitation but noted the condition of his clothes. "I'd best not. I wouldn't want to soil your furnishings or carpets," he replied as he indicated his boots. "Besides, I've an appointment at the office."

"Very well. But we'll see you tomorrow afternoon?"

"Will four o'clock be acceptable?" A quick look at his chronometer had him thinking she would be done with her ride and changed into clothes by then.

"I'll be ready," she replied.

"I'll leave you ladies to it then," he said as he dismounted.

Jemmy hurried up to take the reins as Tom quickly moved to Juliet's side and lifted her down from her mount. He was about to do the same for Victoria when he turned to discover she had already dismounted.

He gave a bow and took her hand to his lips. "My lady. Thank you for the opportunity to ride. You've reminded me of a pleasure I have not had for some time."

Turning to regard Juliet, he gave a bow and lifted her hand to his lips, noting how she curtsied when Victoria didn't offer him the same courtesy.

A moment later, and he was making his way through the house and to his town coach, fighting the urge to simply change his mind and stay for tea. He was about to give in when he noted the other groom, Thompson, driving a cart loaded with hay into the circle drive.

Thompson pulled back on the reins, the single draft horse stuttering to a halt as the groom turned his attention on Tom.

"Afternoon, sir," he called out. "Business with her ladyship again?"

Sensing suspicion in the man's voice, Tom said, "Indeed. Just some paperwork for her to review."

The groom's eyes narrowed. "You won't be taking advantage, if that's what you're thinking to do." He tied the reins to the pole next to his seat and clambered down.

Tom thought the wording of Thompson's warning was odd. "I rather doubt Lady Victoria would allow such a circumstance," he replied as he moved closer to the groom. "Besides, I came at her invitation, and my business with her is honorable."

Although Tom hadn't noticed much about the man the day before, he made a quick assessment of him now based on his appearance—mid-forties, tanned face and hands, and clothes that were appropriate for his vocation but of high quality.

Then he noticed Thompson's bearing. He had either been in the military or held a position as a Bow Street Runner or a magistrate's man.

So why was he a groom at a country estate near London?

He was about to ask when Thompson put voice to his question. "You related to that earl with the Grandby name?"

Nodding, Tom said, "The Earl of Torrington is a cousin, yes." His own suspicion rising, he added, "As is the Duke of Ariley." Although he rarely brought up his family relations, Tom thought it best to do so now. Thompson probably had a pistol hidden in his coat pocket, and if not, his fists could probably take out a man even as tall as Tom with a single punch to the jaw.

Thompson immediately relaxed at hearing the reference to the Duke of Ariley. "Very well, sir. Didn't mean to be pokin' my nose where it doesn't belong, but I try to look out for her ladyship."

Tom allowed a look of relief. "I'm glad to hear it. Out here, she's an easy target for a kidnapper." His eyes darted sideways before he amended his comment. "Well, a target, at least."

Allowing a grin, Thompson agreed but said, "Not on my watch." He gave a wave and led the draft horse to the side of the house and back toward the stables.

Watching him go, Tom wondered if Thompson had been hired by the Duke of Somerset to provide protection or if Lady Victoria had done so. He made a mental note to ask her.

Tom gave his driver instructions to return him to the office and then climbed into the coach.

*V*ictoria watched Tom make his way back to the house, a sense of disappointment settling over her. Although this day was supposed to be for her and her friend to spend together, she had been surprised—pleasantly so—by his appearance, and by his willingness to ride with them despite his lack of riding clothes.

As his parting words replayed in her head—*you've reminded me of a pleasure I have not had for some time*—she wondered if they had been said with the double entendre in mind.

She rather hoped so.

CHAPTER 16

AN EARL ON THE HUNT

n hour later at Fairmont Park

"I've ordered tea and biscuits," Victoria said when Juliet joined her at the top of the stairs. "I think it is warm enough in the orangery for us to have our tea there."

Juliet had changed out of her riding habit into a day gown of pale blue muslin trimmed in vandyke lace. She regarded her hostess with a huge grin. "Blue looks better on you, I think."

Victoria glanced down the front of her darker blue frock, a simple wool gown with long sleeves and a full skirt, and allowed a shrug. "Why, thank you, but I do believe your gown is perfect with your blonde hair."

Displaying a wan grin, Juliet said, "Not that it matters. Who will see?"

As they made their way down to the ground floor, Victoria reached out to grip the handrail and nearly stumbled.

"Are you all right?" Juliet's eyes were wide with fright at the thought of Victoria falling down the stairs.

"I am fine," Victoria replied on a sigh as she reached the bottom. "Although, I do believe I shall have to replace these slippers." She pulled up her skirt and wiggled one slippered foot. Without the other next to it for comparison, it wasn't immediately evident the foot had at one time been crushed, most of the bones broken, and the arch flattened.

"I'm sure there is a shoemaker who can create something that will fit better," Juliet said as she glanced down. "London must have a hundred of them."

"If there is, I haven't found him," Victoria replied. Truth be told, she hadn't exactly spent the time to look. Horses had been her focus ever since she reopened Fairmont Park.

The two made their way to the door leading to the loggia and the orangery, but Victoria paused before going through. "Do you hear that?"

Juliet glanced back toward the hall. "I think you have a caller," she said, the unmistakeable sound of a male voice barely reaching them. "Are you expecting anyone?"

Victoria shook her head. "Mr. Grandby said he wouldn't return until tomorrow afternoon," she murmured as she made her way past a series of paintings featuring ancient relatives to reach the front hall.

Before Clark could announce him, Christopher, Earl of Haddon, appeared, spread out his arms, and gave an exaggerated bow. "Vicky, my darling! It's so good to see you again."

Juliet froze in place behind Victoria. Her startled gaze took in the sight of the dashing earl. Dressed in buff trousers, black boots, a deep green waistcoat, and a black top coat, he appeared far more conservative than he had the day before. And yet, if he had been wearing a cavalier hat adorned with a dyed ostrich plume, no one would have given him a second glance.

Victoria dipped a curtsy as she suppressed a laugh. "You as well, Haddon. I believe you've already met my house guest, Miss Comber?" Even before she finished the introduction, she sorted why the earl had come.

He was there for Juliet, which meant he knew she would be at Fairmont Park, which meant he had spoken with Alistair Comber.

And he had timed his call to coincide with afternoon tea.

Juliet held her breath as she curtsied, sure her face was bright pink. "My lord," she murmured, her eyes widening as the earl bowed over her hand. His grip on her fingers sent tingles shooting up her arm, and when his lips took purchase on the back of her hand, she had to suppress the urge to gasp and pull away.

His kiss was not a simple brushing of lips over skin. He had bestowed the kiss as if he was making love to her hand.

"I have indeed already had the pleasure," Christopher said before his gaze locked onto Juliet's. "Under very unfortunate circumstances, however. May I say you look especially fetching in blue? I do hope you have recovered?"

Juliet said, "I have, thank you. And you?" A flicker of confusion showed in his eyes, and she added, "You hit your head, did you not? I do hope you haven't suffered a megrim as a result."

Christopher tossed his head and aimed his reply in Victoria's direction. "It was terribly clumsy of me—"

"You? Clumsy?" Victoria teased, feigning disbelief.

He pretended offense but took her hand to his lips and gave it a quick peck. "Clumsy, but necessary, it seems."

"Necessary?" Victoria repeated. "You must explain it all over tea. We were just on our way to the orangery."

"Ah, let me say it is an honor to be invited," he said as he held out both his arms. "Shall we?"

Juliet paused before she placed her hand on his arm, her fingers barely resting on the soft superfine of his top coat. Victoria did the same on the other side of him, and the three made their way through the corridor to the door.

As they passed by the loggia, Christopher said, "My ladies, it seems the knock on my noggin has not only left me with a knot, but it has also caused a most fortunate side effect."

"You do seem far happier than you did during our last encounter," Victoria remarked as they entered the orangery. The warmth and tropical scents had all three of them inhaling. "Is there more?"

Christopher dared a glance in Juliet's direction before he said, "The time of my life has been set back several years." He quickly moved to pull two chairs out from the metal table, and the women seated themselves.

"Whatever do you mean?" Victoria asked as she watched him take the chair between her and Juliet—the chair Mr. Grandby had occupied when they'd had luncheon at the same table.

The earl leaned back and said, "I feel as if I have youthened. As if I have not lived the last few years. That their horrid effects on me have been erased."

Juliet considered everything that had happened to her in the last three years—her come-out, a few Seasons of entertainments, a few not-so-serious suitors, and the rest of the time spent with horses—and she couldn't imagine having to live them over again.

"What effects might those be?" Victoria asked as she poured tea.

Christopher furrowed a brow. "Surely you've noticed I was not as you remember me from my last visit to Wiltshire?"

Victoria gave a cup of tea to Juliet and then prepared one for Christopher. "I was hardly in your company, my lord. As I recall, you spent most of the time with my older brother." *Teaching him how to be a brat*, she almost added.

"I was not at my best," he admitted. "My behavior was reprehensible. I look back at that time and feel a good deal of remorse." He paused to accept the cup of tea and then said, "I owe you—and your family—an apology. I fear my influence on your brother had him adopting a life of indolence."

Staring at the earl as if horns had appeared on either side of his head, Victoria said, "I rather doubt you can be at fault for my brother's lack of good judgment," she replied. She held up the salver of biscuits. Both Juliet and Christopher helped themselves, their fingers brushing against one another so that they both gave a start.

"Apologies," Juliet said as she quickly pulled her hand away from the tray.

Christopher stared at her. "I did not mind," he murmured, his words almost a whisper.

A blush colored Juliet's face, and she quickly turned her attention to her tea.

Victoria gave Christopher a sideways glance, which he barely caught given his gaze had lingered on Juliet. "I am responsible for what he became," he insisted. "I am older, and I should have known he might emulate my worst traits. Traits I have recently overcome. I should have provided a better example for him to follow."

Juliet and Victoria exchanged a quick glance before Victoria said, "You really did hit your head, didn't you?"

He nodded and allowed a wan grin. "Indeed, but I am better for it. I promise." Sighing as if a huge weight had been lifted, he added, "Now, you must tell me what you two have been doing on this fine day."

"Riding horses," they said in unison, and then tittered.

"And?" he prompted, his gaze on Juliet.

"Discussing investments."

Christopher blinked before he looked to Victoria.

"I have met with Mr. Grandby regarding an opportunity, but you cannot tell Jerry about it, or I shall be very cross with you," Victoria warned.

"I have not spoken with Lord Jeremiah in over three years, but I promise I shall keep your secret." He turned to Juliet. "Have you done the same? For if you have, you will have my undying admiration."

Juliet shook her head. "I have not, for I have not yet come into my majority. But I'll be reading the contract later today," she replied. "I have agreed to act as a witness when Lady Victoria signs it, so I want to be sure I understand it."

Looking as if he was either in ecstasy or imagining it,

Christopher stared at her until she grew uncomfortable and took a drink of tea. "I should like very much to spend time in your company," he said. "Perhaps you would favor me by agreeing to a ride in the park?"

Juliet swallowed. "I cannot tomorrow, as I won't be taking my leave of Fairmont Park until late afternoon," she stammered.

"The day after, then. May I collect you at three o'clock?"

Deciding she couldn't very well turn down his offer, Juliet tried a different tact. "I'll have to have a chaperone with me," she said, hoping the mention of a companion would change his mind.

It didn't.

"Of course," he replied. "I expect you would. If it's warm enough, I shall drive the barouche, and if it's not, we will ride in a coach."

Juliet once again looked to Victoria, who merely lifted a shoulder and gave her a prim grin.

"Well, if my father allows it, then I shall expect you at three o'clock day after next," Juliet said.

"Capital," Christopher said with a nod. "Ladies, I must take my leave. I've an appointment with my tailor." He leaned over and kissed Victoria on the cheek. "Thank you for tea, my lady."

Juliet squirmed, afraid he might do the same with her. But he merely turned and lifted her hand to his lips. "Day after next, my lady. Good day." He gave them a bow and took his leave as both women watched him go.

Victoria's gaze stayed on the door for a long time before she took a deep breath and returned her attention to her tea. She noticed how Juliet stared at her, and she rolled her eyes. "You are shocked, I can tell."

"Has he kissed you like that before?" Juliet asked in a whisper.

Her hostess nodded. "Once on the lips even," she replied, her brows waggling. "But we are mere friends. Nothing more.

And you must know his mother is Italian, and he's just returned from Paris, so he tends to say or do things that might be considered scandalous here, yet are perfectly acceptable there."

Juliet considered Victoria's comments before she asked, "Did you understand what he was saying about... about *youthening*?"

Sighing, Victoria set aside her tea and interlaced her fingers. "He is nothing like he was when I last spent time in his company," she said quietly.

"What was he like?"

A guffaw escaped Victoria. "A pompous ass," she whispered. "So full of himself as to be completely oblivious to the poor opinions others had of him."

"Has he always been like that?"

Victoria shook her head. "Hardly. He used to be one of the most pleasant men to be with. Very agreeable. Friends with everyone. Educated, of course, so he could carry on a diverting conversation no matter the topic."

"What happened?"

Furrowing her brows, Victoria stayed silent for a long time before an expression of pain crossed her face. "Age, I think. Missed opportunities. Most of his friends have married and already have their heirs and spares while he has yet to have courted a single young woman." For a moment, she looked as if she might cry. "Time passed him by."

"Did you ever want him to court you?" Juliet asked, thinking that might be why Victoria displayed a look of regret.

The older woman shook her head. "Truth be told, I always thought he was too old for me."

"And now?"

Victoria shrugged. "I would not consider his suit, and he knows it." She brightened then. "However, he is definitely enamored with you."

Juliet winced. "I was afraid of that. I'm sure it's just because he feels badly about what happened yesterday."

"Perhaps," Victoria hedged. "But I do think hitting his head knocked some sense into him."

Juliet finished a biscuit. "Then if what you've said is true, let's hope it doesn't get knocked out, for it seems I will be spending an afternoon in his company day after next."

CHAPTER 17

HELP IS SOUGHT FROM AN UNLIKELY SOURCE

*L*ater that night at White's men's club in St. James Street

"I'm rather surprised you two decided to join me tonight," Tom said as Gabe Wellingham took the seat adjacent to his. "I expected the warmth of your future wives to keep you at home." White's wasn't especially busy given the horrid weather that had settled over the city once the sky had darkened. From the snowflakes that still clung to James Burroughs' blond hair, it was apparent it was snowing.

"I am not yet leg-shackled," Gabe replied, a dimple appearing in one cheek. "But come Friday, Burroughs and I will be saying our vows."

James Burroughs gave a nod as he took a seat in a wingback chair. "And I've not yet been to Woodscastle tonight."

"Late night at the bank?" Gabe asked.

"Late night with an agent. I've just acquired a townhouse in Curzon Street," James proudly announced. He gave the waiter his drink order before he turned his attention on Tom. "You cannot tell your sister. It's her wedding present."

Tom blinked at hearing the news. "I don't know when I would have the opportunity," he argued.

"You will be there to pay witness to our vows?" Gabe half-asked.

"Of course, I'll be there," Tom assured them. "Friday. Ten o'clock?"

The two grooms nodded in unison.

"You mentioned in your last note that you had to see someone about a horse," James prompted.

Tom stiffened, sure they would tease him should he mention Lady Victoria. "Indeed."

"And?"

Tom pretended the matter was of little consequence. "A potential client is all. I received a request to meet with someone regarding their investment opportunities," he explained. "They have a fortune that must be protected. They also happen to train horses for the racing circuit."

"Are you buying a race horse?" James asked in surprise.

"No." The word held the sort of finality that suggested James shouldn't inquire further, which instead had him furrowing a brow.

"What's her name?"

His mouth dropping open, Tom straightened in his chair. "Whatever has you asking *that*?"

"If it had been a *man* looking to protect a fortune, you would have said so," Gabe accused.

"You know that I cannot disclose my clients' identities," Tom stated. "Besides, I haven't yet decided if I will take her on." This last wasn't true. He had not only formulated a proposal, he'd had his secretary busy copying it and drawing up a contract just that morning. Then he had dropped off the papers earlier that day.

"Because you have feelings for her?"

"What? No!" Tom replied. Exasperated, he said, "No," one more time.

Gabe's eyes widened in delight, and he said, "Perhaps I should pay a visit to the betting book," he teased.

"Don't. You'll only lose," Tom warned with a shake of his head.

James exchanged glances with Gabe, and the two were up and out of their chairs in an instant, hurrying off to the room in which the betting book was mounted for all to see.

Rolling his eyes, Tom glanced down at the letter he still held.

A letter of apology.

It was the very last thing he had expected to receive from Lady Victoria. Especially when all seemed well upon his departure from Fairmont Park earlier that day. Apparently she was concerned that he had wasted his time on delivering the proposal in person when she was unable to spend time with him right then to review it.

Apparently she didn't understand that she was expected to spend time reviewing the proposal without his counsel. Besides that, she was under no obligation to accept it. However, Tom had every intention of moving forward with the investment—with or without her funds.

Now he had a decision to make.

Once he had made arrangements to invest her funds, could he then propose another sort of arrangement?

He was contemplating writing a letter to both her father and her brother, Lord Michael, when Gabe and James returned, huge grins on their faces.

"You and I have exactly the same problem," Gabe announced.

Tom frowned. "And what is that?"

"We're in love."

"And on that note, I'm off to Woodscastle and the woman I love," James stated. He gave an exaggerated bow as Gabe and Tom watched him go.

Scoffing at the comment—what the hell had happened to his best friend?—Tom turned to Gabe and asked, "Would you like a ride to Trenton House?" Arthurs' was only a ways down in St. James Street, but Tom felt honor-bound to offer his coach.

"I came in the Trenton town coach," Gabe said. "But thank you for the offer." After another moment, he leaned forward and asked, "Pray tell, who is it that warms your bed these days?"

Tom arched a brow, at first tempted to reply that it was none of Gabe's business. But he saw that Gabe wasn't asking for the purpose of teasing him. "Unfortunately, no one," he replied. "Or perhaps it is fortunate. The pursuit of the perfect woman for me is proving rather difficult. So much so, I have ceased thinking about it."

His face displaying a look of disbelief, Gabe said, "You do realize that once you find her, you'll have to chase her until she catches you?" he warned.

His brows furrowing at hearing the odd comment, Tom finally allowed a chuckle. "Perhaps that is what I am doing wrong." The two shook hands, and Tom took his leave of the room.

Heading in the direction of the door, Tom felt a combination of annoyance and regret. The younger man's query not only reminded him that it had been six months since he had quit his mistress, but it also underscored what Tom was coming to believe was a flaw in his character.

When he'd had opportunities to court women—and there had been many—he hadn't taken them.

Not once.

Every time, he'd had an excuse.

Most were valid.

Not enough time when he was in London. His days were filled with meetings and writing letters. Doing research.

Following up on investments scattered across England meant he spent too much time traveling.

When was there time for courting? Enough time for a wife?

He was so deep in thought, he didn't realize he wasn't

walking alone. That is, until he heard the sound of a throat clearing.

Loudly.

Tom stopped, as did the man who was abreast of him.

"Apologies, Mr. Grandby, but I wondered if I might have a word? I'll buy you a drink, of course."

Tom blinked as he stared at the man, for he immediately recognized Christopher, Earl of Haddon.

And couldn't for the life of him think of why the earl might want to have a word with him.

CHAPTER 18

AN EARL PLEADS FOR HELP

A second later

"My lord, I apologize. I did not see you there," Tom said as he gave a bow. Given his height and Haddon's title, Tom made sure the courtesy was deeper than usual.

"Mr. Grandby, it's fortuitous that I find you so close to White's," Haddon said. "I wish to buy you a drink."

Tom didn't try to hide his surprise. "Me, sir?"

"Yes. Will you oblige me?"

The thought of being seen in the company of the future Marquess of Morganfield—in White's no less, given the current marquess was a member of Brook's—had Tom giving the earl a nod. "Of course."

As they turned and headed back to the men's club, Tom was relieved to see Gabe climbing into the Trenton coach. He wouldn't have wanted the young man thinking he hadn't been truthful when he had taken his leave of the club only moments earlier.

Tom followed Haddon into the club, surprised when the earl paused to wait for him to come alongside before they made their way to an alcove at the back. He was also curious as to how Haddon had greeted the butler, his complimentary words leaving the man wide-eyed and tongue-tied.

Haddon indicated a pair of chairs and took one, crossing his legs and steepling his fingers as he rested an elbow on the arm of the chair.

A footman was quick to take their orders and then disappeared.

"I don't mean to be dramatic," Haddon said in preamble. "But I believe you might have the ear of someone I wish to court."

Tom blinked, immediately thinking of his sister, Emily. But given she was only the grandniece of a viscount and a lesser relation to a duke, he didn't think Haddon would even know her. "Not a relative, certainly," he guessed.

"The daughter of a friend of yours," Haddon replied. "Although your last sister is fetching and would no doubt make a suitable wife for any lucky man."

Having a hard time keeping an impassive expression—Tom had thought the earl a pompous man given the descriptions he had heard of late—he said, "I thank you for saying so, my lord."

So much for thinking the earl wouldn't know of Emily.

"Haddon, please." His gaze was intense as he regarded Tom. "The woman I have decided to make my future marchioness is a friend of one of your new investors." He leaned back in the chair, waiting for his guest to guess the young lady's name.

His brows furrowing, Tom considered the identity of his newest investor—Victoria Statton—and then remembered who had been with her when he had paid a call on Fairmont Park earlier that day. "You must know Miss Comber isn't an aristocrat's daughter," he said carefully.

Haddon displayed a look of endearment at hearing her name. "But she is the granddaughter of two earls," he countered. "Her father is a second son, and he served in the British Army in the war against France."

Tom was about to say something when the footman

appeared with their brandies. He allowed the servant to finish setting the glasses on the side tables and then watched as the footman bowed and took his leave of the alcove.

"You don't think she's... too young for you?" Tom asked in a quiet voice. "I would expect your taste in women would tend to someone a bit older. More worldly."

Haddon regarded his brandy as he swirled it in the glass before he said, "I agree, of course. But something happened, and I find myself quite in awe of her skills."

For just a fraction of a second, Tom thought Haddon might be referring to skills for which Juliet Comber should have no knowledge, but then he remembered her horsemanship. "She is quite impressive on a horse," he said.

Furrowing his brows, Haddon said, "Oh, I do not refer to her skills as a horsewoman, although I agree they are impressive. I was referring to her ability to punch."

Tom blinked. "Punch?"

Haddon nodded. "She has a rather effective uppercut." He mimicked her move by balling a fist and then punching it into the air in front of him. "Took me down like a sack of potatoes."

Tom wondered how he was supposed to respond to that bit of news. "I was unaware she possessed those skills, sir," he remarked. Remembering the earl's unusual behavior with the butler, and coupled with his friendly behavior with those they had passed on their way to the alcove, Tom asked, "Did you hit your head?"

A huge grin split the earl's face. "Yes! Yes, I did, thanks to Miss Comber. Best thing that ever happened to me, which is why I have paid a call on Mr. Comber and secured his permission to court her."

Tom dipped his head, not sure what else to do. "And Miss Comber? Given the lack of entertainments in town this month, have you made arrangements for an outing, perhaps?"

"Yes," Haddon replied happily. "I paid a call on Vicky, who was kind enough to include me in her tea this afternoon. After a bit of cajoling, I am scheduled to take Juliet for a ride in the park the day after next," he said proudly.

The mention of 'Vicky' had Tom doing his best to suppress a growl of outrage. How dare the earl refer to Lady Victoria in such a casual manner! "Vicky?" he repeated. And then his mind conjured the absolute worst thought—that the earl and Lady Victoria had at one time been lovers.

Or still were.

Jealousy had the Green Monster rearing up inside Tom. The urge to respond with an uppercut to Haddon's chin was nearly impossible to suppress. "You are referring to *Lady Victoria?*"

If Haddon noticed Tom's growing anger, he ignored it and took a sip of brandy. "Her older brother, Jerry, and I were friends for years," he explained. "I've known Vicky since she was a child. Although it would make sense for she and I to marry, I know she would not be happy with the arrangement, and I do not wish to vex her."

"How considerate of you," Tom murmured, his initial flash of anger settling into a simmering annoyance.

"I don't wish to behave as my reputation would have me behaving," the earl went on. "I am back to the way I was before..." He allowed the sentence to trail off as his eyes glazed over.

Tom sipped his brandy as he watched Haddon slip into a moment of self-reflection, at once relieved the man had no interest in making Lady Victoria his wife, and at the same time, feeling sorry for Juliet Comber. Christopher, Earl of Haddon, was old enough to be her father. If she ended up married to him, the only thing she might look forward to was his early death and the life of a Merry Widow.

He gave his head a shake. Juliet Comber would never behave as a Merry Widow. She was a gently bred young woman, even if she was capable of cursing at a horse when it didn't behave.

Perhaps she would do the same with Haddon. The thought had him suppressing a guffaw.

"I apologize," Haddon said in a quiet voice. "I have not been myself since I suffered this knot on my head."

"Have you seen a physician?" Tom asked, now genuinely concerned. If the earl was concussed, the effects might linger for days.

Haddon shook his head. "I have not, nor do I wish to recover. I do not like what I had become, you see," he said.

"What you had become?" Tom leaned forward, setting his brandy on the side table lest he be tempted to toss it in the earl's face in the event his response impugned a young woman's reputation.

"A pompous ass," Haddon said quietly. "The moment I knew I would reach forty years on this planet was the moment my world changed. And not for the better. I was bitter. All my friends had wed, and they had already populated their nurseries. Lines were appearing on my face that had never been there before. Hairs were growing out of my ears. Out of my *nose*," he said in a louder voice. "I am rich, I've been assured that I am handsome, I dress in the finest clothes my tailor can create, and yet..." He took a deep breath. "I am *alone*." These last words came out in a whisper.

A bit uncomfortable at hearing the earl's complaints—they very well could have been said by him—Tom said, "As I recall, you have not courted anyone." The earl was known to attend all the London entertainments during the Season and sometimes even the Little Season. He danced with eligible young ladies. He acted as host for his mother's charity garden parties when Morganfield would not—the marquess was notorious for drawing the line on what he was willing to do for his wife's charities—and he rode in the park during the fashionable hour during the spring months. "Did not a single young woman catch your eye?"

"Well, of course, but none I was inclined to court."

"Mayhap, were you expecting a young lady to ask for *your* hand?"

At this, Haddon allowed a wan grin. "It would have made things easier," he admitted. "But, no. I think I would not have been happy with any of the young women I was introduced to over the years. Which is why I believe Miss Comber is the one for me."

"Because she punched you?"

Haddon's eyes widened. "Oh, not exactly, but I am glad she did. Knocked some sense into me. I goaded her into it, of course."

"Really? You dared her to punch you?" Tom replied, deciding the earl really had hit his head. "I cannot imagine welcoming such violence upon your person."

"Well, I told her she could slap me, but she refused."

Tom struggled to keep a passive expression on his face. "So, when she punched you, you... fell in love with her?"

Haddon furrowed a brow before he said, "Well, first I fell, hit my head, and then I realized I was quite in love with her... so, yes. I did fall in love, didn't I?"

Clearing his throat, Tom drained his brandy before he said, "When you are courting Miss Comber, you must remember a few things." At the earl's urge to go on, he added, "Horses are not just her... hobby. They are her *life*. You must be willing to share her with them."

"I will. I shall," Haddon said with a nod.

"Lady Victoria is her best friend. You will never replace her in that regard."

"Nor would I expect to. Ladies must have their friends. Their confidantes. Although... I should like to be her next closest friend."

"Then perhaps you should start there," Tom suggested, a strange sensation passing through him as he realized he should be doing the same with Lady Victoria. Even if there wasn't anything romantic betwixt them, he wanted her friendship.

He hoped she wanted his.

"Very good," Haddon replied. "I have decided I shall never again do anything to vex Miss Comber, nor will I behave in the manner to which I have been subscribing these last few years," he vowed.

"Then be sure to tell Miss Comber," Tom replied, deciding he needed to do the same with Lady Victoria.

Given he was set to pay a call on the young lady the following afternoon, he knew exactly when he would tell her.

CHAPTER 19

CONTRACTS AND
QUESTIONS

ednesday, January 9, 1839, four o'clock in the afternoon at Fairmont Park

Despite having downed three glasses of brandy the night before at White's, Tom was in good spirits when he awoke.

As was Jake, who seemed determined to get him to his office as quickly as possible. The gentle giant apparently liked the mews behind his office in Oxford Street, or perhaps just the stableboy, Bobby, who was waiting for them as he parked the phaeton in front of his office.

"He is in fine form today," Tom said as he handed the reins to the young man and then fished a few coins from his waistcoat pocket. "As is the weather." The clouds were clearing, and the sun had begun to warm the air.

"He has a few friends in the stables," Bobby replied with a grin. "And he loves his apples."

"Ah." Tom found some more coins and handed them over. "Then if you could see to keeping him fed, I would appreciate it. Given his size, I fear there isn't enough hay to go 'round at the mews behind Arthur's."

"Very good, sir. When would you like me to bring him back?"

"I've an appointment north of here this afternoon. Say half-past three?"

"I be back at quarter-past, sir."

Tom watched as Bobby hopped up onto the bench seat and expertly merged the phaeton into the busy morning traffic. Then he made his way into his office.

Thick carpet immediately muted the sounds of traffic. The walls—wood paneled on the lower half and silk-covered up to the mouldings—had been chosen by his father, Gregory. The deep green of the fabric reflected a moire pattern that seemed to move with his every step.

Even though he knew his father was in Derbyshire, Tom glanced into his office. A veritable museum given its numerous artifacts from all over the world, the quiet study would be perfect for the likes of James Burroughs. After last night's discussion over drinks at White's, Tom knew he would soon be welcoming the banker as not just a friend, but as a brother.

Although he usually arrived before his secretary, Jasper Adams, Tom was heartened to discover the young man was already at his usual position behind a marble-topped counter.

"Good morning," he said with a nod and a query about the contract for that afternoon's meeting with Lady Victoria. He required his own copy, which was the original, as well as copies for two additional investors.

"I'll have this fourth one finished before you leave today, sir," Jasper said. "Would you like a reminder of your appointments?"

Tom shook his head. "That won't be necessary, but I will be leaving at half-past three to meet with that client," he replied as he nodded toward the paper Jasper was transcribing

"Yes, sir."

His thoughts on his four o'clock meeting with Lady Victoria, Tom moved into his office and went about his day.

· · ·

$\mathcal{D}$espite Tom's anxiousness—he was looking forward to seeing Lady Victoria far more than he ever had any other investor—the day flew by.

He was staring at the Greek pelike of Aphrodite's birth, imagining Victoria in place of the goddess, when Jasper said, "It's nearly half-past three, sir."

Jerked from his reverie, Tom said, "I'll be taking my leave now. I don't expect to return before the end of the day. Could you see to locking up?"

"Of course, sir."

$\mathcal{A}$t exactly four o'clock, Tom halted Jake in the circle drive in front of Fairmont Park. Apparently the horse had been as anxious as he was to arrive. Once they had reached an open road, Tom gave him the rein, and the shire had made up for the delay caused by an overturned drayage cart in Oxford Street.

Jemmy came running around the side of the house, a carrot in one hand. Tom grinned as he tossed him a coin and stepped down from the phaeton.

"Will I find your mistress inside or at the track?" he asked as he pulled his satchel from the back of the phaeton.

"Her ladyship and Miss Comber finished with the horses about an hour ago, sir. I expect they're inside."

Tom sobered at the reminder that Juliet Comber would be paying witness to the contract signing. He had hoped to have Victoria all to himself. "Pray tell, has Miss Comber taken up residence in Fairmont Park?"

Jemmy shook his head. "I think she'd like that, sir, but a coach is comin' to fetch her at five o'clock."

Heartened to hear the news—that meant there might be time alone with Lady Victoria—Tom made his way to the front doors, one of the carved wooden panels already opened. Clark stood aside as he stepped in. "Mr. Grandby to see her ladyship," he murmured as he gave the butler his calling card. "I've an appointment."

"Of course, sir. I'm to escort you to the study."

Secretly pleased he'd be seeing a different part of the house on this visit, Tom followed Clark as he led the way past the library and to an oak-paneled room off the main hall. He removed his driving gloves as he did so.

He half-expected to find the two young ladies still dressed in their riding garb, but both were wearing bright colored gowns, their hair piled into messy buns. Their heads bent over a document, they were murmuring to one another when Clark announced him.

Although Juliet was quick to stand, Victoria merely straightened in her chair as Tom bowed. "Good afternoon, my ladies," he said as he stepped forward. He took Victoria's hand first, brushing a kiss over her knuckles. The slight tremble he felt against his lips might have been caused by his own hand, but he hoped not. Victoria's gaze upon his arrival had suggested she was glad to see him.

He lifted Juliet's hand and gave her the same courtesy, which had the young woman tittering. "Three times in two days," she said when he gave her a questioning look. "I don't think it's ever happened before."

For a moment, Tom wondered at her comment, and then remembered that Lord Haddon had paid a call on them the day before. "You'll have to get used to it should you marry an aristocrat," he said, waggling his brows.

The grin on Juliet's face faltered. "Well, it's not a hardship, I suppose."

Victoria waved at the chair in front of the desk. "Please, have a seat, Mr. Grandby. I rather expect you knew we'd have questions," she said as she indicated the contract.

"Of course. Everyone does," he said, hoping to assuage any

concern she had that only women might have questions. He pulled his copy of the contract from his satchel.

"Would you like tea?"

He glanced at the tray, his mouth watering upon seeing the array of biscuits and cakes. "I would, yes," he replied. "I never once stepped away from the office from the time I arrived this morning."

As Victoria poured his tea, he arranged his copies of the contract on the desk along with an ink pot and some pens.

"Tell me, Mr. Grandby. How many times in a year do you do this?" Victoria asked as she handed him a cup and saucer. She was quick to offer a plate of cake.

"Well, this is my first time for this year," he replied. "Last year, I completed contracts with fourteen... no, fifteen investors, mostly in railway subscriptions."

"Are you an investor as well?"

Tom nodded. "I have always believed, as has my father, that an investment be solid. That if I'm to expect someone to buy into a subscription, then I must be willing to do so as well."

Apparently satisfied with his answer, Victoria held up one of her sheets and began asking questions.

Tom answered each query as well those that Juliet brought forth. He couldn't help but notice that Victoria's attention wasn't on him or Juliet when he was answering the younger lady's concerns, but rather on a different page of the contract.

While Juliet seemed especially concerned with the dividends that would be made as annual profits were calculated, and how much those might be, Victoria seemed more concerned with the end of the contract. What might happen to the investment should she decide to sell her stake.

"At the end of the contract, if you don't wish to renew, your stake is simply sold to another investor," he explained. "Should another party decide they wish to buy up the entire subscription, you'll be asked to cast your votes as to whether or not that can happen."

Victoria's eyes widened. "There are other parties besides you and me in this?"

Tom winced. "Yes, of course. We needed someone to supply the buses as well as be available should something go wrong with them, preferably the inventor. We also needed more money for the initial infrastructure—a bus barn, so to speak, to have a place to park them when they aren't in service—as well as salaries to pay the drivers and the maintenance men."

"How many more? And how much did they invest?" Victoria pressed.

"Besides the inventor and us, there is just one other investor. We needed over a hundred-and-twelve-thousand pounds to fund this venture. You have the majority stake, of course, which carries two votes, while the inventor has agreed to a twenty-five-thousand-pound stake. An earl has invested twenty-five thousand in cash, and I have put in the twelve thousand."

"How many votes do they get?"

"One each. I have no votes."

Victoria furrowed a dark brow. "That seems unfair," she remarked.

"For me? Not really," he replied. "I don't wish to be accused of malfeasance, so I leave the important choices up to the primary investors."

Victoria returned her attention to another page of the contract. "Is investing always this complicated?" she asked as she indicated a series of caveats.

"This particular subscription is actually more straightforward than most. Nothing has to be invented. Just built," he replied before he took a sip of tea.

The sound of coach wheels crunching in the circle drive had Tom's attention going to the window behind Victoria. Juliet followed his line of sight and allowed a sigh of frustration. "My ride is here," she said, not sounding the least bit happy about it.

"My lady, if you require more time to review the contract, we don't have to do the signing today," Tom said. "I can arrange to return another time. I'll need to anyway once I have the copy that includes the inventor's signature."

"Oh, I'm ready," Victoria said. She reached over and took a pen and dipped it in the ink. The scratch of the pen over parchment could be heard across the desk, and Tom watched as Juliet did the same, signing her name on the line marked for a witness. Finally, Tom signed his name and then passed his copy as well as two others for their signatures.

"I must go," Juliet said as she reached over and gave Victoria a kiss on the cheek. "I'll see you again Saturday if you wish."

Tom quickly stood and gave her a bow as she curtsied and hurried out of the office. When he saw that Victoria intended to remain where she was, he returned to his chair. "Did you have other concerns?" he asked as he checked to be sure the ink was dry before he passed back her copy.

"Only about horses," she said on a sigh. "Would you like more tea?"

"I would, thank you. Is Sam still limping?"

She shook her head. "Not when Juliet rides him," she said on a sigh. "Tell me, will you acquire a horse for riding?"

"Not for a time, I think. Mr. Comber has seen to it I have my one and only noble steed. He's doing very well, and he was in a hurry to get here today. As was I."

In the middle of taking a sip of tea, Victoria's eyes widened as she stared at him over the rim of her cup. "You were that anxious to see to it the contracts were signed?"

He shook his head. "I was only anxious to see you," he admitted. Before she could react, he added, "I wondered, my lady, if I might be allowed to escort you to dinner at Rules this evening? A celebratory meal in honor of your investment?"

Victoria hesitated, her eyes darting to one side before she asked, "Is this something you do with all your investors?"

Tom dipped his head and said, "Usually it's drinks at a men's club, but since I cannot take you to White's..." He gave a shrug.

"I suppose you drove your phaeton here?" She knew he had. She had seen him through the window when he arrived.

"I did, but I can return with a town coach," he said, mentally calculating how long it would take for him to get to Woodscastle in Chiswick, change clothes, and return to Fairmont Park.

"We can go in mine," she offered. "But it will take some time for Cummings to doing something with my hair."

"Your hair is quite fetching the way it is," Tom replied.

"Don't be a bounder, Mr. Grandby."

"Call me Tom. Or Thomas, if you must."

Victoria angled her head a bit. "Don't be a bounder, Thomas."

He allowed a grin. "I am telling the truth, my lady." When she didn't reply but merely stood from the desk, Tom was quick to rise. "Might I be allowed to wait for you in here?"

She glanced around and gave a slight shrug. "Of course. Use the desk if you'd like."

He gave a bow as she took her leave of the study, and he watched as she made her way to the stairs.

One thing was certain. She walked with a definite limp. One he found quite fetching.

CHAPTER 20

AN UNEXPECTED CALLER

Six o'clock that evening, Comber townhouse in South Audley Street

Darkness had already settled over Mayfair when the town coach carrying Juliet pulled up in front of her home. A footman saw to opening the door and then collected her valise as she made her way to the house.

The butler stepped aside, and before Juliet could greet him, Williamson said, "You have a caller, miss. Arrived about quarter of an hour ago."

"Me?"

"There you are," her mother said as she hurried through the hall towards the front door. "I was about to send another coach."

"Mother, I was only detained a few..."

"He's in the parlor. I've seen to it he has coffee and walnuts, and, well, I was about to invite him to dinner."

"Who?" But Juliet's eyes widened when she sorted who her caller had to be. "Haddon?" She rolled her eyes. "He wasn't supposed to come until tomorrow afternoon," she complained. "To take me for a ride in the park."

Julia Comber regarded her daughter with an expression of suspicion. "Oh? And when was this arranged?"

Juliet sighed. "Yesterday. He paid a call at Fairmont Park, but it was really to see me, I think. He claims Father said he could."

A guilty look crossed her mother's face. "Perhaps because I encouraged it."

"*What?*"

Julia glanced around the hall before she pulled Juliet into the front salon and closed the door. "I had a caller this afternoon. The Marchioness of Morganfield."

"His mother?" Juliet asked in shock.

Julia nodded. "She's over the moon at how Lord Haddon has changed, and she said it's all because you punched her son."

"He *told* her about that?" Juliet couldn't imagine why a man would admit to being punched. Especially by a woman. "What was he *thinking?*"

"That he wishes to take you to wife. She claims he needs you to keep him humble. He also likes that you can handle a horse."

Juliet knew her mother had never approved of the amount of time she spent in the stables. She had hinted that a young man wouldn't approve, either. After three Seasons, Juliet had begun to believe it, since none of her suitors had been serious about marriage.

Well, Lord Haddon wasn't a young man. He was old enough to be her father. Perhaps the older a man was, the more he appreciated a woman who could handle a horse.

Or a punch in the gut.

Juliet wriggled out of her redingote and removed her bonnet, handing them to her mother. "My hair is a mess," she said. "But I'm not about to have it repaired just for him."

Her mother winced but regarded her daughter with a critical eye. "It's really rather fetching that way. Like you intended it to be a messy bun."

Screwing her face into a grimace, Juliet marched out of the

salon and headed up the steps to the parlor. On the landing, she shook out her coral skirts and straightened the long sleeves. At the top of the stairs, she took a deep breath as if girding her loins and headed into the parlor.

"Good evening, Lord Haddon," she said as she dipped a curtsy.

Christopher quickly stood from the chair he had taken near the fireplace, one upholstered in a floral pattern featuring blue roses. "Ah, Juliet. You are a vision," he said as he gave her an exaggerated bow. "I apologize for my early arrival."

"Did you plan to spend the night?"

The query caught the earl off guard, and he gave a chuckle. "If only I could," he said. "To be as close to you as possible."

Juliet blinked. She had intended for her words to be taken as a scolding. "You didn't say that to my mother, I hope?"

"Would it have helped my suit?" he asked, with far too much enthusiasm.

"Lord Haddon—"

"Haddon, please. And when we're *really* alone, I would ask that you call me Christopher. Or Chris. Or whatever you wish, really."

Juliet could imagine a half-dozen words she might call him, but none of them would have been appropriate for an earl. "May I inquire as to why you have arrived..." She mentally calculated just how early the earl was. "Twenty-one hours early?"

Looking thoroughly besotted, Christopher stepped up to her and took both of her hands in his. "You are so quick with arithmetic. And you did it without a pencil and paper," he murmured in awe.

At first, Juliet thought he might be teasing her, but then she watched as he gave a shake of his head. "Of course you can. Forgive me. You no doubt had a tutor in addition to a governess."

Well, she'd had the benefit of a tutor, but only because her younger brother, Jamie, had a tutor. She had sat in on his lessons when boredom threatened her sanity.

"Something like that," Juliet agreed. "But I know what I need to know to run a household. How to keep the books, of course. Like any young woman would." She had a thought to shake off his hands—he still held her fingers draped over his index fingers, his thumbs barely brushing her knuckles.

A slight tremble vibrated there, and Juliet sucked in a breath. "You still haven't said why it is you have come twenty-one hours early."

An odd expression crossed Christopher's face, and Juliet stared at him. She had never really looked at him up close like this. Now that she studied his features, she found she could not look away.

He was handsome, his hair almost as dark as his mother's and tinted with hints of red and gold. The waves in it meant he could never sport the latest fashionable hairstyle for men, and there was one forelock that seemed determined to decorate his forehead.

His complexion was almost the olive of an Italian—he had inherited that from his mother as well—and his eyes were a chocolate brown with hints of gold speckles in their depths. Damn it, but if he didn't have long lashes, too, tipped in gold.

Juliet was sure he had inherited his nose from his father, for there was the hint of generations of aristocracy in its shape.

But what had her attention just then was his lips, for they were parted slightly. They barely hid teeth bestowed by the dental gods on only those they deemed worthy.

Apparently, Christopher, Earl of Haddon, was worthy.

"I couldn't wait to see you again," he murmured, finally answering her question.

Juliet watched his lips form the words, her brows furrowing when they lowered to hers.

Soft, she thought first, rather stunned they weren't more firm. That the kiss he was bestowing on her wasn't hard or more urgent or crushing in its intensity. Instead, it was simple and respectful, almost innocent.

When he pulled away, she had to stop herself from leaning forward to recapture his lips with hers.

"I couldn't wait to do that, either," he whispered.

"Oh," Juliet managed to say before she swallowed. When she noticed his attention had gone to the door—her back was still to it—she glanced around to find her father leaning against the jamb, his arms crossed over his chest.

Panic gripped her, but Christopher was quick to say, "Good evening, sir. I was just bidding Miss Comber good night." He turned his attention back to her. "I shall return for you tomorrow at three o'clock." Then he once again lifted both of her hands to his lips and kissed her knuckles.

Juliet watched him go, watched as he gave her father a deep nod as he passed him on his way to the stairs. She listened as his footfalls faded down the steps, and then she finally took a breath.

She blinked a few times as she stared at her father. "How long were you standing there?"

Alistair uncrossed his arms and moved to join her in the parlor. "Long enough to know that he is thoroughly smitten with you," he replied.

"How do you know that?" she asked, hoping her embarrassment wasn't evident. Her coral gown certainly didn't help. Her face was probably doing its best to match the color.

"Because I'm quite sure I looked exactly like he did the first time I kissed your mother."

Juliet swallowed. "How much longer after that before you knew you loved Mother?"

Alistair's eyes darted to one side. "An hour, mayhap? Probably less." He sighed as he turned his attention back to his daughter. "If you cannot abide another moment in his presence, I will write and let him know he's not welcome tomorrow."

Juliet stared at him for a long time before she shook her

head. "There's no need. I'll go on the ride in the park with him," she said. "As will my maid. At some point, he'll either show his true colors, or he'll prove that he really has changed for the better."

After that kiss, though, Juliet didn't know which one to want more.

CHAPTER 21

DINNER FOR TWO

eanwhile, at Fairmont Park

"Have you ever been to Rules for dinner?" Tom asked as he opened and held Victoria's redingote for her. The establishment was London's oldest restaurant and featured different game meats according to the season.

"Of course. Father has taken us many times," she replied. She had changed into a more formal gown, a deep blue watered silk trimmed with tiny blue fabric flowers along the neckline and the seam of the flounce. Her maid had done her hair in an elegant chignon, and ringlets bobbed from both temples.

"Did you like it?" Tom asked as he helped her into the redingote, a deep blue wool that fit to perfection. Clark stood off to one side, holding a matching hat and kid gloves.

She buttoned the coat. "I did. I cannot say if I still do as I've not been there since my return to the capital." She pulled on the pair of black gloves and then took the hat from the butler.

Tom watched in awe as she set the hat at a perfect angle on her head—without the benefit of a mirror. His mother would have fussed over the positioning and attempted several angles all while putting voice to a number of complaints. Then his father would simply lift her into his arms and carry her to the coach, essentially ensuring she would forget about her hat and instead focus her energy on berating him until he could silence her with a kiss.

Tom blinked at the memory of how his father had behaved with his mother—still did, for all he knew. He had half a mind to try it on Victoria, just to discover how much she might complain—or not.

But if she didn't complain, then he wouldn't have a motive to kiss her.

Dammit.

He offered his arm, and Victoria placed a hand on it.

"Let Cummings know I won't need her assistance when I return," Victoria said to Clark. "I'd rather she spend some time with her family."

"Very good, my lady," Clark replied with a bow. Although he opened the door for them, his expression suggested he was none too happy about Lady Victoria stepping out with a gentleman—and no chaperone.

"I'll have her home before one o'clock," Tom murmured as he passed the butler.

Victoria gave him a quelling glance. "Clark is not my protector, and I am old enough to go out without a chaperone."

"You are a duke's daughter, though," Tom said as the footman opened the door of an unmarked town coach. He turned his attention to Cummings, remembering the footman was married to Victoria's lady's maid. "Could you let the driver know we're going to Rules in Maiden Lane?"

"Aye, sir," the footman replied.

Tom turned back to Victoria. "A rogue intent on kidnapping an aristocrat's daughter might decide you are the perfect mark. You are, of course, under my protection on this night—"

"I rather doubt anyone will attempt a kidnapping," Victoria said. She stumbled a bit before stepping up and into the coach. "It's far too cold for anyone to be waiting in a hedgerow, and besides, the coach has no markings. Deliberately," she added as she took the seat facing the direction of travel.

"I had wondered about that, my lady," Tom said as he took the seat that faced her. "I suppose it is wiser than traveling in a coach emblazoned with Somerset's crest." He glanced around the roomy interior, impressed by the light blue velvet squabs. It was also warmer than he expected on a wintery night. "On my visits here, I have not noticed anyone seeing to your safety." The comment was a white lie, but he was curious to hear how she would respond.

Victoria furrowed a brow. "The groom carries a pistol in his pocket, and Jemmy hides a knife in a boot. On the days Juliet is here, she sports a small lady's pistol—"

"Does she know how to use it?" Tom asked in surprise as the coach lurched into motion. As far as he knew, none of his five sisters had ever learned how to wield a gun. They could operate microscopes and telescopes, though, and identify some fossils and indigenous plants, but those skills would hardly ward off an attack.

He supposed if they had to, they could throw agates at a ruffian, or they could bonk a would-be kidnapper over the head with the tube of a telescope, although the tripod would prob-ably do more damage.

"Miss Comber is an excellent shot," Victoria replied. "Her father taught her how to shoot. He wouldn't let her spend Tues-days with me if she wasn't capable of defending herself."

Tom had a brief thought of Haddon, his arms held up, as Juliet Comber threatened him with a pistol. The earl would probably enjoy the experience, though, thinking it was some sort of foreplay.

"Hardly anyone knows I live at Fairmont Park, which suits me just fine," Victoria continued as she adjusted her coat to cover her half-booted feet. She angled her head to one side. "Where do you call home, Mr. Grandby?"

Tom winced at hearing the query, but decided truth was

best. "I have a room at Arthur's, although I can still call Wood-scastle in Chiswick my home should I require the comforts of a larger estate."

"Arthur's?"

He nodded. "It's a men's club that is owned by its members, and there are a few of us that have taken rooms above it," he explained.

"In St. James Street?"

"Indeed. Makes for a quick ride to my office in Oxford Street in the mornings. It usually takes longer to get back there at night, depending on traffic," he explained.

"And here I thought you might live in a mansion in Mayfair," she said.

Although he thought she might be judging him based on where he lived, Tom didn't hear any censure in her voice. "I have considered it on occasion," he admitted. "But given the amount of time I spend in my office, I have concentrated my efforts on making it as comfortable—and presentable–as possible."

"Oh?"

"I do have to consider the first impression my office makes on a potential investor," he explained. "I rather doubt a man of means would be comfortable leaving his money in the hands of someone occupying a shabby cubbyhole."

"Goodness. I didn't even see your office, and yet I have turned over a considerable sum to your care," she said, sounding in the dark as if she might be chiding herself.

"About that. May I inquire as to who recommended you invest in steam buses?"

Victoria seemed to ponder the question for a time before answering. "Not yet," she replied. "I think it best he remain unknown to you."

"And why is that?" Tom asked in alarm.

She allowed a sigh. "Because I prefer there be no..."

"Collusion," he finished for her. "Of course. You're absolutely right." Still, it rankled that whoever had recommended the investment knew *his* identity.

"Will you take me there?" she asked after a few moments of silence. Although the exterior lanterns were lit, she was barely visible in the darkened interior.

"To the office? Certainly. After dinner, perhaps?"

"If it's not too close to one o'clock," she countered.

Tom could imagine her dark eyebrows arching in a tease, his parting words to Clark coming back to haunt him.

"Do you drink brandy, my lady? As an after dinner drink?" He kept a bottle of the best that Berry Brothers offered in their Jermyn Street store. "Or do you prefer... champagne?"

"We've not yet had dinner, and you're already planning on how you're going to seduce me?" she countered.

Tom cleared his throat. Loudly. "My lady, I—"

"I'm teasing, Mr. Grandby," she scolded.

Hating that he couldn't see her in the dark, Tom asked, "Are you? Because..." He inhaled. "I like you."

"I should hope so. I just signed over most of my inheritance—"

"That's not why," he countered. "I like your confidence. You're a refreshing change from the parade of helpless females I tend to meet."

"You cannot hold it against them, Thomas," she argued. "They've no choice in the matter of their upbringing, no choice in their education—or lack thereof—and certainly no choice in how they shall live their lives. Marriage is their only option."

Tom wondered at the odd sensation he felt when he heard her say 'Thomas.' Usually he didn't care for the formal version of his name, but the way she said it, in the dark, had him wishing she would continue saying it. "Forgive me. I tend to forget that my sisters had the benefit of an education because my father wouldn't have had it any other way."

She furrowed a brow. "'Tell me truthfully, do they think he's done them a favor?"

Hearing the chiding tone in her voice, Tom asked, "Are you implying ignorance is bliss?"

"Perhaps," she hedged. "If you do not know what you are missing, then you never miss it."

Tom inhaled softly. "And what are you missing, my lady?"

He heard her soft chuckle and winced when she said, "The world."

For a moment, Tom imagined what it would be like to travel with the woman. What it would be like to show her the wonders of the world. To be the first one to see her reactions to the sights and sounds of foreign lands. To eat strange foods and dance to music unlike any played in a ballroom.

To share in her awe.

"I'm of a mind to send your father a letter asking if I—"

"Don't you dare," she said quickly.

Tom straightened in the squabs, just as the coach came to a stuttering halt. Glancing out the window, he was stunned to discover they were already in Maiden Lane, the restaurant only a few doors down from where the coach had parked.

He stood, bending over nearly in half due to his height, and opened the door before the driver could step down from his seat. Turning around, he offered his hand, and Victoria placed hers on it.

"As you wish, my lady," Tom conceded, concerned when she seemed to need him for support as she struggled while stepping down from the coach. "I've got you," he whispered, as his other arm wrapped around her waist to steady her until she had both feet beneath her.

He closed the door and gave the driver a nod. "We'll either be ten minutes or two hours," he said before he offered his arm.

Victoria inhaled sharply. "An hour-and-a-half," she called up to the driver. "Mayhap two."

"Yes, my lady," the driver acknowledged.

It was then Tom realized the driver was Thompson, the groom from the stables at Fairmont Park.

No wonder Lady Victoria wasn't concerned about high-waymen or would-be kidnappers. Her driver was armed.

"Shall we?"

Victoria regarded him with an expression that might have been capitulation or resignation. "Lead the way, Mr. Grandby."

Tom winced. "Would you consider calling me Thomas on this night? Or Tom?" He nodded to the footman who opened the door of the restaurant.

"Only this night?" she countered as she stepped into the dimly-lit establishment.

The scents of freshly-baked bread and grilled meats filled the air, and Tom surreptitiously inhaled as he allowed his eyes to adjust to the dark interior. "For the rest of time, if you'd like," he replied as he gave a nod to the host who acknowledged their arrival.

They were quickly led to a table in the corner, a single candle lamp providing the light by which to read the menu board. Before the waiter could step away, Tom said, "A bottle of champagne and some oysters, if you would."

"Right away, sir."

The waiter hurried off as Tom held Victoria's chair. "Are we in a hurry?" she asked as she settled into the chair.

"You told our driver an hour-and-a-half," he reminded her as he took his seat across from her, a grin teasing the corners of his lips.

"I didn't mean to be difficult," she said, her haughtiness from their moment outside of the coach replaced with what seemed like doubt.

"I think your definition of 'difficult' is different from mine," Tom replied lightly. "I merely wanted him to stay put for a time until I knew if tonight's fare suited you." He picked up the menu board and held it to the light from the candle lamp. "What do you like? Or what has been your favorite when you've eaten here in the past?"

"Do they have quail? Or pheasant?"

Tom scanned the list. "Seems they have both on this night. Have you a preference?"

Her gaze darted about the dining room before she turned her attention back to him. "Pheasant will do fine."

Tom furrowed a brow. "Is something wrong, my lady?"

She seemed about to answer and then her eyes once again scanned the room. "Are people staring?"

"I rather imagine the men are," he said with a quirked brow.

Her eyes widened. "Why? Is there something—?"

"My lady, you are a beautiful woman. A man would have to be a monk not to notice you, and I rather imagine there are a few of those who would regret having taken vows if they saw you."

Victoria straightened and stared at him. "Do you say that to flatter me?"

"Of course not. I say it in defense of those of my sex," he replied as a waiter appeared with a bottle of champagne. He poured two glasses and set the bottle on the table before another waiter set a plate of oysters between them.

The half-shells were artfully displayed on a scalloped ceramic dish. Tom had a mind to ask from where the restaurant might have acquired the serving tray. He thought of the pottery restorer at the museum, the one that had captured Gabe Wellingham's eye, and apparently his heart. She might have made dishes such as this when she was employed at Wedgwood's studio in Staffordshire.

Tom offered Victoria a glass of the champagne and she took it, her attention going to the the rising bubbles. "Shall we toast to our business arrangement?" he asked as he touched the rim of his glass to hers.

"Indeed. May it go as planned," she said before taking a sip.

Watching as she sampled the bubbly and then an oyster, Tom grew more curious about the young lady. He was about to ask her why she had decided on steam buses as an investment when there were so many other options, but the waiter returned to take their order.

Tom spoke in low tones, ordering the pheasant and a few side dishes, as well as a white wine.

"I've not had oysters served like this," Victoria commented. She helped herself to another as Tom downed one.

"They offer a variety. If you don't care for them like this, I can have them bring something different."

"Oh, these are fine," she insisted, bringing another to her lips. About to swallow, her eyes suddenly widened, and she quickly brought her napkin to her lips.

"I'll have them taken away—"

"No," she said as she held up a hand. "It's..." She paused to surreptitiously pull something from between her lips. She held the white sphere between her thumb and forefinger, bringing it next to the flame of the candle lamp.

"A pearl," Tom said in awe. A huge grin split his face. "Congratulations."

Victoria blinked, quickly glancing around as if she feared others might have seen what had happened. Then she stared at the jewel for a moment before lifting her gaze to Tom's. "A pearl? What's it doing in my oyster?"

Tom blinked. "It's where they come from," he replied.

"Oysters?" she questioned.

Thinking of the Ancient Greek vase in his office, the one depicting Aphrodite's birth, Tom realized he had never thought of the goddess as a pearl. Perhaps she was the embodiment of the iridescent gemstone. "Indeed. The jewel of the sea," Tom said with a grin.

"But... but how?"

For once glad his father had seen to an education that included the natural sciences, Tom said, "A pearl is the result of a mere grain of sand."

"What?"

"It's an irritant to an oyster. When sand makes its way inside of an oyster shell, the oyster coats it with a substance that smooths and hardens over time," he explained. "So if you were able to break that pearl in half, you would probably find a grain of sand at its center."

"I had no idea," she murmured.

"You'll have to take it to Ludgate Hill. Have a jeweler make it into a pendant or a brooch," Tom said. "If you—or I—find another on this night, you can have them made into earbobs."

Victoria grinned in delight. "Are they really so common?"

Tom sobered. "Probably not," he replied. "Or they would not be worth so much." He motioned to the one she still held. "Do you have a pocket where you might safely stow it away?" he asked. "If not, I can hold it in my waistcoat pocket for you."

Victoria took a moment to consider his offer before she held it out to him. "Could you keep it for me?" she asked. "I did not bring a reticule."

"Of course," he said as he took it from her. He studied it a moment, heartened to see that it was perfectly round and evenly colored. Flanked by a pair of diamonds or rubies or sapphires, it would make a beautiful ring. He stuffed it into his pocket. "Shall we see if we can find a match?"

But Victoria was already helping herself to another oyster, her enthusiasm for the shell fish apparent.

"Tell me, my lady, how could a father in his right mind allow his youngest daughter to move to London to manage one of his estates? Without so much as a brother living nearby?"

Sobering, Victoria stared at Tom, the oyster on her fork forgotten. "Well, it's as you say," she replied before allowing a long sigh.

Tom stared at her, reviewing the words he had just spoken.

In his right mind.

"Oh, I'm so sorry," he whispered, remembering what Lord Michael had said about their father. That he was forgetful. Confused. Apparently Jeremy Statton was no longer in his right mind. Tom's brows furrowed. "What's happened to Somerset?"

Victoria's shoulders slumped. "At first, he was just... forgetful. He would walk into a room and glance around as if he had no idea why he was there," she said in a quiet voice. "Then he didn't know what day of the week it was." Her eyes brightened with unshed tears. "One day, he didn't recognize Mother. Accused her of being a thief."

Tom groaned, already knowing what came next. "I'm so sorry," he murmured.

"It would not have been so bad if Jerry hadn't taken advantage of the situation," she said, referring to her oldest brother and the heir to the Somerset dukedom. "He saw it as an opportunity to pilfer from my father's accounts and squander it. To gamble away a fortune. To behave as a... as a *rake*," she whispered.

"When was this?"

"Last spring. Even before that," she quickly amended.

"Your father did have moments where he was aware enough to see what was happening?" Tom hinted. The kind of dementia she was describing rarely happened all at once.

"A few," she agreed. "At times he admonished Jerry. Threatened to cut him off, but..." She shook her head. "My younger brother, Michael, knew what had to be done. He saw to dividing the three unentailed properties. I took Fairmont Park because I knew I could raise horses there, and Father, in one of his more lucid moments, signed over my inheritance to me," she explained. "My sister and her husband see to an estate with farms in Wiltshire. And Michael manages the townhouse in Mayfair as well as some cottages down in Hove. He lives in our summer house in Brighton."

"And your mother?" Tom thought of Elizabeth Cunningham Statton, the Duchess of Somerset, remembering when her older brother, Michael Cunningham, had once introduced them in Brighton. A vivacious woman, the duchess was a close friend of the Earl of Haddon's sister, Elizabeth Bennett-

Jones, Viscountess Bostwick. Tom secretly hoped the duchess had sought help and solace from the viscountess.

"She sees to my father. There are good days and some... not so good," she murmured. "She'll never leave him, of course. She lives for the moments he is himself."

"He's not that old," Tom murmured.

"True. But the dukedom will surely be lost when Jerry inherits. Lost due to debt."

Tom's eyes suddenly widened. "Which is why you invested your inheritance. To keep it protected from him," he claimed, once again remembering Lord Michael's reason for his visit the week before.

Victoria nodded, her mood brightening at hearing his words. "You have the right of it," she agreed, just as a waiter appeared with their meals. "Oh, my," she murmured, her gaze taking in the array of foods that were set before them. "Were you expecting others to join us?"

Tom allowed a guffaw. "My appetite may have been larger than my stomach," he said as he grinned. "I expect you to help, my lady."

Victoria dropped her gaze on the oysters, intrigued at the thought she might find another pearl. Instead, she concentrated on the pheasant and potatoes as Tom put voice to assurances that her investment would be safe from her brother.

They spoke of steam buses and Brighton, of horse racing and life outside of London, and finally of her friendship with Juliet.

"Kindred spirits, I take it?" Tom suggested.

Victoria grinned. "We are, all because of horses, I suppose. And because..." She stopped, her eyes darting to the side. "Because of our marital status."

Tom dipped his head. "If the Earl of Haddon has his way, Juliet will eventually be the Marchioness of Morganfield."

Blinking, Victoria took a breath and then sighed. "He fell

and hit his head and... now he's... he's back to being the agreeable man he once was."

"So I noticed. I had drinks with him last night at White's."

"Oh?"

"I had just come out of White's after having drinks with a couple of my cousins when Haddon stopped me. He looked so young, and he was dressed so conservatively, I almost didn't recognize him."

Victoria grinned. "I'm not sure what I think of his infatuation with Juliet," she murmured. "Of course I wish her the best match. And Haddon has made it known he will allow her whatever she wants, but—"

"Which means she could still spend Tuesdays at Fairmont Park," Tom suggested.

Brightening at hearing his comment, Victoria said, "True." Her expression grew thoughtful. "He's old enough to be her father."

"I thought that, too," Tom agreed, "But it's not so unusual. If she can keep him in his place, she might find marriage to him preferable to spinsterhood."

Victoria's eyes widened before she hid her mouth behind a hand. "Thomas!" she scolded. "I rather doubt *you* would ever allow a woman to keep you in your place," she countered.

He stared at her a moment, thinking she had been quite successful with him a few times. If by some strange or unusual circumstance the two of them were ever to end up together, he feared they might end up at odds with one another more often than not. "Depends on the woman, I suppose," he said, one brow arching. "I used to think my mother managed my father, but... then something would happen, and all I would notice for a time was him managing her."

"And now?" she prompted.

Tom allowed a shrug. "Now I think they trade off managing one another."

She grinned. "What you're missing is what each of them has

taken to managing," she remarked. "My parents are the same... *were* the same way. Mother sees to what's important to her and father... father saw to all the rest."

"It sounds as if Lord Michael may have taken up your father's mantle."

Nodding, Victoria allowed another sigh. "I really wish he was the heir and not the spare."

"Like your father?"

Victoria's head jerked up. Jeremy Statton—Lord Jeremy—had been the second son, inheriting the dukedom when his father and older brother had both drowned in a boating accident. "Exactly," she whispered. "Do you remember that?"

Tom gave a start. "I'm not *that* old, my lady." In fact, he was fairly sure he hadn't yet been born when Lord Jeremy inherited. He cleared his throat. "Do I look that old?"

Victoria tittered. "No, of course not. I forget sometimes that there are people here in London who read *deBrett's.*"

"Required reading for one in my line of work," Tom replied. "I shouldn't wish to offend an aristocrat looking to invest in a lucrative railway endeavor."

"So... you read about me... about my family? Before you met with me?"

Tom shook his head. "Truth be told, I did not. Lord Michael... he's already an investor," he explained. "Has been for a couple of years. He paid a call at my office last week and asked if I might meet with you. He seemed especially concerned about Lord Jeremiah's plans, and wanted to be sure he was prevented from undermining yours."

"Deliberately so," she said. "I did not wish to do business with you if... what if you and my older brother were known to one another? I could not take the chance he would discover what I was planning with my inheritance."

Tom gazed at her with appreciation. "Well done, my lady," he said as he refilled her wine glass, the bottle emptying as he did so. "Would you like me to order another?"

She shook her head, aware of the distant buzz from having drunk too much champagne and then the wine. "Only if you want more. I fear I will be foxed should I drink another glass."

Attempting to suppress a grin, Tom said, "Have you ever been foxed?"

Victoria rolled her eyes. "Once. With Juliet. And I shall never do it again."

He chuckled and then sobered. "There's still brandy to be had at my office," he reminded her as he passed some bills to the waiter who appeared to clear their dishes.

"Then let's not keep it waiting," she said as she moved to stand.

Tom was immediately by her side, holding out a hand to assist her. He felt her grip on him tighten as she rose and was about to take a step.

"Apologies, but my foot—"

"I've got you," he said as he reached out with his other hand, placing his body so she was shielded from the gazes of other diners.

"You're terribly close," she whispered.

"Just until you're on your feet," he murmured.

When she was standing and he was sure she could walk, Tom gave her more space. The two made their way to the exit, several patrons acknowledging Tom with nods or quiet greetings.

Outside, Thompson was quick to jump down from the box and open the coach doors. "We're going to stop at my office on the way back to Fairmont Park," Tom said as he helped Victoria into the coach. "Number three-hundred, in Oxford Street."

Thompson acknowledged the instructions with a curt nod and closed the door behind Tom.

CHAPTER 22

A GRECIAN GODDESS CASTS
A SPELL

few minutes later, in 300 Oxford Street
Victoria angled her head back as she regarded the Portland stone building before her. The dim light from the gas lamps at the corner and in front of it made it hard to see the shingle. Hanging from a decorative rod that protruded from the white stone, the sign's lettering, *Grandby & Son*, gave no hint as to the nature of the business located there.

"It looks new," she remarked as Tom offered his arm.

"Father had the façade cleaned last year. Made a world of difference," he replied as he led them to the entrance. He extracted a key from his waistcoat pocket and was quick to open the door. He held it for her and then moved to turn on the gas sconces along the corridor. Light bloomed, revealing the green moire silk walls and thick carpeting, and Victoria inhaled softly.

"It looks as if *this* is new," she commented as Tom led her to the end of the corridor. His secretary's desk and counter were clear of papers. Only a green-glass shaded lamp sat on the counter. "Who was your decorator?"

Tom allowed a guffaw. "Father said he wanted green, Mother chose the silk, and a month later, it was done. But that was years ago." He turned up the gas for the next set of lights and entered his office. He stepped aside and waved an arm for Victoria to join him. "This, my lady, is where I spend most of my time when I am not traveling."

He moved to the credenza behind his desk and poured brandy into two crystal glasses as Victoria gingerly stepped into the office, her gaze quickly taking in the masculine surroundings. He offered her a glass, and she took it.

"Do your clients usually meet you here?" she asked when she noticed there were two chairs placed in front of the desk.

"They do," he replied.

Her eyes widened as she moved to one of the artifacts he had on display. "And yet you came to me."

Tom took a swallow of his brandy and allowed a shrug. "It wasn't an inconvenience, my lady," he said. "You served an excellent luncheon. I find doing business over a meal far better than across a desk," he added.

Victoria remembered her appointment at the bank with Mr. Burroughs. Food—or at least drinks—would have made the awkward meeting less so. "Is this yours?" she asked as she indicated a globe of the earth mounted at an angle in a decorative brass stand.

Joining her at the wall of shelves holding his library and a number of artifacts and *objets d' art*, Tom nodded. "It was a gift from a Brazilian client, made entirely of a lapis lazuli agate found in one of his mines."

Victoria leaned over and studied the globe more closely. "How is it possible?" The gleaming surface displayed light and dark blue that matched the shape and size of the continents and the oceans.

"Well, it would be worth far more if the other side had the American continents," he said with a chuckle as he gave the globe a slight shove. The orb turned, revealing that the other side was almost entirely dark blue. "Even so, it's a beautiful piece."

"Very unusual, it is not?"

He considered the query a moment. "Not for Brazil, I suppose. The gemstones they're pulling out of the mines there certainly keep the jewelers in Ludgate Hill in business."

"Gemstones?"

"Amethysts, citrine, emeralds, tourmaline, topaz... they all come from various regions of the country."

Victoria shook her head. "I had no idea." She turned her attention to the next curiosity. "And this?" she asked, her gloved finger nearly touching the mid-section of a marble statue depicting Dionysus. His fully-erect penis was mostly missing.

Tom's face reddened. "The god of wine and..." He paused, about to add 'fertility' when he noted her expression of amusement. "Grape cultivation."

She arched a brow before taking a sip of her brandy. "It seem Dionysus has been dismembered."

Covering a guffaw by clearing his throat, Tom finally gave up trying to hide his humor. "He arrived like that. From an archaeological dig in southern Greece." He held his breath when he saw that her attention had moved to his latest acquisition.

The *pelike* featuring the birth of Aphrodite held a spot dead center in the oak shelving, lit by a nearby gas chandelier. "Now I understand what you meant about pearls," she murmured. "Do you suppose Aphrodite was an irritant to Poseidon?" The forefinger of her free hand had moved to hover next to the god of the sea while her other hand gripped her glass of brandy.

Tom considered the query a moment. "Doubtful. She bore him two daughters. Rhodos and Herophilos," he replied.

Victoria pointed to the figure on the left side of Aphrodite. "Hermés seduced her, and she bore him a son."

"How did you know that's Hermés?" Tom asked in surprise. He'd had to be told the figure's identity by Gabe Wellingham.

"He's holding a herald's wand," she murmured. "He was the herald of the gods," she added as she pointed to the staff he carried. "And he," she pointed to the boy with wings next to Poseidon. "Is Eros."

Tom gazed at her in awe. Even when she turned to ask him about the next curio, he continued to stare at her.

She lifted a finger to her face. "Do I have something...?"

She couldn't complete the sentence. Tom's lips had captured hers in a most unexpected kiss.

For just a moment, Victoria thought to lift a hand to his shoulder and shove him away, but then his lips moved over hers in a most delicious way, his tongue urging her lips to separate. All at once, she tasted brandy and champagne as the scents of sandalwood and musk surrounded her. She nearly dropped her glass, now empty of brandy, barely aware of anything but him and his lips and what they were doing to hers.

She was so lost in the kiss, she would have allowed him to do whatever came next. But the distant sound of a closing door brought her back to her senses. Before she could step away, though, Tom ended the kiss and quickly stepped back. He inhaled sharply and then turned his attention to his office door.

Thompson appeared in the opening a moment later, his eyes darting about. "Pardon, my lady, but..." He paused. Having expected to find his mistress in a compromising position, he was suddenly at a loss for words.

Victoria turned from the Greek vase and regarded her servant with an expression of curiosity. "Yes, Thompson?" she prompted. "Is something wrong?"

"You mentioned midnight."

Blinking, Victoria glanced around the office until her gaze fell on a Baroque clock near the desk. "Oh, my," she murmured. "Is that the correct time, Mr. Grandby?"

Tom pulled his Breguet from his waistcoat pocket. "It is midnight, my lady," he said in surprise. "I've kept you far too long." He angled his head in the driver's direction. "I got carried away showing off my collection of antiquities," he said lightly.

"At my insistence," Victoria said, placing the brandy glass on his desk. "But I must go now. I have an appointment with a horse in the morning."

"Lucky horse," Tom murmured under his breath.

Victoria gave him an arched brow before she headed toward the door. "Are you coming?"

Tom considered how uncomfortable their trip to Fairmont Park might be after what had just happened. "If my shire might be allowed to spend the night in your stables, I think I shall take a hackney back to Arthur's. I can send a man for my phaeton in the morning."

As soon as he finished the comment, he knew he had made a mistake. Victoria's expression shifted from disappointment to suspicion.

Her chin lifted, Victoria said, "Very well. I appreciate the dinner, Mr. Grandby. Good night."

She turned on her heel and paused as if she had to catch herself. But Tom was already there, shoving an arm beneath hers as his other hand came to rest atop her arm. "I've got you," he whispered.

Victoria's first reaction was to pull away, but her foot protested with an ache that nearly had her staggering.

Thompson had already moved to the front door, holding it open for her. He frowned at seeing how she leaned on Tom for support as she made her way down the corridor and out the door.

"Are you all right, my lady?" Thompson asked as he aimed a quelling glance in Tom's direction.

"I'll be fine, Thompson. Just as soon as I'm off my feet."

"Perhaps I will come with you," Tom whispered as he opened the coach door.

"That's really not necessary—"

"Can you climb the stairs to your bedchamber?"

Victoria inhaled sharply. "I'm not above crawling up them if I must," she countered, sounding annoyed.

Tom stepped up and into the coach. "That's it. I'm coming with you," he said as he settled onto the opposite seat from hers, bending his knees as much a possible lest his feet tangle with hers. Thompson shut the door behind him.

In the sudden darkness, Victoria turned her gaze out the window. "I shouldn't wish for you to miss your appointment this evening."

Tom blinked, wondering at the odd comment. "The only appointment I had scheduled this evening was with you, my lady." He paused and then finally sorted what she implied. "Well, there is the one with my bed, but as is the case every night, I shall be the only one in it."

*V*ictoria inhaled sharply, glad for the darkness that hid her combination of relief and surprise. She had been sure Tom's reason for staying in town had to do with a mistress.

Why had she reacted with such sudden anger, though? Their dinner was merely an occasion to celebrate a business transaction. Nothing more.

But that kiss in his office? That hadn't been a celebratory kiss. Or a kiss of friendship. That look on his face—when she had put voice to the identities of the gods on the Greek vase—that look had been filled with wonder. With awe. As if he couldn't believe she would know such a thing, and the fact that she did must have raised his opinion of her.

Or aroused him.

The last thought had heat rushing through her entire body. That knowing a bit of Greek mythology might elicit such a reaction from a man seemed odd to her. But then Tom Grandby was obviously well-educated. A man of the world. She knew that from their meeting at Fairmont Park. Their conversation over dinner reinforced it.

The few minutes in his office? That had felt as if she had been invited into his sanctuary. The place he spent most of his days. The place where his clients usually met with him. Clients who were probably all men.

"Tell me, Thomas. Am I the first woman who has ever been in your office?" she asked, her query breaking a silence that had grown uncomfortable.

"Except for my mother and a few of my sisters, yes," Tom replied. He paused a moment before adding, "My lady, I should apologize for what happened, but I cannot help but think that if I do, I will only anger you more, and I do not want there to be any animosity between us. Just the opposite, in fact."

Victoria inhaled softly, stunned he would so perfectly guess her reaction should he put voice to an apology. But then, he did have lots of sisters. He had probably learned long ago never to antagonize a female lest he suffer their wrath. Or their thorns.

"I am not angry with you, Thomas," she murmured, realizing it wasn't anger that had her reacting when she had thought he would be meeting a mistress.

She had been jealous.

"I am relieved to hear it, my lady."

"Answer me this, please," she said, grateful for the dark and the sound of the coach wheels that kept their conversation private. "Why did you kiss me?"

She heard him inhale to respond, but no words came at first. When they did, they were impossibly close, and she realized he had leaned forward as far as he could to respond. "I could not help myself, my lady. I have never known a woman like you."

Victoria knew if she leaned toward him, their faces would be close enough that they might continue what had been interrupted in his office. But with the sway of the coach, the kiss would be awkward.

Instead, she lifted a gloved hand to his face, felt his hand cover it and bring her palm to his lips. "Because I happened to recognize a few Greek gods on your favorite vase?"

He kissed her gloved hand and said, "Yes," he replied. "How... how did you know them?"

Allowing a chuckle, Victoria said, "My brothers had tutors, and I suffered from boredom. My governess gave up on trying to keep me out of their classroom, and my mother..." She allowed a long sigh. "My mother just gave up."

Tom tightened his hold on her hand. "I rather doubt that last," he whispered.

"She is beside herself that I live without a paid companion and train horses. I won't even tell her of my arrangements with you lest I further distance our relationship."

The coach turned, and a quick glance out the window showed they had pulled into the circle drive of Fairmont Park.

Tom straightened and gave up his hold on her hand. "Do not think ill of her. She only wants what she thinks is best for you," he murmured, just before the door opened. "I'll see you inside."

He made his way down the step to the crushed granite drive and then turned to help her down. Light from a couple of lanterns flashed, and he whirled to discover Jemmy pulling Jake and his phaeton from around the side of the house. One of the lanterns hung from the side of his phaeton. Grateful for the boy's thoughtfulness, he paused to give Jemmy a coin before he escorted Victoria to the door.

When Victoria's walk didn't suggest she was favoring her foot, he lifted her hand and kissed the back of it. "Thank you for joining me this evening. I'll see you again when I have news from our partner."

She nodded, a bit dismayed that Thompson seemed intent on hovering nearby instead of returning to the coach. "I look forward to it. Good night, Mr. Grandby." This time, she curtsied to his bow and disappeared into the house.

As Tom made his way toward his phaeton, he called out a thanks to Thompson. The groom seemed perplexed, but finally gave him a nod. "G'night, sir." A moment later, and Thompson was driving the town coach toward the side of the house.

Tom inhaled and turned to regard Jake. The huge beast was

obviously not pleased at being hitched up for a post-midnight ride. "Come, let's get you home," Tom said as he stepped up into the driver's seat.

It was nearly half-past one when Tom pulled into the mews behind Arthur's.

The very last person he expected to find waiting for him was the Earl of Haddon.

CHAPTER 23

A PLEA FOR HELP

In the mews behind Arthur's, in St. James Street

"The gent's been waitin' for ya for nearly an hour," the stableboy, Bobby, said when Tom pulled up to the mews behind Arthur's. He jerked his thumb over his shoulder. "I sent him into the club. Told 'im I'd come for him when you arrived, but he came back out a few minutes ago."

Tom's first thought was that the Earl of Haddon was foxed and had simply gone the wrong direction after leaving White's. But then he noticed occasional puffs of smoke surrounding Christopher's head as the man leaned against the club's back wall.

The faint scent of a cheroot reached his nostrils as did the hint of snow that might start falling at any moment. Despite the earlier evening's clear skies, winter was once again settling over London.

"Haddon? Is that you?" Tom asked as he turned the reins over to the stableboy. He clambered down from the phaeton and hurried toward the club.

"Grandby. I was about to give up on you," Christopher said as he crushed the stub of the cheroot beneath a boot. He held out his right hand. "I do hope she was a beauty and a good tumble."

Tom shook the hand and indicated they should go inside. "*She* was Lady Victoria, and I assure you, my lord, there was no tumbling involved," he replied. Even if there had been, he wouldn't admit it to the earl.

Christopher looked suitably chagrined. "Apologies. Did you want there to be?" he queried as they made their way to a pair of chairs near the back. At this late hour, only the die-hard card players and a few younger bucks remained in the club.

Deciding it better he not answer the earl's question—Tom feared his words might find their way back to the duke's daughter since Haddon was a friend—he said, "We had dinner. To discuss business." He turned his attention to the waiter who had just joined them. "Ah, Watson. Surprised to see you still about at this late hour."

When the waiter recognized Tom, he displayed a look of surprise. "You're up late as well, sir," Watson commented.

"Indeed," Tom replied. "Two brandies, if you would," he said, glad when the waiter hurried off.

Tom turned his attention back to Christopher. "I do hope you weren't waiting long. What's the matter?"

"I think I made a mistake."

Tom stiffened. "With Miss Comber?"

Christopher nodded. "I paid a call at her home this afternoon."

Tom furrowed a brow. "Had she even returned from Fairmont Park?"

His eyes darting about before he leaned in closer, Christopher said, "I deliberately timed my arrival so that I would be there when she returned."

Wincing, Tom said, "You wished to lie in wait for her? I take it she was not pleased to see you?" he half-guessed.

The earl seemed to think on the query for a time before he said, "She didn't seem *displeased*."

"Ambivalent, then," Tom murmured, his expression suggesting the young lady had every right to be. "Why did you go?"

Christopher allowed a shrug. "I had to see her, of course."

"Won't you be seeing her tomorrow?"

"Well, yes, but... one-and-twenty hours? I could not wait that long," Christopher admitted before he took an unsteady breath. "I don't know what's happened to me, but—"

"You hit your head, and you're not thinking straight."

"I'm thinking far straighter than I have in years," Christopher countered, his voice rising for a moment. He quickly settled back in his chair when the waiter returned with their drinks. "And it's all because of her. I want her. I *need* her, Mr. Grandby."

Tom was about to chide the earl for his obsessiveness, but after his evening with Victoria, he was beginning to understand. He had never wanted a woman more than he wanted Victoria Statton.

Gabe's words from a few nights ago came back to him, and he allowed a chuckle. "I have it on good authority that you must chase her until she catches you."

Christopher stared at him and then blinked. He looked into his brandy glass and then into Tom's. "How many of these have you had?"

"Apparently not enough," Tom murmured. "Look, it's just a suggestion, of course, but perhaps it would behoove you to give the young lady a few days to catch up to your affections. If you're too aggressive with your pursuit of Miss Comber, you will only annoy her," he explained. "Now that she knows you are enamored with her, you may need to allow her to decide that she has feelings for you."

"And if she does not?"

The look of desperation on the earl's face had Tom swallowing. "You must be prepared to give up your pursuit of Miss Comber. Turn you attentions to another young lady who might better suit you and the position she must fill as your wife. As your countess."

An audible moan erupted from Christopher. "Oh, I suppose there is always Vicky," he said on a sigh.

Tom blinked. "Lady Victoria?" he questioned, attempting to tamp down his alarm.

Christopher nodded. "We would vex one another, but I believe she would agree to a betrothal. I would have to make concessions, of course."

"Concessions?"

"Well, she has to have her horses, which is fine, really."

"Go on," Tom prompted, his alarm turning to something palpable.

"I would have to agree to forgo any claim to her dowry, since she's made it quiet clear no man will take it from her," Christopher continued. "I have my own fortune, of course, so that wouldn't be a hardship. As for Fairmont Park, I really don't like the place—it's too far from town and terribly rustic—but she seems determined to live there." He sighed. "So I suppose I would keep the house in Mayfair and then pay calls on my wife when I wish to see her."

Tom stared at the earl, at first wondering if Christopher was teasing him. Did he know that Tom had come under the woman's spell? If not, Tom needed to dissuade the earl from considering the duke's daughter as his future marchioness. "You do realize there are literally hundreds of daughters of the *ton* in need of husbands?" Tom half-asked. "Young ladies who would love to be wed to you. Who would worship the ground you walk on and never vex you. Who you would grow to adore over time. Love, even, as they bestowed you with lots of babies."

Women who are not Lady Victoria.

Christopher drained his brandy. "I want Juliet Comber." He set his glass on the table and lifted his gaze to regard Tom. "No other woman will do."

Tom stared at the earl, somewhat relieved but now grasping at ideas that might change the young lady's opinion of the earl.

For once, he wished Cupid could be summoned.

"Perhaps you just need to be... *you*," Tom suggested. When Christopher grimaced, he added, "Friendly. Obliging. Generous. Humble."

"You mean anything but a pompous arse?"

Tom jerked at hearing the earl's self-assessment. "Exactly."

Christopher inhaled and allowed a nod. "I shall endeavor to do so."

Tom watched the earl take his leave, a sense of calm replacing his momentary foreboding.

He knew one thing for sure.

He was not going to allow Christopher, Earl of Haddon, to marry Lady Victoria.

But did that also mean he had to see to it Juliet Comber agreed to marry Haddon?

He hoped not. He really hoped not.

CHAPTER 24

A RIDE IN HYDE PARK

Thursday, January 10, 1839, three o'clock in the afternoon

Juliet nervously watched the clock on her bedchamber's fireplace mantel. She couldn't decide if she wanted the hands to move forward or backward.

Her lady's maid, Beeker, chattered away as she styled Juliet's hair, well aware of who was scheduled to take her mistress for a ride in the park.

"An earl! And a rich one," Beeker said with excitement.

Juliet managed a wan smile. For some reason, she had decided this ride in the park would be much like the last trips to the park made by those who were hung at the gallows. The thought of such finality had her daring another glance at the clock.

"Are you finished?"

"Oh, if I must be," Beeker replied, inserting one last pin in Juliet's hair.

"You do realize I have to cover most of my hair with a hat?" Juliet asked rhetorically. "It's freezing out there."

"But when he brings you back, it will be time for tea, and you can show it off then."

Juliet blinked. She hadn't thought about what came *after* the ride in the park. "I don't know that I'm to invite him to tea," she said with uncertainty. "I'll ask Mother."

Williamson's footfalls sounded from the corridor, and Juliet allowed a sigh of resignation. "I suppose I must go."

"Well, ye needn't say it like ye was going to the gallows," Beeker scolded.

Juliet gave her maid a quelling glance and met the butler at the door.

"I know," she said before Williamson could announce her caller.

The butler blinked and then nodded. "I put him in the salon."

Halfway down the stairs, Juliet realized Williamson might have put Christopher in the salon, but Christopher certainly hadn't stayed there. He was standing at the bottom of the stairs, looking up with an expression much like that of a puppy dog. The sight had her smiling despite her earlier sense of foreboding. "Good afternoon, Haddon." She managed a curtsy on the last step.

"My Juliet, you are a vision," Christopher said as he leaned over her hand and kissed the back of it. "I regret it's not a warmer day, so that you might be spared the need to cover your gorgeous hair with a hat."

Juliet blinked as color suffused her face. Had he been listening in on her conversation with Beeker? "You are kind to make mention of it, my lord," she said as she regarded him. "My maid has been fussing over it for some time."

Still standing on the last step, her eyes were even with his. For a moment, Juliet could not have looked away if she wanted to, for he seemed determined to mesmerize her with his gaze.

"Will she be joining us on our jaunt this afternoon?"

Juliet had completely forgotten about the need for a chaperone, but before she could respond, her father appeared from the study and said, "I think we can forgo a chaperone just this once."

Awestruck, Christopher turned and nodded to Alistair. "Your trust is noted, Mr. Comber. I shall comport myself with the utmost propriety," he claimed.

When her father turned his gaze on her, Juliet had to quickly hide her own shock and say, "As will I."

"Have her home in an hour, my lord," Alistair said. "Tea will be served at four o'clock."

"I will, sir." With that Christopher offered his arm to Juliet, and she took the last step down.

"Will we be riding on your phaeton?" she asked, concerned about how heavy a redingote to wear.

"I brought the barouche and unfolded the hood. There's a hot brick for your feet and plenty of quilts to keep us warm," he said as they paused in the entry so Juliet could don a coat and hat.

The mention of quilts sent an odd sensation fluttering through Juliet's mid-section. Although they would be riding in an open carriage, his barouche's hood would essentially hide them from anyone except those riding toward them.

Williamson helped her with her coat while Christopher pulled on his black wool greatcoat and then his black riding gloves. With the addition of a low profile top hat, he cut a fine figure.

He once again offered his arm, and Juliet placed her hand on it, managing to grab a muff just before they took their leave.

"You must let me know if it becomes too chilly for you," Christopher said as he held out a hand to help her into the barouche. But Juliet's attention had gone to the perfectly matched pair of horses in front.

"Where did these black shires come from?" she asked in awe. She lifted a gloved hand and slid it up the first horse's head, cooing softly as she did so. She repeated the move with the other horse, angling her head in delight when the first horse nickered. "They're gorgeous."

Christopher joined her, secretly thrilled she seemed so impressed with his team. "At Tattersall's. Your father helped me pick them out," he replied. "I bought them for my phaeton, but they do just as well for the barouche."

"They are stunning with your black barouche," Juliet remarked as she fished for a carrot in her redingote pockets. She pulled one out and broke it in half, immediately endearing herself to the matched pair.

"You needn't curry favor, my sweet. They already adore you," Christopher said with a grin. "As do I."

Juliet inhaled softly upon hearing his endearment and then dipped her head when he made his claim. "You hardly know me," she murmured.

"Nor you me, I suppose. Which is why I wanted to spend the afternoon in your company." He led her to the side of the barouche and assisted as she stepped up and into the equipage. He followed her in, and they settled onto the single seat lined with several quilts. At their feet were bricks, still warm in their wrappings.

The earl quickly unfurled a quilt and settled it over their legs while he reached behind her to wrap the edges of the quilt around Juliet's shoulders. "Are you warm enough?"

Between inhaling the Bay Rum scent of Christopher's cologne and sensing the close proximity of his body, Juliet felt a sudden rush of heat. "I am. And you?"

Christopher unwrapped the reins from the pole. "I have felt nothing but warmth since the moment I laid eyes upon you, my sweet," he replied. He set the horses into motion, merging them into the afternoon traffic in South Audley Street.

Despite the layers of quilts, Juliet was sure her thigh was touching the earl's. Given the quilts and the size of the bench, she feared if she attempted to shift away, Christopher would notice. She was arguing the merits of moving in her head when she realized he had turned his head in her direction.

"I do hope you're not uncomfortable sitting so close to me."

Juliet sighed. "I wouldn't be, except I cannot help but think someone will notice."

"And if they do?"

Her eyes widened with a combination of shock and annoyance. "There will be gossip," she countered.

Christopher seemed about to agree—happily—but then he settled back in the seat and took a deep breath, his broad shoulders brushing against hers. "No one will see us tucked in here," he assured her, moving his free hand to take one of hers. He brought it to his lips and kissed the back of her kid glove. "You needn't concern yourself, my sweet."

Juliet was sure the space under the hood seemed to warm considerably more. For a moment, she imagined what life would be like with such a doting husband. 'My sweet' were words of endearment she hadn't expected to hear from the earl, especially this soon in his pursuit of her.

Struggling for a topic of conversation, she remembered what had them meeting each other in the first place.

Fencing.

"How long have you been fencing?"

Christopher's face lit up with his smile. "Since I was at Eton," he replied. "At one time, I thought I might enjoy bare knuckle fighting, but I have since decided I prefer a more elegant sport. There is a version of fencing that I find very challenging, though—more physical, if you will—and I prefer it to the classical version practiced here in town."

Juliet gave a start. "Bare knuckle fighting? Have you ever punched someone?"

Christopher dared a glance in her direction before he saw to turning the team south onto Park Lane. "Indeed. I punched Lord Wessex once, much like you did me."

"Whatever for?" she asked in surprise.

"He thought I was pursuing Lord Lancaster's daughter with the idea of ruining her. And although I liked—*like* Analise—"

"Lady Wessex?" Juliet countered, just then understanding to whom he was referring. "Soon to be Lady Middleton?" There was talk Lord Wessex' father, the Earl of Middleton, was quite ill and might die at any time.

"The very one. I never *once* did anything to besmirch her reputation, nor did I have a thought of making her my wife," Christopher claimed. "I was fresh out of Oxford. Far too young to be marrying."

Juliet did the math. Lady Wessex had probably been married as long as Juliet had been alive. "She has four children now," she murmured.

He nodded. "I am well aware. You reminded me of her that day in front of Angelo's."

"Oh?" Juliet couldn't imagine how she could be compared to Analise Lancaster Merriweather, Viscountess Wessex. The viscountess always seemed so elegant, so refined.

"She knew what she wanted. *Whom* she wanted, I should say," he explained.

"And who was that?"

"Well, Wessex, of course. I knew the first time I met Miss Analise at a ball that no one else would do for her," he explained. "Wessex was of the same mind about her, so I only had to pretend a *tendre* for her. Tricked her father into believing I might have designs on her. His attentions were entirely on me, which allowed Wessex to court Analise right under her father's nose."

Juliet's eyes widened. "So... you *helped* Lord Wessex? Despite having punched him?" Her opinion of the earl shifted slightly. Perhaps he wasn't as selfish as she might have first thought.

Christopher allowed a shrug. "I thought of it as helping Miss Analise, if you must know," he said, a dimple appearing in one of his cheeks.

Remembering his earlier words, Juliet asked, "What do you

think it is that *I* want?" She wasn't about to ask *who* he thought she wanted. She certainly didn't want to offend him, but she had no intention of claiming to *want* Christopher.

Once again turning his attention to her, the earl said, "To own and run your own stables, of course. Much like Vicky does."

Juliet inhaled sharply. "You say that as if you don't mind."

Christopher allowed a shrug. "Why would I? I want you to be happy. I wouldn't think to deny you anything you wanted." His face suddenly displayed a more serious expression. "Although I would deny you the freedom to take a lover. There will be no other man allowed in your bed. Nor would you be allowed in his."

Incensed by his even suggesting such a situation might occur, Juliet straightened on the bench. "How *dare* you think such a thing," she scolded.

Christopher blinked. "I didn't," he argued, his gaze quickly darting to the side when a sudden movement caught his attention. Another horse had pulled up directly on his left.

"You just did, or you wouldn't have mentioned it," Juliet countered, her ire evident.

Leaning forward, Christopher peered out around the front edge of the unfolded hood of the barouche and allowed a curse. "Hold on, my sweet!"

A phaeton heading in the same direction as they were going nearly collided with them, and Christopher was forced to pull back on the reins. One of the ribbons slipped through his gloved hands, though, and the barouche suddenly swerved as the horse on the left continued his trot while the one on the right attempted to slow down, the pole between them shifting.

Both Christopher and Juliet were jerked sideways in the barouche, which left Juliet leaning heavily against him. She struggled to right herself, but Christopher took hold of the ribbons in one hand and wrapped his arm around her shoulders, forcing her to his side in order to protect her from being slammed against the side of the barouche.

Juliet wriggled in his hold. "Unhand me," she demanded.

Still holding the reins one-handed, Christopher found he needed both hands in order to control the team. "Hang on, my sweet," he said as he gave up his hold on her at the very moment the horses straightened in the yoke and once again resumed their original course.

The barouche swayed to the right to compensate, and Christopher was sent sliding sideways, crushing Juliet against her side of the barouche. "Get off me!" she cried out, attempting to push the earl away, her hands still stuffed in her muff.

Meanwhile, the phaeton pulled by a single horse moved ahead of them by a few feet, and one of the occupants glanced in their direction.

"Why, good afternoon, Haddon!" a woman called out.

Juliet leaned forward, mortified to see Lady Parkerhouse. She quickly leaned back, right onto Christopher's outstretched arm.

"How do, my lady? Fine day for a ride, is it not?" he called out.

"Well, it would be if I could drive this beast," the young widow replied, her words followed by a titter. "Why, I nearly ran you off the road."

"No harm done," Christopher said with a nod as he waved a gloved hand. He directed the horses to take the turn into Hyde Park while the phaeton sped on its way down Park Lane. Once they were through the gate, he pulled the barouche to a halt.

The earl turned to Juliet, his eyes wide. "Are you all right, my sweet? I am so sorry about what happened."

Juliet stared at him. "Sorry?" she repeated in disbelief. "You were *flirting* with her!"

Christopher blinked. "I was most assuredly not," he replied, sitting up straighter on the seat.

"Which has me thinking you've been warming her bed," Juliet went on, ignoring his denial.

"But... I haven't," he insisted. "I wouldn't. I promise," he continued.

"You were thinking about it," Juliet accused. "Here you are, telling me I cannot take a lover, and yet you wouldn't hesitate to tumble Lady Parkerhouse. I suppose you have a *mistress*, as well."

Wide-eyed, Christopher stared at Juliet, his head shaking from side to side. "No. No, I was not. I do not." He took a deep breath. "I would not. Juliet, I have thought of no one but you since the moment I hit you with my foil."

Juliet tore her gaze from his and faced forward. "Perhaps it would be best if you took me home, my lord."

His shoulders slumping, Christopher settled back on the seat and sighed.

When he didn't make a move to put the horses back into motion, Juliet dared a glance at him. His downcast eyes and slack expression had him looking far older than when he had been smiling only a few minutes earlier. Given what she had said—what she had accused him of—she expected he would react with anger. Instead, he looked as if he might shed a tear.

Had she overreacted?

She remembered his denials. Remembered seeing fear in his eyes as he attempted to pull her to his side. Had he thought that the barouche was about to tip over? That the horses might bolt? Given the way the team was hitched to the barouche, it was unlikely either event would occur, but perhaps he didn't know that.

Then she remembered his other words.

I have thought of no one but you since the moment I hit you with my foil.

For just a moment, she felt elation. The Earl of Haddon, heir to the Morganfield marquessate, had put voice to a claim that he only had thoughts of her since the day they had met.

If Lady Parkerhouse hadn't attempted to drive them off the road, Juliet wouldn't have thought to accuse him of infidelity. They weren't even betrothed. But the thought of Christopher in bed with Lady Parkerhouse had her reacting in a manner most unexpected.

Why would she care if the earl had a lover?

She had lashed out at him with words that suggested she was jealous of the widow.

Was she?

Juliet continued to stare at the earl for a moment before she removed a hand from her muff and laid it atop one of his. "I apologize. It's none of my concern if you have a lover."

Christopher regarded her with furrowed brows. "But it is, my sweet. I want desperately for you to be my wife," he said in a quiet voice.

Juliet stared at him a moment before giving her head a shake. "I think it best we discuss matrimony another time," she suggested. "One turn about Rotten Row, and then you shall see me home."

A glimmer of hope appeared in Christopher's eyes, which seemed to warm both her and the barouche. The ride along the entire loop of the King's Road would take at least a half-hour. "Agreed," he said, lifting the reins and setting the shires into motion. "If we cannot speak of our wedding, then may we speak of horses?"

Allowing a brilliant smile, Juliet said, "Yes. I wish to know all about yours."

For the next half-hour, Christopher recited the names and breeds of all the horses in the Morganfield stables, describing how they had been acquired and how they were used. He finished with the story of his racehorse, Thunder, a Thorough-bred he had purchased from Lord Reading.

"The Marquess of Reading?" Juliet questioned in disbelief. Victoria was training two of the marquess' colts for the racing circuit, and it was well known the Reading stables featured a number of racehorses of different ages. "But, why would Lord Reading sell one of his racehorses? I shouldn't think he would want the competition."

Christopher grinned. "He already had two the same age, one for the distance races and one for the short track," he replied. "I don't think he believed I would succeed in running Thunder in either sort of race even though the beast has been bred for both."

"Will you race him?"

"Oh, yes. I intend to enter him in as many races as he can manage when the season starts," Christopher replied.

"Who trains him?"

"One of the grooms in my father's stables at the country estate in Morganfield," he explained. "Thunder is a bit on the large size compared to most racers, but I've been assured he'll be competitive."

Juliet delighted in hearing the earl's descriptions of his horses, and she felt relief that he no longer seemed so glum. When the barouche turned to exit the park, she was surprised when he asked about her horse.

"You do have a horse of your own, do you not?" he added.

"I have two Irish walkers, only because they were twins from my mother's mare, and I would not allow father to sell one of them," she replied.

"How often do you ride them?"

"Every day, unless I'm at Fairmont Park."

Christopher seemed impressed. "Should we wed, you will always be allowed to ride," he assured her. "I hope I shall be welcome to join you." He steered the horses to take the turn that would lead to South Audley Street.

Juliet couldn't imagine how she could deny the earl and said so. "Besides, I rather think you will simply do as you wish."

Furrowing his brows, Christopher shook his head. "It's true I might have done so in the past. But I think it's past time I do what's best."

"And riding with me would be best?" she queried, her voice sounding doubtful.

He nodded. "Spending as much time in your company as I am allowed, surely, whether it be riding or..." Here he stopped and regarded her with a hopeful look. "I need an heir and a spare, and I would like a daughter or two as well."

"So... would we share a bed?"

He gave a start and the barouche nearly passed the Comber townhouse as he stared at Juliet. "Could we?" He quickly pulled the team to a halt at the edge of the pavement.

Juliet considered how to respond. "Wouldn't we have to?"

She wasn't prepared for what came next, but she thought later it was best she wasn't. Christopher wrapped an arm behind her shoulders and turned in her direction, his lips taking hers in a kiss that was at first urgent and then slowly softened until he pulled away on a sigh. "You needn't give me an answer now, for I do not expect one," he whispered. "But promise me you'll think about marrying me?" He reached into his waistcoat pocket and pulled out a gold band festooned with sapphires and diamonds.

Juliet's eyes widened at seeing the gemstones. She was barely aware of him pulling her glove from her hand and slipping it on her finger until he lifted the same hand to his lips and kissed the back of it. "Oh, Christopher, it's beautiful," she murmured.

"But not as beautiful as you," he replied. He leaned over and stole another kiss, this one a quick peck. "I think I shall never tire of kissing you."

The sound of a clearing throat had the earl straightening to discover Alistair Comber peering into the barouche, his arms crossed in front of his chest. "Good afternoon, my lord."

"Likewise, Comber. As you can see, I've brought your daughter back in one piece and in just under an hour's time."

Alistair allowed a nod. "If you've the time, her mother insists you come in for tea. It's freezing out here."

Until that moment, Juliet hadn't given the weather a single

thought. But without the warmth of the quilts and the earl's hold on her, she shivered. "Will you join us?"

Christopher nodded. "I will, thank you." He wrapped the reins around the pole and stepped down. Turning to assist Juliet, he noted how she had already pulled her glove back onto her hand, covering the ring.

"Just until we're out of the cold," she murmured.

Ever so satisfied with himself, Christopher helped her down and escorted her to the house. Once inside, he behaved as the perfect guest during tea.

But even more importantly, he secured permission to take Juliet for a ride on horseback the day after next, probably because Juliet's mother spied the ring and surreptitiously pointed it out to her father.

Christopher really wanted to take her the following day, but he remembered Tom's suggestion that he give the girl some time to consider his suit. And to consider him.

Chase her until she catches you.

CHAPTER 25

A TWO-FOOT TUMBLE

*M*eanwhile, at *Fairmont House*

Having finished her luncheon whilst reading that day's issue of *The Times*, Victoria was on her way up the stairs to change into riding clothes when she heard a commotion at the front door.

The sound of a familiar man's voice caused a slight smile to form on her lips, a sensation of excitement skittering under her skin.

Mr. Grandby had returned.

Clark admitted him into the house, but when the butler made his way toward the stairs to announce her caller, Victoria lifted a hand to wave him off. "Mr. Grandby! To what do I owe this honor?" she asked as she moved to pivot on the stairs and make her way back down.

Tom's long legs carried him to the base of the stairs in just a few strides. "Lady Victoria," he said as he gave a bow. "I bring good news."

Victoria allowed a brilliant smile and started her descent. The slipper of her crushed foot caught on a runner, though, and she pitched forward. Reaching out to grasp the railing, she missed and fell.

. . .

atching as if the events happening before him were occurring in slow motion, Tom knew exactly the moment Victoria lost her footing, knew exactly which way her body would twist as it tumbled forward, knew exactly where to place his arm to catch her shoulders, knew exactly how to brace his body to stop her downward fall so her head wouldn't hit the bottom step.

At the last second, his other arm reached beneath her knees in an attempt to keep her perfect bum from hitting the stairs, and he almost succeeded.

Victoria stared up at him, her mouth forming a perfect 'o.'

Tom stared down at her, his brows furrowed in worry. "Are you all right?"

Blinking, Victoria stiffened in his hold. "I... I think so."

"I've never had a woman fall for me before," he said, a teasing grin replacing his serious expression. He lifted her from the stairs and turned so they were away from the bottom step, his gaze never leaving her eyes.

"Put me down," she ordered, as she began to struggle in his hold.

"Oh, of course," he replied as he bent and lowered his one arm so her feet could touch the ground. As soon as she put weight on them, though, she winced and nearly fell against him.

He wrapped his arms around her waist and pulled her close. "What hurts?"

Victoria's hands moved to his shoulders, gripping them to lift herself in an effort to relieve the pain. "My foot... or my ankle. I think... I think I twisted it."

Lifting her into his arms, Tom started to climb the stairs.

"What do you think you're you doing?"

"Taking you to... to someplace where I can examine your foot."

. . .

*V*ictoria thought to protest, but they were already halfway up the stairs, and he carried her as if she were nothing more than a feather. "Second door to the right," she murmured. For just a moment, she had considered giving him directions to the guest bedchamber, but she didn't want him thinking she slept in a room decorated in every imaginable shade of pink.

*T*om stepped over the threshold and paused a moment to get his bearings. An immediate calm settled over him as the various shades of soft blue surrounded him. "Is this your bedchamber?" he asked as he moved to the bed and set her on it. He had expected to see pink, and lots of it. He had five sisters who tended to favor the feminine color.

"It is," she admitted, her response sounding defensive.

"Unexpected, but rather elegant," he murmured as he knelt before the bed and placed his hand beneath the misshapen foot. He pulled the slipper off.

"Oh, please don't," she said, and then winced when her attempt to free her foot from his hold sent pain radiating up her leg. "What do you think you're doing?"

Tom ignored her protest, one hand cupping the heel of her foot as he used his thumb and forefinger to knead her flat foot through her silk stocking. "Does this hurt?" he asked as he pressed the area near her largest toe.

"No," she replied, her brows furrowing when she leaned over to see what he was doing. Her skirts prevented her from seeing her foot, though, so she pulled them taut over the front of her lower legs. She watched as he moved his thumb, rotating it over the top of her foot and gently pressing as he did so.

Tom marveled at the distance between the bones, realizing several had to have been crushed or broken.

"And now?"

"No," she said on an exhalation of breath.

"What about now?"

"Are you a doctor, Mr. Grandby?"

Tom lifted his eyes to meet hers, wincing when he noted the tears that had collected in their corners. "No, but... my father made us learn about all the bones in a body. Muscles and ligaments. How everything is connected," he said as his ministrations moved farther up her foot towards the ankle. "With five boys in the family, we frequently suffered sprains and scrapes," he added with a grin. "What about now?"

Victoria grimaced and inhaled sharply, and Tom was quick to release the pressure he had put on the inner ankle.

"I apologize. I don't wish to hurt you, but can you wiggle your toes?" He turned his attention back to her foot, noting how broad it was where it had apparently been crushed.

"Why?"

"I wish to ensure there's nothing broken," he replied. "Nothing torn."

"*Everything* was broken," she countered in a huff, but she did as she was told and attempted to wiggle her toes. Only three complied as she winced again and sucked in air between her teeth

"I can see that... or feel it, rather. It's a wonder you can walk at all, let alone move your toes as you just did." He once again moved his hands into place around her foot, gently massaging it. "What happened to crush it?"

No longer able to hold back the tears, Victoria whispered, "My brother's horse stepped on it."

"When did it happen?" he asked as he absently pulled a handkerchief from his waistcoat pocket and offered it to her.

"Seven or eight years ago, I think." She sniffled and took the square of fabric, staring at the embroidered initials in one corner.

TRG.

"Was he being especially cranky that day?"

"How did you know?" she asked in a huff, sniffling as she dabbed her eyes.

Tom didn't, but he remembered some of what he had learned from Alistair that day at White's. "Were the mares in heat?"

Victoria inhaled on a sob. "How did you know?"

Giving his head a quick shake, he said, "The stableboy at the mews behind Arthur's has mentioned how unruly the stallions can be in the early spring. I do hope you weren't otherwise injured?"

*V*ictoria hated thinking of that day. After spending nearly four months with a dance master, she had been scheduled to attend her first ball the following night. The injury had left her bedridden for a month and unable to ride for another month after that. "My pride, of course." At seeing his questioning frown, she added, "I had been around horses my entire life, and never once had one do such a thing."

"You think he did it deliberately?"

Her eyes darting to one side, Victoria sniffled and said, "I remember it felt like it at the time. I was so hurt because I spent more time with that beast than my brother did."

Tom gazed at her a moment, noting her appearance didn't suffer due to her tears. Except for his youngest sister, Emily, his sisters had all been ugly criers. "They say being hurt by the one you love hurts twice as much," he murmured as he returned his attention to her foot. "Does this hurt?" he asked as he pressed on her outer ankle bone.

"No. What are you doing now?" she asked. Although his ministrations weren't unpleasant, she knew he shouldn't be doing them at all. He shouldn't have had her foot in his hands. And he certainly shouldn't have been in her bedchamber.

"Can you feel this?" he asked as he pressed a thumb into the ball of her foot.

"Of course."

"And this?" He moved the thumb to where her arch would have been if it had not collapsed from the pressure of a horse's hoof stepping on it. Her foot jerked.

"Did you just do that because it tickled? Or... or because it hurt?" he asked.

"Neither," she replied.

He pressed the area again and once more, the foot jerked. "You didn't feel that?"

"I have no control over it," she argued.

"When your foot is in a riding boot, do you feel the stirrup through the boot? The pressure of it?"

She straightened and considered the question for a long moment. "Not as much as I do with my other foot, I suppose," she admitted. "Why do you ask?"

Although he was prevented from seeing the details of her foot—the white silk stocking was opaque—Tom tried to imagine how the skin would appear stretched over the broadest part of her foot. Curious, he slid the hand at her ankle up the back of her calf and asked, "Is it possible Sam senses that?"

Victoria inhaled at the sensation she felt as his warm hand smoothed up her leg. "What ever do you mean?"

Tom untied the ribbon at the top of her stocking. "Do you suppose Sam limps because he senses that the pressure from that stirrup is different from the other one?"

Caught between imagining what he was describing and knowing that his fingers had just untied the ribbon at the top of her stocking, Victoria struggled to come up with an answer. "It's possible, I suppose," she murmured. She closed her eyes as she felt the stocking catch at the top of her knee.

"Fascinating," he replied.

"It's hideous," she countered, thinking he referred to her foot.

"It is not hideous," he argued. "It's just a foot."

Shivering as his finger once again touched bare skin, she asked, "Now what are you doing?"

"Removing your stocking," he whispered. He moved his other hand up the inside of her leg to where the top edge of the stocking had just crested her knee and was on its way down.

"Why?"

Using the tips of his fingers, he rolled the stocking all the way down her calf, over the heel of her foot and past the broadest part. The knit silk popped off her foot, and he was quick to once again cradle her foot in one hand. "So I can do this." He leaned down and kissed the top of her foot.

Victoria gasped, torn between jerking her foot from his hold or allowing a moan of pleasure to escape. "Why?"

He kissed the knuckle of her largest toe, ignoring her half-hearted attempt to pull her foot from his grasp. He kissed the next knuckle and then the next before planting another one on the top of her foot again. "So I can test if you have feeling there," he whispered. "Do you?"

The warm wash of his breath cascaded over the taut skin, and Victoria inhaled softly. "Yes," she said on a sigh.

*T*om kissed her ankle and then the space above it. When the hem of her skirt prevented him from going higher, he straightened one of his bent knees and rose to lean over her. One hand moved to her cheek and then he touched his lips to hers.

The kiss was light as a feather, a barely-there wisp of a kiss that left him wanting more when he knew damned well he wasn't entitled to the intimacy.

When he pulled away, he thought to apologize, but Victoria asked, "What was that for?"

"To soften the blow of what I'm about to tell you," he murmured as he straightened and then sat down next to her on the bed.

Her eyes widened. "What?"

"Could you ring for your maid? You've a sprained ankle. I'll wrap it, but you'll have to stay off it for two or three days—mayhap longer."

"Two or three *days*?" she repeated in horror. "But, I have horses to train. Surely I can just—"

"Have your grooms and stableboy exercise the horses for a few days," he said, sounding ever so reasonable. "If you'd like, I can ask Alistair Comber to pay a call every day just to see how they're progressing," he offered.

Her eyes still wide, she asked, "How do you know Mr. Comber?"

Glad he had taken her mind off her injury for just a moment, Tom said, "Why, I just bought a horse from him a few days ago. A shire to pull my phaeton."

Victoria furrowed a dark brow. "What kind?"

"It's a Tilbury," Tom replied. "Nothing fancy. Just black with red spokes. High perch." At seeing her quelling glance, he allowed a teasing grin. "He's a shire. Name's Jake."

"Jake?"

"Jake," he affirmed. "He's nineteen hands and a true gentle giant."

Victoria inhaled. "A giant, indeed," she murmured in awe. "I don't think my father ever had anything that large in his stables in Wiltshire. When can I meet him?"

Tom angled his head to one side. "Well, you could meet him right now, but I rather doubt I could get him up the stairs and through that door. I'm quite sure he'd get stuck."

A pillow hit his chest, nearly knocking him backward onto the bed. "You're incorrigible," she accused. She started to get up, but Tom wrapped an arm around her waist to keep her sitting on the bed.

"Have a care, my lady. You'll not be able to walk let alone go down those stairs."

Victoria's eyes blazed. "Just for that, I should make you *carry* me down them, for tempting me..."

Her words cut off when she was whisked up into his arms. Tom carried her through the door and down the hall to the steps, happy to know he could do so without banging her foot against the door frame.

"Put me down, Mr. Grandby," Victoria ordered, although she did nothing to struggle in his arms. She had wrapped her hands around his neck, as if she feared he might drop her.

"I will when we're in front of Jake, but then you shall lean on me and keep your foot from touching the ground," Tom said as he descended. "Where's your lady's maid?"

"Here, sir," Cummings said from the bottom of the stairs, her mouth open as she watched him carry her mistress.

"Her ladyship has a sprained ankle. I need a long strip of stiff fabric so I can wrap it," he said, authority sounding in his voice. "Clark?"

"Sir," the butler replied, joining the lady's maid.

"Send a footman to Mr. Alistair Comber's residence in South Audley Street with a note requesting Mr. Comber pay a call on her ladyship when it's convenient."

"That's really not necessary," Victoria argued as they passed the servants and headed for the front door. Clark was quick to follow.

"But you don't trust your grooms or the stableboy to see to the training of the horses," he countered when he reached the door. He turned his attention on the butler. "Could you toss a wrap or shawl over her ladyship? She wishes to go out for a moment, and I don't want her to catch a chill."

Victoria huffed. "This from the man who removed my stocking," she whispered. "My foot is bare."

The oddest sensation passed through Tom just then. The half-tease, half-admonishment spoken in a whisper had him wondering what else he could do to have her scolding him again. "As I recall, you did not protest overmuch," he whispered back. He did take a quick glance to ensure the hem of her gown hid her bare foot, though.

*I*ncensed, Victoria was about to respond when Clark returned and unfurled a shawl so it covered most of her.

"We won't be long. My lady would like to take a look at my horse," Tom said as Clark opened the door.

They found the stableboy, Jemmy, lifting a carrot in front of Jake, the horse quickly downing the treat before Jemmy's attention turned to his mistress.

"My lady?" he asked as he stepped back.

"She has a sprained ankle," Tom was quick to say. "Which means you and the grooms will need to see to the horses for a few days."

"Yes, sir," Jemmy replied with a bow.

"What do you think you're doing giving orders to my...?" Victoria's scold stopped when Tom turned her so she could see Jake. She inhaled sharply. "Oh! Oh, he's magnificent!" she murmured.

Tom moved so he stood directly in front of the shire. "Lady Victoria, may I have the honor of introducing you to Jake the Gentle Giant?"

"Oh, you may," she murmured as she reached out with a hand and stroked the horse's muzzle and then slid her fingers up as far as she could reach. Even with his head slightly lowered, she wouldn't have been able to reach the top of Jake's head. "You are a sweetheart," she breathed.

Jake nickered, obviously enjoying the attention. "I wonder where Mr. Comber found him?" she asked.

"He was up for auction, but Mr. Comber allowed me to buy him outright. He feared he would be bought for hard labor otherwise."

"And there was not another horse this large to make a

matched pair," she guessed, her hand continuing to stroke the horse's head. "His coat is perfect," she murmured, noting the shiny black hair and white stockings.

"Matches your hair," Tom remarked. "You would look stunning riding him."

"Is there even a saddle large enough for him?" she countered, knowing she would have to ride him sidesaddle. She couldn't imagine riding such a broad-backed horse astride.

"Good point," Tom replied.

"Your arms must be tiring. You can put me down," she suggested.

"If I do, promise me you will lean on me and not put any weight on your bare foot?"

"I promise," she whispered, well aware Jemmy watched them from where he still stood.

Tom lowered her until her slippered foot touched the crushed granite, and then he helped with wrapping the shawl around her shoulders. Standing upright didn't provide any more height when it came to stroking the horse, though—given Tom's height, she was as tall in his arms as she was standing.

"You won't use him for anything but pulling the phaeton?" she asked.

"I have a town coach with a matched pair," he replied. "No other equipage, though, so just the phaeton."

"He should have some time in a pasture. You're welcome to bring him here if you don't plan to use your phaeton for a few days in the spring," she offered.

"It's very kind of you to offer," Tom murmured.

"Is the mews at Arthur's even large enough to board him?"

"It is. Just barely. He just has a few stablemates. My other two horses, and there are two shires that belong to the club."

"As long as he's not alone," she said before turning in his arms. Given how she had to use him for support, Victoria thought they stood impossibly close.

• • •

"*D*o you suppose that's true for people as well?" Tom asked in a quiet voice. He felt her tremble and wondered if she was cold. At the moment, despite the winter chill in the air, he was blissfully warm, and he knew it was because she stood so close. Because she leaned against him.

"I suppose it could be," she replied. When he didn't respond but merely gazed at her, she asked, "Why do you stare at me so?"

"So I can remember every detail of you. Of your beauty. The scent of you," he whispered, leaning forward so he could breathe in her light perfume. The scent of lilies wafted past at the moment a blush colored her face.

"Why?"

"So I can fall asleep thinking of you," he replied quietly. He kissed her then, the firm pillows of his lips colliding with her softer ones as her hand reached up and wrapped around the back of his neck for support.

Although Tom was aware of the stableboy attempting to avert his eyes, he knew the youngster was peeking. And then, apparently to cover his embarrassment or perhaps to appease Jake's sudden lack of attention, Jemmy took the reins and began leading the shire around the circle drive in front of the estate.

When Tom finally ended the kiss, he dipped his head so his forehead touched hers. "I'd ask for forgiveness, but I surely don't deserve it," he whispered, his breathing labored.

"Forgiveness for what?"

He gave a start and straightened slightly. "You're not... angry?"

"Do I look angry?"

"You're not... offended that I have taken liberties?"

Her eyes narrowed. "You consider bestowing a single kiss taking a liberty?"

Tom furrowed his brows. He was fairly sure there had been more than one kiss just then. In fact, there had been several of them, although one did just sort of merge into the next and the one after that. "Does that mean you would allow me to do it again?"

Victoria visibly swallowed and her gaze moved to his lips. "Perhaps," she hedged, shivering slightly as a wintery breeze kicked up.

"Come. Let's get you inside where it's warm," Tom said as he turned, intending to lift her into his arms. But Victoria had quite forgotten her injured foot and made to take a step toward the door. She inhaled sharply and cried out in pain even as she was being lifted into Tom's arms.

"I've got you," he murmured, hurrying to the door. He only had to knock once and both doors were opened by Clark, the elderly man stepping aside to provide a broad entry.

"This is all my fault," Tom said on a sigh as he aimed for the stairs. "I didn't send word ahead of my intent to pay a call. I interrupted your climb up the stairs. If I hadn't, your poor foot wouldn't have twisted so badly, and your ankle wouldn't be injured."

Victoria angled her head away from his body and nodded. "This *is* all your fault," she accused, although there wasn't any malice in her tone.

"I was so excited about the news I had received, I only wished to share it with you as quickly as possible."

"Which you have yet to tell me," she reminded him.

Tom blinked. "We've received a response from our steam bus inventor. He is amenable to our terms and is anxious to begin a limited service as soon as facilities can be arranged," he explained as he took her back to her bedchamber. He set her on the bed, heartened to discover a length of starched muslin on the counterpane.

"That's most excellent," Victoria said with excitement. "He was not put off of the idea of the project when he learned of my sex?"

Tom's eyes darted sideways. "I don't know that the topic

even came up," he replied as he found the end of the muslin. "Can you pull up your skirts, please?"

Victoria did so without protest, but her thoughts were still on the project. "He doesn't know I am an investor?"

Holding the end of the fabric with one hand as he pulled the remainder around her leg, he said, "Most investors in such a scheme are unknown to one another. It's better that way. Trust me," he said as he concentrated on wrapping her ankle.

"Why?"

He gave a shrug. "Not everyone is invested to the same degree. With the same amount of money," he replied, thinking that he had only ever discussed money like this with his mother and grandmother. For some reason, it was easier to do so with Victoria. "Which means the returns will differ as well."

"How so?" she asked, only vaguely paying attention to what he was doing with her ankle. Despite the pressure he was applying, he wasn't causing as much pain as she expected.

"Your investment is the largest at seventy-five percent," he said. "Your return will be seventy-five percent of the total when the periodic payouts begin."

"When will that be?"

Tom paused his wrapping. "As per the contract, probably as soon as the end of next year."

Her eyes widened in alarm. "Well, that won't do," she murmured.

Sitting back on his haunches, Tom came to the end of the muslin strip and threaded it under her foot and tied it off just above her ankle. He was examining his workmanship when his gaze moved up to her knee.

Although he had seen a woman's knee before—he'd employed a mistress, after all—the sight of Victoria's had him swallowing. He wanted nothing more than to touch it. To run his finger along the top and over the sharp bend and down the front of her perfectly formed shin bone to where the muslin encased her ankle and half her foot.

Without even thinking, he was lowering his head so that he might place a kiss on her knee when the hem of her skirts and petticoat suddenly dropped in front of him. A second later, and one of her fingers was beneath his chin, forcing it up.

"I said that won't do."

Tom blinked as he struggled to remember what she had asked him. "You don't wish to receive dividends?" When she shook her head, he said, "But... they were listed in the contract. A dividend paid out every year."

"I read the contract," she argued. "I don't recall a mention of any payouts."

Trying a different tact, Tom asked, "My lady, will you have enough funds to live on as well as those you need to continue the restoration on the house and grounds?"

"I thought I made it clear that I did," she replied.

Tom wrapped his fingers around the one that was still beneath his chin. He brought it to his lips and kissed the tip of it. "I recall you mentioning—"

"Does everyone have this... this clause in their contract?"

He inhaled and cleared his throat. "Of course. Most investors require some monies to be paid out from their investments on a regular basis. As proof the enterprise is operating as planned. That it's profitable."

"Well, *I* don't require it." The hint of annoyance in her voice could not be missed. "You didn't believe me, did you?"

Tom dipped his head and allowed a long sigh as he moved to join her on the edge of the bed. "It wasn't a matter or believing you or not, my lady. I just wanted to be sure you weren't left destitute should this investment not provide some funds before it ran its course or... or was sold for a profit." He paused and then added, "I know a banker who can see to an account where we could store the funds until you truly need them."

"I have my own banker," she said in a huff.

"Do you trust him?"

Victoria's eyes were still wide as she turned to regard him. "I do. He's the one who…" She paused, not about to admit that James Burroughs had been the one to suggest she invest in steam buses. "Who I've had handle my funds since father turned them over to me."

"Perhaps he can set up a second account on your behalf?" Tom suggested.

"Oh, if he must," she said on a sigh, crossing her arms to further punctuate her annoyance.

Tom looked as if he'd lost his best friend, or at least the opportunity for the two of them to ever become best friends.

Or perhaps something more.

"I will be sure to send future updates by way of a courier or the post," he said before he stood. He reached for her hand and kissed the back of it, heartened she didn't try to pull it away. "Leave the wrap on your ankle for a few days. It will help keep the the swelling down," he said before he gave a leg and then took his leave of her bedchamber.

CHAPTER 26

AN HEIRESS REGRETS

A moment later
Victoria listened as the sound of Tom Grandby's retreating steps faded. She imagined the front door opening and closing. Imagined him climbing onto his phaeton and setting Jake into motion.

If she could have walked without having to hop on one foot, she would have followed him—run if she'd had to—called out to him to wait so that she might apologize.

The terms of the contract had been quite clear. She had asked the important questions, and Juliet had asked the others, but at no point could she remember a section about periodic payouts.

Dividends, he had said.

Damnation, she thought in dismay. She hadn't questioned the dividends, and neither had Juliet.

Her overreaction had bothered him. Offended him. She might never see him again if he was true to his word about sending future updates by way of a courier. Or the post.

Falling back onto the bed, her legs still hanging over the edge, she cursed in a whisper.

Why had she lashed out at him? Her clumsiness wasn't his fault, even if he thought it was.

And he had apologized.

Victoria sighed as she closed her eyes and replayed her time with Tom.

No man had ever touched her as he had. Other than her father, no man had ever carried her in his arms. No man had ever removed her stocking and held her misshapen bare foot. Other than her boot maker, no man had ever even *seen* her foot, and the boot maker had most assuredly never removed her stocking. He had never massaged her foot or kissed the top of it.

Thank the gods.

When the stocking had come off, Tom never once showed disgust. Pity, perhaps, and genuine concern. Curiosity, for why else would he ask so many questions? Spend so much time studying her foot?

Kiss her foot and then kiss her lips?

His kiss hadn't been her first, nor had his kiss in his office, but it had certainly been the longest. The most curious. The most exciting.

There was the briefest of moments when she was sure his tongue was going to invade her mouth, but then didn't. The briefest of moments when she was sure he was aroused. Hoped he was, because she knew she was. Her breasts had swelled, her nipples had tightened at the thought he might cover one with his hand. Knead it through the fabric of her gown with his thumb. He had to know she wore stays and not a corset.

Or mayhap he didn't.

But what did it matter now?

From his parting words, she was sure he would never again pay a call at Fairmont Park.

Tears slid down her temples at the thought she would never see him again. Sobbing quietly, she sniffled and thought about sitting up but then decided she would rather just cry herself to sleep.

She lifted the handkerchief she still gripped in one hand to her temples and then inhaled the scent of *him*.

Sandalwood and spices, musk and wool. Her eyes closed as she held the linen square over her face and inhaled slowly.

Him.

I still have his handkerchief.

Inhaling again, she opened her eyes and blinked at seeing the face that hovered over hers.

"Are you all right, my lady?" Cummings asked in alarm.

Victoria allowed a long sigh. "Other than a sprained ankle, I am fine," she replied as she moved to sit up. Cummings assisted her, a look of worry causing her features to appear older than usual.

"Mr. Grandby explained what I must do for your ankle for the next few days," the lady's maid said.

A flash of anger speared Victoria before she quickly quelled it. Hadn't she just been mourning the loss of Mr. Grandby? Of his friendship and his kisses?

"He's ever so sorry," Cummings continued. "He feels at fault for what happened to you."

"He was not at fault," Victoria said on another sigh. "As much as he insists on claiming responsibility, he has no control over my unfortunate foot."

Cummings regarded her mistress with a furrowed brow. "I really thought he might be the one," she murmured.

Victoria frowned. "The *one*?" she repeated.

Her lady's maid dipped her head. "I was sure you saw him differently than you did your last suitor—"

"Mr. Grandby was not a suitor. He's merely my invest-ment... *advisor*." The angle of Cummings' head had Victoria's eyes widening. "What?"

"I'm not blind, my lady."

"I never said you were."

"He feels affection for you," Cummings stated.

"He does not," Victoria countered, even though a part of

her reveled in the thought that, just maybe, he did. Surely he wouldn't have kissed her if he didn't feel *something* for her.

She winced at thinking what he felt for her now. Tom Grandby probably despised her. Sorted she was a typical female who didn't pay attention to the terms of a contract, and who behaved as a spoiled brat when she didn't get her way.

"Do *you* feel affection for *him*?"

The query had Victoria lifting the handkerchief to her eyes once more. "I rather doubt it," she replied as she glanced around the room. "Could you bring my lap desk and a sheet of parchment? It seems I shall be staying in here for the next few days, so I need to write a note to Juliet."

"Of course, my lady," Cummings replied. She took her leave of the bedchamber, a sense of profound disappointment settling over her.

She was sure her ladyship was in love, but it wasn't as if there was anything she could do about it.

CHAPTER 27

ARRANGEMENTS ARE MADE

n hour later, at the Comber townhouse in South Audley Street

A footman opened the door and stepped aside as Tom held out a calling card and said, "Tom Grandby for Mr. Comber. It won't take long."

"Come in, sir. I'll find out if he's still in residence." The servant set off through the hall as Tom waited near the front door. His attention went to the stairs when he spied Juliet standing at the top of them.

"Miss Comber," he said as he bowed. "So good to see you again." Then he grimaced. "Might I have a moment of your time?" He hated to be the bearer of bad news, but he knew she would want to know about what had happened to Lady Victoria.

Juliet hurried down the stairs. "Of course," she said, as she dipped a curtsy. Tom was quick to take her hand. He was about to brush his lips over the back of it but paused. "This is a lovely ring," he said just before he kissed her knuckles and straightened.

"Thank you. Lord Haddon just gave it to me this afternoon

after our ride in the park. He left here, in fact, just a few minutes ago. He joined us for tea."

"So... he has proposed?" Tom asked, wondering if she had put off the earl or if she had accepted the suit. He wasn't sure what to hope for now that he knew Lady Victoria felt nothing for him. Nothing but contempt.

Juliet nodded. "In a manner of speaking, but I have not yet given him an answer. We're to go riding in a couple of days."

Tom nodded his understanding. "He adores you." He paid witness to her sudden blush and added, "He sought me out for advice, although I'm still not quite sure why he thought I would have your ear."

"That does seem rather odd," Juliet remarked. Then she recalled what he had said when she was still at the top of the stairs. "Was that why you wished to speak with me?"

Giving his head a quick shake, Tom said, "I came with news of Lady Victoria. She has a sprained ankle—"

"Oh! Is she all right? Otherwise, I mean?"

"She is, although... I think she could use a friend, as well as someone to help with the horse training. At least until she can walk again. I thought of your father."

"Was it her bad foot?" Juliet asked in a whisper.

He nodded. "Happened on the stairs. I cannot help but think it was my fault, since I had just paid a call regarding our investment."

"It was not," Juliet said as she shook her head. "The only footwear she owns that allows her to walk properly are her boots —they were custom-made for her feet—but she cannot wear those all the time."

Tom frowned. "Surely there is a... a cobbler or a shoemaker who could make a proper pair of shoes for her situation."

"If there is, she hasn't found him," Juliet replied. "I'll find out from my father if I can pay a call right now. Mayhap spend the night at Fairmont Park. She'll go mad if she's not able to ride."

His attention on something in his mind's eye, Tom furrowed a brow. "Do you suppose you could bring her boots back with you when you return from Fairmont Park?"

Juliet's eyes widened. "Whatever for?"

"I think I may know of someone who could direct me to a custom shoemaker," he murmured. "If he can use the boots as a model of sorts, he may be able to make slippers that do what those boots do for her."

A smile split Juliet's face. "Why, that's brilliant, Mr. Grandby," she gushed. "How long do you suppose he would require the boots? I'm quite certain Vicky won't be bedridden for long, even if she does have a sprained ankle."

Tom knew she spoke the truth. "A few days, at most."

"What's this about a sprained ankle?"

The two turned to find Alistair Comber quickly making his way down the stairs.

"Mr. Comber," Tom said with a nod. "I've just come from Fairmont Park."

He explained what had happened, but before he could ask if the equine expert could see to paying a call and working with the horses, Juliet begged her father to let her stay with Victoria. "At least for tonight."

"I think that would be acceptable," Alistair replied. "You'll need to have your lady's maid pack a valise—"

"Oh, thank you, Father," Juliet said before she kissed him on the cheek, gave a quick curtsy in Tom's direction, and hurried up the stairs.

Alistair blinked before he turned his attention back to Tom. "When you finally decide to take a wife, do be sure to sire more boys than girls," he suggested as he motioned for them to continue their conversation in the front salon.

Tom displayed a wide grin. "You are speaking to a man who has four brothers and five sisters." He took a deep breath and let it out slowly. "Can you afford the time to work with Lady

Victoria's horses? She's desperately worried about their training being interrupted—"

"Despite the fact that she has two grooms and a stableboy who could see to it?" Alistair half-asked, although he did so with a measure of amusement. "Though I'm not quite sure about the one." He indicated a couple of floral chairs near the fireplace and paused at a sideboard to pour brandy into two crystal rummers.

"Thompson?"

"Yes. He's obviously been around horses and knows how to ride—"

"And drive a coach," Tom put in, acknowledging the offer of the glass of brandy with an appreciative nod.

"But—"

"He's not a groom," Tom finished for him. "Truth be told, I think he might have been hired to provide protection for her ladyship."

Alistair arched a brow. "By her father, do you suppose? I don't know Somerset at all. He hasn't been to London in an age."

Tom explained what he knew of the man, and Alistair allowed a sound of despair. "Do you suppose Lady Victoria knows of his situation?"

Dipping his head, Tom said, "She's the one who told me." At Alistair's continued look of concern, he allowed a sigh. "Anyway, I feel awful about what happened to her, and I would be happy to compensate you for any time you spend out there."

"I'm sure she's most concerned about Reading's colts," Alistair replied, absently swirling his brandy. "I'm already on retainer with him—have been for... twenty years, so there's no need to pay me."

"Are you quite sure?"

Alistair nodded. "This time of the year is slower for me at the auction house. It will be good for me to get out on a track instead of spending the day behind a desk studying lineages and filling out paperwork for the Jockey Club." He leaned closer to Tom and added, "Besides, I just found out my daughter has had the opportunity to ride Sam, and I find I'm quite jealous."

Tom laughed out loud and then sobered. "You'll have to discover if he limps for you or not," he said, before enjoying a swallow of brandy.

"I'm looking forward to it," Alistair claimed. "I'll go there tomorrow. Spend the day and then bring Juliet home."

"Very good."

Alistair gave him an assessing glance. "When will you go back there? Juliet mentioned you were there on business with Lady V. Now I have her asking about my investments."

A rock seemed to drop into Tom's stomach as he considered the question. "Probably not for a very long time, if ever," he replied. "After my discussion with Lady Victoria today, I don't believe I'd be welcome."

Alistair furrowed both brows, but he didn't press the issue.

"I appreciate your time," Tom said as he drained his brandy and then stood to go.

"Any time," Alistair replied, his expression still showing concern as Tom took his leave.

Given what Juliet had said when she first returned from Fairmont Park the day before, he had been left with the impression Tom might be courting the duke's daughter. Now he wondered what had happened between Lady Victoria and Tom Grandby that had him believing he wasn't welcome.

Alistair was fairly certain it had nothing to do with the sprained ankle.

CHAPTER 28

COMMISERATING AT WHITE'S

*L*ater that night

"Lord Bostwick. I was hoping to find you here tonight," Tom said as he made his way to where George Bennett-Jones, Viscount Bostwick, was reading *The Times* in a small salon at White's. "Might I have a moment of your time?"

"Grandby! Of course. Have a seat," the older gentleman said as he set the paper aside. "And be warned. My brother-in-law will be here soon. Said something about needing to speak with you."

Tom furrowed a brow and then thought of Juliet Comber and the ring she was wearing. "Ah. Probably wishes to crow about his good fortune with Miss Comber."

George blinked. "Good fortune?" Then his eyes widened. "Oh, by the gods, did he propose?"

Recalling Juliet's comment, Tom carefully replied, "In a manner of speaking. She hasn't yet given him an answer, but he's to take her riding in a couple of days."

"Huh." The viscount shook his head. "I thought for certain she would beg off."

"He adores her. She knows it. And even though he's old

enough to be her father, I think she would make a fine countess."

"Agreed," George said. "Did you know he hit his head?"

Tom grinned. "Indeed. He seems as if he's quite back to the way he used to be, is he not?"

"I thought so, too. Even Elizabeth noticed it," George added, referring to his wife and Christopher's sister. "Said he's youthened at least a decade, as if the pursuit of a wife will do that."

"Speaking of pursuits, might you know who your wife's charity employed for making custom shoes? For those who had foot injuries from the wars?" Although *Finding Work for the Wounded* wasn't as busy these days with finding employment for injured soldiers and sailors, they did so for anyone who had some infirmity that made it difficult for them to be hired.

George considered the question a moment. "There must be five thousand shoemakers in London," he replied. "I suppose almost any of them could do a custom shoe."

"But who does your viscountess use?"

"Well, I know she had one of Hoby's men making men's boots, but for shoes and slippers and such, she used to go to Wood over in Cornhill Street. He closed up shop some time ago, though."

"They sell clocks in that shop now," Tom said, recognizing the location. "Savory. He's a watchmaker."

Nodding, George said, "Damned good ones, too. I bought a clock under glass for my study last year. Keeps perfect time."

"Good to know," Tom replied, not mentioning that the clock in his office had come from the same shop. Since his secretary saw to winding it every day, Tom never knew if it needed adjusting.

"As for shoes these days, Elizabeth has been using a man named Shoemaker over in New Bond Street. She claims he has the best clickers, closers, and makers," he explained, referring to the tradesmen who cut the leather for the upper, lining and sole, stitched the upper and linings together, and finished it with a heel into a final product.

"Shoemaker?" Tom repeated in disbelief. "That's his name?"

Allowing a grin, George said, "That's his name. Fourth-or fifth-generation shoemaker who specializes in making odd-sized shoes and slippers. For club feet and the like. Is that what you're looking for?"

"Indeed," Tom replied, well aware the viscount was surreptitiously glancing at his feet. "They're not for me but for a..." He was about to say *friend*, but instead said, "Client."

"Must be an important client," George remarked.

Remembering what had happened earlier that afternoon, Tom merely nodded and said, "Indeed. I thank you for your time. Good night."

He stood and gave the viscount a slight bow before finding one of the doormen. "Should anyone be looking for me, I think I will be in the back," he murmured.

The doorman furrowed a brow, knowing Tom usually spent his evenings at White's in the front room. "Very good, sir."

Although he had an excuse to drink for celebratory reasons—his latest investment was fully funded and would no doubt be a resounding success—Tom found he only wanted to drink to get drunk tonight.

A half-hour later

A happy Christopher, Earl of Haddon, greeted the footman at White's with an uncharacteristic, "How do?" and practically bounded into the men's club. "Has Mr. Grandby made an appearance this evening?"

The footman blinked. "The tall one?" he responded, holding his arm up well above his head.

Christopher's grin widened, just then remembering there were a number of Mr. Grandbys that might be members of the club. "That would be him."

"Arrived a while ago, my lord. Said if anyone asked for him to send them to the back salon."

Glancing toward the area where Tom Grandby usually held court with fellow investors and bankers, Christopher was surprised to find the chairs empty. "Private meeting?"

Shaking his head, the footman said, "He was alone and looking rather glum when he arrived."

"Glum?"

"Like he had lost his best friend."

Christopher straightened. He knew that look. He'd been displaying it himself just the night before. "I'm on it," he stated before he gave up his hat and coat to another startled footman.

The earl made his way through the club, calling out greetings and patting fellow aristocrats on the shoulder as he went. In his wake, those same aristocrats stared at his retreating figure in various states of wonder, suspicion, confusion and curiosity.

Haddon was not himself. Or, at least, he was back to being himself after several years of bad behavior.

*A*s promised, Christopher found Tom in the very last salon, the very room in which his brother by marriage, George Bennett-Jones, had thoroughly admonished him for his bad behavior. Across from him sat Gabe Wellingham, the oldest son of the Earl of Trenton, and next to him stood James Burroughs, his banker.

Christopher halted and gave a slight bow as the three turned to regard him. "Gentlemen," he said as he straightened.

Gabe quickly came to his feet. "Lord Haddon." He bowed in greeting.

"Haddon! Care to join us?" James asked as he moved to shake Christopher's hand. "I have to warn you. Two of us are over the moon in love and celebrating the acquisition of special licenses and appointments with the priest on the morrow whilst Mr. Grandby here is—"

"Despondent," Gabe interrupted. "He won't tell us why."

Tom rolled his eyes and was about to say something in his own defense, but Christopher's elation bubbled over. "I should have joined you two in Doctors' Commons," he exclaimed before turning his attention to Tom. "I'll admit, I nearly bungled it, but I managed to save the day and gain an appointment with Miss Comber for another ride in the park the day after tomorrow. This time on horseback." His happy countenance sobered, and he furrowed his brows. "You look as if you've lost your best friend."

"He hasn't, since that would be me," James said quickly. "What's this about a ride in the park with Miss Comber?"

"Juliet Comber?" Gabe asked in surprise. When James and Christopher both turned to stare at him, he added, "Her father is one of my father's best friends."

"She is the one," Christopher affirmed. "And I have Mr. Grandby to thank for my success today."

"You're welcome," Tom said on a sigh.

The three directed their gazes onto the only seated man in the salon. "Out with it, Tom. You're starting to scare me," James ordered as he moved to take a chair adjacent to Tom's.

"Indeed," Christopher said as he settled into an upholstered chair. He crossed one ankle over the other knee, his fingers steepling as he rested his elbows on the arms of the chair. "When last I saw you..." He paused to pull out his pocket watch. "At two o'clock this morning, you were in fine form."

"Two?" James repeated, turning to Tom for affirmation.

Tom nodded. "That's because I'd just had one of the best nights of my life."

Christopher allowed a huff. "You said your dinner with Vicky was merely a business meeting!"

"Vicky?" Gabe repeated, his gaze going from Tom to James. When the banker displayed the same look of shock as Gabe and merely shrugged, Gabe turned his attention back to Tom. "Who's Vicky?"

"That would be *Lady Victoria* to everyone but Haddon," Tom replied, directing a frown in the earl's direction.

James' eyes widened. "What about Lady Victoria?" Concern was evident in his voice.

"Are you her banker, too?" Christopher asked.

"I am," James replied. "What's this about?"

Tom inhaled and let the breath out slowly. "A misunderstanding is all," he said on a sigh.

"About an investment?" James asked. He knew the duke's daughter had withdrawn a substantial sum from her account, but he also knew why.

"I cannot discuss my clients," Tom said quietly. "And shouldn't you be at Woodscastle? Making love to my sister?"

James blinked and then stared at his future brother-in-law.

Gabe blinked and then pretended to study his fingernails.

Christopher blinked and then laughed out loud. "If you wish to court Vicky, you only need let me know," he said as he leaned forward.

Tom's expression darkened. "She is a *client*. Nothing more," he murmured, just before he drained a glass of brandy.

"And the misunderstanding?" James queried.

Tom sighed again. "She didn't understand that dividends would be periodically paid out." He directed his attention on his second cousin and narrowed his eyes. "She doesn't want them, but she signed the damned contract. They were described in detail."

James furrowed a brow. "Oh." He gave his head a shake. "That's easily solved, though. We'll just open an account where they can be deposited," he offered. "She can access it whenever she is in need of funds."

"Which is exactly what I told her," Tom replied. "Nicely. But she is not happy about it."

"Was she angry about the prospect of dividends?" Gabe asked in confusion. "I should think she would welcome them."

"She was, and she does not."

James and Christopher exchanged curious glances. "There's more to this than you're telling us," Christopher accused.

"Of course there is. She's sprained her ankle on account of me. I wrapped it and gave her lady's maid instructions on how to care for it."

"And?" Gabe prompted, his eyes wide with the thought that his second cousin might finally have found a potential wife.

"She's a client, dammit, and I really shouldn't have said anything."

"Oh, no," Christopher said as his eyes widened. "Poor Vicky. Can she ride?"

Tom shook his head, bristling at the earl's continued use of the nickname. "She won't be able to walk for at least a few days."

"Well, good," the earl replied.

Three sets of eyes turned on him, all wide with shock. "What are you saying?" James asked.

"Vicky, bedridden, means Vicky cannot ride a horse. She will be desperate for company..." He stopped when he noticed how Tom stiffened. "Desperate for someone to pay a call. *Desperate* for attention," he went on, his eyebrows waggling. "Buy her a bauble, Grandby, and she'll forgive your damned dividends."

The mention of a bauble had Tom giving a start. He reached into his waistcoat pocket, relieved to discover the pearl Victoria had found in her oyster the night before was still there. The need to return it to her would be a valid excuse to pay a call at Fairmont Park. She might even agree to see him.

Perhaps he could do one better.

"Gentlemen, I must take my leave," Tom said as he stood. He pulled his Breguet from his pocket, his brow furrowing. "How late is Rundell, Bridge and Company open?"

The other three inhaled sharply, the sound of their collective gasps resulting in a series of guffaws. "Ten o'clock, although I hear they'll stay open as late as need be should a customer wander in," Gabe replied. When the others gave him looks of surprise, he said, "I have wandered in on occasion. Like last night." At James' arched brow, he added, "I wanted to get a bracelet for Frances. And a silver rattle for David."

"What's this?" Christopher asked, obviously not familiar with the arrangements Gabe had made to marry Frances Longworth and take on her son as his own. "You mean you have a bride and a babe to go with the special license?"

"Well, of course I do," Gabe replied, wondering if others acquired marriage licenses without having prospective wives. "She's a fellow employee at the British Museum. She has a son who I will claim as my own. The wedding is tomorrow."

Christopher smiled, impressed by the young man's enthusiasm. Had he done something similar when he was Gabe's age, he would already have a nursery full of babes and toddlers. Perhaps by now a schoolroom full of children.

He thought of Juliet. He was of an age where he could have daughters old enough to be courted by the likes of him. Men old enough to be their fathers.

The thought had him sobering for the first time all day.

When he noticed Gabe waving a hand in front of his face, Christopher murmured, "You are a better man than I," pretending to ignore Tom's quiet departure from the salon as Gabe and James' attentions were on him. "I do not know that I could adopt another man's babe."

"Would you if Miss Comber had a child?" James countered.

The earl regarded him with an expression of shock and gave the question a moment of thought. "I would," he admitted in a quiet voice. He glanced at Gabe. "Oh, I would," he reiterated. "What does that mean?"

James and Gabe exchanged quick glances. "You're in love," Gabe said.

"Doomed, my lord," James added. He turned back to Gabe. "Shall we take this to the betting book?"

"Indeed," Gabe replied happily. "Perhaps I can win back

what I will lose to you and Tom when I marry Frances on the morrow."

Before Christopher could put voice to a protest, the other two quickly stood and left the salon.

When they returned, Christopher was gone.

The reminder of baubles had him heading for Ludgate Hill. If he intended to formally propose while he and Juliet were on their ride in the park, he required another ring.

CHAPTER 29

COMMISERATING AT
FAIRMONT PARK

eanwhile, at Fairmont Park
Under a cloudy sky that had darkened with the setting sun, Juliet stepped out of the Comber town coach with the assistance of the Fairmont Park footman, Cummings. She glanced up the Portland stone edifice and wondered at why all the windows were dark.

"Her ladyship will be glad to see you," Cummings remarked as he lifted her valise from the town coach. "And right quick, too, seeing as how the courier hasn't been gone that long."

Juliet furrowed a brow. "Courier?" she repeated.

"Her ladyship's letter for you. One of the grooms took it not even an hour ago. It's why you've come, is it not?"

Juliet shook her head, realizing whatever letter Victoria might have sent had probably been delivered to the townhouse after she had already departed. "Uh, yes," she answered, not about to tell the footman it was Mr. Grandby who had shared the news. She hurried to the front door. Then she turned around and called to the driver to hold for a moment. "I need to send you back with some boots. Be sure they're given to Mr. Grandby just as soon as possible."

The Comber groom acknowledged the odd comment with a tip of his top hat.

Clark already had the door open, and Juliet paused only to allow him to help with her redingote. She also handed him her muff while keeping her reticule's handle around her wrist. "Where are her ladyship's boots?"

The butler blinked, but Cummings heard the query and said, "I've been polishing them, my lady."

"Could you go get them and give them to the driver, please?"

Cummings gave a start, but said, "Right away, my lady." He hurried off to the back of the house, and Juliet turned her attention back to the butler.

"Is she in her bedchamber?"

"I believe so, my lady," Clark replied. "I will announce you—"

"No need," Juliet said as she turned and rushed across the hall and up the stairs. She paused a moment outside the closed door of Victoria's room, straightening her skirts as she caught her breath. Then she knocked.

"Really, Cummings, I don't need more tea," she heard from the other side of the door. "I'll drown."

Juliet opened the door and peeked around the edge. "Maybe you don't need tea, but *I* could use a cup," she said with a wink. At the sight of Victoria in bed, surrounded by papers, with her wrapped ankle propped on a pillow, and her eyes red-rimmed from crying, Juliet sobered and added, "You poor thing."

"Juliet!" Victoria's face lit up as she straightened. She winced when her injured ankle protested the move. "However did you get here so quickly?"

Juliet remembered the footman's comment. Apparently the courier—whoever he was—had just departed Fairmont Park in the last hour. "Mr. Grandby told me what happened," she said as she hurried to the bed and lifted a hip to sit on the edge. She leaned over and kissed Victoria on the cheek.

"What? When?" Victoria asked in shock. "He only just left here—"

"And headed straight to my house. He was still speaking with Father when I took my leave," Juliet explained. "Thank the gods the team was still hitched to the town coach. Mother had just returned from paying afternoon calls."

"How fortuitous. Can you stay the night?" Victoria asked hopefully. "Or two or three?"

"Of course. At least until the day after tomorrow afternoon." Juliet suddenly inhaled as her brows drew together. "Haddon has invited me for a ride in the park at three o'clock, so Father and I will have to take our leave around one o'clock, I expect." She regarded her friend for another moment. "Or I could send a note to Haddon and beg off—"

"No! You'll do no such thing," Victoria insisted. "You really must go with him, or he'll be beside himself with worry that he's done something unpardonable." She arched a brow. "He hasn't yet, has he?"

Juliet dimpled, remembering the earl's behavior in the barouche earlier that day. Remembering the kiss. "He's been the perfect gentlemen, actually. Not at all what I expected. He's really rather charming."

"That sounds like the old Christopher," Victoria said with a wan grin. "So, I will simply have to do without you for a time," she added as she lifted the back of her hand to her forehead and feigned despair. Then her gaze fell on Juliet's hand and her eyes widened. "What's this? Has he already proposed?"

Inhaling and about to hide her right hand, Juliet realized it was too late. "He has only threatened to do so. Gave me this as some sort of promise, I suppose," she admitted as she wiggled her ring finger.

"It's gorgeous," Victoria murmured as she lifted Juliet's hand and examined the sapphire and diamond ring. "And familiar."

"I thought so, too. It looks like almost every other betrothal ring I've seen, including my mother's, although I couldn't help but notice she seemed a bit jealous at seeing this one."

"That would be because of the size of the sapphire," Victoria scolded with a grin. "For a promise ring, it makes me wonder what he has in mind for the real thing," she added.

"About that," Juliet said, dipping her head. "Would you tell me truly? Did you expect to become his countess? I cannot help but think his true affections lie with you."

Victoria sighed as she shook her head. "He has teased me for years with the threat of a betrothal, but he knows we would not suit. We would argue more than we would agree on any matter, from what he should wear to a ball to what I should serve at a garden party," she replied. "You, however, have truly captured him in a way I've not seen before."

Juliet blinked. "I have not *captured* him," she argued. "And I have no idea what I'd serve at a garden party."

Victoria tittered. "Mayhap you don't think so, but he's made it quite clear he is yours to command. Given his manner the other day, I cannot help but think he really has returned to his better self."

"Because he hit his head on the pavement?"

Shrugging, Victoria said, "Or because he's finally found the woman he wishes to make his countess."

Juliet's face bloomed with color. "Because I punched him," she murmured.

"As for the garden party, you can always ask him what he would like served."

Rolling her eyes, Juliet scoffed, and then she glanced at the papers strewn over the bed's counterpane and frowned. "Is that the contract for your investment?"

"It is," Victoria acknowledged with a sigh. "After my unfortunate conversation with Mr. Grandby, I realized I needed to learn more about dividends."

"Oh. The periodic payouts?"

Victoria's eyes widened. "You remember reading about them?"

"Well, of course. I thought it rather a clever concept."

"How so?" Victoria asked, her dark brows furrowing.

"Well, think about it. You give all this money toward an investment that is due to last a decade or more. The only way you'll know if it's truly succeeding is if you're getting something out of it on an ongoing basis."

"The dividend, you mean?"

"Yes. If you don't get anything, then you would have to wonder if the investment is sound. If those who are running the scheme are doing their jobs. In which case, at the end of the contract, can you hope to get back what you've paid into it if you sell your shares? Or will the whole investment be a total loss?"

Victoria listened to the argument, understanding now why Juliet hadn't questioned that portion of the contract when Tom Grandby was there for the signing. "I comprehend it now. But... earlier today... I fear I did not, and poor Mr. Grandby... he suffered my wrath. My terrible wrath."

Juliet remembered how concerned Tom Grandby had been when he had spoken with her and her father. At no point had he seemed upset with Victoria.

Just the opposite.

More as if he was upset with himself, convinced he was the cause of Victoria's sprained ankle.

"He can't have suffered overmuch," Juliet murmured. "He's gone to the trouble of arranging for Father to take over the horse training—at least for Lord Reading's horses—and for..." She stopped, deciding not to inform Victoria of his plan to have a shoemaker make her some custom shoes.

What if he intended for that to be a surprise?

Victoria blinked several times. "So... your father is coming here? Tomorrow morning?" she asked in surprise.

"Yes. That's part of why Mr. Grandby paid a call. Asked if

my father could see to training the horses while you're unable to." At Victoria's look of disbelief, she admitted, "I may have eavesdropped a bit whilst I waited for the coach to pull around front. I even heard him offer to pay my father for his time."

Victoria stared at her, a myriad of emotions playing over her face. "Well, that was entirely unnecessary," she replied.

"Exactly. Father said he's already paid by way of a retainer by Lord Reading, so he didn't accept the offer."

Blinking back tears, Victoria struggled to breathe.

"Vicky, what's wrong?"

"I said things to him... he looked so hurt, and when he left..." She sniffled as she lifted a sodden hanky to her face. "He said he would send future word by... by way of the... the *post*."

Juliet stared at Victoria. "I rather doubt he meant that," she hedged.

Victoria's sobs increased in intensity.

"He obviously cares about you," Juliet insisted.

"If only that were true," Victoria whispered between sobs.

"You're in love with him." The statement wasn't a question.

Hiccuping, Victoria shook her head. "I cannot be."

"Oh, this is *wonderful*," Juliet breathed as her eyes widened in delight. "We'll be betrothed at the same time. Perhaps we could have a double wedding!"

The keening sound merely increased in intensity at the same moment Victoria's lady's maid appeared at the door with a tea tray. "Tea will make everything better, my lady," Cummings said as she set the tray on the nightstand.

"I'll serve," Juliet offered.

"That will be all tonight, Cummings," Victoria said between quiet sobs.

"But... but what about dinner?"

Victoria and Juliet exchanged quick glances. "Bring trays, and we'll eat here," Juliet ordered. "But not until seven o'clock. And there will no changing clothes for dinner on this night."

Her eyes wide at hearing the decisiveness in Juliet's voice, Cummings said, "Yes, my lady," and hurried out of the room.

Victoria stared at her friend. "What's gotten into you?" she asked in alarm.

"Whatever do you mean?"

"Why, for a moment there, you sounded like... like me."

Juliet dimpled as she prepared the cups for tea. "I'm practicing. I might be a countess before the end of the year," she said with a grin

Victoria allowed a wan smile and then said, "Poor Christopher. He has no idea, does he?" she asked rhetorically.

Pouring a cup of tea for Victoria, Juliet considered the teasing comment before displaying a brilliant grin. "Actually, I think he does," she murmured. She took a sip of tea. "And I think he likes it."

Victoria sniffled and directed her attention to the bottom of her cup of tea. Although she had no idea how to read tea leaves, she hoped Juliet's words were true.

Every one of them.

CHAPTER 30

JEWELRY AND A PEARL

Half past nine o'clock, 32 Ludgate Hill, London
The light snowfall had ceased by the time Tom's town coach was parked in front of Rundell, Bridge & Co. Given that the displays in the front windows that flanked the doors were lit from behind, Tom knew the jewelry and gift shop was still open.

He bounded down from the coach and hurried inside, happy for the warmth and relieved to discover two jewelers behind the back counter. He knew they were related to one another, and they looked it. "Apologies for my late arrival," Tom said as he approached the men. "I wondered if you might have a gold ring on which a pearl could be mounted?" He pulled the pearl from his waistcoat pocket and set it on a black velvet-covered box on the counter.

The older of the two jewelers bent down and examined the orb. "How have you come by this?" he asked, lifting the pearl and moving it closer to a lamp.

"I was holding it for my dinner guest. She found it in an oyster."

"Rules, by chance?"

"Indeed. How did you know?"

The man allowed a shrug. "Oysters are their speciality," he murmured. "Good size, good color, excellent shape."

The other man disappeared for a moment. "Nephew's been working on some designs. Perhaps he has a setting it will work with."

"How soon could you have it mounted?" Tom asked. He knew it wouldn't do any good to get the ring that night—he wasn't about to pay a call at Fairmont Park this late and risk getting shot by Thompson—but he could deliver it on the morrow.

The nephew reappeared with a tray of rings, none of which included any gemstones. "Are you just wanting the pearl, sir? Or were you thinking to add some sapphires or—?"

"Emeralds," Tom interrupted, remembering the color of Victoria's eyes.

"Ah, I have this ring, which will accommodate your pearl and two smaller emeralds," the younger man murmured as he lifted a gold ring from the tray. The setting was simple. No filigree decorated the gold posts that would hold the stones, nor was there any flourish on the band. Tom tried to imagine what the ring might look like when completed. Depending on their cut, the emeralds might indeed look like green eyes.

"Or there's another here that can feature a ring of small emeralds all around the pearl." The older jeweler pulled that setting from the tray and held it up with the pearl. Tiny leaves extended from the gold band, suggesting the setting would look like a flower once completed.

"Do you have the emeralds?" Tom asked.

"Of course, sir," the older one replied, his tone suggesting he had taken offense.

"I meant to ask, do you have emeralds ready to use in either of these settings?"

The younger man disappeared behind the curtain again and

emerged with a flat drawer lined in velvet and dotted with dozens of emeralds. The green gems were of various shapes and sizes.

"Oh," Tom said as he gazed at the selection. His attention went back to the two settings. He tried to imagine Victoria wearing them. Tried to imagine which would suit her better. Although he favored the idea of a flower, he also thought the three-gem ring would suit her tastes better.

"This one," he said, pointing to the first option. "With the two best of those," he added as he pointed to the drawer of emeralds. "I can pay cash on the morrow if you can have it done by five o'clock." He had thought to ask for it to be ready sooner, but he didn't want to pay a call at Fairmont Park whilst the Combers were there.

The two jewelers exchanged quick glances. "I'll have it ready by four," the nephew promised. "What name shall go on the receipt?"

"Grandby. Tom Grandby."

Eyebrows raised, the older said, "Is the Earl of Torrington a relative, perhaps?"

"Cousin, yes. Why do you ask?"

The two jewelers both looked crestfallen. "My uncle fears we have fallen out of his favor."

"Given he was not in to buy his countess a Christmas gift last month," the older one added.

Tom shook his head. "I can explain. Torrington's son and daughter both married last month, and the earl and his wife accompanied them on their wedding trips to the Kingdom of the Two Sicilies. I'm quite sure the earl will return here before they head north to Hexham."

"Ah, that is a relief to hear," the nephew said.

The sound of the door opening had the two jewelers glancing toward it to discover Christopher, Earl of Haddon, making his way to the counter.

"Haddon?" Tom said with some surprise. "Don't tell me you're already buying baubles for Miss Comber?" he asked, well aware the two jewelers knew the identity of the newest arrival to their store.

"I would deny it, but I would be lying," Christopher said. "I am here to procure a betrothal ring."

"Congratulations, my lord," the uncle said as he dipped his head.

"If not a betrothal ring, then what was Juliet wearing on her finger this afternoon?" Tom asked, his voice almost a whisper.

Christopher allowed a shrug. "That old thing? Just one of the rings my father's mother's aunts insisted I have on hand should I ever find someone to marry."

"Old thing?" Tom repeated. "It looked as if it's worth a fortune." And it looked suspiciously like the ring James Burroughs had bestowed on Emily's finger when he asked for her hand in marriage.

"Probably is. But I wish to give my prospective bride something new," he argued. "I plan to propose whilst we're on our ride in the park. There's a hedgerow near the Serpentine with a bench. Very secluded."

"Sounds cold," Tom murmured.

Doubt appeared on the earl's face for a moment, but he gave his head a shake. "Miss Comber's genuine warmth will make it seem positively tropical," he claimed. "Then we shall return to the Comber residence and make our announcement over tea."

"Sounds perfect," Tom replied, deciding not to put forth any more thoughts on the subject. If Juliet Comber agreed to marry the earl, then the earl wouldn't turn to Lady Victoria as a last-ditch means of gaining a countess.

But Christopher had turned his attention on the drawer of emeralds and the gold rings the jewelers still held. "Gold and emeralds?" he asked as he turned his attention on Tom.

"And a pearl," Tom said as he nodded to the white sphere resting on a velvet-clad box.

"A betrothal ring, perhaps?" Christopher asked, his brows furrowing.

Tom shook his head. "No, just a gift is all."

Christopher regarded him a moment before he said, "She might say 'no' the first time you ask, but my money is on a 'yes' the second time."

"And who might you be putting that money on?" Tom asked.

"Why, you and Vicky, of course," Christopher replied before he leaned in closer and whispered. "Her first betrothal was a disaster. Hence the reason you will need to be firm with her on this one."

First betrothal? Tom felt the rock drop in his stomach as he stared at the earl. "Anyone I know?"

The earl shook his head. "Doubtful. Arranged by her older brother to help one of his friends. A rake, as it happens." The comment was accompanied by an arched brow, as if to drive home his bad news.

Tom nodded, immediately understanding why it was Victoria seemed so distrustful of him. Of men in general. The rake had no doubt ruined her before she'd had a chance to beg off, which explained why her father had settled her inheritance on her rather than holding out for another betrothal.

Christopher turned his attention back on the jewelers, his brilliant smile once again on display. "Gentlemen. I would like to see all your sapphire and diamond rings," he announced.

"You might ask about a horseshoe motif," Tom suggested before he gave a parting nod to the jewelers. "Remember, Haddon, it's the little things that matter." He gave a slight bow to Christopher before he headed towards the door.

"Oh, that's brilliant," the earl replied, his eyes widening in delight. "You have my gratitude, Mr Grandby. And my assistance should you require it."

Tom took his leave, grinning when he overheard Christopher asking about horse-related baubles.

He soon sobered as he considered Christopher's news about Victoria. A few moments alone in his town coach had him deciding the news changed nothing.

He still wanted Victoria.

Now he just had to make sure she wanted him.

CHAPTER 31

SHOES MAY BE A
GENTLEMAN'S BEST FRIEND

L *ater, at Arthur's in St. James Street*

Bone tired and weary from his day, Tom was about to head up to his rooms at Arthur's when Watson, the waiter, caught him.

"Mr. Grandby. You had a delivery this evening."

Tom paused on the stairs, resisting the urge to snap at the servant. "Delivery?" he repeated, suddenly intrigued.

"Some boots, sir. Rather odd, if you ask me. Pardon me for saying, sir, but there ain't no way they would fit you."

Understanding immediately whose boots they were, Tom quickly descended the stairs. How Juliet had managed to procure them and have them delivered so fast, he had no idea. He had just asked if she could take possession of them this afternoon!

His opinion of the young lady went up a few notches. She was obviously resourceful. And a good friend to Lady Victoria.

Perhaps she was exactly what Christopher, Earl of Haddon, needed in the way of a countess.

"Where did you put them?"

"Right back here, sir." Watson hurried off to the tap room and returned with the pair of polished black riding boots.

"

Although they appeared identical from the side, the box of one was considerably larger in the front.

"Thank you," Tom said as he took them. "Seems I'll be paying a call in New Bond Street on the morrow."

Watson bid him good night and watched as the tall man climbed the stairs. Although he was curious, he resisted the urge to ask why the one boot was so different from the other.

The following morning, Shoemaker's in New Bond Street, London

The odors of leather and shoe polish assaulted his nostrils as Tom entered the shoe shop recommended by Viscount Bostwick. Lady Victoria's riding boots hung from one leather glove-clad hand.

A pair of older ladies were ensconced on a velvet settee, a young man kneeling before one of them with a selection of slippers at hand. He was attempting to push a blue satin shoe onto a foot that was entirely too long for it, the woman insisting it would fit if he just pushed harder.

Suppressing the urge to grin, Tom captured the attention of a man whose hands were stained with polish.

"How do?" the older man said as he approached Tom.

"Good morning, sir. I wondered if I might speak with Mr. Shoemaker about having some custom slippers and shoes made?"

"You're speaking to one. There are three of us who answer to that moniker," the man replied with a grin. His attention went to the boots. "Using those as a guide, perhaps?" He winced at seeing the wider boot.

"Yes," Tom hedged. "But only if these aren't destroyed in the process." He gave up his hold on the boots as the man reached for them.

"Let's see what we have here," Mr. Shoemaker murmured as he set them on a nearby counter. "Looks like Hoby's work."

"It is," Tom affirmed. "They fit her ladyship perfectly, but she has no other shoes for day or evening that allow her to walk as well as she can in these."

The shoemaker was studying the sole of the larger boot. "Crushed foot?"

"Indeed."

"Well, the other one seems a common size and shape. But I'll have to take this one apart to make the pattern."

Tom sucked in a breath. "Is that really necessary?"

"I'll stitch it back together again, of course," the shoemaker replied, apparently offended. "They'll be good as new. And it looks as if the smallest toe is a bit cramped. I can account for that when I make the pattern," he commented absently. "I suppose she needs these back right away, though?"

Shaking his head, Tom said, "She has a sprained ankle, so she won't be needing them for a few days."

"Oh. I was about to ask if her ladyship would be in to choose what she'd like."

"She won't. But if you have some samples, I can select a few to have made."

The shoemaker gave him a dubious glance. "That's what all the husbands say. And then the wives are in here a week later choosing something different."

Color suffused Tom's face. He was about to deny being a husband, but thought better of it. "I have five sisters," he said instead.

"You have my sympathy," Mr. Shoemaker said with a grin. He led Tom to a display of slippers. Some were simple, some ornate, and some were intended for dancing. On a separate shelf were several styles of half-boots. "Well, then. What does her ladyship need?"

Tom glanced over the array of choices and then noted the man didn't have a paper and pencil in hand. "You may wish to write this down," he warned.

The shoemaker blinked. "I thought you said a few."

Clearing his throat, Tom said, "That's before I saw what you can do." When Mr. Shoemaker shrugged, he added, "I'll pay cash now, of course."

Rushing off to the counter, Mr. Shoemaker returned with an order form in hand. "Very well. What can I make for her ladyship?"

Recalling the gowns he had seen Lady Victoria wearing, he pointed to one sample and said, "This one in sapphire blue and a second pair in garnet." He pointed to the next pair. "Black. And let's do this in white, too." He moved to the next one and gave a shake of his head, deciding it was far too ornate for Victoria's tastes. The next pair were simple satin slippers, void of decoration other than a band of satin around the top edge. "These in all the fashionable colors."

"All"? Mr. Shoemaker repeated in shock.

Tom's confidence faltered. "Is... is that a lot?"

The older man's jaw dropped. "I must have twenty bolts of satin in the back. Had a modiste select them to match what she was making for this Season's gowns," Mr. Shoemaker replied. "Then she sends her clients to me to make the matching shoes."

"Then one pair of each," Tom said with a shrug. He turned to the other shelf. "These half-boots. Brown and black." He glanced around the shop. "Can you do another pair of riding boots to match hers? She wears them every day, and I expect that pair will be worn out before next year."

Mr. Shoemaker glanced over at the ones made by Hoby. "I can. And I'll do a better job on the stitching, too. Sixty-four to an inch," he bragged, referring to the number of stitches for every inch of leather.

"Then do two pairs of those."

After writing furiously, the shoemaker lifted his gaze and regarded Tom with a look of awe. "That's eight-and-twenty pairs!"

Tom shrugged. "Are you aware of any women of quality

who have less than that?" he asked, an eyebrow arching with his tease.

Mr. Shoemaker allowed a slight grin. "None, sir."

"How much do I owe you?"

The older man took the form to the counter, adding the amounts and double-checking his total. He hadn't even completed the arithmetic when Tom dropped two twenty-pound notes on the counter.

"Will you have any of them ready by tomorrow afternoon?" He remembered Haddon's comment about taking Juliet for a ride in the park. That would mean Victoria would be alone sometime before three o'clock. The jeweler had promised the pearl ring would be completed later on this day.

"I can have the Hobys ready, and mayhap a few of the slippers finished by noon," Mr. Shoemaker replied. "All the rest in a week. Will that do?"

Tom nodded. "I'll be back at noon tomorrow."

"But... what about your change, Mr...?"

"Grandby. Tom Grandby. You can leave it on my account."

"Yes, sir," Mr. Shoemaker replied, recognizing the name. His eyes were wide as he watched the tall customer take his leave.

An hour later, Mr. Shoemaker had Victoria's wider boot disassembled to make the patterns for the other shoes. By closing time, his crew had completed some of the slippers and the black pair of half-boots. And by noon the following day, the Hobys were restitched and ready.

CHAPTER 32

A RIDE ON HORSEBACK

The following day, Comber townhouse in South Audley Street

Julia Comber regarded her husband with a smirk as she watched him pace across his study for at least the tenth time.

"Are you worried because she's about to become a countess? Or because it's Haddon?"

Alistair stopped in his tracks, the well-worn carpet beneath his feet showing that he had made this trek many times before this day. "Both," he replied. "I cannot believe you are so calm about this. Our daughter might hear a marriage proposal on this day, and after spending time with her in the town coach earlier this afternoon, I cannot help but think... she's looking *forward* to it."

He had spent that morning as well as the morning before at Fairmont Park exercising the horses with the help of a groom and the stableboy. Besides being impressed by the stables and the horseflesh, he was left wondering how and where he might construct a track of his own.

Unable to suppress her grin, Julia allowed a sigh. "I know. Isn't it wonderful? Did you see the ring he already gave her?"

Her husband blinked. "What? No!"

Julia rolled her eyes and continued to grin. "Of course, you didn't. Her glove would have covered it," she said as she resisted the urge to say something about men ignoring the little things in life. "Well, it has a sapphire and diamonds, but apparently it's not the real betrothal ring," she added with some excitement. "I had tea with Haddon's mother this afternoon. Adeline is over the moon about the possibility of her son marrying our daughter. As is his sister, Elizabeth. She was there as well. Said that Juliet's punch to her brother's gut is the best thing that could have happened to him."

Alistair blinked. "Punch to the gut?" he repeated in disbelief. "She *said* that?"

Her titter turning into a giggle, Julia nodded. "Elizabeth said her brother is back to behaving as he used to a few years ago, all because of our daughter."

"But what if that doesn't last? What if he... what if he turns back into a pompous ass?"

The sound of a clearing throat came from the doorway, and Alistair gave a start. Williamson stood there, his eyes darting toward the entry. "Lord Haddon has asked for Miss Comber," he said in a quiet voice. His eyes darted sideways again, this time with a bit more urgency.

Julia was about to ask if he had something in his eyes when she realized the earl was probably standing nearby. Possibly right next to the butler. "Oh, do fetch Juliet, and I'll see to his lordship," she said as she directed a knowing look toward her husband and then arched a brow. "I'll inform him of his options," she added, *sotto voce*.

"Options?" Alistair repeated in alarm. "Julia..." But his wife had already taken her leave, her bell-shaped skirts disappearing beyond the door.

Alistair wondered if he should join her. Wondered if he should rescue the earl from his wife.

Whatever could she mean by her comment?

She would no doubt inform Haddon of the options in the

front salon. Alistair hurried to the study's door and peeked around the jamb to see Julia and Haddon making their way into the makeshift parlor. If he stayed close to the wall, he could sneak toward the salon and eavesdrop on their conversation. And he was about to do so when the salon door shut with a resounding *thud*.

Oh, dear, he thought, realizing his wife was doing what he should be doing. Laying down the law. Threatening bodily harm. Describing the size and shape of what the earl could expect to become should he do anything untoward. The size of his plot in the Morganfield cemetery should he be guilty of any crime against Juliet.

But Alistair held his ground, deciding his wife was probably doing all of the above in a more socially acceptable manner than he would.

So he was entirely unprepared for how the two emerged from the salon—the earl all smiles and Julia looking as if she was the one who was to marry him.

Alistair stepped out of the study and regarded the two with a quizzical expression. "Good afternoon, Haddon," he said as he gave a slight bow.

"Mr. Comber. I was just telling Lady Comber of my intentions for this day. For this ride in the park." He reached into a waistcoat pocket and pulled out the ring he had acquired at Rundell, Bridge & Co. just the day before. One of the jewelers claimed to have worked through the night to fashion the unusual setting. "I'll give her another ring on our wedding day, of course, but I thought this might do for a betrothal ring. What do you think?"

Julia gasped as he held the ring between his thumb and fore-finger. "Is that a... a *horseshoe*?" she asked in awe, her head bending to study the series of sapphires in the shape of a U atop a gold band.

"Indeed. The wedding band is still being fashioned, as is the complete parure."

"Parure?" Julia repeated in awe.

"Of course. There will be a bracelet and earbobs, a pendant much like this, but far larger on a gold chain," he explained. "A tiara with a series of horseshoes—one she can wear to balls and such—and a variation of the Morganfield coronet to include horses in brown diamonds."

"Coronet?" Alistair repeated.

Christopher nodded. "She will eventually be a marchioness, so although there is already a coronet, I think I shall allow my mother to keep that until her death and have Juliet wear the new coronet of the Morganfield marquessate." He was about to say more, but his gaze had lifted, and his jaw dropped.

Alistair followed his line of sight to discover Juliet standing on the last landing of the stairs. Dressed in a sapphire velvet riding habit, with her hair piled high atop her head and a small hat mounted at a jaunty angle, Juliet Comber looked every inch a countess. "Oh, God," he whispered.

"Oh, my goddess," Christopher corrected him.

"You promise to do as I said?" Julia asked, her attention turning to the earl.

"Oh, I do, my lady," he replied, his gaze following Juliet's descent down the stairs. At the last moment, he hurried forward and lifted her hand to his lips. "You are a vision, my sweet," he murmured.

Juliet's eyes swept down and then back up to regard the earl with amusement. "Whatever did you have to promise my mother?" she asked in a whisper.

Christopher gave a start before he realized she had overheard Julia's query. "That I would allow you to do me bodily harm should I ever vex you. Preferably with a slap to the face, but a punch to the gut... *stomach*... should I behave as a pompous ass. Please pardon the language."

Juliet's gaze moved to her mother before she said, "Since I require a working hand to ride a horse, I may have to forego doing you bodily harm, darling," she replied, a dimple appearing in her cheek. "In favor of demanding a different sort of recompense."

Christopher stared at her for a full five seconds before he blinked. "Recompense?"

Rolling her eyes, Juliet whispered, "I'm not really sure what that means, but mother said I would sort it at some point."

A slow smile appeared on Christopher's face before he allowed a nod. "If that is the case, I may go out of my way to vex you, my sweet."

Juliet's eyes widened before they lifted to find her father and mother staring at her. Although her mother displayed a sweet smile, her father looked as if he might faint. "Perhaps we should go," she suggested.

"Of course," Christopher agreed as he offered his arm.

The two made their way through the hall and out the front door, well aware her parents watched them as they took their leave.

*O*n the pavement in front of the Comber townhouse, a Comber groom stood with Juliet's horse while the stableboy held the reins of Lord Haddon's Thunder. A mounting block had been positioned next to the gray Irish walker named Sean.

Juliet stepped up onto the block and settled herself into the sidesaddle, Christopher standing at her side. "You look stunning," he murmured, once she had her right leg wrapped around the pommel and her skirts spread out in an arc along the side of the horse.

"Thank you, my lord," she whispered. "Now stop fawning and mount your gorgeous horse," she demanded with a teasing grin.

Christopher held a hand to his chest. "I am yours to command on this day," he replied, rather wishing she were demanding he mount her. If his ride with her went well this day, such an event might just be in his future.

He was quick to settle himself on the saddle before he had Thunder pulling up next to her smaller horse. When she indicated she was ready, the two urged their mounts into a walk that took them in the direction of the park.

"I was unable to tell you before, but I want you to know how stunning I find you in your riding habit."

Juliet grinned, a dimple appearing in one cheek. She was about to remind him that he had seen her in a riding habit at Fairmont Park, but then she remembered that she and Victoria had already changed into day gowns when the earl had paid his call. It was Mr. Grandby who had joined them on a ride around the track. "I appreciate the compliment. This is my favorite habit," she acknowledged.

"I expect you have one for every day of the week—"

"I do not," she replied.

"Then I will see to it you have as many as you want. Every color you like," he claimed.

"Haddon!" she admonished him.

"It's not as if they will be packed away for long periods of time. You ride so frequently, I know you will wear them all," he replied.

Juliet furrowed a brow. "It's true. I do ride often. Every day if I can. You're not... bothered by that?"

Christopher glanced at her, surprised by the query. "Not at all. I think it a noble choice."

"Choice?"

"Well, others of your sex spend their days in more domestic pursuits. If you were not spending time with your horses, what would you do instead?"

She considered his question a moment before replying. "When I am not riding or spending a day with Vicky, then I embroider or practice dancing or read or draw—"

"You draw?"

Juliet nodded. "Father has complained about the number of sketch books he must buy since I fill them up so quickly."

Christopher stared at her a moment, and then had to return his attention to the street when Thunder angled toward a huge flower pot on the pavement in front of a townhouse at the corner of South Audley and Curzon. "Not yet, Thunder. I've only just made arrangements to purchase it," he scolded his horse.

Juliet glanced from the flower pot to the earl. "You're buying a flower pot? For your horse?"

Christopher blinked and then allowed a guffaw. "I am. Along with the townhouse to go with it," he said as he pointed to the white four-story building trimmed in blue and black. "What do you think?"

"It's quite grand," Juliet remarked in awe. "Lots of windows, and I suppose it even has a vantage of the park."

"Oh, it does, my lady. From the mistress suite," Christopher replied.

Juliet swallowed. "You're going to live there?"

"I am," he acknowledged. "There's plenty of room at Carlington House, of course, but I decided that I should have a house of my own until I inherit. Or until my father decides to rusticate in the country."

Juliet didn't know the Marquess of Morganfield well, but she couldn't imagine him ever moving to the country. Or his wife. Adeline Carlington was one of Mayfair's premiere hostesses.

Juliet took another look up at the front of the townhouse.

"Could you imagine drawing it?" Christopher asked as he drew his horse alongside hers.

"I could, but I rarely draw things."

"Pray tell, then what do you use for subjects?"

Giggling, Juliet said, "Horses, of course. And someday I may paint them, but I've not yet developed my skills enough with a brush."

"I should like to see your art," Christopher said. "I will of course keep you in sketch books. As many as you need."

"That's very kind of you, my lord," Juliet said, her attention going to a passing town coach. She displayed a brilliant smile and waved.

"Who was that?" Christopher asked.

Juliet laughed. "Lady Bostwick. Your sister," she replied. "You did not see her?"

Christopher shook his head. "I see little else when I am with you," he murmured as they crossed onto Park Lane and headed north toward the Stanhope Gate. "I think of no one else."

"Haddon," she said softly. "Have a care with your words, or you'll have me thinking you feel affection for me," she added in a tease.

They crossed under the gate and followed the crushed granite path toward the Serpentine. "But I do," Christopher insisted, when they were once again riding abreast of one another. "I have for... well, ever since you punched me."

She gave him a quelling glance. "Toadie," she accused, and then she dimpled. "I do not mind, you must know. But I will admit, I did at first."

"I did not mean for my attentions to vex you," he said. "But I know I am different because of having met you."

"Because I punched you?" she teased. "Nonsense."

He gave his head a shake. "Because when I fell, I hit my head, and it was as if the last three years were banged out of it."

"Three years?" she repeated, sobering. "Do you remember any of it?" she asked, worry evident in her voice.

"I do, although in a very different aspect from how I experienced it. As if I'm watching myself from afar, remembering how I was saying and doing things I at one time would never do or say. And thinking what a horrid man I had become."

"Horrid might be overstating it," Juliet argued.

"Not at all. I've been told I was behaving like an idiot. A pompous, mean-spirited idiot." At her look of shock, he added,

"My sister could always be quite cross, but I knew she spoke the truth when Bostwick had words for me that day."

"What happened to change you three years ago?" Juliet asked gently.

He glanced in her direction and then faced forward. "Besides growing old? Without so much as a wife by my side?" he asked rhetorically. "I thought it was that at first, but there is more."

"Will you tell me?"

Nodding, he directed Thunder to take an intersecting path toward a hedgerow that bordered the King's Road. "As an heir to a marquessate, I have known my whole life I would one day have to marry and sire an heir," he said. "I never resented that. I know it's a privilege to be an aristocrat. My sister's charity has reminded me of it every year of its existence. But as I grew closer to the age of forty, I grew resentful. Angry. I had always been sure that at some point, I would find someone to marry, and I would do my duty and all would be well."

"But you didn't," she murmured.

"I attended every ball for which I received an invitation. I went to soirées. I attended the theatre. I met I cannot tell you how many young ladies. Perfectly good young ladies who would have made perfectly suitable wives," he claimed. "I thought it would be easy to simply pick one and go on with life."

"Then why didn't you?" Juliet asked in awe.

Christopher blinked. "I didn't like any of them."

"What?"

"Not a one," he insisted, shaking his head. He glanced around and then led them off the path toward the hedgerow. "Well, I liked them in that they were pleasant and all, but I couldn't imagine eating dinner with them, or having tea in their company, or spending a morning with them in the breakfast parlor. Every day for the rest of my life."

"Oh." Juliet grew nervous, wondering if she was merely a

means to an end for the earl. If she had just happened to be at the right place at the wrong time.

"Meanwhile, all my friends were married," Christopher continued. "Most to amiable women who they seemed to adore, especially after they'd been made fathers," he complained. "I directed all that anger and resentment towards them and anyone else I was around."

"You were jealous," Juliet said as she pulled her walker to a halt to stare at him.

Christopher followed suit and dismounted, then quickly moved to lift Juliet from her horse. "Possibly," he responded as he offered his arm. "Probably," he amended.

"Then what did you do?"

"I stopped going to so many entertainments, since they only reminded me of what I didn't have," he replied. "Instead, I starting fencing as if my life depended on it. But after I was practically skewering my opponents, I found only my brother-in-law would agree to a match with me."

He sighed as he indicated a secluded park bench. Pulling a handkerchief from his pocket, he used it to dust the snow from the bench and indicated she should sit.

Juliet settled onto the bench and waited until he was seated next to her before she said, "All because you could not decide on a woman to marry?"

Dipping his head, he said, "That day you punched me would have been the last day Bostwick ever fenced with me. He left Angelo's in a huff—I cannot blame him—and I was chasing after him when I nearly skewered you."

They sat in silence for a moment as Juliet considered his words. At no point had he displayed anger or resentment in her presence, and if he felt any jealousy, she was unaware of it.

"You have said you will propose marriage, which now has me wondering, why *me*? Of all the young ladies you might possibly like if you would only take a few minutes to—"

"Because I can imagine having breakfast with you every

morning," he said as he lifted a gloved hand to her face. "I know, because I have done so every morning since we met," he replied. "I've taken tea with you on several occasions now, and I would like to continue doing so." He took a breath. "I've imagined dinner together, but I admit I haven't thought through a seven-course meal just yet. But besides the eating and drinking, I rather enjoy our conversations. You have opinions. You're not an insipid empty-headed female—"

"I should hope not!"

"—And I like that you're not cowed by my rank. That you're a member of the *ton* but not so closely related as to show privilege. But I especially like that should I ever again display my less likable qualities, you will see to it I'm put in my place, whether that be a slap across the face, or a punch to the gut, or just a stern word of warning."

Juliet stared at him for a long time before a smile lifted her lips. "Oh, dear. I think I may be feeling some affection for you, Christopher. And mayhap a desire to have breakfast in your company."

Christopher's eyes widened, not only by her use of his Christian name. "Oh?" he replied, straightening on the bench. "May I ask what has changed?"

Juliet swallowed as she continued to stare at him. "You," she said, a twinkle appearing in her eyes. She leaned over and kissed him on the corner of his mouth.

Not about to let the moment pass without some sort of acknowledgement, Christopher took her lips with his.

He meant for the kiss to be but a short one. A simple kiss that would segue into the real reason he had brought her to this specific location in the park. To surprise her with her real betrothal ring and tell her what he had in store for her in the way of jewelry. A bit of bribery, to be sure, but what else did he know how to do to entice her to be his wife?

After a few moments, though, he was so engrossed in the kiss, he forgot all about the ring. Forgot where he was. Forgot there were two horses standing not five feet away. Forgot about the flakes of snow that had begun falling. Forgot about time and the rest of the world as his gloved hand moved from her cheek to the back of her head.

The slight moan Juliet made in the back of her throat might have been the reason he suddenly pulled away, but the wash of warm air on his forehead had him leaning back even more.

"Oh, Sean," Juliet murmured, "Must you?"

Christopher blinked. The Irish walker was nibbling on the silk flowers in Juliet's small hat, his nostrils flaring when Juliet leaned toward Christopher to save her hat from further destruction. "Who's Sean?" he asked as he glanced around where they were sitting. "Do you kiss him, too?"

A series of discombobulated thoughts flew through Christopher's injured head as jealousy replaced his feelings of love and devotion.

What if Sean was her real lover, and she was imagining Sean whilst kissing him? What if Sean was somewhere nearby, spying on them? What if Sean was about to challenge him to a duel, and not with swords...?

"My horse, of course," Juliet replied, her eyes fluttering open. "And I rather doubt I've ever kissed him." Her blonde brows furrowed when she noted Christopher's odd expression. "Who did you think I was scolding?"

Christopher experienced a sort of relief he had never before felt. He stared at the horse, who once again snorted so a blast of warm air surrounded him. "You named your horse Sean?" he asked, hoping to hide his momentary flight of fancy.

"Well, he is an Irish walker," she replied as she pulled an apple from a pocket in her habit and offered it to the horse. Sean quickly captured it with his flat teeth and stepped back. "I named his brother Seamus."

Christopher allowed a sigh of relief. "Oh."

Juliet stared at Christopher for a moment, concern still

etched on her face. "Did you think...? Did you think I was speaking of another... man?" she stammered.

Bobbing his head first one way and then the other, Christopher said, "I did. And truth be told, I've never been so jealous in all my life."

Inhaling slowly, Juliet allowed a wan grin and settled her head into the small of his shoulder. "Oh, really, Christopher. You needn't be jealous of Sean. Or of Seamus."

Christopher wrapped his arms around her shoulders and pressed a kiss against her coiffure, heartened she had used his Christian name—even if she'd been admonishing him. "I would not if I knew you would always spend your nights with me," he whispered. "Your mornings, during breakfast."

"Tea and dinner with you?" she murmured, lifting her head to regard him with a smirk.

"Indeed. Will you marry me?" He fished the ring from his waistcoat pocket and held it close to his chest.

Juliet's eyes widened. "Is that... is that a horseshoe?" she asked in awe. She quickly straightened on the bench and continued to stare at the ring.

"It is," Christopher acknowledged. "Do you like it?"

Juliet turned her attention to him and then back to the ring. "I do." She watched in wonder as he pulled her glove from her left hand and slid the ring onto her finger. "It's perfect with this riding habit," she whispered. "You had it made special, didn't you?"

"I did," he admitted. "There will be more, of course," he murmured before he kissed her forehead. "Will you marry me?"

"If I do, will you always kiss me like you did a few minutes ago?"

"Will you marry me if I do?"

She nodded. "I will."

"Then of course I will," he replied. "So... you will marry me?"

Juliet giggled. "Yes. Yes, I will."

He pulled her close and held her for a time until Thunder nudged his shoulder, nearly knocking him over.

Juliet giggled again and pulled a carrot from another pocket. She held it out for his horse, who quickly downed it.

"You do realize you'll forever be his favorite now?" Christopher said in a scolding voice.

"Will I always be yours?" she countered, a brow arching.

Christopher nodded. "Always," he replied. He gave her another kiss and then glanced around to discover snow falling all around them.

"It's magical," she murmured, lifting her face so the flakes settled on her chilled skin. She took a deep breath and regarded him a moment. "I can hardly wait to tell Vicky, and I know she'll be happy for me—for us—but I can't help but think she will assume I'll no longer visit Fairmont Park as often."

"Of course you will," Christopher assured her. "I shall put forth no impediment to you continuing your weekly trip there." He leaned forward and added, "Besides, I do believe Vicky will have a man of her own very soon."

Juliet's eyes widened in delight. "How do you know that?"

He chuckled but didn't provide a reply. "Come. Let's get you back and share our good news with your parents," he suggested, offering a hand to assist her from the bench. He lifted her onto Sean and made sure she was settled in the saddle before he mounted Thunder.

Despite how hard the snow fell, the two took their time returning to South Audley Street.

CHAPTER 33

BOOTS, A BATH, BUBBLES
AND A BAUBLE

eanwhile, at Fairmont Park
As the unmarked town coach lumbered into the circle drive in front of Fairmont Park, Tom glanced out the window and wondered if his arrival could be seen by the lady of the house. Nervous, he couldn't decide if he wanted her to be forewarned or taken by surprise.

If she was still bedridden, her only view would be toward the stables and the track, given her bedchamber faced that vantage. She had probably been watching Alistair Comber from her window as he put the horses through their paces these past two days.

Given the snowy weather and the number of pasteboard boxes he had for Victoria, Tom had opted to have his town coach deliver him to Fairmont Park. He had hoped to drive the phaeton and then pay the stableboy to see to Jake's care, but the snow had dashed those plans.

The coach door opened and his driver began collecting the boxes into a stack. "Should I wait out front here or... pull around to the back?" the driver asked as Tom stepped out and then took the boxes from him.

"Neither," Tom replied. "Come back for me tomorrow in the morning. Say... nine o'clock."

"Very good, sir."

The driver moved to step up to the seat and Tom said, "Make that ten o'clock," he amended.

"Very good, sir," the driver replied, a smirk barely hidden as he took the reins from the pole and set the team in motion.

Tom watched as the coach departed and then turned his attention to the front door.

Clark stood there, an expression of curiosity crossing his face. "Mr. Grandby? Is that you?"

Leaning his head around the stack of pasteboard boxes, Tom said, "It is. Might her ladyship be in residence?"

The butler nodded as he stepped aside. "She hasn't left her bedchamber since you were last here, sir."

Tom quickly stepped inside so the servant could shut the door against the flurry of snowflakes that followed him in. He winced at the thought that Victoria's ankle might still be too painful for her to at least limp around the first floor. "I'll see if I can't assist in that regard." He set the boxes on a chair and then divested his coat and hat into the butler's waiting arms.

"Would you like me to announce you?"

"No need."

Tom once again lifted the boxes and made his way toward the stairs. "But do send up a tea tray, won't you?"

The butler visibly winced. "I don't think that would be a very good idea, sir. Her ladyship has not been pleased at the prospect of more tea since Miss Comber's departure a few hours ago."

About to argue, Tom reconsidered his request. "Then send up a cup of chocolate and the brandy with two glasses."

"Very good, sir." The butler hurried off as Tom carefully made his way up the stairs, balancing the boxes against the front of his body and securing the top one with his chin.

When he reached Victoria's door, he paused and attempted to knock with the back of his hand.

"I said I do not want more tea," he heard from the other side of the door. He silently thanked the butler for having warned him and then managed to lower the door handle with his elbow. He gave the door a slight shove and entered the room.

He leaned against the door to shut it, prepared to greet Victoria formally and then beg forgiveness for not having sent word ahead that he would be paying a call.

But he was suddenly tongue-tied.

Victoria was propped up against a mound of pillows, the likes of which had probably required the feathers of the entire goose population of Devonshire. Her dark hair was down past her shoulders, and she wore a pristine white nightrail that featured only a small ruffle at the neckline and three pearl buttons down the front of the bodice.

She was staring at him as if he were a ghost, and for a moment, he did the same with her. When he finally found his voice, he said, "You're gorgeous."

Victoria blinked and then set aside the book she'd been reading. "You might be in need of spectacles," she countered. "I'm in desperate need of a bath, as is my hair. What are all those boxes?"

Pulled from his stupor, Tom straightened from the door and said, "Footwear."

"Footwear?" she repeated, her brows furrowing.

"Slippers, boots, shoes." He moved farther into the room and set the boxes on the end of the bed, careful they were well away from where her feet were tucked under the covers. Then he leaned down and kissed her on the cheek.

She stared at him. "I never thought I'd see you again," she whispered.

Tom sat on the edge of the bed and took one of her hands

in his. He kissed the back of it. "About that. I was a fool to have left the way I did."

She shook her head. "Thomas, I behaved terribly towards you. I've reread the contract—several times—and now I understand what divi—"

The rest of her words were cut off when Tom's lips took hers in an urgent kiss, his hand moving to the side of her face to cup her cheek. After a moment, he slowly pulled away, but he left his forehead pressed against hers. "I am here to do your bidding, my lady. If a bath is what you want, you shall have it."

Victoria stared at him, her lashes nearly brushing his, they were so close. "That bad, am I?"

Thomas blinked. "What? Oh, no," he assured her as he straightened. "I meant what I said when I arrived. You're gorgeous."

"You said it as if you were surprised," she accused, her lower lip protruding.

"I was," Tom admitted. "Clark said you hadn't been out of this bedchamber since I was last here."

"Oh, dear. I think he might be right," she murmured.

"I was imagining you all old and withered, your hair turned white," he teased.

"You mean how you'll look when you're eighty?" she countered, a dimple appearing in one cheek.

He afforded her a brilliant grin. "I can only hope you'll still love me when I'm that old," he whispered.

Victoria sucked in a breath, about to chide him for his cheekiness. "What about you?"

"I came in here despite what I was imagining," he reminded her with a grin.

Her gaze moved to the pasteboard boxes. "Are those yours?"

He shook his head. "They're yours, actually. I rather doubt they would fit me."

"May I see?"

"Of course." Tom reached over and selected the largest box,

knowing they contained her riding boots. He placed it on her lap.

Victoria watched him as she lifted the lid. She gave a start when she lifted one of the boots from the tissue. "Isn't this... isn't this *my* boot?" She pulled the other one out of the box and held them up. "This one, too?" Her eyes widened. "What were you doing with my boots?"

"I wasn't doing anything with them. Mr. Shoemaker was. Is. Did," he stammered.

"How...?"

"Miss Comber arranged for their delivery to me a couple of nights ago." When he noted Victoria's look of disbelief, he said, "She's a resourceful young woman. She'll make an excellent countess." He pulled his chronometer from his waistcoat pocket. "I rather imagine Haddon is about to propose to her this very moment," he added.

"She's going to accept his suit," Victoria whispered, a hint of sadness creeping into her voice.

"With the caveat that she'll still be allowed to pay calls on you every week," Tom murmured, heartened when he saw how her expression changed. "And now you won't have to accept his suit."

She displayed a smirk. "What a disaster we would be," she whispered.

Tom was about to pull the pearl and emerald ring from his waistcoat pocket, but a knock on the door had him standing up from the bed.

Cummings poked her head around the door. "It's not tea, I promise, my lady," she said as she moved to set the tray on the nightstand. "Will there be anything else, my lady?"

Victoria stared over at the tray and furrowed her brows. Then she glanced at Tom and grinned. "Will there be anything else, Mr. Grandby?"

Tom turned his attention on the lady's maid. "Tonight's

dinner will be served at seven o'clock in the dining room. There will be two of us."

Cummings blinked. "Should I come to dress her ladyship at six?"

Tom glanced over at Victoria. "Your services won't be required again until tomorrow at ten o'clock," he replied. "But let the cook know breakfast will be served at nine."

"Yes, sir," Cummings replied happily. She curtsied and took her leave of the bedchamber, fairly bouncing as she did so.

When he returned to his place at the edge of the bed, Tom found Victoria staring at him. "Please, don't be angry with me," he pleaded.

"Oh, I'm not," she replied. "You just do it so... easily. I always feel as if I'm imposing on them." She lifted one of the boots. "Since you dismissed my maid, could you...?"

"Oh, of course." He reached over and took the boots from her. "Where would you like them?"

"In the dressing room," she said, pointing to a door in the opposite wall from the bed.

Tom entered the long, thin room, taking in the rows of colorful gowns hung from pegs along the wall. There were several pairs of misshapen slippers, but none looked quite like the ones Mr. Shoemaker had created. He hoped the man had been successful with copying the pattern of her riding boots.

When he emerged from the dressing room, he found Victoria staring at a pair of sapphire slippers. She looked up at him. "You did this?"

He shook his head. "Mr. Shoemaker made them. In New Bond Street. Shall we see if they fit?"

Victoria nodded, her eyes still round in awe.

He flung the covers from her feet and undid the wrapping from around her ankle, heartened to see that any swelling had subsided. "Does this hurt?" he asked as he pressed on her inner ankle bone.

She shook her head. "I've been moving it about. Stretching

it," she replied. "I will probably have pain when I put weight on it, but I do think it's much better."

"Well, this is good news," he said as he slid the larger of the two slippers onto her foot. It went on without much effort.

Victoria inhaled and watched as he slid the smaller one onto her other foot. "It fits," she breathed. "They both fit." Then she leaned over and grabbed another box from the stack. She opened it, her eyes wide with wonder. Inside was a pair of black half-boots. "Thomas," she whispered. She was about to reach for another box, but Tom stilled her hand. "Later," he said.

Victoria pretended to pout. "Just one more?"

He gave her a grin. "Oh, all right." He peeked into one of the boxes, his brow arching. "You can open this one," he said as he passed the box to her.

Victoria removed the lid and stared at the silver satin dance slippers. "Oh," she whispered. "But, I cannot dance," she added, as she raised her gaze to his.

"Tonight, you will. Even if I have to carry you through a waltz," he replied.

She seemed to think on it for a time before she finally nodded. "These will be perfect with my orchid gown, I should think," she murmured.

"Then I shall dress you in the orchid gown for dinner." Before she could remind him that she needed a bath, he added, "But first, I shall draw you a bath and wash your hair."

A frisson had Victoria trembling. "Are you going to undress me, too?"

Tom allowed a shrug. "If you'll allow it. Otherwise, I shall drop you into the tub with you still in your nightrail." He disappeared into the bathing chamber, and Victoria settled back into the pillows. Her gaze fell on the other boxes. She once again leaned forward and peeked into the top box.

"No peeking," Tom called from the bathing chamber. The sound of running water came from the tub, and Victoria grinned as she pulled a pair of scarlet satin slippers from the box. She knew in an instant which gown he'd had in mind when he ordered the shoes.

"I'm not," she called back, reaching for the last box. She opened the lid and sighed at the sight of another pair of day slippers, these in black satin. "But do tell me. Just how many shoes did you order from Mr. Shoemaker?"

Tom appeared in the door to the bathing chamber. "Eight and twenty," he replied. "And I expect to see you wear each and every one of them sometime in the next year."

Victoria blinked. "Noted," she said as Tom moved to the side of the bed and lifted her into his arms. "However did you choose the style and colors?" She wrapped her arms around his neck, glad to finally be out of the bed.

Tom carried her into the bathing chamber. "Fashion, I suppose," he replied after a moment of reflection. "Mr. Shoemaker said a modiste chose all the colors for the Season, so he has satin in all of them. And I do have five sisters," he added when she gave him a dubious glance. "Now, what do you like in your bath water?"

Victoria pointed to a glass decanter on the dressing table. "Bubbles, I should think," she replied, hoping they might hide most of her nakedness whilst she was in the water.

Tom set her down into the chair in front of the table and grabbed the bottle. "How much?" he asked as he started to shake the powder into the tub, just beyond where water emerged from a tap. Bubbles immediately appeared on the surface of the water.

"Oh, that's quite enough," she said, her eyes wide. "Any more and you won't be able to find me in the water."

Tom gave her a smirk and then moved to the dressing table. "How many strokes?" he asked as he lifted the hair brush from the table.

Victoria eyed the way he held the brush and wondered if he intended to spank her with it. "Ten or twenty," she murmured.

"My sisters always insisted on a hundred strokes a day. Can

that be good for hair?" He pulled the brush through the bottom half of a section of her dark locks, heartened when there weren't any snarls to impede the brush.

"It cannot be too bad, since that's the last thing Cummings does before I dismiss her at night," she replied as she kept an eye on the rising bubbles.

Victoria thought it odd that the way he brushed her hair felt entirely different from when her lady's maid did it. Sensual. Slow and hypnotic. The fingertips of his other hand stroked her scalp as the brush separated the strands from the top of her head to their tips.

It would have been easy to simply close her eyes and revel in the sensations, in the skitters that darted beneath her scalp and the frissons she felt from his nearness. But all she could think about was what would happen when the tub was full.

"Shouldn't you be testing the water?" she asked, her words sounding strangled. "Cummings always complains about how hard it is to get the temperature right."

Tom dipped his hand under the faucet. He was about to test the water in the tub, but first he removed his topcoat and rolled up the sleeves on his shirt before he dipped his hand into the tub. "It's rather warm, but not hot. By the way, where is your water heating device?"

"Just there," Victoria replied, pointing to where a series of pipes went in and out of a metal box just beyond the tub. Beneath it, he could see tiny flames erupting from a pipe with holes. "Does this stay lit all the time?" he asked, intrigued by the arrangement in the plumbing. He followed the pipes back until they disappeared through a hole in the wall. "And what's beyond this wall?"

"The bathing chamber for the bedchamber next door," she replied. "Juliet's room. I just had a few of them done on this floor," she explained. "The man who installed it said to just leave it set like that. Heats the water for the tub as well as the faucet for the washbowl just above it. He said the water will never get hotter than boiling since it's not a pressurized system. Does that sound right?"

"It does," Tom replied, impressed. "There must be a vent here somewhere." He found a pipe that went straight up the wall. "Here. Now, from where does the gas come?"

Jealous of the hot water system—Tom seemed entirely too fascinated by it—Victoria rolled her eyes. "Father arranged for it years ago when the lines for the lights in London were being dug," she replied. "The nearest gas main is not far." She watched as he continued to study the arrangement, finally amused by his interest.

If she could walk on her own, she would simply remove her nightrail, step into the tub, and hide her nakedness beneath the bubbles. But then she noted how the bubbles in the tub were nearly to the top edge. "Thomas, the water," she warned.

He let out a guffaw and quickly turned off the water source. "There may be more bubbles than water in here," he said with a smirk. He dipped his hand into the airy orbs of delight and announced that the water was a fine temperature. "Now, let's get you in here." He moved to lift her from the chair, but she shrank back from him. "What is it? What's wrong?" he asked.

"I... I don't want you seeing me... *naked*," she whispered.

Tom frowned, his lower lip protruding in a pretend pout. "Oh, all right. Hands around my neck," he ordered. When she did as she was told, he lifted her and carried her to the tub. "Now, when I lower your legs, you're just going to put down your good foot until it touches the bottom. I'll hold on whilst you remove your gown," he explained.

"Close your eyes," she ordered.

"I will. Just..." He sighed and did as he was told, giving up his hold briefly as the fabric of her nightrail slid up and over her body. His hands tightened around her bare waist, and he felt the warmth of her skin. He was aware of a *whoosh* of air as the gown descended to the floor. Struggling to keep his eyes closed, he bent and lowered her into the tub until she let go of his neck.

"May I open my eyes now?"

Victoria giggled. "This is positively heavenly."

Tom stared down at her, laughing when he saw that the bubbles were up to her chin. "I shan't make that mistake again," he murmured. "Now. Where's the soap? And what do you like to use on your hair?" He glanced around and found a small pail. He filled it with hot water from the sink and set it aside.

"Just there," Victoria said as she pointed to a ball of soap on the dressing table.

Tom plucked the ball from the table and sniffed it. "French, I suppose?" he asked as he knelt next to the tub.

"Of course."

"I'll do your hair first."

Victoria disappeared beneath the bubbles, her knees appearing for a moment before she re-emerged, her hair soaked and slicked back from her face.

For a moment, he simply stared at her, reminded of the Greek pelike in his office. Of Aphrodite stepping out of an oyster shell. Of the pearl ring that was tucked into his waistcoat pocket.

He handed her a small linen. "I have something for you."

She blinked away the water droplets that clung to her eyelashes and then dabbed at her face with the linen. "More shoes?"

He shook his head. "I forgot to give you your pearl. The other night, after dinner," he whispered.

"You still have it? I thought perhaps it was lost."

"No, but I did take the liberty of having it made into something I hope you'll like," he said as he reached into his waistcoat pocket. He pulled out the gold band, watching her reaction as she straightened in the tub and stared at the ring.

"Are those emeralds?" she asked, one of her hands gripping the side of the tub. The other one joined the first as she leaned in his direction.

"To match your eyes," Tom replied. He touched the fourth

finger of her right hand with the tip of his finger, and then slid the ring on it when she straightened it.

"Oh, Thomas, it's beautiful," she whispered. "I don't remember the pearl being this large."

"The jeweler is quite good with his settings," he replied. "Marry me, Victoria. I'd ask you, but I have reason to think you would turn me down."

Victoria swallowed. "Oh, Thomas. I would turn you down, as I would anyone else," she said, a pained expression crossing her face. "You deserve a woman who hasn't been ruined, and who has two good feet."

"But I want you, and I don't care about the first man you were betrothed to, except—"

"Who told you?"

"—should I ever meet him, he will suffer a fist to the face." He actually imagined a knee to the groin, but he didn't want her knowing it.

"Haddon? He told you?" she asked, obviously angry. "How *dare* he?"

"He dared because he knows how much I love you, Victoria. He even warned me you would turn me down."

She shook her head as tears brightened her eyes. "I broke off an engagement to Viscount Upton. He said he was sure I was no longer a virgin. Because he paid witness to me riding astride." She wrapped her arms around her knees and pulled them to her chest, the bubbles no longer so thick as to hide her nakedness.

"And then he ruined you. To prove his point?" Tom guessed.

Victoria recoiled in horror. "How—?"

"When I next meet Viscount Upton, he shall suffer far more than a fist to the face," Tom said quietly. "Haddon mentioned your brief betrothal—"

"Damn him!" Victoria cursed.

"—which positively makes no difference to me. Other than

an overwhelming desire to have Upton forced to learn female anatomy at a medical school."

She furrowed her dark brows as tears collected in the corners of her eyes. "You *knew?*" she asked in a whisper. "And yet you still proposed?"

He shrugged. "I love you, Victoria. As long as you no longer harbor feelings for the man—"

"Contempt, of course," she replied. "Anger. Betrayal—"

"I was thinking more along the lines of affection."

"I cannot say I ever felt *affection* for him. He was merely the one Jeremiah thought best for me. Father only agreed because..." She sighed. "Because Upton will be a marquess one day."

"And now?" Tom prompted, when she didn't offer more.

"Only contempt, I suppose."

"Then it matters not. Other than the knowledge that you shouldn't feel pain when I make love to you for the first time. Tonight, if you'll allow it?" he suggested in a hoarse whisper. At seeing her widened eyes, he added, "I cannot help but think that I owe you two hours of pleasure for every hour of pain you have suffered because of me."

Victoria stared up at him. "Oh, Thomas, I have not suffered pain because of you," she countered in a quiet voice.

His eyes darted sideways. "Could we... pretend you have?"

"Thomas!" she scolded as she slapped his chest.

Tom raised the hand to his lips and kissed the back of it. "I'll take that as a yes."

Victoria stared at him, her expression still displaying her indecision.

"I've arranged with your brother, Michael, to buy Fairmont Park from your father."

"What?!"

"And I've drawn up a settlement whereby everything you own here, as well as the house and grounds, will remain yours, for you and our children," he went on. "My business and half the earnings will go to you upon my death."

"Thomas—"

"The other half will go to the children, one of whom I hope will aspire to take it over."

"You're *buying* Fairmont Park?" she asked in a pained whisper.

"As a wedding gift. For you," he replied. "I love you, Victoria. I think we suit quite well, and I have to believe you must feel some affection for me, or you wouldn't have allowed me to kiss you so many—"

His head was suddenly pulled toward hers, her hand having moved behind it and her lips settling onto his in an awkward kiss that soon was not.

Tom reveled in the feel of her lips on his while he ignored the bubbles that cascaded over the edge of the tub and dripped onto his thighs. When their tongues tangled and she moaned, he responded in kind. When she finally ended the kiss to take a deep breath, he asked, "Is that a yes?"

She nodded. "With one caveat."

"Only one?"

She gave him a quelling glance. "You'll allow me to continue training horses?"

"I will. But when you're with child, you'll stop when the physician says to and resume when he allows it."

Victoria considered his conditions and finally nodded. "Agreed. And Juliet?"

"Is always welcome, of course. Which means I may have to spend more time in Haddon's company."

"I would give you my sympathies, but—"

"He's not a bad sort when you get to know him," he said on a sigh. "I'm not exactly sure why I thought him a pompous arse, but by now," he pulled his Breguet from his waistcoat pocket and said, "he has no doubt asked Miss Comber for her hand in marriage."

"Why do you say it like that?" Victoria asked, her eyes

lighting up with his news. She turned his chronometer so she could read the time.

"Because he would be here, asking for your hand if he had not. I would have to challenge him to a duel, and although I can wield a sword, he's much better with a foil than I." When he noted her expression of amusement, he added, "I was never a cavalier, but I'm a crack shot with a pistol."

"My hero," she murmured, a grin lighting her face. "Now given the time, and the fact that you ordered dinner be ready at seven, I think you best wash my hair."

Tom leaned over the tub, noting how half of the bubbles had disappeared. "I look forward to it," he said with a grin.

"Thomas!" she replied, covering her breasts with her crossed arms.

"Lean back, my lady. I'm about to play lady's maid."

Once again, Victoria dunked her head in the water, and this time when she emerged, Tom was ready with a kiss and soapy hands.

CHAPTER 34

AN EARL MAKES AN ANNOUNCEMENT

eanwhile, at the Comber townhouse in Mayfair

Giggling as she brushed the snow from her riding habit and then from Christopher's coat, Juliet felt positively giddy. She was betrothed to a man who would one day be a marquess. A man who was proving to be agreeable and who seemed to adore her. A man who could ride a horse without bouncing about in the saddle. A man who had already bestowed her with not one, but two rings.

A man who not only didn't mind her fascination with horses, but honored it by having a horseshoe of sapphires included on her betrothal ring.

She took his arm and gave him a brilliant smile. "Do come in for tea," she insisted. "And a chance to warm yourself before you take your leave." Carlington House was not far in Park Lane, but the snow was coming down in huge flakes.

"I will come in, of course. But I've no need of your home's warmth. Your smile is providing all I need on this auspicious day," Christopher said with a grin. The front door opened, and Williamson stepped aside to allow them in. "You seem truly happy, and I hope you are," he remarked, handing his top hat to the butler before he brushed the flakes from his shoulders.

"Oh, I am, Christopher. I only wish..." Juliet sobered as she sighed.

"What is it?" he asked, pulling off his gloves and his coat. The butler was quick to take them.

Juliet removed her own gloves and held out her hands as she angled her head. "Victoria was so sad when I left her earlier today. She is convinced she has lost the good opinion of a man I think she was coming to like very much."

Christopher furrowed a brow. "So Mr. Grandby hadn't yet paid a call before you took your leave today?"

Juliet's eyes widened. "How do you know it was Mr. Grandby?""

A grin split the earl's face as he lowered his forehead to hers. "I do. We have been plotting these past few days," he admitted, just before he stole a kiss. "When I last saw him, he was at Rundell and Bridge with a tray of emeralds and a pearl before him."

"A pearl?" Juliet repeated. "The one Vicky found in an oyster at Rules? She had him hold it for her and then forgot he had it."

Christopher's eyes darted to the side. "He did not say from where it had come," he murmured, and then he grinned in delight. "The rogue."

Juliet gasped. "But he seems like such an honorable man."

"That's because he is," Christopher assured her. He pulled his chronometer from his waistcoat pocket. "By now, I expect Vicky is betrothed to him. That is, if he asked for her hand more than once."

Staring at Christopher with a combination of confusion and shock, Juliet finally sighed. "She was so sure she would never see him again."

"We men are not that easily denied," Christopher replied, once again stealing a kiss. "Especially when it comes to the women we love. Wild animals cannot tear us from—"

The sound of a clearing throat had him stepping back in an

instant, his attention—and Juliet's—turning to discover her father standing in the hall with his hands on his hips.

"I'm hardly a wild animal," Alistair said, barely able to suppress a grin at the expense of his future son-in-law. Then he gave a bow. "Haddon," he said, his gaze on Juliet.

Christopher gave him a bow. "Mr. Comber. Your daughter has graciously accepted my offer to be my countess."

"Your wife, actually," Juliet whispered.

"That, too," he replied with a dimple.

"Best wishes to you both," Alistair replied, apparently resigned to his daughter's fate. "Join me in my study, my lord, and we can go over the settlement and the dowry."

"Haddon, please." Christopher said as he dared a glance at Juliet.

"I'll order tea," Juliet said. "You two won't be long, I hope." She was about to head to the front salon to ring the bell, but Williamson motioned for her.

"What is it?"

"Tea has been ordered by Mrs. Comber. She's been in there for at least a half-hour," he replied, indicating the salon.

"Is something wrong?"

He shook his head. "Nerves, perhaps?"

Juliet had never had the impression her mother was nervous about a possible marriage proposal from the Earl of Haddon, but now she was left wondering if the woman had only been putting on a show of confidence for her sake.

She found her mother sitting in the middle of the room's only settee, staring into a cup as if she was reading the tea leaves at the bottom of the porcelain bowl.

"Good afternoon, Mother. May I join you for a cup?"

Julia very nearly sent the remains of her tea onto her peach day gown. "Oh, you scared me," she accused.

"You did look as if you were far away," Juliet said as she sat down next to her mother.

The older woman turned in her direction. "I fear I was

entirely too familiar with the earl this afternoon," she whispered. "I warned him he couldn't behave badly with you. That he had to allow you to set him straight should he do anything... untoward. Has he... has he begged off?"

Juliet gave as start. "Hardly," she replied as she held up her left hand. When she saw that the horseshoe of sapphires was upside down, she quickly re-angled her hand so the ends of the horseshoe were pointed up. "I accepted his offer."

Julia blinked and then leaned in closer to the ring. She angled her head first one way and then the other to confirm it was the ring he had shown her earlier. "It's much lovelier on your finger than it was when he was holding it in his thumb," she murmured.

"You already saw it?" Juliet asked in dismay.

Her mother nodded. "He has an entire set of jewels under construction for you," she warned.

"A parure?" Juliet asked in a whisper.

Julia nodded. "I was quite excited about the prospect of you marrying an earl," she admitted. "About you becoming a marchioness someday. But now—"

"*You're* having second thoughts? Mother!"

"I know. Your father reminded me that you'll be moving out soon—"

"Oh, I'll just be down the street."

"What?"

"Christopher is purchasing a townhouse right where South Audley meets Curzon Street. He pointed it out to me as we were on our way to the park."

"Oh, well. That makes all the difference, doesn't it?" Julia replied, looking as if she was trying hard to stave off tears.

"Oh, Mother," Juliet sighed. "I thought you would be happy for me."

"I am," Julia sniffled, her expression the exact opposite of happy. "By the way, what have you done with him?" she asked as she glanced toward the hall.

Juliet was tempted to tease her by telling her she had relegated the earl to the dungeon for having taken liberties with her in the park, but she had enjoyed his kisses and thought better of it. "He's in the study with Father."

Her mother sighed. "The settlement papers."

"The dowry," Juliet murmured. "Can Father afford it?"

Julia's eyes widened. "Of course, he can. Your grandfather Aimsley was quite generous with his inheritance, and my father pays him for running the Harrington House stables. Then he earns consultancy fees at Tattersall's, and—"

"Which you're not supposed to know anything about."

The two looked up to discover Alistair regarding them from the doorway, a smirk lifting the edges of his lips.

"Then you shouldn't mention it as the reason when you're giving me a new bauble every now and then," his wife replied with a smirk of her own. She leaned forward on the settee and glanced past her husband. "Oh, dear. What have you done with the earl?"

"Well, I haven't relegated him to the dungeon, if that's what you're thinking," Alistair replied.

"We don't have a dungeon," Julia said, her eyes widening in alarm. She turned her attention to Juliet. "Did he do something... *naughty*?"

From the way her mother said the word, Juliet thought she meant something far worse than a kiss. "Mother, it's cold outside. We were on horseback. It's snowing. Hard. Whatever could he do that would be considered *naughty*?"

Julia could think of a dozen things a man might do to keep himself warm with a woman. She knew because her husband had taken such liberties with her in the past. And just that morning when they woke up in a cold bedchamber.

"Don't answer that, darling," Alistair said before he turned his attention on his daughter. "Could you join the earl and me in the study?"

Juliet exchanged a quick glance with her mother and stood.

"Yes, of course." When she was alone with her father in the hall, she asked, "Is there something wrong?"

He paused when they were halfway to the study. "No, but I don't want there to be, either."

Alarmed, Juliet fairly tiptoed into the study, her intended quickly coming to his feet and hurrying to kiss her hand.

"My sweet Juliet. Your Father wishes for us to wait a bit before we marry. I have secured a special license that would allow us to wed on the morrow—"

"Oh. But I don't yet have a gown."

"—or anytime we wish."

Juliet turned to her Father, her brows furrowed. "How long must we wait?"

Alistair crossed his arms over his chest. "A week?" he suggested, a bit surprised Juliet seemed so eager. He had thought that by making the two wait to wed, they might reconsider their decision.

"What if Vicky is getting married, too? And what if she does so sooner than a week? I should like for her to be my witness," Juliet countered.

Her father gave a start. "You have reason to believe Lady Victoria is being courted?" Then he remembered his afternoon spent at Brook's with Tom Grandby. Remembered how he accused Tom of being in love with Lady Victoria.

Had Tom already proposed to the duke's daughter?

Christopher straightened and said, "Mr. Tom Grandby has been doing so under the guise of business meetings. Vicky is one of his clients, you see."

"I'm well aware," Alistair replied, a grin slowly appearing. "Let us discover if he and Vicky are betrothed before we discuss a date, shall we? Once we know their plans, then perhaps you two can arrange a wedding on the same day."

Juliet beamed in delight. "Oh, that would be perfect, Father. Don't you think so, Christopher?" she asked as she turned her brilliant smile on the earl.

"More than you might realize," he murmured, deciding it best he not share what he and the investment advisor had been doing these past few days. Then he allowed a guffaw. "My sweet, we must hire London's best modiste on the morrow to make you a splendid gown," he stated. "Mother will wish to host us for a dinner party so that the announcement can be made formally. I expect that will probably happen the day after tomorrow, given how quickly she can manage such entertainments."

"That soon?" Juliet's eyes widened in wonder.

"My mother is an efficient woman." He turned to Alistair. "You and Lady Comber really must attend, of course."

"I wouldn't miss it," Alistair replied. He took a deep breath. "Well, then, I suppose this is when I say my best wishes."

"Oh, Father, you needn't look so glum," Juliet murmured. "I'll just be down the street, and I'll still pay calls on Fairmont Park every week."

"I already told him about the townhouse," Christopher said as he leaned toward Juliet.

She sighed. "Then I do believe it's time for tea," she said as she reached for the bell.

Alistair glanced over at Christopher. "We can certainly imbibe in something a bit stronger," he suggested. "Brandy?"

Julia appeared on the threshold. "I cannot help but feel as if I'm being left out of important decisions," she complained. Her red-rimmed eyes betrayed a recent cry, but her expression suggested she had recovered.

"My lady," Christopher replied as he moved to take her hand. "Your words of earlier have not been forgotten. In fact, I have taken them to heart—"

"Oh, Haddon, I feel awful about what I said," Julia said as her hands crossed over her chest.

"You needn't, my lady."

"Bodily harm is the very last condition I should wish on the man who is marrying my daughter."

"We have sorted what it is she must do," he replied, his face taking on a reddish cast as he dared a glance in Juliet's direction.

Juliet blushed. "He's right, Mother. I know exactly what to do," she claimed, not having the foggiest idea.

But she would learn. Probably in a week's time.

Williamson appeared behind Julia, burdened with a tea tray that seemed to display every variety of biscuit and cake.

"We'll take tea in here," Alistair said as he indicated his desk and the leather sofas and chairs near the fireplace.

The butler hesitated, but an encouraging nod from the lady of the house had him doing Alistair's bidding. Once he took his leave, Juliet stepped up to the desk and began preparing the cups for tea. "I've got this," she said when she saw her mother's startled look. "Please, do be seated, and I'll see to the brandy for the gentlemen and tea for us."

Julia exchanged glances with her husband as Christopher stared at his betrothed with eyes that might have belonged to a love-sick puppy. "I love you," he whispered.

A blush once again colored Juliet's cheeks. "Toadie," she replied before blowing him a kiss.

CHAPTER 35

DRESSING FOR DINNER AND
A DANCE

*M*eanwhile, at Fairmont Park

Tom stared down into the bathtub as his betrothed stared up at him, her arms crossed over her breasts. The bubbles had long since dissipated, and the water was cool to the touch.

Although he had already wrapped a linen around her wet hair and held another for her to wrap herself in once he had her out of the tub, she refused his assistance.

"Please let me help, my sweet. I'll close my eyes, I promise."

"Then close them now."

"But, how am I supposed to—?"

"Thomas," she scolded.

"They're closed," he said, clamping his eyes shut. He swept a hand down and out in front of his thighs until he felt her hand grasp it. "Do you wish me to...?" But he couldn't complete the sentence when she pulled on his hand in an effort to hoist herself up to stand on only one foot.

For a moment, Tom thought he might be joining her in the tub, but he managed to right himself at the same time she grabbed for the linen. A moment later, and he wrapped both arms around her as the front of her body collided with his. "Can

I open them now?" he asked as his hands skimmed down her uncovered back and over the globes of her bare bottom.

The bottom he had found rather fetching when it was clad in riding breeches. 'Fetching' didn't really apply now.

'Arousing' was a far better term.

"Bounder," she murmured.

Tom opened one eye. "I'm quite sure there would have been a more elegant means of lifting you from the tub," he claimed with a grin. "Had I been able to see what I was doing." He kissed her forehead. "Why so modest?"

"Contrary to what you seem to think, we're not married."

"Yet," he replied defensively. "Could we pretend we are?"

"Besides, it's too light in here with the lamp lit," she argued, ignoring his query.

"Noted. Next time I'll turn down the lamp, and we can do this in the dark."

"You would do this again?" she countered, still leaning against him for support as she wrapped the damp linen around her body.

"Of course. I rather like washing your hair. It's a bit like taking a shower bath with my clothes on." He had shed his waistcoat once he had begun rinsing her hair and she had flung water at him from her wet fingertips. "Next time I'll get into the tub with you."

Despite the protest she was about to make, a frisson shot through Victoria, and she could only continue to stare up at him. "You're terribly tall," she murmured. "I don't think the tub would be large enough."

"You're not so short yourself, thank the gods, but I think we could manage," he countered playfully. "Come. Let's get you dried off and into a gown before you catch your death." He bent down and lifted her into his arms.

"I can dress myself."

"Oh."

The word was said with such sadness, Victoria was forced to

add, "But you can help with the fastenings, and the gloves and the shoes."

Tom immediately brightened. He set her on the edge of the bed. He disappeared for a moment and came out with the orchid gown. "I'd love to see you in this."

She inhaled softly, remembering her thought about that exact gown when she had spied the silver slippers. "Very well. Then I'll need the petticoats. All of them," she added when he held out only one set. "And a pair of stockings. They're in the top drawer, and there's a corset—"

"You don't need one of those. Not tonight." At her look of shock, he added, "I think a sprained ankle is quite enough discomfort already. No need compounding it with a garment that restricts your breathing, too." He moved to the dresser and pulled a pair of light hose from the top drawer, their ribbon ties fluttering as he unrolled them. "Do you require assistance with these?"

She shook her head as she took them and began pulling them on, struggling to keep the linen from slipping from her body. "Perhaps you could comb out my hair while I do this?" she suggested, knowing if she didn't give him something to do, he would merely hover about much like her lady's maid.

Grinning, she watched as he disappeared into the bathing chamber. Wearing only a shirt and trousers, and given his height, she could easily imagine the shape of his body beneath the clothes—broad shoulders, thin hips, and thighs that were probably larger than his waist.

Wanting to be sure her crushed foot was covered before he returned, she concentrated on its stocking first. When he climbed onto the bed behind her, Tom removed the linen turban he had wrapped about her head and began combing out her hair.

"I don't suppose you would know how to pin it up," she teased as she pulled on her other stocking.

"I could probably do a manageable job, but I would prefer

you leave it down." At her over-the-shoulder look of surprise, he added, "Just for tonight," in a whisper. "And maybe a few nights in the future?"

Victoria swallowed, the strange frisson once again shooting through her body. "If that's what you wish."

"Then I won't have to fish about looking for all the pins later tonight." When she turned around on the bed to stare at him, he added, "I'll have to help you get ready for bed." When he saw how nervous she suddenly looked, he leaned over and kissed her on the temple. "I should bring you over by the fire. I don't want you to catch a chill."

Tying the ribbons at the top of her stockings, Victoria wasn't about to tell him she wasn't the least bit cold. Her entire body felt as if there had been a fire inside, smoldering, ever since his arrival. "Then could you bring my dressing gown?" she asked. Although she would have been fine with him seeing her in a corset and her petticoats, she wasn't comfortable wearing only her chemise and petticoats. The silk fabric of her chemise was nearly translucent.

He was quick to do her bidding, helping her into the garment and then taking the damp linen from her when she wriggled out of it from beneath the dressing gown. A moment later, and she was sitting before the fire.

"Tell me, did you often see your sisters in their undergarments?" Victoria asked as Tom went about pulling on his waistcoat.

"All the time," he replied, rolling his eyes in mock dismay. "Such drama over what to wear."

"You men have it so easy," she complained.

"I'll not argue with that," he said as he finished buttoning his waistcoat. He rolled down his sleeves. "I just have to decide which color waistcoat to wear. Now, do you think you'll be able to stand? To pull on your undergarments?" He lifted the chemise and petticoats from the bed. "I'm happy to help," he said as he waggled his eyebrows.

Victoria was about to claim she could do it herself, but she remembered the feel of his hands as they skimmed down her bare back. "Perhaps if you just allow me to lean on you," she said. She gripped his arm and pulled herself up and then turned so her back rested against his chest.

"I've got you," he whispered, wrapping an arm around her waist, the chemise dangling from his fist.

The dressing gown slid from her shoulders, and Tom let go his hold until the satin fabric slipped down her body and ended up as a puddle on the floor at her feet. "Does it hurt for you to put weight on your foot?" he asked, his warm breath washing over her shoulder. He kissed the top of it, his eyes closed lest she scold him for peeking.

Victoria immediately suspected he was seeing more than he should. But when she turned to discover his eyes were closed, she leaned her head back and kissed him on his jaw. "Would you tell me if you found me... lacking in some regard?"

Tom's eyes opened in astonishment. "I rather doubt that's possible—"

"Besides my foot, I mean," she said as she placed one of her hands on the back of his and moved it up from her waist to cover one breast. She sucked in a breath as his hand molded the mound, the tips of his fingers barely caressing her skin. Her puckered nipple slipped between two fingers, and she nearly wept when his thumb brushed over the tip of it.

His breath ragged, Tom gave her breast a gentle squeeze. "I don't doubt it's possible, Victoria. I *know* it's not possible," he murmured as his hand moved to the other breast. "Besides, I already know you have a perfect bum," he added as he gently kneaded the breast.

"Bounder," she murmured, gasping at the sensations created by his touch.

"If I don't get you dressed right now, I shall be having my way with you," he warned as he lifted the chemise and placed it over her head. "And our dinner will be cold."

Realizing the moment of intimacy was over, Victoria mewled and turned to face him. She finished pulling on the chemise, her eyes never leaving his. When it was time for the petticoats, he raised them over her head and dropped them, one after another, their volume of fabric briefly coming between them until all three were settled on her hips.

"Something tells me that if I let go, you won't topple over," Tom teased as he hesitantly stepped back and grabbed the orchid ball gown from the bed. "Your petticoats will hold you up."

"I'll simply aim for you should I topple over," she murmured, wavering a bit as she balanced on her one good foot and the ball of her crushed foot.

Yards and yards of orchid satin and sarcenet fell around her. When her head finally appeared through the neckline, she gave Tom a quelling glance. "There are more fastenings you could have first undone in the back."

Given the layers of petticoats and gown that threatened to separate them, Tom said, "Now I know why it was so easy for my parents to court one another," he said with a smirk.

Victoria giggled, the first sound of amusement he had heard from her since her bath. She finished dressing and then turned her back to him. "My ankle does not pain me much," she claimed. "Perhaps I can ride tomorrow?"

"Me? Or a horse?" Tom asked with a teasing grin as he did up the few fastenings.

Her eyes narrowing as she glanced at him over her shoulder, Victoria asked, "If I do the one, will I be allowed to do the other?"

Tom blinked, wondering if she was teasing him. "Always," he whispered. "Anytime." He paused a moment. "Well, when we're alone, of course."

Suddenly embarrassed by her flirtatious behavior—Victoria couldn't believe she had put voice to such a scandalous suggestion—she quickly faced away from him. "I've never said anything like that before," she whispered.

Tom leaned his head down, her silken hair brushing his cheek. "I'm relieved you've made that clear, but I rather like knowing you would say it to me."

She turned and regarded him, her brows furrowed. "You must think me fast."

He shook his head. "No. In fact, I've just this moment realized that you are nothing like any of my sisters."

"They were fast?" she asked, astonished.

Tom shook his head. "No, but... well, yes."

Victoria blinked. "All of them?"

"No, oh, God, no. Just the youngest. I learned last Sunday morning that Emily has already been intimate with her betrothed," he said on a sigh.

"Well, isn't that to be expected?" Victoria countered. At his look of surprise, she added, "My mother told my sister and I we wouldn't make it to our wedding nights with our virtues intact. She said it was a man's right to bed his betrothed before the wedding." She furrowed a brow. "Surely, you are expecting to do the same with me, or you wouldn't keep suggesting we're going to make love tonight."

Tom blinked, thinking about what he was hoping to do with Victoria later. Even if they didn't make love, he had planned to stay with her for the night. At least under the same roof. "Guilty as charged," he admitted. "If you're amenable."

Victoria inhaled softly, skitters of delight racing down her spine and through her belly. Upton had never had this effect on her. She had barely known the man. But from the first day she had met Tom, it didn't seem to matter if she liked him or not—her body reacted as if she should.

And who was she to argue?

"Do you still expect me to dance with you?"

Dipping his head—the query was entirely unexpected—

Tom said, "If not tonight, then sometime soon, when your ankle is healed."

"Hmm," she murmured. "I was looking to forward to it."

"You minx," he replied with a grin. "We'll dance tonight. I'll carry you if you're ankle is not up to it."

"I'll need to wear something on my feet," she reminded him.

"Ah, the silver satin slippers," he remembered as he tipped the lids on several of the boxes until he found the right pair. He knelt before her. "Hang on to my shoulders," he instructed as he saw to helping her into the shoes.

"They both fit perfectly," she breathed. "I may even be able to walk."

"I'll carry you until it's time to dance," he countered.

"Will you take me to the stables?"

"Now?"

"No. Later. I like to take a walk after dinner, visit the horses before Jemmy goes to bed."

"Very well," he replied, curious if the grooms were present when she was out after dark. Hopefully, Thompson had been keeping watch.

Tom pulled his Breguet from his pocket. "We have a few minutes before dinner." He reached out and slid his fingers through her hair. Although it was combed out and nearly dry, he thought it lacked something. "Have you a purple ribbon? For your hair?"

It was Victoria's turn to blink. "All my ribbons are in the top drawer," she murmured.

Tom confirmed she was standing upright with a hand on the nearest chair before he quickly moved to the dresser. He opened the drawer to discover ribbons of every imaginable color rolled into circles. "Well, I can see I won't be spending much blunt on fripperies," he remarked as he found the matching ribbon for her gown.

"Surely not after all the blunt you've spent on shoes," she

reminded him as Tom moved behind her. He grinned as he gathered hair from her temples and pulled the two swaths of black silk to the back of her head. He secured them with the ribbon and then tied a bow. Then, because there was enough ribbon, he tied another atop the first.

"You've done this before," Victoria accused, a streak of jealousy tingeing her voice.

"I have five sisters," he reminded her. "I used to have to do this for the youngest one—the fast one—before she had her own lady's maid."

He dipped his head, remembering the morning before when he had watched as Emily and James exchanged vows at the same time Gabe and Frances exchanged theirs. Even without many people in attendance—until the rest of the family returned from Derbyshire, he was Emily's only close relative in town—the double ceremony had been simple and memorable. He hoped Juliet had agreed to wed Haddon so that their double ceremony would be much the same. "By the way, Emily married James Burroughs yesterday morning," he added.

Victoria whirled around, nearly toppling when she didn't catch herself before Tom did. "She married my banker?" she asked in surprise.

"My best friend," he countered, surprised by her words. Then his brows furrowed, reminded of their first afternoon together. "Tell me, my love. How was it you came to learn enough about steam buses to want to invest in them?"

Her eyes darting sideways, Victoria attempted to suppress a grin and could not. "My banker?" she replied sheepishly.

"That blighter!" he replied with a huge grin. At no point during their evenings at White's had James Burroughs admitted his role in Victoria's choice for an investment.

A knock at the door had the two calling out, "Come" at the same time. And they chuckled.

Clark gingerly opened the door. "Dinner is served, my lady, sir." His expression of trepidation was soon replaced with surprise at seeing his mistress dressed for dinner—and in good spirits.

"Thank you, Clark," Tom said. He turned to Victoria, a frown slowly forming. "However am I to find you in all of this fabric?" he asked as he moved to lift her into his arms.

She wrapped her hands around the back of his neck. "Just like this," she replied as one of his arms found the back of her knees while the other settled against the back of her waist. She reached up and kissed him on the corner of his mouth.

"Careful, my lady, or we shall be foregoing dinner all together," he warned.

"We shall not," Victoria whispered. "I'm *starving*."

"A man can try," Tom said as he carried her down the stairs.

CHAPTER 36

WINTER WEDDING VOWS
BEFORE THE CEREMONY

*M*eanwhile, at the Comber townhouse

"I cannot help but fear that I have overstayed my welcome," Christopher said when Juliet accompanied him to the front door. Her mother had insisted the earl stay for dinner, and he had, even though he had complained about his lack of proper dress.

"Nonsense," Juliet replied. "It was good we discussed the wedding plans, such as they are. And truth be told, talk of our wedding has me rather excited."

Christopher's eyes widened. "Truly?"

She dimpled. "The sooner we're wed, the sooner we can begin work on populating your nursery," she whispered.

Blinking, the earl seemed to have difficulty breathing. "True, but you needn't make it sound as if it will be a *chore*."

Juliet regarded him with an arched brow. "My mother has said that having babies is quite taxing—"

"I'll make it worth your while," he assured her.

"That it can be quite painful."

"I'll provide you two hours of pleasure for every hour of pain," he promised.

"That you might take a mistress should you find my body

too terribly misshapen after a few babies, with my breasts overly large and my hips wider."

"Never," he vowed, rather liking the image she was creating with her words.

"You swear to that?" she asked in surprise, her eyes wide.

"I do," he replied, holding up his right hand.

"I would call you a toadie, but I do believe I feel too much affection for you to call you such an awful name," she murmured.

"Too much?" he repeated, thinking he hadn't really minded her occasional nickname for him. She had always said it with such affection. "Truly?"

Juliet nodded as she seemed to struggle for her next words. "If you had asked me just three days ago if I could imagine myself married to you, I would have said no," she whispered. "But now... now it's as if I have seen our entire future together, and I rather like it."

"As do I," Christopher said, hoping he was imagining the same scenarios.

"We'll pay frequent calls on Vicky and Mr. Grandby."

"I will allow you spend an entire day with Vicky every week, as you do now," he assured her.

"But only while you're stuck in Parliament," she replied. "Or meeting your friends at your club."

"And we'll pay calls on your parents and mine," he offered.

"Agreed."

"Four days."

"Four days?" she repeated.

"Until we wed. I must send a missive to Tom Grandby to let him know. I'll be sure my mother invites him and Vicky to the dinner party. I expect that will be the night before the ceremony."

"I will send a note to Vicky," Juliet said. Then she blinked. "Does my mother know all this?"

A dimple she had never noticed before appeared in Christopher's cheek. "She does. As does my mother."

Juliet furrowed a brow. "Christopher Carlington, just what have you been up to?" she asked, as she moved close enough to raise her hands to his shoulders.

Christopher grinned and began to explain.

*H*er mother, who hadn't been in the study when her father and Christopher were discussing such details, had insisted on learning the earl's intentions.

Had he a date in mind for the ceremony?

"Tomorrow," he had replied, as if that were possible. And then he added, "I have a special license, as does Mr. Grandby. The women will insist on a double wedding, but I understand from my mother that we have to wait at least three days and possibly up to a week before we can wed."

Lady Comber had blinked. "Oh. I can work with that. Although we surely don't have a large enough dining room to host a wedding breakfast."

"But Carlington House does," he assured her. "Mother will insist on hosting, if you're of a mind to allow it."

Considering Julia had conferred with the marchioness earlier that morning over tea—she had received an invitation only the day before—she was already apprised of Adeline's desire to play hostess for both a dinner party announcing the betrothal as well as the breakfast.

"I've not had a wedding party at the house since Elizabeth married, and that was *ages* ago," Adeline had complained, despite Elizabeth having been right there in the parlor with them.

Even now, Julia could still hear Elizabeth's scolding, "Mother!"

Elizabeth wasn't *that* old.

So how could Julia argue with the generous offer?

. . .

id he have a place in mind?

"My mother will insist on St. George's, but—"

"As do I," Julia had said.

"Which is available to us in four days," Christopher had said, rather proud of his role in the arrangements. "I've already paid the priest to hold the church for us."

Julia had given him one of those approving looks he so needed to see now and again. A look that suggested he had done something right. "Four days, then," she had said. "I'll leave you to inform your bride."

*fter a moment of enduring his lingering gaze, Juliet dimpled and said, "Four days. I shall be there, with bells on."

"And a gown, I should hope," he said. His expression was so serious, as if he were attempting to memorize everything about her face, Juliet nearly laughed.

Instead, she asked, "Well, are you going to kiss me? Or are you in need of a pen and paper so you can do a drawing of me?"

A grin of delight appeared on Christopher's lips. "The latter I may do when I am next in your company," he replied, "But right now..." He bent and covered her lips with his own, heartened when she pressed her body against the front of his. At hearing her soft moan, he deepened the kiss and then finally, reluctantly, pulled away. "I promise, making love will not seem like *work*," he whispered.

"I should hope not," she replied with a wink.

"I'll be just down the street. At our townhouse, should you wish to pay a call and take a tour," he suggested, his eyebrows waggling. "I took the liberty of ordering the same sort of chairs your mother has in the front salon," he went on. "But you'll have to choose which color of peony you'd like on the fabric."

Juliet giggled. "I really don't care," she murmured.

"You're welcome to move in anytime."

"Toadie," she accused, her eyes widening in delight.

The sound of a clearing throat had Christopher taking his leave of the Comber townhouse in a hurry.

"Father!" Juliet complained. "I've almost got him eating out of my hand."

Alistair shook his head. "He's a man, Juliet. Not a horse," he admonished her.

Juliet's eyes darted sideways, not about to counter his claim.

The training methods the two species required seemed so much the same.

CHAPTER 37

DINNER AND A DANCE

*M*eanwhile, at Fairmont Park

"Which way?" Tom asked as he reached the bottom step.

Victoria pointed to the right. "Second door."

He entered the dining room, soon realizing it was more of a dining hall. The pale green walls were long—almost the length of half the house—and the room was thin. Ornate white plasterwork featured on all the walls as well as the ceiling. Two white marble fireplaces interrupted the short walls, and long carpets stretched the length of the long walls on either side of the massive oak table. "Entertain much?" he teased.

"If you're asking if I've ever hosted a dinner party, then no," she replied. "Although my mother used to, back in the day."

"But you've had guests in here," he insisted.

"Only Juliet. Michael, of course. And now you." Tom was about to lower her into a carver at one end of the table, but she said, "Don't you dare. That's your chair. For tonight, mine is to your right."

"Not at the other end of the table?" he teased.

With twelves chairs on either side, the other carver was a long ways away.

"Only if we host a dinner party," she replied.

Not about to argue, Tom set her into the chair next to the right of the carver and took the carver for himself. He held one hand to his brow while he stared down the length of the table, sure it was as long as the one in his great-uncle Milton's house in Park Lane. "Ah, I can make out the opposite end," he murmured playfully as he settled into the armed chair, surprised that it was more comfortable than he expected. "I already feel like the man of the house. But perhaps we should procure a shorter table."

"It needs one," Victoria whispered.

Tom furrowed a brow. "Are you speaking of the house? Or the table?"

"Both," she replied, just as Clark appeared with a bottle of wine.

Warmth spread through Tom just then. He had rarely thought such a moniker as 'man of the house' might one day apply to him.

"I suppose I've known it since I moved in," Victoria murmured. Clark poured glasses for them both. When Cummings, the footman, appeared with bowls of soup, she avoided his questioning glance.

"Would you be amenable to marrying this week?" Tom asked. "Monday, perhaps?" He attempted to suppress a grin when he noted how Cummings nearly upended his bowl of soup at overhearing the comment.

"The day after tomorrow? How is that even possible?"

"Special license. I was able to pay a call in Doctors Commons yesterday afternoon to secure one. As was Haddon," he added, not surprised when she didn't immediately react. "I can't imagine him being allowed to use it quite so soon, though."

Victoria gave a start. "You don't think Juliet will agree to wed him?"

Tom was relieved when Cummings returned to the kitchens,

leaving him and Victoria alone in the dining room. He was sure the footman would see to it everyone in the household was informed of their mistress' betrothal. "I don't think Lady Comber will allow her daughter to wed quite so quickly," he finally replied. "She'll want a few days to prepare. Send out invitations. Make it less likely the *ton* think it a scandalous marriage."

"Of course," Victoria agreed. She thought of her own mother and how she would react at learning her youngest daughter had finally agreed to wed. The duchess had come to believe Victoria would end up a spinster. "I know you said Haddon would have asked for Juliet's hand—"

"Five or six hours ago."

"So I suppose it's possible she's already given him an answer," she said in a quiet voice. "I wonder if she did so while they were on their horseback ride in the park this afternoon?" Tom remembered Haddon's complaint about having to wait an entire day before seeing Miss Comber. He had felt the same anxiousness, though. The same urgent need-to-know the earl had experienced that night he had made an appearance at Arthur's. The same night Haddon had threatened to wed Victoria if Juliet didn't accept his suit. "Do you think Lady Comber would be amenable to a double wedding for her daughter?" Tom asked. "I may have promised to pay witness to Haddon's nuptials."

"As did I," Victoria countered, her gaze lifting to his. "Which is awfully convenient." She gave him a look of suspicion. "You've been spending more time in Haddon's company than I thought," she accused.

"Couldn't be helped," Tom replied. "He was determined to marry Miss Comber and sought my assistance in that regard. And I am just as determined to marry you."

"So you sought *his* assistance?" she asked in alarm.

He shook his head. "He offered. I wasn't about to turn him away. He has your ear as well as your brother's."

Victoria inhaled. "Which brother?"

"Lord Michael, of course."

She seemed to relax a bit, but then her brows furrowed. "Pray tell, when did you have occasion to arrange for the purchase of Fairmont Park?"

Tom stiffened, knowing she wouldn't be pleased to learn what her brother had intended for the estate. "Lord Michael has been here in London for over a week," he replied. "I should also mention that he is one of my investors, Victoria. He had contracts to sign. Alliances to arrange on behalf of your father. It was during our meeting when he brought up the need to sell Fairmont Park."

She winced. "He thought to force me out?"

Tom shook his head. "Not at all. He wanted to protect it from being gambled away by your brother whilst finding an investor who would allow you to continue living here." He straightened and then gave a shake of his head. "When he brought it up, I didn't think *I* would be the one buying it," he murmured. "But now... I cannot imagine Fairmont Park in anyone else's hands." He felt some relief at seeing Victoria's expression soften.

"Lord Michael intends to pay a call on you on the morrow."

"I am aware," Victoria replied. "He spent his first night here in his old bedchamber when he arrived in London. A couple of days before you came for the first time," she added, remembering Michael had been as concerned about her inheritance as he was about his own. "He arranged for you to pay a call on me here, did he not?"

"He did. I think he feared you might not go to my office of your own accord."

She inhaled, obviously annoyed at having been managed by her brother. "He could have stayed here at Fairmont Park instead of in town. There are several completed bedchambers. I even invited him to do so."

Tom shook his head. "He's frightened to death of you," he said with a grin.

Victoria's mouth dropped open. "But, why?"

"You, my lady, have been a formidable woman when it comes to your family. Which I find simply perfect, since he will be my brother in a few short days."

Despite her initial anger, Victoria allowed a wan grin. "Serves him right."

"He only wished to protect your fortune from Lord Jeremiah," he murmured.

"And his."

"So... you don't hate me for having purchased Fairmont Park for you?"

Victoria sighed, her shoulders drooping. "Tell me. Did you agree to buy it *before* you met with me that day?"

"Of course not. I never buy anything sight unseen."

"Then you learned of my plans for the place that first day you were here. Knew I had already invested a good deal into the stables and the track... and yet, you still decided to buy it? Knowing all that?"

She looked so crestfallen, Tom leaned over placed a hand over hers. "Only after our dinner the other night. When I knew I wanted you to be my wife. And then only as a gift for you, of course," he whispered.

Pulling her hand from his hold, she stared at him. "But, what if I *hadn't* agreed to marry you?"

Tom's eyes darted to the side. "I... I can be very persuasive," he hedged. "If you had turned me down, I... I don't know what I would have done. Maybe requested I be allowed the use of a few common areas? Taken a bedchamber and moved in? Vexed you incessantly until you agreed to marry me?"

Victoria gave him a dubious glance. "What a scandal that might have caused," she whispered, a grin finally appearing to brighten her face. She was about to return her attention to her soup, but paused. "Speaking of moving in, when might that happen?"

Relief settled over Tom, and he once again grasped one of her hands in his. "Whenever you allow it. Tomorrow, perhaps? My coach will be here at ten in the morning."

"You'll be leaving then?"

Hesitating to answer when he heard the surprise in her voice, Tom asked, "That all depends. Will I be welcome to stay?" He didn't add that the coach would be arriving with a trunk of his clothes and another filled with items from his rooms at Arthur's. The last-minute packing had been done on a whim, one he was now glad he had entertained.

He had no intention of returning to town until Monday, and only then because he would need to pay a call at the office.

"I'm not yet sure if you'll be welcome, exactly," Victoria teased. "But surely I can find a suitable bedchamber for you."

"Next to yours, I hope. Although I expect I'll only use it to dress."

"Oh, so you think you're going to spend your nights in my bed?"

His eyes darted sideways again before he said, "Only if you're not spending your nights in mine."

She swallowed. "The first room at the top of the stairs has a connecting door to my bedchamber," she said in a quiet voice. "I cannot say that it's a master suite, exactly."

"It will do," he said with a grin. "Or is it pink?"

Chuckling, Victoria said, "That's the third bedchamber. The one Juliet sleeps in when she's in residence."

"Perhaps we can see to renovating the suites at the end of the hall. To create an apartment if there isn't one already."

Victoria's eyes widened at hearing his suggestion. At hearing him say "we." The word seemed to have come easily to his lips. "Did your parents share a bed?"

Tom nodded. "They still do. Which is probably why I have five sisters and four brothers."

"Noted," she replied with a smirk.

The bedchamber arrangements settled, they spoke of her plans for the other rooms in the house. For new furnishings for the parlor and modern plumbing for the rest of the bathing chambers.

When they finished dessert, Tom refused the offer of port and asked that Victoria show him the ballroom.

"There's a piano-forté in there, but no one to play it," she said as Tom lifted her into his arms.

"Then we shall have to hum the music," he said. "Point the way."

"It's not large," she warned as she directed him down the hall to the opposite end of the house. "And it's rather... gold," she added. "Lots of gilt. I cannot decide if I like it or not, so I have done nothing to it."

Tom stopped in front of the carved double doors and carefully lowered Victoria until she could stand. She turned the handles and pushed the doors open to reveal the dimly lit room.

An Axminster carpet stretched over the length and most of the width of the floor. Wider than the dining room by half, it wasn't quite as long, but it was bathed in gold. As Victoria turned up the gas for the chandeliers, the full effect of the gilt became apparent.

"Blazes," Tom murmured as his gaze swept the ballroom.

"It does sort of look as if it's on fire."

"It reminds me of one of the salons in a palace I once toured," he remarked.

"I think Father bought the house because of this room," Victoria explained. "Thought to impress my mother."

"Did it?"

Victoria grinned. "Not in the way he imagined. But she did host a ball here once when I was a child. I remember hiding near the top of the stairs so I could watch the couples as they made their way down the hall."

"Aristocrats, no doubt," Tom guessed.

She nodded. "That was the first time I saw her best friend from when she attended finishing school."

"Oh?"

"Lady Elizabeth Carlington," Victoria said as she arched a brow.

"Now Viscountess Bostwick," Tom offered.

"She was then as well. Lord Bostwick was escorting her, and I remember thinking he looked so besotted. As if he truly loved her."

"That's because he does," Tom replied. "I had drinks with him at White's earlier this week."

Victoria gave a start, glad when he wrapped an arm around her waist and pulled her close. Although she had been able to balance her weight on her one good foot, she feared it would grow tired before they had a chance to dance.

"Is he a client?" she asked.

"Yes, but that's not why I met with him," he replied. "I wanted to discover which shoemaker his wife employed for her charity, so I would know where to have your shoes made."

Victoria winced.

"I knew she would only employ the best," he quickly added.

"Of course," she replied, heartened he didn't say it was because she had a misshapen foot.

Tom suddenly allowed a chuckle. "I wondered how it was you knew Haddon. It's because of your mother's friendship with Viscountess Bostwick, is it not?"

She nodded. "Christopher is younger than Elizabeth, of course. In so many ways. And despite his being seventeen years older than me, I can remember when he had just finished university," she murmured. "He came to Wiltshire with Elizabeth and George for a house party. Every day he played with my brothers as if he was still a little boy. I remember feeling jealous of my brothers because he showed them so much attention."

Tom regarded her a moment before he asked, "Were you in love with him?"

Pulled from her reverie, Victoria blinked. "I think I was four years old at the time, so perhaps," she admitted as a teasing grin appeared.

"You minx. You had me rather worried just then," Tom admitted. He glanced around the room, taking in the ornate fireplace and the upholstered chairs that lined one wall. "May I have this dance?"

Victoria faced him and placed a hand on his shoulder. "Are we doing a Viennese waltz?"

Tom's gaze suggested he was considering how best to respond. "It's the only one I know," he said sheepishly.

"You'll remind me of the steps?"

"I won't need to," he replied. He began to count, "one-two-three," in a whisper, humming as he took her other hand in his and led her through the first three steps. "Is your foot all right?"

Victoria nodded, and then joined in the humming of the music. She nearly giggled as they circled the room, the feeling of euphoria making her feel as if she was weightless. Despite Tom's rapt attention on her, he kept them from colliding with the furniture or dancing into the walls. His hold on her—his hand at her waist and the other supporting her hand—was firm and sure as he led them in the circles that made up the invigorating dance.

"One-two-three," she whispered, when she could no longer hum the music.

"I love thee," he countered in a quiet voice, just as they had completed a second circuit.

Victoria nearly lost the count, her gaze locked on his. Their moves slowed until they nearly stopped. When she suddenly winced, and Tom quickly took her up into his arms.

"That's enough for tonight," he whispered, bestowing a kiss on her forehead. "Stables next?"

Victoria had forgotten her earlier request to visit the horses. "Could we?" she asked, her voice breathy.

"Of course," he replied as he took her out to the vestibule

for a wrap. Once they were bundled up against the cold, he carried her down the corridor to the back door. Several lanterns were still lit in the stables, providing enough light to illuminate the pavers as Tom made his way.

Their arrival had several horses nickering and Tom grinning. "They look forward to your visits, don't they?" he whispered as he lowered her until her feet touched the hay-strewn floor.

"Especially when they think I have treats for them," she replied.

"Jake apparently has a preference for apples," Tom said, making his way to a wooden bucket half-filled with the fruit.

"I think they all do," Victoria replied as she stroked the cheek of the nearest beast. Tom handed her an apple, and she in turn offered it to the horse, watching as he devoured it. She moved to the next, grinning as Tom continued to hand her apples. "You do realize you could be making friends with all of them if you were the one doing this."

"Ah, but I think they know *I'm* the one giving them to you," he countered, admiring how at ease she was with the animals.

When Victoria had finished greeting every horse except Sam, she allowed a long sigh as she confronted the Thoroughbred. "You haven't limped once while Mr. Comber has been seeing to you," she accused. "I know because he told me so."

Sam neighed.

"You'll not limp with me. Ever again. Understood?" She held the apple beyond his reach until the horse nickered. When she offered it to him, he nickered again before noisily downing the fruit.

Allowing another sigh, she turned and found herself engulfed in Tom's arms. "I don't care if you always limp with me," he whispered, just before his lips covered hers.

Victoria mewled as she returned his kiss, finally understanding just how different her life would be going forward.

She had just pulled away and was about to suggest Tom take

her back to the house when the sound of a clearing throat had her giving a start.

"Mr. Thompson," Tom said as he turned, not at all surprised to find the groom holding a gun. "Her ladyship has just been saying her good-nights to the herd."

The groom relaxed his stance. "You're here awfully late."

Tom dipped his head. "As I will be every night from now on."

When Thompson's expression darkened, Victoria said, "Mr. Grandby has just purchased Fairmont Park."

"As a wedding gift. For my bride to be," Tom added, glad when Thompson seemed to relax and finally lowered the gun.

"Oh. Well. That's a relief," the groom replied. "Perhaps I'll be allowed to return to my usual assignment. After you're wed?"

Tom furrowed a brow and gave Victoria a quick glance. "Usual assignment? What might that be?"

Thompson glanced about, as if ensuring no one else was listening. "Investigations, sir. On behalf of Lord Michael."

Victoria stiffened in Tom's arms. "What... what sort of investigations?" she asked.

When Thompson didn't answer right away, Tom inhaled. "Would your... *employment* have anything to do with Lord Jeremiah?" he ventured.

The groom nodded. "Lord Michael is trying to stay a step ahead of his brother's expenditures, you might say. I let him know what and where there's been a transaction, and he sees to cancelling the orders 'afore they cost Somerset any blunt."

"Which means you haven't been able to do that for the last few months," Victoria reasoned. "Seeing as how you've been working here."

Thompson's eyes darted to the side before he said, "Actually, I still do what I can, which is why I've been gone missing at times," he admitted.

Victoria stared at the groom, her brows furrowing. "So... my brother hired you to... to provide protection for me?" she asked as a pained expression crossed her face.

Nodding, Thompson said, "Lord Michael, yes. He wanted to be sure you was protected from any fortune hunters. And from Lord Jeremiah. Mr. Grandby here gave me a bit of a worry 'til I learned he had a fortune of his own. Doesn't gamble, neither."

When Victoria noticed that Tom didn't seem surprised by the groom's comment, she said, "You knew."

"I *guessed*," Tom countered. "The night we went to dinner at Rules."

Victoria stiffened in his arms. "I do not appreciate being managed—"

"Nor will you be," Tom said quietly. "But your brother was right to have someone on the premises looking out for you and your servants," he added. He turned his attention back to the groom. "I'll see to returning Lady Victoria to the house now. I expect you and Lord Michael to make some new arrangements for your time when he's here on the morrow."

"Yes, sir."

"Good night, Mr. Thompson."

The groom nodded and took his leave of the stables, heading for the manse just beyond.

Without a word, Tom lifted Victoria into his arms and made his way back to the house. "Will someone put out the lanterns?" he asked once they were just inside the corridor. He turned to close the door and noticed the stables were already dark.

"Jemmy sees to it," Victoria assured him.

Tom lowered his gaze to meet hers. "May I take you to bed now?"

"Are you coming, too?"

Wondering if she intended her comment to be a double entendre, Tom replied, "In more ways than one."

CHAPTER 38

PAYING A DEBT

wo hours later, in the bed in Victoria's bedchamber
Tucked against the front of Tom's bent body, Victoria was quite sure she couldn't move.

Not that she wanted to move. Not when her entire body felt as if it were floating, despite the weight of an arm that was wrapped around her waist. The hand at the end of it held one of her breasts.

Perhaps that's why Tom held her like this. So she wouldn't float away.

She grinned as her entire body vibrated with an unfamiliar *thrum* of excitement. Even though she should feel exhausted—experiencing wave after wave of pleasure was rather taxing—she didn't wish to sleep.

She also didn't wish to forget what Tom had done to her on this night. His kisses had her aroused even before his tongue saw to pleasures she had not imagined. When his tall body covered hers, she wrapped her legs around his long thighs and allowed him entry into her most private space.

After his tentative start, his thrusts had grown stronger, his penetration into her deeper, until all at once a pleasure so intense, she could not breathe, had overwhelmed her—and apparently him, for he had said words that might have been a curse combined with a prayer of thanksgiving.

Nor would she forget what she had done to him as she sat on him, astride. Her hands had been braced on his shoulders as she rode him, her body lowering with each of his upward thrusts until her nipples had grazed the dark, crisp curls on his chest. Delightful frissons raced through her at the very moment her mount seized and nearly bucked her off.

Not once had she detected a limp.

Then she remembered what he had threatened to do to her before the sun lit the sky. Only a day ago, she would have been scandalized. Now she looked forward to it with every fiber of her being.

Two hours of pleasure for every hour of pain I have caused you, he had said between his series of kisses.

At the rate they were going, she feared his bill would be paid before the month was gone.

What then?

Before she could spend another moment wondering, she felt the slightest touch between her shoulder blades as his lips traced the bumps of her spine. She shivered in response, and then tried to suppress a giggle when his lips took purchase on one of her shoulders. The arm around her waist tightened its hold, and his manhood suddenly stiffened, lengthening between her thighs to rest against her honeyed folds.

The memory of how it had felt when he entered her the first time had Victoria inhaling sharply as her insides reacted. That sense of invasion, of taking in the entire length of him in only a few slow movements, of the careful thrusts meant to avoid causing pain, nearly had her pleading for him to stop.

But then he had done something to bring on a series of delicious sensations beneath her skin. The frissons that had her lower body trembling. Her womanhood throbbing. Her desire for him cresting. A moment later, and any thoughts of asking him to stop had flown from her mind, replaced with words of encouragement and pleading and begging him to go on.

"My apologies for having fallen asleep," he whispered as he raised himself onto an elbow. He lowered his lips to her ear and nibbled on the lobe.

Victoria turned her head and stared at him from the corner of her eye. "I could not sleep if I tried," she whispered in return.

"Then you will not mind if I pay down my debt more this night?"

Turning her body so she lay on her back, Victoria furrowed a dark brow. She loved the way his appreciative gaze moved to her breasts and belly, and secretly chided herself for having been so modest before dinner. "That all depends."

Tom's expression mirrored hers. "On what?"

"What happens after you have paid your debt in full?"

Thinking on the query for a moment, Tom chuckled softly. "Then I shall begin banking credits for the future."

Victoria inhaled sharply when he dipped his head and nipped one of her breasts with his lips. "You expect to cause me pain in the future?"

Tom's attentions had moved farther down the front of her body, but he paused in his ministrations to say, "I'm a man. It's inevitable I will do something stupid," he murmured. He lifted his head from her belly to remind her of the times she would be with child. "All those little aches and pains will add up quickly," he warned, reminding her of how the little things mattered. "I would rather I never be in debt with you for the rest of our lives."

She was about to put voice to a protest that *she* would be in debt to him, but thought better of it. Or at least she would have, if she'd had any mental faculties about her.

Whatever Tom was doing to her left her quite unable to think.

EPILOGUE

hree months later

"What is it, my love?" Tom asked when he found his wife staring at the floor in her bedchamber. He was dressed for the first ball of the Season in a black topcoat, white cravat, white tie and black satin trousers. She was dressed in the orchid gown she'd been wearing for their first dance together.

Her lady's maid had apparently been dismissed, since Cummings wasn't in the bedchamber.

Victoria furrowed her dark brows. "I cannot decide," she complained.

Tom frowned and joined her, attempting to suppress a chuckle when he discovered various colors of dance slippers arranged in a long line. "The sliver ones, dear heart," he said as he knelt and helped her into them.

"I don't understand what's wrong with me," Victoria said, placing her hand on his shoulder for support. She leaned over him, admiring his backside as he saw to helping with the slippers.

"Are you staring at my bum?" Tom accused, his attention still on one of her feet.

"If you didn't want me to, you shouldn't have bent down

like that, especially whilst wearing satin trousers," she replied in a teasing voice. She sobered, though and said, "Other than matters of a carnal nature, I cannot seem to think straight."

Tom finished putting on the slippers and leaned back on his haunches, her comment bringing back memories from his childhood. "There's nothing *wrong*, exactly," he said, his gaze moving to her midsection, where the orchid satin skirts flared out from a fitted waist. Although she was as trim there as she had been since their first night together, he remembered his mother never showed evidence of a pregnancy until she was five or more months along.

"Exactly?" Victoria repeated in alarm. "What does *that* mean?"

Tom straightened and pulled her into his arms. "There's a colt on the way, my love. Six months, mayhap?"

Victoria's eyes widened, and she leaned back to stare at Tom. At seeing her look of shock, he allowed a huge grin. "Or it could be a filly," he offered. "Truth be told, I'd welcome either one. Or both," he quickly added. "I should warn you that twins do run in my family."

Blinking, Victoria looked as if she were about to faint. "I'm with child?"

Tom pulled her into his arms again and kissed her forehead. "I'm fairly certain you are."

"There are six colts due to be born in the next couple of months," she argued. "Who's going to train them?"

The query had Tom wondering how best to respond. "You are, of course. I don't expect to have to hire a replacement for you until... until you're no longer able to sit atop a horse," he lied.

Victoria stared at him a moment. "You're lying," she accused.

"I am," he agreed. "It will probably be the moment you go into labor. Until then..." He sighed, a grin still lighting his face. "You and Countess Haddon can commiserate together."

"Commiserate?"

Tom nodded. "Haddon is sure she's with child. At least, his mother is fairly sure—"

"Thomas!" she scolded. "How long have you known?" Juliet had just been to Fairmont Park this Tuesday past.

She hadn't said a thing.

"About you? Or Juliet?"

Victoria angled her head to one side in an attempt to be cross with him. She couldn't be, though. Not with the way he beamed in delight.

"You'll probably deliver your babies on the same day," Tom said with a shrug. "At least, that's what Haddon seems to think."

"You bounder," she accused, a fist pounding his chest.

There wasn't much force behind it, though, and Tom caught it in one hand and kissed the back of it, still grinning. "You can find out tonight. That is, if we're not too late. We may have already missed the entire ball," he teased.

An hour later

The Weatherstone manor was ablaze in lights as the Morganfield town coach came to a halt in front of it. David Carlington, Marquess of Morganfield, was the first to step down, followed by his marchioness, Adeline. Then their son, Christopher, looking as if he wasn't a day past thirty, jumped down and turned to lift his wife from the coach.

"Christopher," Juliet chided him. "You'll wrinkle my gown," she complained, her tone more of a tease than a complaint.

"No one will notice," he countered as he set her down so her slippered feet touched the ground. "You glow as if you have a thousand lights inside you."

"That's because the gown is covered in gold sarcenet," she argued. "And I'm wearing most of the parure you had made for me."

"Actually—"

"Let's go inside, shall we?" Morganfield suggested, his wife's hand already on his arm. "I'd like to get to the library before anyone else," he added as his eyebrows waggled in Adeline's direction. "Lock the door and—

"David," Adeline scolded. But she hurried alongside her husband as they made their way to the front door of the Weatherstone mansion.

Juliet glanced up at her husband. "Was he... serious?" she asked.

Christopher nodded. "They rather enjoy this first ball of the Season, and it's not because of the orchestra or the dancing," he murmured as he offered his arm.

Blushing at the thought of what the Morganfields intended to do in the library, Juliet struggled to keep a straight face. "About that," she said as they made their way. "Did you intend to...?" She paused, unsure of how to finish the query.

"Intend to?" he prompted.

"Have your way with me? In the gardens? I hear they are legendary for illicit kissing. Forbidden fondling. Copious couplings."

Christopher blinked. "Would... would I be allowed?" he asked. "It's terribly chilly."

Juliet suddenly screwed her face into a pout. "I cannot believe I just put voice to all that," she claimed. "I don't know what's gotten into me."

"Oh, I do," Christopher replied, just as they reached the front door.

"Oh? Do tell."

"Me. And now my heir," he said as he handed their coats to a footman. "Oh, look. The Grandbys are here," he added, before Juliet could form a coherent response. "I'll put money on a bet they have similar news," he added as a dimple formed in his cheek.

"You toadie!" Juliet said in a hoarse whisper, but her smile was bright as she and Victoria embraced.

"Am I the last to know?" Victoria asked in a whisper.

"Apparently, *I* am," Juliet complained on a sigh. "But it matters not," she added as she released her best friend. "We're with child. At the same time."

"Well, it's the little things that matter most," Victoria replied as she let go her hold and regarded Juliet with a brilliant smile.

"He's not *that* little," Juliet argued.

Victoria stared at her friend for a moment before she burst out laughing.

Tom exchanged a quick glance with Christopher. "You look as if you've hit your head."

Christopher waggled his brows. "Every night, damned headboard. So, shall we start our evening in the gardens?" he asked.

"The gardens," Tom agreed, rather glad Victoria's headboard was upholstered.

They took the hands of their wives and quickly made their way outside.

None of them complained about the cold.

AUTHOR NOTES

Illegitimacy in the Aristocracy

During the time in which this book takes place, a child born before his parents were married was considered illegitimate even if his parents married after his birth. For purposes of inheritance, the father could recognize the child as his own and provide a settlement for him, but *the child could not inherit any aristocratic titles.*

Do horses mimic human behavior?

They certainly can!

Horses are social creatures. They learn from other horses, even when they're being trained by humans (and more easily if they've had human interaction since birth). When they are consistently fed and trained by the same handlers, they will recognize them on approach and usually move toward them.

The study, *Effects of size and personality on social learning and human-directed behavior in horses (Equus caballus)* by Josefine Henriksson, Mathilde Sauveroche & Lina S. V. Roth, showed that full-sized horses, but not ponies, showed more human-related behaviors when presented with an unsolvable problem, and they found several correlations between these behaviors and personality traits. Also, size and personality had an impact on the human-related behavior in the two experiments they performed.

Arthur's

Established in 1811, Arthur's was a London gentlemen's club that lasted until 1940. Between 1827 and 1940 it was based in a custom-built clubhouse designed by Thomas Hopper located at 69 St. James Street—the location of the current Carlton Club. The club was first formed at a meeting at a bank at 16 St. James Street on May 8, 1811, with the resolution 'That a New Club be forthwith established, to consist of 300 Members.' The club is notable for being the first to be a members' club wholly owned by the members, as opposed to the proprietary clubs which previously existed, like White's, Boodle's, and Brooks', and it was avowedly non-political.

Betrothal Rings

During the Regency and Victorian eras, sapphire rings were highly valued, more so than diamond rings since sapphires were considered a much more valuable gemstone. DeBeer's, the firm credited with having created the market for diamond rings, wasn't founded until 1888.

ABOUT THE AUTHOR

A self-described nerd and student of history, Linda Rae spent many years as a published technical writer specializing in 3D graphics workstations, software and 3D animation (her movie credits include SHREK and SHREK 2). Getting lost in the rabbit holes of research has resulted in historical romances set in the Regency-era as well as Ancient Greece.

A fan of action-adventure movies, she can frequently be found at the local cinema. Although she no longer has any tropical fish, she follows the San Jose Sharks and makes her home in Cody, Wyoming.

For more information:
www.lindaraesande.com
Sign up for Linda Rae's newsletter:
Regency Romance with a Twist
Follow Linda Rae's blog:
Regency Romance with a Twist

www.ingramcontent.com/pod-product-compliance
Lightning Source LLC
Chambersburg PA
CBHW032100180726
48284CB00002B/381